Jack Hight

Jack Hight is an American historian. He lives with his wife and dog in Washington DC, where he is currently writing a trilogy about the Crusades, the first volume entitled *Eagle*. When not writing in the neighbourhood coffee shop, he enjoys good books, bad movies and trying to recreate medieval recipes.

Visit his website at www.jackhight.com

SIEGE

JACK HIGHT

JOHN MURRAY

First published in Great Britain in 2010 by John Murray (Publishers)
An Hachette UK Company

First published in paperback in 2010

2

© Jack Hight 2010

A CIP catalogue record for this title is available from the British Library

B-format ISBN 978-1-84854-296-9
A-format ISBN 978-1-84854-504-5

Typeset in Monotype Sabon by Ellipsis Book Production, Glasgow

Printed and bound by Clays Ltd, St Ives plc

John Murray policy is to use papers that are natural, renewable
and recyclable products and made from wood grown in sustainable forests.
The logging and manufacturing processes are expected to conform to
the environmental regulations of the country of origin.

John Murray (Publishers)
338 Euston Road
London NW1 3BH

www.johnmurray.co.uk

For Cate

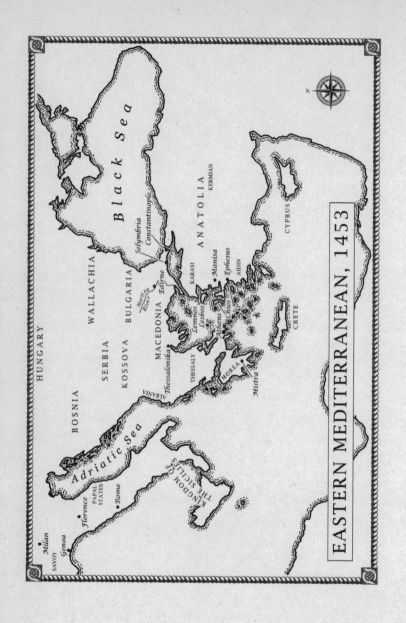

EASTERN MEDITERRANEAN, 1453

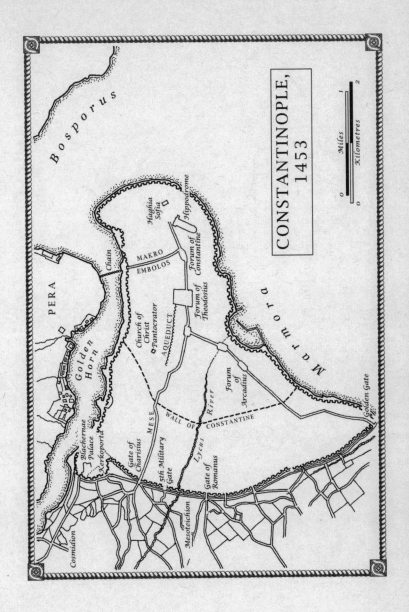

CONSTANTINOPLE, 1453

Bosporus

Miles
Kilometres

PERA

Chain

Haghia
Sofia

Hippodrome

MAKRO
EMBOLOS

Forum of
Constantine

Golden
Horn

Church of
Christ
Pantocrator

Forum of
Theodosius

AQUEDUCT

Forum
of
Arcadius

Marmora

Blachernae
Palace

Kerkoporta

MESE

Gate of
Charisius

5th Military
Gate

WALL OF CONSTANTINE

Lycus River

Gate of
Romanus

Golden Gate

Cosmidion

Mesoteichion

Prologue

Longo lay still under the bodies of two dead soldiers and waited for the last of the Turkish army to pass. The Christian crusade had been routed, and now the enemy marched around and over him, their boots squishing in the blood-drenched earth. He could just hear the distant horns of the scattered Christian army as it fled, followed by the cries and drums of the pursuing Turks. Finally the field fell silent save for the moans of the wounded and the harsh cries of the ravens that were arriving to feast upon the dead. One settled on a corpse near Longo and began to peck at the soft flesh of the face. If the ravens were here, then the battle was truly over. He had waited long enough.

He rose, stiff from lying so long on the cold, wet ground. He kicked at the raven, sending it flying away cawing in protest, and then drew his sword, a long thin blade of dark-grey steel. The battle might be over, but Longo was not done fighting. He scanned the horizon and saw a few distant enemy soldiers, pillaging amongst the thousands of dead. He ignored them; they were not the prey he sought. He was looking for one man: a Turk with pale-grey eyes

I

and a gruesome scar stretching down the right side of his face from his temple to his jaw.

At the height of the battle, Longo had seen his quarry behind the Turkish lines, wearing chainmail covered in scarlet fabric. He rode beneath a golden standard from which hung three horsetails – the mark of a vizier. Longo had no sooner spotted him, however, than the Christian line had broken and the retreat had been sounded. In the ensuing chaos, Longo had played dead. He had searched for this man for years, and now that he had finally found him, he would not let him escape.

Stepping over the bodies of the dead, Longo strode towards the Turkish camp. As he neared the first of the tents, five Turkish soldiers came out to meet him. They were ragged bazibozouks, peasant soldiers who were recruited to the defence of Islam whenever the Ottoman Empire went to war. Two carried heavy axes, better for chopping wood than fighting. One held a sword, while the last two carried crude wooden clubs studded with protruding nails. As they rushed Longo, they screamed the *Allah! Allah! Allah!* battle cry of the Turks, but Longo did not hear them. He heard only the blood pumping in his ears as he stood his ground and readied his shield and sword.

At the last second, Longo sprang to his left, outflanking the group so he only had to face one man. He knocked the Turk's club aside with his shield and then slashed down with his sword, dropping his enemy. Then he waded straight into the rest: at close quarters the clubs and axes would be less effective. He sidestepped a clumsy axe blow and spun away in one fluid motion, slashing across the face of his attacker before thrusting up past the guard of the next man. Leaving his sword embedded in the Turk's chest, Longo drew a dagger from his belt, turned, and threw. It caught the second to last Turk in the throat. The dying man's club dropped from his hands, and he fell in a mass of blood.

Longo felt the hard slap of a sword glancing off the chainmail along his side. He turned just in time to raise his shield and deflect another blow, this one aimed at his face. He stepped back, weaponless, and faced his final assailant, a huge Turk who wore a long beard. The man grinned, revealing yellow, rotting teeth. 'Now you die, infidel!' he roared and swung in a huge arc for Longo's chest. Longo feinted as if to block the blow, then ducked and came up under it, smashing the Turk in the face with his shield. The Turk staggered backwards, his broken nose pouring blood, then turned on his heel and stumbled away, fleeing for his life.

Longo retrieved his sword and grimaced as he reached over to feel the bruise that was already forming along his side. He had been lucky. A more experienced swordsman would have killed him. Offering up a prayer of thanks to the Virgin, he stepped into the shadow of the nearest tent and peered deeper into the camp. Cooks were busy tending dozens of cooking fires, but there were relatively few soldiers and no sign of his quarry. He had almost given up hope when he heard a horse whinny behind him. Turning, he saw the vizier riding towards the camp, surrounded by some two-dozen black-armoured janissaries.

With no thought to anything but his blazing need for revenge, Longo raised his sword and charged. The janis-saries saw him coming and formed a square of bristling spears around the vizier. Longo hurled himself into the guards. He deflected one spear with his shield and knocked another aside with his sword before charging into one of the janissaries, knocking him backwards and whirling away just in time to avoid a spear thrust. He hacked down, snapping the spear shaft in two, and then waded deeper into the fray, spinning and slashing in a mad frenzy as he pressed his way towards the vizier, each foot forward bought with blood and death.

A spear skipped off Longo's shield and drove into his shoulder. Oblivious to the pain, he grabbed the spear and jerked on it, pulling the janissary forward and then slashing down to finish him. Longo saw a flash out of the corner of his eye and narrowly ducked a blow that would have decapitated him. He turned quickly, swinging his sword in a wild effort to keep the janissaries at bay. Swords were glancing off his chainmail, but Longo ignored them. A spear drove into his leg and he dropped to one knee. Still he kept fighting, striking out again and again as he yelled with rage and pain. The vizier was now only a few yards away. The man's thin face was lined and his beard and moustache had turned grey since Longo last saw him all those many years ago, but there was no mistaking his pale eyes or the jagged scar that Longo had left on his face. Longo crawled towards him, but a janissary stepped in front, blocking his path. Longo tried to stab at the man, but someone grabbed his arm from behind and wrenched away his sword.

As Longo raised his eyes, he saw death towering over him: a janissary with his long *yatağan* raised high, the sword's inward-curving blade showing dark against the bright sun. He felt no fear, only bitter disappointment at having failed. He noticed a nick on the long blade, the smooth black leather of the pommel, the janissary's bulging arm, and then the sword began its fatal descent.

'Stop!' The sword froze inches short of Longo's neck. 'Leave him to me.'

The janissaries stepped away to reveal a huge man, well over six feet and barrel-chested, wearing the black armour of a janissary, with the fur-trimmed cloak and yellow boots of a general. The man spoke briefly to the vizier, who turned his horse and rode away. 'Go! Escort him to the sultan,' the general commanded the janissary troop as he pulled an impossibly long *yatağan* from the scabbard at his side. 'I will finish this one.' He swung his huge sword lightly from side to side as he approached Longo.

The general waited until the other janissaries were well away and then sheathed his sword. He offered Longo his hand. 'Get up,' he ordered. Longo hesitated, then took the hand and pulled himself to his feet, wincing at the pain of his injured leg. He stared into the janissary's face, trying to understand. 'You haven't forgotten me, have you?' the general asked.

Longo blinked, his pain momentarily forgotten as he remembered where he had seen this face before. It had been a younger face then, thinner and unscarred – a boy's face. Long ago in the godforsaken camp of the janissaries, this was the one man he had called friend. 'Ulu,' Longo whispered.

'You saved my life once, Longo,' Ulu said urgently. 'Now I have returned the favour – but if you wish to escape, you must go quickly. Head south and pray to Allah that we never meet again. For my debt is paid, and the next time we meet, it will be as enemies. Now go!' Turning his back on Longo, the general strode away.

Longo watched him disappear into the Turkish camp. As his blood rage vanished, he felt the pain from his wounds flood back, mixed with the familiar cold ache of vengeance delayed. He turned and limped away from the camp, to the south. If he hurried, perhaps he could catch up with his men. Otherwise, it would be a long, lonely walk to Constantinople.

Part I

Chapter 1

Sofia Dragases, Princess of the Eastern Roman Empire, walked through the dark hallways of the emperor's palace in Constantinople, hurrying to keep up with John Dalmata, the commander of the emperor's guard. As they passed a window, she glanced out to where a full moon hung heavy in the night sky over the waters of the harbour. It was several hours until dawn. The emperor, John VIII, had been ill for weeks, and Sofia would only have been summoned so late if he were on the verge of death.

The antechamber of the emperor's apartments was crowded. Most of those present knelt on the hard stone floor, whispering prayers for the health of their emperor. They spoke in Greek, for although the people of Constantinople still called themselves Romans, Greek had replaced Latin as the language of the empire centuries ago. As she passed through the crowd, Sofia noticed the emperor's mother, Helena Dragases, seated in a corner, speaking with George Sphrantzes, the emperor's most trusted minister. Dalmata led Sofia to the door of the emperor's bedchamber, which was guarded by the *praepositus sacri cubiculi*, a balding eunuch who controlled

9

access to the emperor. 'He is very weak. Do not stay too long,' the eunuch told Sofia as he ushered her through the door.

The room was lit only by the flicker of a few candles near the entrance. At first Sofia could not see the emperor, but she could hear his laboured breathing – a series of rattling gasps coming from the darkness on the far side of the room. She moved towards the sound, and as she approached, she made out a large, canopied bed and then the emperor himself. John had been a large man, but now he had wasted to the point where she scarcely recognized the skeletal figure before her. His face was waxen and his eyes closed. Were it not for the horrible rasping of his breathing, Sofia would have thought him dead. As she watched him sleep, she fought back tears.

She did not love her uncle. He was temperamental and drank too much. Nevertheless, John had been a good emperor, and he had allowed Sofia her freedom. She was nearly twenty-four, well past the age when a princess of the empire should have been married, yet her uncle had never broached the subject. He had allowed her to study, not just the literature and philosophy normally taught to women of the court, but also mathematics, government and languages – Italian, Arabic, Latin and Turkish. At the urging of the Empress-Mother Helena, he had even allowed her to join him in council meetings, where she had learned the art of politics. Whoever succeeded John, Sofia doubted that he would be so accommodating towards her.

Sofia gently smoothed back the emperor's hair. 'I have come, Uncle,' she whispered.

John opened his eyes. 'Sit beside me, Sofia,' he gasped.

'I want to ask . . .' John stopped short, his words lost in a long fit of coughing. 'I want to ask your forgiveness,' he continued at last, 'for any wrongs that I have done you.' Such a request was traditional for emperors in their last days. It was clear that John knew his time was near.

'You have no need to ask, Uncle. You have done me no wrongs.'

He frowned and shook his head. 'No, Sofia. I fear I was wrong to raise you as I did. You reminded me so much of my poor dead wife, Maria. I wished to keep you near me, as a reminder of her, and to give you all you wished, as I failed to give her.' He sighed. 'I did not prepare you to be a princess, to be a wife. You have not learned your place in this world.'

'I wish for no other place than that which I have,' Sofia told him. 'I do not regret what I have learned.'

'Nor do I, Sofia,' John wheezed between ragged breaths. 'These are difficult times, and the empire has need of you. There are those in Constantinople who would sell the city to the Turks to feed their ambition. We must stop them. Our empire has stood for over a thousand years. We are the heirs of Rome. We must not fall!'

'But what can I do?' There was a trace of bitterness in Sophia's voice. 'I am a woman, Uncle. I will have little influence at Constantine's court.'

John shook his head as he was seized by another fit of coughing. 'No, you are more than that. Look at my mother, Helena. She is a better statesman than any of my councillors. You have her same spirit, Sofia. My brother Constantine is a good man, but he is not a subtle one. When I am gone, he will need your help, even if he does not wish for it.'

'I will do what I can, Uncle.'

'You must swear to me, Sofia! Give me your hand . . .' Sofia placed her hand in his, and the dying emperor gripped it with surprising strength. His eyes burned with urgency as he met Sofia's gaze. 'Swear that when I am gone, you will do all you can to protect this city from those who would destroy it.'

'I swear it,' Sofia replied solemnly. 'I will defend Constantinople with my life.'

John released her hand and lay back, suddenly small and fragile. 'Good. Now go,' he said. 'And send in my mother.' Sofia nodded and left. In the antechamber, she told the empress-mother that John wished to see her, and then knelt, joining the others in silent prayer.

Sofia knew they were praying for themselves as much as for the emperor. John had no sons and three brothers, and the people feared civil war if he died. And with civil war came the threat of another Ottoman invasion. The Eastern Roman Empire was only a shadow of what it had been when Constantine the Great moved the imperial capital from Rome to Constantinople in 330 AD. The current Turkish sultan, Murad II, had taken the great cities of Adrianople and Salonika. Now, nearly all that remained of the once great Empire of the Romans was the imperial city of Constantinople. It was the last link to a glorious history that reached unbroken to the Caesars; the last barrier between the Turks and the rest of Europe. The sultan's armies had already gathered in the north to confront the crusade called by John before he grew ill. News of a battle had not yet reached Constantinople, but if the Turks were victorious, and John died, then there would be little to stop the sultan's armies from marching on Constantinople.

Sofia's thoughts were interrupted by a loud wailing from the emperor's room. It was the Empress-Mother Helena mourning her son. The emperor was dead.

The evening sun hung low in the sky when William Whyte reached the top of a long rise and saw Constantinople for the first time. The city was still several miles off, but even at this distance, the majesty of it caused him to stop short. Fields of wheat and herds of roaming cattle lay spread out before him, running right up to the city's towering walls. The walls stretched for miles, from the Golden Horn, its waters glinting to the north, to the Sea of Marmora to the south. Beyond the walls, the city rose high on its seven hills. Squinting, William could just make out a few monuments: domed churches, sprawling palaces and thin columns towering above the city. It was no wonder they called Constantinople the Queen of Cities. William had never seen anything like it.

William took his eyes off the city as the long rope that led from his bound hands to the saddle of the horse before him went taut, jerking him forward so that he stumbled down the far side of the hill. The man riding the horse – a Turk named Hasim, who had rotten teeth and a greying beard – turned back and shouted something in his strange tongue. The man's meaning was clear: speed up, or else. He had already beaten William more than once during the long journey from Ephesus to Constantinople – seven days of hard marching across brutal dry lands, and seven cold nights spent huddled on the ground beneath the unforgiving autumn sky. Thin already, William had lost more weight, and now his ribs showed clearly through his skin. He spat at Hasim but quickened his pace.

It was barely two months since William had joined the crew of the *Kateryn*, sailing for the East from his home, the English port of Fowey. He had thought he was sailing to riches. Carlo Grimaldi, an Italian who claimed to be an exile from Genoa, had promised that he could lead the *Kateryn* safely past the Genoese and Venetian galleys that dominated the eastern spice trade. Captain Smith, William's uncle, had been sceptical, but the opportunity was too good to pass up. If they could make a direct connection with the eastern spice traders, cutting out the Italian middlemen, then they would make a fortune. It had been a kindness of Captain Smith to ask William to join the crew. William's father had died almost ten years ago, when William was only five, and for the past year his mother had suffered from a wasting sickness. The little that William earned as a water-porter, even when combined with his winnings at the knife fights, was barely enough to feed them and pay rent for the draughty, damp room they shared. With the money from the voyage, William had hoped to find proper lodgings so that his mother could spend her last days in comfort.

But his plans had gone awry even before they left port. The day before they sailed, William's mother died. Once in the East, Grimaldi had led them to a small cove south of the Turkish town of Ephesus, where they had found the tents of a Turkish caravan set up on the shore. Smith had anchored far out, and William had watched from his position in the crow's nest high above the deck as Smith, Grimaldi and four heavily armed crewmen had rowed ashore to negotiate. They had hardly stepped out of the boat before archers hidden in the tents cut the crewmen down. Grimaldi had killed Captain Smith himself, striking him down from behind. The remaining crew onboard the *Kateryn* had hurried to set sail, but two Turkish long-boats had cut off their escape. The ship had been boarded, and after a brief, bloody fight they had surrendered. William had been lucky; he was young enough to be sold as a slave. So while the old and injured crewmen were lined up on the beach and executed, William had been given to Hasim, who had set off immediately for the slave markets of Constantinople, where a fair-skinned European like William could be expected to fetch a high price as a house slave for some Turkish or Greek family.

Now, as they covered the last few miles to the city, William kept a careful eye on his captor. Whenever Hasim was not looking, William worked at the bonds that tied his hands. It was nervous work. Just yesterday, Hasim had caught William at it and had whipped him, then tied his hands so tightly that the ropes cut into his skin. William ignored the pain as he continued to work the ropes, pulling this way then that as they slowly loosened. If he did not escape soon, it would be too late. Already the Golden Gate leading into Constantinople was looming before him.

The gate's three archways were each over thirty feet high, and the central gate was wide enough to allow twenty men on horseback to pass through side by side. Beyond the gate was a walled courtyard, filled with pedlars' carts and a milling crowd. William had never seen so many different kinds of people in one place: local peasants in belted tunics and leather breeches; wealthy Greeks wearing wide-sleeved caftans of blue or red silk, embroidered with threads of gold and silver; Turks in turbans; bearded Jews in skullcaps; and olive-skinned Italians in trimmed velvet doublets and tight hose. There were blued-eyed men from the Caucasus, Wallachians with their dark hair, pale skin and pointed features, and Africans as black as the night sky. They spoke a bewildering variety of languages, none of which William could even identify, much less understand. And the goods being hawked were just as varied: exotic spices whose powerful scents competed with the general odour of unwashed humanity and animal excrement; steel swords short and long, curved and straight; nervous horses and camels impassively chewing their cuds; meat roasting on spits; and dirty prostitutes caked in unnatural-looking makeup. Hasim did not pause to look. He spurred his horse through the market and into the city.

William found himself on a broad, paved avenue. The street was crowded on either side by low buildings, and looking past them to his left, William could see broad fields where cattle and sheep grazed on the dried wheat stalks left from a recent harvest. To the right, the land sloped down to the sea wall and the Sea of Marmora beyond, blazing red under the setting sun. William watched a ship sail slowly across the water and thought of how it would be to be onboard, tasting the sea spray as he sailed back to England. The ship disappeared from view behind a low but massive church, fronted with fat columns and topped with a broad dome. It was nothing like the tiny chapel at home.

Past the church, the road began to climb, passing a sprawling monastery and several more churches. At the crest of the rise, they came to a gate set into the crumbling ruins of an ancient city wall. Past the gate, William was assaulted by a nauseating odour. The city was denser here, with houses built one upon the other, and the streets ran with filth – a foul mixture of emptied chamber-pots, animal manure and offal from a nearby butchery, all draining away towards the sea. At intervals, narrow alleyways led away from the main road. In one of them, William saw wild dogs snapping at each other as they tore at an animal carcass.

The road emptied into a wide square crowded with shouting merchants and squealing pigs packed into pens. In the middle of the pig market, a column soared high above even the tallest trees in the square, its entire length decorated with spiralling bands of stone-carving depicting battles and ceremonies, their meanings long lost. Hasim did not pause. He rode on, pulling William behind him, deeper into the city. They climbed another hill to a square that looked out over a valley spanned by a monumental aqueduct, well over a hundred feet tall. At the square, they turned right. On the distant hills before him, William saw a massive church, its many domes gilded by the last rays of the setting sun, and to the church's right the crumbling ruins of a huge Roman arena.

As the twilight gloom began to settle around them, they turned on to a wide street that ran down towards the Golden Horn, the inlet that bordered Constantinople to the north. The street was lined on both sides by columns that supported sheltered promenades. After a short time, Hasim dismounted and occupied himself with his horse's saddle, unknotting the rope that had pulled William across Anatolia to Constantinople. He took the rope and pulled William after him into the dark shadows under the promenade on the right. Before William's eyes could adjust to the dark, he found himself shoved forward, and he stumbled until he ran hard into a stone wall. The lead-rope landed next to him, and he heard the clang of an iron gate as it slammed shut behind him. William turned and slumped to the ground with his back to the wall. He was sitting in a small cell, no more than three feet deep and three feet wide and closed off by iron bars.

Peering through the bars, he could just make out Hasim as he walked out of sight. From the darkness to either side of his tiny cell, William heard hushed noises – muffled crying, whispers, scuffling feet, occasionally punctuated by a loud curse in some foreign tongue, or, further off, the baying of dogs. William drew his knees to his chest and sat shaking. Cold had descended along with night, and with it fear. Yet, even as he shook, he permitted himself a smile. After hours of struggle, he had finally managed to slip the bonds that tied his hands.

The sun had only just risen, casting the world in a grainy golden light, when Longo splashed across a ford on the Lycus river and Constantinople came into view. He reined in his horse on the far bank and breathed a sigh of relief. He had caught up with his men several miles from the battlefield, but it had been a tense journey from Kossova. They had passed through the heart of the Ottoman Empire, travelling within fifty miles of the Turkish capital at Adrianople. It was land that held bad memories for Longo – dangerous land, too, overrun with bandits and thieves, not to mention Turkish troops. Longo had pushed his men hard, avoiding towns and driving them as far and as fast as their horses would allow. Now that they had reached Constantinople, they were as safe as they would be anywhere. But how long Constantinople would remain a safe haven, Longo could only guess. In Selymbria, he had heard that the emperor, John, was dead. If his brothers fought over the throne, then the ensuing civil war would leave Constantinople an easy target for the Turks.

Longo's men came up behind him, joining him on the riverbank. He had taken over one hundred men from Italy to the fields of Kossova, and just over fifty remained. Their armour was battered and dented. Many were wounded and some might not survive the sea voyage back to Genoa. Most were long-standing veterans of Longo's campaigns; a few, like Tristo, had fought along-side him since they were boys. Longo had led the survivors safely out of the Turkish lands, but he knew that would be little comfort to the wives and children of the men who had died. They would blame him, and he did not begrudge them their anger. He blamed himself as well.

Tristo interrupted Longo's sombre thoughts. 'It's good to see the old city again, eh friend?' he said. A notorious joke-teller and wit even in the midst of battle, Tristo could always be counted on to brighten Longo's mood. 'We'll finally have some easy living after all these months of war,' Tristo continued with a grin. 'No more stale bread and dried meat.'

Longo eyed Tristo critically. He was a huge bear of a man – a good two hands taller than Longo and almost twice his weight, and Longo was not small. 'Easy living is the last thing you need,' Longo told him. 'I should put you on half rations.'

'Nonsense,' Tristo replied. 'I need to keep up my strength. I have a duty to the women of Constantinople.'

'I thought you had a duty to your wife.'

19

'I do, indeed. That's why I need the practice: to make sure I get the rust off before we return to Genoa.'

'We'd best hurry then,' Longo said with a grin. 'I'm sure you're very rusty.'

'I am indeed,' Tristo said and spurred his horse down the hill and towards Constantinople. Longo shook his head and galloped after him.

William woke with a start to find the day already bright and the street before him bustling with life. Outside his cell, a stooped Greek in a dirty linen caftan had begun loudly hawking a collection of clay pots.

William stood gingerly, stretched his stiff legs, and peered out of the cell. To his left, other merchants lined the street, peddling their wares to passers-by. Far to his right, the street opened into a small square, where a large crowd had gathered around a raised platform. A portly Turk wearing a blue silk caftan and a towering turban stood on the platform, and as William watched, he hauled up a dazed, naked young boy to stand beside him. Immediately, men in the crowd began pointing and shouting. It was a slave auction, William realized. The boy sold quickly to a Greek and was dragged off. William turned away and sat down. If he did not want to share that boy's fate, then he would have to be ready when Hasim came.

William took the rope that had bound his wrists and wrapped it around both arms so that it appeared as if he were still bound. Last night, he had made a noose of the long rope that Hasim left behind, and now he placed the noose in his lap, hiding it from view under his hands. He did not have to wait long before Hasim arrived, accompanied by the portly man from the auction and a large, well-muscled Turkish guard. Hasim and the slave-trader were arguing loudly. Hasim smiled and pointed repeatedly at William, and each time he did so, the slave-trader frowned and shook his head. William's heart pounded in his chest, but he forced himself to stay still. Finally, an agreement was reached. The slave-trader produced a pouch and carefully counted out a dozen coins.

Hasim pocketed the coins, then unlocked and opened the cell door. As he turned his back, William sprang up, dropped the noose around his neck and pulled it tight. As Hasim clawed at the rope that was strangling him, William took the dagger from Hasim's belt and cut his throat. Hasim slumped to the ground, blood pouring from him. The slave-trader, white with shock, had recovered from his initial surprise and drawn his sword. He swung for William's head. William ducked the blow and slashed out with Hasim's dagger, opening a long cut along the slave-trader's cheek. Grabbing his face, the trader staggered back as his burly guard surged forward. William threw his dagger, catching him in the throat and dropping him. Then he turned and ran, dodging between people and around pedlars' carts. He could hear the shrill voice of the slave-trader calling for someone to stop him. A Greek merchant tripped him, and William went sprawling. But when the merchant tried to grab him, William slipped away and dashed to his right down a wide avenue. There were fewer people here, and he sprinted unimpeded. He ran until he reached a large square, where he paused, bending over to catch his breath. Looking back, he saw the slave-trader some fifty yards back, now accompanied by two more guards. William straightened and ran on.

Past the square, he left the main avenue, turning off

into a maze of narrow alleyways. His pursuers' footsteps echoed between the tall buildings so that they seemed to be everywhere at once. William ran hard, turning frequently until he was completely disoriented. He kept running even as the guards' footsteps faded and his lungs began to burn. Finally, he turned a corner and found himself facing a dead end. He slumped against the wall and sank to the ground, breathing heavily. He listened intently, straining to hear approaching footsteps over the drumming of blood in his ears, but all was silent. William offered up a prayer of thanks to Saint William of Bury, his patron saint. He had escaped.

A mangy dog entered the alley where William sat and sniffed cautiously at him from a distance. William thought of the carcass he had seen yesterday being torn apart by wild dogs. A night spent alone on these streets, and he too might end up prey to the dogs. He would have to find some place to sleep and food, too. He remembered the monastery he had seen upon entering the city. They might take him in, if only for the night.

He rose and made his way through the warren of small streets to a broad avenue, pausing in the shadows of an alleyway until he was certain that there was no sign of the slave-trader or his brawny Turkish guards. Then he set out in what he hoped was the direction of the monastery. He had only walked for a few minutes when he came to the square with the towering column that he remembered from the day before. Fortune was with him. He quickened his pace, but just then, on the far side of the square, he spied the slave-trader on horseback. William froze, but it was too late. Turning to flee, he ran straight into one of the Turkish guards.

The guard grabbed William's right arm and twisted it behind his back, while with his other hand he held a knife to William's throat. William struggled briefly, but the knife dug in, drawing blood, and he stopped. As a crowd of onlookers gathered, William watched the slave-trader canter up to them and dismount. He said something to the guard, who twisted William's arm further back, forcing his head down. William looked up to see the slave-trader standing above him, a dagger in his hand. William spat at the trader, who slapped him and then put the dagger to William's nose.

'*Serbest birakmak onu*!' someone shouted at the trader in Turkish, and he pulled the dagger away. William twisted around to see a lean, square-shouldered man striding through the market towards them. The man wore dark chainmail, and at his side swung a sword that, judging from his strong hands and thickly muscled forearms, he knew how to use. He was strong-jawed and handsome, although the deep creases on his forehead told of a life that had been far from easy. His hair was a sandy colour, surprising for the East, and his eyes were a piercing blue. The slave-trader looked at him for a moment, then spat and put his dagger back to William's nose.

Longo looked from the well-dressed Turk to the bone-thin boy with fair skin, reddish-brown hair and not the first hint of a man's beard. He looked no older than fifteen, and he was certainly not from the East. Whoever he was, Longo was not about to let this fat Turk torture and kill him in public.

'Please, sir. Help me!' the boy pleaded in English.

'I said, release him,' Longo said again in Turkish and drew his sword.

'The boy is a slave, bought and paid for,' the fat Turk replied. 'I will do with him as I wish.'

'Then I will buy him from you.' Longo took a pouch from his belt and tossed it so that it landed heavily at the Turk's feet. A few gold coins flashed in the sun as they rolled free from the bag. 'I trust that will be more than sufficient.'

The Turk lowered his dagger as he glanced at the pouch – easily four times what the boy was worth. He touched the long gash that William had opened on his cheek. 'The boy has drawn my blood. He has killed one of my men. His life is forfeit.' He raised his dagger, preparing to strike.

'My name is Giovanni Giustiniani Longo, and if you kill that boy, then you will have a quarrel with me.'

The blood drained from the Turk's darkly tanned face, leaving it a sickly yellow colour. He stared from the sword to Longo's worn chainmail and then to Longo's hard face. '*Katil Türkin,*' he whispered. He lowered his dagger and shoved the boy roughly towards Longo. 'The boy is yours, *effendi*. Take him!' The Turk scooped up the pouch, not even bothering to collect the loose coins, and hurried off down the street, followed by his guard.

Longo looked at the boy. 'Well boy, what did you do to make him so angry?' he asked in English.

The boy spat after the retreating figure of the slave-trader and then turned to face Longo. 'He wished to sell me as a slave. I did not wish to be sold.' He looked at Longo suspiciously. 'What did you say to him that made him leave? What does *Katil Türkin* mean?'

'It means "Scourge of the Turks". It is what I am known as amongst their kind.'

'What are you going to do with me?' the boy asked.

'I have no need for slaves,' Longo told him. 'You are free to go.'

The boy did not move. 'I have nowhere to go. I have no money, no food. At least give me a weapon so that I can defend myself.'

Longo looked hard at the boy. Something about him, perhaps the flash in his eyes or his belief that with a weapon in hand he could make his way in the world, reminded Longo of himself at that age. 'What is your name, boy?'

'William, sir.'

'And how old are you, William?'

'Sixteen,' William replied. Longo eyed him sceptically. 'Fifteen, sir. Fifteen next month.'

'You are very far from home, William. How is it that you came to be in Constantinople?'

'We sailed looking for spices, but our ship was captured by Turks. I was brought here to be sold as a slave.'

'Can you fight?'

William nodded. 'I can hold my own with a dagger.'

'Can you, now?' Longo pulled a dagger from his belt and tossed it to William, who caught it deftly.

'The life of my men is not an easy one, William,' Longo warned. 'We fight many battles, and we are often on the move. I will not lie to you: you are not likely to live to an old age. But if you do live, then there is glory to be won in battle against the Turks. What do you say?'

'I hate the Turks. They killed my uncle and my ship-mates. They beat and sold me. I will fight them gladly.'

'Very well.' Longo took William's arm and clasped him by the elbow. 'You are my man.' Longo turned to shout to Tristo, who was standing some twenty feet away, his arm around a rather buxom woman selling bread. 'Tristo! Come here.'

Tristo kissed the woman he was holding on the cheek, while his hand slipped from her waist to her bottom. 'Sorry, love,' he told her. He gave her bottom a squeeze, and then ducked away before she could slap him. He approached Longo with a grin on his face. 'What is it? She was just about to ask me home.'

'Tristo, this is William, a new recruit.'

'Glad to have you with us, boy,' Tristo said, and he slapped William on the back so hard that the boy stumbled and almost fell.

'Tristo will take care of you, William,' Longo said. 'And your task is to keep Tristo out of trouble. He's a little too fond of women and dice. Can I rely on you?' William nodded, and Longo turned back to Tristo. 'Take him to the ship and prepare to sail. We leave tonight.'

'Where will you be?'

'At the royal palace. I should pay my respects to the empress-mother. With the emperor dead, she may have need of our services.'

Sofia stood at the window of her bedroom within the women's quarters of the Blachernae Palace and looked out at the market square beyond the palace courtyard. The view – normal people going about their lives – had always comforted her, but it could not do so now. Many of the people she saw were dressed in black, returning her thoughts to the grim events of the past few days. It was less than a week since the funeral of Emperor John VIII, and her future and the future of the empire were both uncertain. Constantine, the eldest of John's brothers, was far away in Mistra, at the heart of the Peloponnesian peninsula. The second brother, Thomas, was rumoured to be closer. As for Demetrius, the youngest and most ambitious of the three, nobody knew where he was.

The sound of a horse's hooves interrupted Sofia's thoughts, and she looked out to see a man approaching the palace. He was tall and rode with a warrior's ease, a sword swinging at his side. His hair was light and even from a distance Sofia could see that he was not Greek. He was a Latin, perhaps northern Italian, Sofia guessed as the man drew nearer. He was strikingly handsome, but hard, too. There was something about his face, the grim set of his lips . . . her uncle's face had been like that.

Who was he? she wondered. The Italian ambassadors had already been to the palace, expressing their grief at the death of the emperor and making empty promises of assistance. This Italian would not be coming on behalf of Genoa or Venice. Why, then? Sofia watched him enter the palace courtyard and dismount. She prayed that he was not bringing more bad news.

The Italian looked up suddenly, and his gaze landed on Sofia in her tower room. Their eyes met, and he did not look away. Sofia stepped back from the window and drew the curtain shut. When she looked out again, the Italian had gone.

'Count Giovanni Giustiniani Longo of Genoa and Chios.'
 Longo followed the herald's voice into the great octagonal hall of the palace. Its bright interior was ringed with

27

high windows and the walls were lined with Varangian soldiers – the royal family's private guard. Before him, the Empress-Mother Helena sat upon an ornate throne, the back styled as a lion's head, the arms its clawed feet. Over seventy, white-haired and wrinkled, Helena nevertheless held her head high and sat straight, conveying an air of command. To her left and right stood members of the royal court. Longo recognized the Patriarch of the Orthodox Church by his tall conical hat, and the captain of the Varangian guard, a stern, square-built man bearing the insignia of the emperor's personal bodyguard. Near the empress-mother stood the woman that Longo had seen in the tower as he arrived. She was slim and carried herself with a dancer's grace. Her olive skin was flawless, and she had wavy chestnut brown hair, and bewitching eyes of light brown shot through with flecks of gold and green. Longo realized that he was staring at her and turned his attention back to the empress-mother.

'Your Highness,' he said in Greek and bowed with a flourish, his right foot forward and his head lowered to his knee. With a wave of her hand, Helena bade him stand. 'I am honoured to be allowed into your august presence,' Longo continued. 'My condolences on the death of your son, God rest his soul.'

'I have had enough of condolences, Signor Longo,' Helena replied in flawless Italian. Longo was surprised, as much by her directness as by her command of his language. 'You speak Greek well,' Helena continued, this time in Greek.

Longo bowed again in recognition of the compliment. 'Thank you, Your Highness. I spent my childhood in Thessalonica.'

'Ah, yes, before the wars no doubt,' Helena murmured,

her eyes closed in memory. When she opened them again, they were cold and stern. 'But you did not come here to discuss your childhood.'

'No, Your Highness. I come bearing important news and to offer you my services, if you have need of them.'

'Very noble of you, Signor Longo,' Helena said. 'What then is your news?'

'Forgive my presumption,' Longo replied. 'But I wish to speak to Your Highness privately.'

Helena studied him closely, her eyes narrow. She nodded, satisfied with the results of her inspection. 'Leave us,' she ordered. The courtiers and soldiers filed quietly from the room. Only the captain of the private guard and the beautiful young woman stayed. Who was she?

'The Princess Sofia is very wise,' Helena said, answering his unspoken question. 'You may speak freely in her presence.' She gestured to the captain of the private guard. 'And I would trust John Dalmata with my life. Your secrets are safe here.'

'Of course, Your Highness.'

'Very good,' Helena said. 'You may proceed, Signor Longo.'

'I come bearing unwelcome news, Your Highness. The crusade led by King Ladislas and John Hunyadi of Hungary is no more. Their armies were surprised and routed by the Turks at Kossova. King Ladislas is dead, and Hunyadi has returned to Hungary to rule as regent. He will no doubt be forced to make peace with the sultan.'

Helena was silent. To her left, Sofia's eyes were wide with disbelief. It was Dalmata, the captain of the guard, who spoke first. 'Hunyadi defeated? We have heard nothing of this.'

29

'I witnessed the defeat with my own eyes,' Longo responded. 'My men rode hard to reach Constantinople. We arrived only today.'

'If Hunyadi has been defeated,' Sofia began, 'then there is no one left to stand between us and the Turkish army. They will not be quick to attack so soon after a major campaign, but if they sense any weakness – a struggle for succession, civil war – then they will strike.' Longo nodded. The girl's grasp of the situation was perfect.

'And Constantinople would fall,' Helena concluded. Good, Longo thought. They understand the danger. 'I will see to it that the succession is handled swiftly,' Helena continued. 'My oldest son, Constantine, shall be named emperor, and there will be no dissension, no civil war. I thank you for your news, Signor Longo. We are in your debt.'

'You do me too much honour, Your Highness,' Longo said. 'But I have one more piece of news to deliver. My men and I passed through Selymbria on our way to Constantinople. Your son, Demetrius, was there. He will arrive before Constantine even knows of the emperor's death.'

'Of course,' Helena replied coolly. 'We are expecting Demetrius any moment now. But do not fear. I will deal with my son when he arrives, and I will send a messenger to Constantine informing him that he is now the emperor.'

'Demetrius will no doubt arrive with force, Your Highness,' Longo said. 'My men are at your disposal, if you have need of us.'

Helena shook her head. 'Thank you, Signor Longo, but I believe I know how to handle my son.'

'Then may I offer the services of my ship? She is fast,

and Mistra is on the way to Italy. Allow me to carry your message to Constantine.'

'I accept your gracious offer,' Helena replied. 'John Dalmata will travel with you. Constantine trusts him. I will send two officials, Alexius Philanthropenus and George Sphrantzes, with the crown. Constantine shall be crowned emperor as soon as you arrive.'

Longo nodded his agreement. 'I will await Lord Dalmata and the officials at my ship. It is harboured in the Golden Horn, at the Port of Pera. We will set sail this very night.'

'Very well,' Helena said. 'May God go with you, Signor Longo.'

The sun had set by the time Longo's ship, *la Fortuna*, got under way. Tristo and the other soldiers were already below decks, drinking and playing dice. The ship's crew scurried about the deck, preparing the rigging. The two ambassadors from Constantinople were in their cabin, suffering from seasickness. Longo had stayed on deck to talk with Dalmata. He was a man of few words, but forthright and intelligent. Like all of the Varangians, Dalmata's ancestors were Saxon nobles who had come to Constantinople generations ago, after King William conquered England, and Dalmata retained the brown hair, grey eyes and lighter skin of his kinsmen. He had been raised in the imperial household and trained in combat by his father, the emperor's personal bodyguard before him. Dalmata told Longo that Constantine was a strong man and would be a good emperor. They had grown up together in the palace, and Dalmata counted Constantine as a friend. Longo was glad to hear that Constantine was capable. He would need to be if his empire were to survive.

Dalmata excused himself to see after the two ambassadors, and Longo was left alone on deck. He stood near the rail, alone with his thoughts as a strong westerly wind hurried *la Fortuna* across the Sea of Marmora. Longo had been campaigning with Hunyadi for nearly a year, and it had been much longer since he had last set foot in Italy. He was eager to feel the warm sunshine of his homeland, eager to walk his fields once more and to watch his grapes as they ripened in the sun. But looking towards Constantinople, dark on the horizon with lights shining here and there, Longo felt something pull at him. A part of him always felt more at home in the East, far from the shores of Italy and the squabbles of his countrymen. Perhaps things would be different if he married, as his chamberlain Nicolo had been urging him to do for years. He thought of the Princess Sofia, with her bright, intelligent eyes, and then laughed at himself. He would never see her again, and he knew better than to wish for things he could never have. He had learned that lesson long ago.

Longo turned away and made his way to the ladder leading below decks, but before he could descend he was stopped by a noise so unexpected that it took him a moment to identify it. Floating in and out of the myriad noises of a ship at sea – the creaking of wooden planks, the slap of waves and the constant roar of wind in the sails – was the barely audible sound of someone crying. Longo looked around him, but saw only a few sailors coiling ropes. He listened more carefully. The sound was coming from above him.

Curious, Longo mounted the ratlines and climbed up to the crow's nest, high above the deck. He hauled himself over the side and found himself face to face with William, who looked away as he wiped the tears from his eyes. 'Why aren't you below with the others, William?' Longo asked.

William wiped away a last tear. 'I was just watching the city, the lights,' he said, struggling to master his quavering voice. 'It's like nothing I've ever seen.'

Longo looked out to where the city was still floating past, visible only as a thousand flickering flames from torches lining streets or fires burning in hearths. Its sea walls rose abruptly from the waves, giving it the look of an island, or some fantastic city afloat at sea, another Atlantis. 'Constantinople is magnificent, isn't she?' Longo reflected.

William nodded. 'Why do they call themselves Romans? They don't live in Rome.'

'They are the heirs to the Roman Empire, with an unbroken line of emperors all the way back to Augustus,' Longo explained. 'In some ways, they have a greater claim to the name *Romans* than the people of Rome themselves.'

'Is Rome like Constantinople?' William asked.

'Like Constantinople? No,' Longo laughed. 'But it is a magnificent place. It is filled with palaces, fountains, markets where you can buy whatever your heart desires, and beautiful women. I will take you there someday. You will like it.'

'I know I will. And yet . . .' William looked at Longo steadily, and Longo was surprised to see that the young man's eyes were filled not with sadness, but with anger. 'Part of me does not want to leave this place. The Turks killed my crewmates, my friends. It is my duty to avenge them. I owe them that.'

33

The blazing eyes, the hatred, William was so much like Longo at that age. 'Do you know, William,' Longo said, 'that I too took up the sword looking for vengeance? I have killed more men than I can count, more than I dare remember. War is all I know.' He looked closely at William. 'Vengeance will not bring your friends back, nor will it bring you peace.'

'You don't understand,' William snapped, shaking his head. 'The Turks betrayed us. They cut my friends down in cold blood. They killed my uncle, my last family in this world, but they let me live.' William fought back tears. 'I cannot live in peace until they are dead. All of them.'

'I do understand, William,' Longo said. 'Better than you know. I was only nine when a Turkish raiding party came to my family's home outside Salonika. The sultan had claimed Salonika, and I was to be forcibly recruited into the janissaries as part of the *devshirme*, the gathering. My older brother fought, hoping to save me. He was killed, and as punishment for his defiance, the Turkish commander had my parents gutted and left for the wolves to finish. I took up my brother's sword, thinking I could save them. I surprised the Turkish commander, and had I not been so clumsy, I would have killed him. Instead, I left an ugly gash on his face. In his rage, he beat me almost to death. When I came to, I swore that someday, somehow, I would kill that man. I still see his face in my dreams.'

Longo paused. The lights of Constantinople had been swallowed by the darkness and grey, barely visible land rose from the sea on either side of them – the walls of the Dardanelles Strait. 'But my vengeance had to wait,'

Longo continued. 'I was taken to Edirne, the Turkish name for Adrianople, and placed in the *acemi oğlan*, the school for young janissaries.' Longo fell silent. He had never told his story to anybody. He rarely allowed himself to think of it. Now, he gazed into the darkness beyond the reach of the ship's lamps and battled with old memories.

'You were a janissary?' William asked. 'What did you do? How did you get out?'

'Three years after my capture, when I was twelve, I escaped. I tried to reach Constantinople, but I never made it. I lost my way and spent nearly a year wandering the countryside, stealing food and sleeping in barns. I passed through Athens, Kossova, Thebes. Eventually, I stowed away on a ship and ended up on the island of Chios. I lived on the streets until one of the Italian families that rule the island – the Giustiniani – took me in. My parents were Venetian and I could speak Italian, so they made me a house servant. Eventually the head of the family, who had no children of his own, adopted me.'

'And the man who killed your family, did you ever find him?'

'Yes, I found him,' Longo replied quietly. He thought again of the battle of Kossova, of how close he had come to the scar-faced man, of how he had failed. Longo closed his eyes against the pain of the memories. 'Get below,' he told William. 'That is enough talk for one night.'

Later that night, long after the streets of Constantinople had been abandoned to thieves and packs of wild dogs, a lone traveller dressed in black spurred his horse along

35

the deserted avenue that wound up the fourth hill, high above the waters of the Golden Horn. The traveller's face was invisible, swallowed up in the shadows of his hood. He kept to the darkness, carefully skirting the intermittent pools of light that spilled on to the road from open windows. At the top of the hill the Church of Saint Saviour Pantocrator came into view, its many domes rising high above the road. The traveller quickened his pace, riding at a gallop into the church courtyard.

Two monks in long, black cowls stood waiting. One took the traveller's horse and led it away to the stables. The other led the traveller into the monastery, along dim passages and down a short flight of stairs to a low-ceilinged cellar, where they stopped at a heavy, wooden door. The monk took a lantern from the wall and opened the door, leading the traveller into the catacombs beneath the church. The catacombs had been built above an ancient cistern, and the air was cold and wet, thick with the smells of rock and decay. Their path twisted and turned amongst the crypts before coming to an end at another thick, wooden door. The monk knocked, twice slowly and then three knocks in rapid succession. Then he pushed the door open, and the traveller stepped inside. The monk closed the door behind him.

The small, brightly lit room was dominated by a rectangular table of rough-hewn stone. Around the table stood three men. To the traveller's left was the rotund Patriarch of the Greek Orthodox Church, Gregory Mammas, a nervous man with small, darting eyes. He had only been named Patriarch after the more influential bishops had refused, not wanting to be associated with Emperor John VIII's policy of unifying the Greek and Catholic churches.

The two churches had been separate since 1054, when the pope and the Greek patriarch had excommunicated one another, and the rift between them had only deepened over time.

To the traveller's right stood Lucas Notaras, a tall man with chiselled features and dark, brilliant eyes. Only forty, Notaras had shown himself both an able warrior and an implacable foe of union. John VIII had placed him in charge of the city's defence, a position he had filled capably. As megadux of the empire he was second in power only to the emperor.

George Scholarius Gennadius, a small, wiry man with bright, penetrating eyes, stood across the table from the traveller. Gennadius wore the simple black robe of a monk, his mode of dress ever since he had rejected the patriarchy and retired to the monastery of Saint Saviour Pantocrator. He was the leader of those who opposed union, and he commanded the support of nearly all the Orthodox clergy. From his small cell in the monastery, he wielded far more power than the actual patriarch and almost as much as the emperor himself. It was Gennadius who had called this meeting. He spoke first.

'Welcome to Constantinople, Prince Demetrius,' he said. 'You honour us greatly by accepting our invitation.'

'The honour is mine, Gennadius,' Demetrius replied, pushing back his hood. He had dark black hair, cropped short, and a small beard, immaculately groomed. 'Forgive the late hour of my arrival, but you all understand the importance of my entering the city unseen.'

'Of course,' Gennadius agreed. 'None can know that our next emperor has already arrived in Constantinople.'

Demetrius's eyes glittered. 'So it is true. You wish to

37

offer me the crown.'

Gennadius nodded. 'There are conditions.'

'I expected as much. What are they?'

Lucas Notaras leaned forward, his hands gripping the table. 'We all know your brother, Constantine, wants union with the Catholics. He would have us licking the pope's feet the day after he took the throne. Union is a fool's dream. We will make you emperor, Demetrius, but you must swear on your life to never accept union with the Catholic Church.'

Demetrius looked at their expectant faces. He had never shared this religious fervour, this blind faith that led men to such foolish acts. Still, if religion would make him emperor, then he would embrace it. 'I swear on my life, on the blood of the Saviour himself, that as emperor, I will never allow union with the Catholics.'

Gennadius's lips pulled back in a predatory smile. 'Very good,' he said. 'But I believe Mammas has one more condition.'

Mammas nodded and licked his lips. 'There are many in the Church who wish to see me removed for having supported union.' He glanced at Gennadius, then back to Demetrius. 'You must promise to maintain my position as patriarch, and in return, I will crown you emperor.'

'Very well,' said Demetrius. 'It shall be as you say.'

'Then you shall be emperor,' Gennadius confirmed. 'It will take several days to gather all of the nobles who are loyal to you. In one week's time, Patriarch Mammas will proclaim you emperor in the Forum of Theodosius. From there, you will parade to the Blachernae Palace, where you will take the crown.'

'What of my mother?' Demetrius asked. 'Constantine

is her favourite. Surely she will not accept me as emperor.'

'She will have no choice,' Notaras replied. 'Helena is only a woman. She thinks the palace guard can protect her, but in a week we will have gathered over five hundred nobles to support you. If it comes to a fight, we will win.'

'And Constantine?' Demetrius pressed. 'He will not sit idly by in Mistra after I take the throne. He will bring an army against me.'

'The walls of Constantinople have stood for over a thousand years, they have defeated Huns and Turks alike. They will defeat Constantine and his army, too.'

Demetrius nodded.

'Until next Sunday then, when we shall greet you as emperor,' Gennadius said. 'In the meantime, I suggest you stay here, out of sight. Nobody must know that you are in the city.' He pulled a long bell rope that hung from a hole in the ceiling. They heard no sound, but a second later the door to the room opened to reveal the monk who had led Demetrius into the catacombs. 'Eugenius,' Gennadius called to the monk. 'Lead Demetrius to the guest quarters.'

Demetrius followed the monk out of the cell, and the two disappeared into the darkness of the catacombs. Patriarch Mammas hurried to close the door behind them. 'Do you think supporting Demetrius is still wise?' he asked, turning back to Gennadius and Notaras. 'You have heard the news that the Turks have defeated Hunyadi. If we put Demetrius on the throne, then we will have civil war. The Turkish army will come for us. Demetrius is no leader. The Turks will push him over like a toy.'

Gennadius and Notaras exchanged a glance. 'Better the sultan's turban than the cardinal's hat,' Notaras said.

Gennadius nodded in agreement. 'My thoughts exactly. Leave politics to others, Mammas. You are a man of God. These matters are not your concern. Simply do as we ask, and you shall keep the patriarchy. Otherwise, we are prepared to act without you.'

Mammas stood silent, wringing his hands. 'I will do it, but with a troubled conscience,' he said at last. 'I fear that we are inviting our destruction at the hands of the Turks.'

Chapter 2

Mehmed, prince of the Ottoman Empire, stood outside his tent on a hilltop overlooking Edirne and surveyed the vast army camped all around him. The morning was crisp and clear, and he could see all the way to the jumble of bazibozouk tents that ringed the camp at over a mile's distance. There was little movement. The indisciplined peasant soldiers were no doubt still sleeping off the previous night's celebrations. Closer in to the centre of camp, the more luxurious tents of the Anatolian cavalry formed a wide ring around the hill where Mehmed stood. The Anatolians were nobles, who, in return for absolute control over their lands, fought for the sultan in times of war. The janissaries were camped closest, in a tight ring around Mehmed. Cooking pits had been set up at intervals amongst the uniform grey tents, and they were crowded with janissaries in black chainmail, quietly sharing their morning meal of bread and watery gruel. Just below Mehmed, a dozen of the highest-ranked Anatolians sat in the saddle beside a hundred janissaries of his personal guard, all ready to accompany Mehmed on his triumphant march into Edirne. All they awaited was his signal.

Mehmed turned and entered his tent. Gülbehar, his new favourite concubine, or *kadin*, lounged nude and seductive on his bed. She was stunning, tall and lithe with blonde hair, a light complexion and wide green eyes. He had found her at Kossova after the battle. She claimed to be a princess descended from Albanian royalty, but Mehmed's advisors whispered that she was a slave girl, the whore of the Christian commander. Mehmed was sure that his father, the sultan, would say that it was a bad match: the heir to the empire and an Albanian slave girl. But Mehmed did not care who Gülbehar had been. She was his now. He had chosen her, unlike the wife his father had foisted upon him.

'Come here,' Mehmed commanded her. 'Arrange my turban.' He sat while she stood before him. Her ripe breasts, large on her lean frame, hung tantalizingly close as she wrapped a long white turban around his head. When she had finished, Mehmed pulled her on to his lap and kissed her hard. Her hand moved between his thighs, and Mehmed felt his *sik* harden. But this was no time for play. His men were waiting. 'Up, woman,' Mehmed told Gülbehar. He pushed her aside and rose to examine his reflection in the mirror. He was proud of his unusual appearance. He had light skin – the heritage of his mother, an Italian Jew – and delicate features: almond-shaped eyes, a narrow nose and full lips. He wore the gold-trimmed black armour and towering turban of the sultan, but he was sultan in name only. When Mehmed was only twelve, his father, Murad, had abdicated and retired to a life of pleasure, leaving Mehmed the throne. But Mehmed's reign had been a short one. He had never won the support of the army or the people, and two years ago, when another European crusade was launched against the empire, the Grand Vizier Halil had called Murad back to rule. Now sixteen, Mehmed was a sultan without a throne.

'You look magnificent,' Gülbehar whispered in his ear in her heavily accented Turkish. 'When the people see you, they will know that you are the true sultan, not that weak old man who will not even leave the palace to lead his armies.'

Her words were dangerous, treasonous even, but Mehmed did not correct her. Gülbehar had voiced his own thoughts. Maybe now that he had led the armies of Islam to victory on the field of battle and killed one of the Christian commanders in single combat, his father would finally step aside.

'Go and prepare yourself. My father will want to examine you,' Mehmed told Gülbehar. 'And send in Halil and the generals.'

Halil entered first, wearing a ceremonial robe of brilliant *serâser* – a heavy cloth of white silk woven through with gold – with an interlocking pattern of sharp teeth etched in scarlet silk at the cuffs. The ageing vizier was tall and bony, with a long face and narrow lips encircled by a moustache and the faint outline of a beard. He would have been handsome were it not for the ugly scar that marred the right side of his face. Ulu, the supreme *aga* of the janissaries, followed. He was as tall as Halil, but thick, with bulging arms and a bull-like neck. Like all janissaries, he was clean-shaven. The other generals trooped in together: Mahmud Pasha, the bazibozouks' short, fiery commander; Boghaz Pasha, the proud commander of the Anatolian cavalry; and his second-in-command, Ishak Pasha, an older man with greying hair and the scars from many battles lining his face.

'Your Highness,' Halil pronounced and bowed profoundly.

'My Lord,' the generals said and knelt.

Mehmed motioned them to their feet. 'Halil, all is ready in Edirne for my arrival?'

'Word of your glorious victory has preceded you, My Lord. The people will fill the streets.' Halil smiled, wolf-like, his thin lips stretching back from sharp teeth. 'Gold has been distributed. The crowd will cheer.'

'The people do not need to be paid to cheer,' Ulu barked.

'Peace, Ulu. Halil has only done as I asked,' Mehmed said. He turned back to Halil. 'And has my father sent any word from the palace?'

'None, My Lord, but I am sure he only awaits your return to greet you properly.'

'I am sure,' Mehmed said. He turned to the generals. 'We will leave immediately. I will ride first, alone. My guard will come next, followed by the Anatolian commanders and then Halil and my servants.'

'Forgive me, My Prince,' Boghaz Pasha said, although there was nothing humble about his tone. 'But should I not ride with you? As the commander of the Anatolian cavalry, it is beneath me to ride in the rear, following a prince as if I were his servant.'

'A prince, you say?' Mehmed asked, his voice controlled and calm, although inside he felt the old anger begin to boil. It was never far from the surface. 'Perhaps you have forgotten, but I was proclaimed sultan in the mosque of

Eyub four years ago. Nothing can change that, even if I now rule beside my father.'

'There can be only one sultan,' Boghaz Pasha replied. 'And he sits in Edirne.'

'I see. Thank you for enlightening me, Boghaz Pasha,' Mehmed said coldly. Boghaz smiled and bowed. 'Ulu,' Mehmed called. 'Cut off his head.'

Boghaz laughed, but when Ulu drew his sword, the mirth faded from his face. He backed away, but Ulu stood between him and the only exit. There was nowhere for him to run. Boghaz turned to Mehmed.

'You cannot do this, I fought with your father at Varna. He appointed me pasha of the Anatolian cavalry. He would never allow this.'

Mehmed turned his back on Boghaz as Ulu advanced upon the Anatolian commander. Neither of the other generals made a move to help.

'My Lord, I beg you . . .' Boghaz began again, then stopped. In one fluid motion he unsheathed his sword and swung it at Mehmed's back. The sword stopped just inches short, blocked by Ulu's blade. Mehmed turned as Ulu stepped between him and Boghaz.

'How dare you!' Mehmed hissed.

Boghaz's only reply was to renew his attack. Gripping his sword with both hands, he slashed at Ulu's face, but Ulu deflected the blow easily, wielding his huge scimitar one-handed. Boghaz attacked again, feinting low and then bringing his sword up towards Ulu's chest. Ulu knocked the sword aside with his blade and then kicked out, catching Boghaz in the stomach. As Boghaz doubled over, gasping for breath, Ulu brought his sword down hard, decapitating him. Boghaz's head rolled to a stop at

45

Mehmed's feet, while his body lay still, spilling its blood on the thick carpet.

Mehmed kicked the head aside and turned to Ishak Pasha. 'You have command of the Anatolian cavalry now,' he said to the grizzled Anatolian general. 'May Allah guide your sword.'

Ishak Pasha bowed in recognition. 'Many thanks, My Lord Sultan,' he replied, laying particular emphasis on the last word.

'Now, we shall ride,' Mehmed said. 'I do not wish to keep my people waiting.'

'Mehmed *fatih*! Mehmed *fatih*!' the crowd chanted as Mehmed rode along the broad avenue leading to the palace. There were thousands there to cheer him. They stood several rows deep on either side of the street, loudly proclaiming him *fatih*: conqueror. Yet Mehmed found that their cheers did not please him as much as he had hoped. He could not forget that only four years earlier, these same people had jeered and called for his head as he left Edirne in shame. In his mind, Mehmed could see still see their angry faces, spitting hatred as he rode away. He felt more comfortable now in far-off Manisa, but Manisa would not do for a capital. When he was sultan, Mehmed would leave Edirne behind and make himself a new capital in Constantinople.

Mehmed rode into the courtyard of Eski Serai, the palace built by his father when he moved the capital to Edirne. The palace's huge central dome dominated the city, and smaller buildings and towers spread out around the dome on all sides, like the arms of an octopus. Mehmed dismounted and hurried up the steps. Halil joined him as they entered the great hall housed under the dome. The hall was empty, or almost. In the dim light shed by two lamps, Mehmed saw a single man waiting: Mahmud, the Kapi Agha, or chief eunuch.

'Welcome home, Prince Mehmed,' Mahmud said in his high voice. 'The sultan awaits you in his chambers. Halil Pasha is also expected.'

Mehmed dismissed Mahmud with a nod and began the long walk to his father's quarters, with Halil following close behind. How typical of his father, Mehmed thought, to send only Mahmud to greet him. Murad was never one for ceremony, but Mehmed had thought that this one time, after his great victory, he might be met with the pomp that his station demanded.

'I lead his armies, defeat his enemies, and still he treats me like a child,' Mehmed complained.

'But one does not place a child in command of armies,' Halil countered.

Mehmed held his tongue. Perhaps Halil was right. Still, he wished his father would see that he was no longer the boy he had been four years ago. He was a man now and wished to be treated as such.

They entered a covered walkway and passed through a courtyard garden before stepping into the dark entry hall of Murad's private residence. They paused there while a eunuch announced them: 'Prince Mehmed and Grand Vizier Halil Pasha!'

Mehmed stepped into Murad's private audience chamber and bowed low before his father, taking the opportunity to observe his surroundings. Little had changed in his absence. The room, dimly lit by a few hanging lamps, was richly appointed with scarlet satin

47

draperies on the walls and thick Persian carpets covering the floor. Murad sat in the middle of it all, propped up by a mound of pillows. He was dressed in pale-blue silk robes and from his neck hung a chestnut-sized ruby as dark as blood, the *kumru kalp*, or 'dove's heart'. At forty-four, the sultan showed the effects of a life spent at battle. The scars on his cheeks now intersected with deeper creases around his eyes and his thick black beard was laced with grey. His joints ached so that he could barely rise in the morning unless he was massaged first. And in recent years he had been afflicted by a burning pain in his stomach, which at its worst left him doubled over in bed, retching and cursing Allah. It was this last pain that had led him to abdicate four years ago. His doctors had suggested that a peaceful life far from court would end his torments, and, indeed, his condition had improved before his return to the throne. Now, though, he suffered nightly. Still, he carried himself with an air of command and his piercing eyes retained their youthful vigour. His mouth was set in a thin line. Mehmed could read nothing in Murad's face.

'Welcome home, Prince Mehmed,' Murad said, his voice deep and flat, the voice of a general barking orders. 'Now, sit. Have a drink of wine. You must be parched after your long journey.'

'Thank you, Father.' Mehmed sat down and drank deep, thankful that his father shared his impious love of alcohol. He had not had a drop of wine during the entire campaign: his father had told him again and again the importance of following the dictates of Allah while leading the armies of Islam. Now he was surprised how quickly the wine went to his head.

'I am told that you executed Boghaz Pasha today,' Murad

48

began. 'A good general dead simply because he insulted you.' He shook his head. 'You must learn to control your passions, Mehmed. A wise sultan must sometimes bear insults patiently. Otherwise, he will find himself surrounded only by honey-tongued courtiers, afraid to speak the truth.'

'I am not afraid of the truth,' Mehmed replied. 'But nor was I raised to suffer insults lightly.'

'I am your father, boy. You will suffer insults gladly if I command it. Now tell me. Is it true that the people proclaimed you *fatih* today?'

'They did, Father.'

'Nonsense,' Murad snorted. 'What have you conquered? You defeated a ragtag band of mercenaries, nothing more.'

'I defeated Hunyadi, the Christians' greatest general,' Mehmed protested.

'And tell me, how many bazibozouks did you lose?'

'I am not sure of the exact numbers . . .' Mehmed hesitated.

'Out of over fifty thousand bazibozouks, we have not twenty thousand left who will ever see battle again,' Halil said.

Mehmed flashed him an angry look. 'But I won,' he insisted. 'And I killed the Polish king, Ladislas, myself. It was at the sight of his head raised on my spear that the Christian army fled.'

'King Ladislas is a formidable warrior,' Murad said. 'It is no small feat to have defeated such a man.' Mehmed smiled and nodded, happy to at last receive the praise that was his due. 'But a sultan must seek more than personal glory. Your tactics were clumsy, you wasted count-less lives, and you were lucky not to have been killed.

What does victory mean when it comes at the cost of so many men?'

Mehmed took another drink. 'At least I am not afraid to fight,' he retorted. 'I did not stay cowering in the palace.'

The words were hardly out of Mehmed's mouth when Murad slapped him hard across the face. The blow stung, and Mehmed fought back tears.

'Watch yourself, Prince. Do not forget I have another son.' Murad's voice was hardly raised. 'Now, what is this I hear that you wish to make a common whore your favourite?'

'Gülbehar is no whore. She is an Albanian princess.'

'She is an Albanian whore who barely speaks Turkish, and you wish to make her the mother of the empire.' Murad shook his head. 'You should spend more time with your wife, Sitt Hatun. She at least is worthy of you.' Mehmed had married Sitt Hatun, the daughter of Suleyman Bey of Dulkadiroglu, over a year ago, but the marriage was an empty formality for both of them. Mehmed sometimes pitied his young wife; she was so beautiful, but was kept locked in the harem like a bird in a cage. He pitied her, but he would never lie with her, never allow Sitt Hatun to produce an heir. He would not give his father the satisfaction.

'I will decide who is worthy of me, Father. Gülbehar is my *kadin* and will have a place of honour in the harem. I love her.'

'Love?' Murad scoffed. 'You were not born to love, Mehmed. A sultan has no family, no friends, no lovers. You know that.' Murad sighed. 'Have this Gülbehar sent to me today. I wish to inspect her.'

'Very well, Father.'

'Good,' Murad concluded. 'Now, you have heard that the Greek emperor is dead?'

Mehmed nodded. 'With his death, Constantinople is vulnerable. I already have an army at my command. Let me lead it against the Greeks. I will win victory for you there just as I did at Kossova.'

Murad smirked. '*Kizil Elma*, the red apple. It is a great prize. When I was your age, I too longed to take it, but this apple is sour, I fear. I laid siege to the city for months, but I put not a single dent in those walls. To take Constantinople requires planning, years of preparation, a fleet to block their supply ships, a huge army.'

Mehmed opened his mouth to protest, but his father held up a hand, silencing him. 'Still, you are right,' Murad continued. 'If there is civil war amongst the Greeks, then we would be fools not to take advantage of it. Keep your army, Prince Mehmed. Drill the men. Show me that you know how to make soldiers as well as how to destroy them. If I am pleased with your progress, then perhaps I shall allow you to attack Constantinople.'

Mehmed bowed at the waist, as low as he could while sitting. 'Thank you, Father.'

'Now, off to your wife,' Murad ordered. 'She has waited long for your return and must be eager to see her husband.'

Sitt Hatun sat motionless amidst a profusion of silk cushions, waiting patiently while two *jariye* – female house slaves – applied her makeup, highlighting her dark, oval eyes and her small, full mouth. Sitt Hatun was accustomed to waiting. After her marriage to Mehmed, she had waited in vain, night after night, for him to lie with her. When Mehmed had been sent in shame to Manisa,

51

she had waited for him to call her to him from Edirne. Then, she had waited for Mehmed to return from war in Kossova. Now, that wait was over.

Mehmed would be joining her soon. Murad would make him spend his first night in Edirne in her bed. But while he might allow her to pleasure him, he would not fulfil his duty as her husband. Mehmed had made it clear from the first that he was not interested in giving her a son. At first, his rejection had confused Sitt Hatun. Petite but with a curving figure, golden skin and slender limbs, Sitt Hatun drew envious stares from the other women of the harem, and before her marriage she had received her share of suitors. Even now, living in the harem where entry meant death for any man who was not a eunuch or of the royal family, there were men who had risked their very lives to make their interest in her known. Mehmed, however, was not interested. Sitt Hatun knew now that he preferred another type of beauty.

From the window of her chamber, Sitt Hatun had watched Gülbehar enter the harem. Tall and blonde, with fair skin and high cheekbones, Gülbehar was everything that Sitt Hatun was not. She was a nobody, a slave girl whose father was not even a born Muslim. Yet Mehmed had chosen her as his favourite, and there were even rumours that Gülbehar was pregnant with his child. As *bas haseki* – mother of the heir – Gülbehar would be entitled to honours that Sitt Hatun would never receive. Sitt Hatun would be sultana in name only, just as she was now wife only in name. Unless she listened to Halil . . .

'Wife,' Mehmed called, snapping her from her thoughts. He was there, in the entrance room to her chambers. Sitt Hatun waved her attendants away and moved to greet him, gliding through her chambers in a transparent, silken gown.

'Greetings, husband,' she said and curtsied low before him, revealing her ample cleavage. 'I am overjoyed at your safe return.'

Mehmed took her hand and raised her up. 'You have been well, wife?' he asked, stiff and formal.

'As well as I can be, with my husband gone,' Sitt Hatun replied with a smile. Mehmed did not smile back.

'I am sorry to inform you that you will be moving to smaller apartments,' he said. 'You will have to reduce the size of your court.'

'But why? Have I done something to displease you?' Sitt Hatun prostrated herself, even though she knew she had done no wrong. 'If I have, then punish me.'

'No, you have not displeased me. Gülbehar will be taking your apartments. As mother of my child, she will need a large court.'

'I understand,' Sitt Hatun replied. So it was true. This Gülbehar already bore the child that should by right be Sitt Hatun's, and now she took her apartments as well. It was almost too much to bear. Sitt Hatun dug her nails into her palms as she struggled to control her anger. Finally, she stood and managed to ask demurely, 'Would you like to sit? Some wine?'

'No,' Mehmed said. 'I wish to sleep. I am tired.'

'Shall I give you a massage, to help you rest more peacefully?'

Mehmed gave her a long look – whether of desire, pity or both she could not tell – and shook his head. 'I wish to sleep, wife.'

In their large bed, with its silken sheets and elaborate

53

canopy, Mehmed lay rigidly still, an arm's length from Sitt Hatun. She listened as his breathing slowed to the rhythmic cadence of sleep. She had hoped that tonight would be different, that his great victory would have changed Mehmed, allowing him to put aside his rivalry with his father. She still hoped that someday he would give her a child. Maybe he only needed some encouragement.

Sitt Hatun eased herself across the bed towards Mehmed. Gently, she placed her hand on his bare chest. He did not move; his breathing was still easy. She stroked his chest gently, and then moved her hand down slowly, slowly. Mehmed stirred in his sleep, but made no move to stop her. Sitt Hatun leaned forward and kissed his ear, moving her hand still lower, past his stomach.

Mehmed's hand caught hers, gripping it painfully. He was awake, his face right beside hers, his breath hot on her face. 'Wife,' he whispered, his every word a threat, 'you know the punishment prescribed in the Koran for taking that which is not yours?'

'Yes, husband.'

'Good,' Mehmed said. 'Then keep your hand to yourself if you wish to keep it.' He continued to look at her, and the anger faded from his eyes. He ran his hand along the length of her side and then stroked her black hair. 'But if you insist,' Mehmed continued, his voice altered, deeper now, 'then you may pleasure me.' He gripped her hair and forced her head down. Sitt Hatun grimaced in distaste as she placed the tip of his *sik* in her mouth. She knew better than to refuse.

Mehmed hardened immediately and arched his back, thrusting against her so that she gagged. Within minutes he climaxed and collapsed back with a moan of pleasure. Sitt Hatun turned aside and spit out his seed, wasted. When she turned back, Mehmed had already settled in to sleep, his back to her. Sitt Hatun lay back, tears in her eyes. It was humiliating to be treated as little better than a concubine, good only for pleasure. She knew now that Mehmed would never lie with her. Nothing would change that, not success at war, nor even his father's death. She would be locked away in the harem all her life, shamed and childless.

She thought once more of the proposal that Halil had made to her. If Mehmed died, and she had a son, then her child would be the sultan. No matter that the child would be Halil's and not Mehmed's. That secret would be theirs alone. Sitt Hatun would be the *valide sultana* – mother of the sultan – and Halil the ruler until their son came of age. And Gülbehar? Sitt Hatun would enjoy devising a suitable end for the Albanian whore and her bastard child.

But no, Sitt Hatun sighed. These were just dreams. Reality was sleeping right there beside her. She would be mad to join Halil's plotting. Mehmed was a vengeful man. Sitt Hatun had heard of Boghaz Pasha's gruesome death. Mehmed would not hesitate to do the same to her if she did not keep her place.

Still, to see her own son seated on the throne, to take her rightful place in the harem, to no longer have to serve as Mehmed's whore . . . Sitt Hatun wiped away her tears. Crying would not change her fate. Only she could do that.

Chapter 3

'I proclaim you, Demetrius Dragases, Emperor of Rome, heir to Caesar, ruler of Constantinople, Selymbria and Morea,' Patriarch Mammas intoned. His gold-embroidered white robe was heavy with rain, and tiny drops of water ran off his nose in a continual stream as he made the sign of the cross over the kneeling Demetrius. 'Rise, Emperor Demetrius.'

Demetrius stood to the half-hearted acclamation of the nobles who surrounded him. Notaras had promised five hundred men, but the day had dawned grey with a drenching rain that had turned the streets to mud and the forum of Theodosius into a quagmire. Less than four hundred nobles had braved the weather, and they were soaked and cold. 'Hail Demetrius, Emperor of the Romans,' they grumbled once or twice. It was clear that they were ready to move on to the warmth of the Blachernae Palace.

'May God grant me the wisdom to rule with justice and the strength to guard with steel the empire of which he has made me the emperor,' Demetrius declared, his words concluding the ceremony. All around him, men

56

were already hurrying to their horses. Patriarch Mammas had disappeared, no doubt eager to dry off. The moment was not how Demetrius had envisioned it. He had dreamed of cheering crowds, proud speeches, himself framed majestically in the towering Triumphal Arch of Theodosius. Instead, the ceremony had been cut short, and other than the nobles, there were only a handful of citizens who had come out in the rain to watch the spectacle. Behind him, the Triumphal Arch had been transformed into a waterfall, with rainwater cascading down the front from its broad, flat top. Still, he was emperor, rain or no.

A servant handed Demetrius the reins to his horse. He mounted and led a dreary procession through the city and to the imperial palace. He arrived in a foul mood and stormed into the great hall, followed closely by the nobles. The hall was dim, the high windows shuttered. In the flickering torchlight, Demetrius was surprised to see his mother, Helena, seated on the throne with the entire court flanking her.

'Welcome, my son. I have been expecting you. I am disappointed that you could not arrive in time for your brother's funeral. Selymbria is so close.'

'I came as soon as I heard the tragic news, Mother,' Demetrius said.

'Of course,' Helena replied. 'Fortunately, you have arrived well in advance of your brother, Constantine. You will not also miss the entrance of our next emperor.'

'You are in error, Mother. It is I who am to be crowned. Surely you have heard that I was proclaimed emperor this morning.'

'Were you indeed?' Helena feigned surprise. 'And who

57

was it that proclaimed you emperor?' Demetrius thought he saw her make a single, sharp signal with her right hand, and behind him he heard a muffled thump, as if something very heavy were being moved into place. What was it? he wondered. No matter, he had more than enough men to subdue the palace guard. His mother could do nothing to stop him.

'The very men who stand before you, nobles all, proclaimed me emperor. Patriarch Mammas gave his blessing to my reign.'

'Did he?' Helena arched an eyebrow. 'I fear your reign will be a short one.'

'Do not fear, Mother. The men with me are sworn to protect their emperor, with their lives if needs be.' Demetrius drew his sword, and the nobles gathered behind him followed suit. 'I have come for the crown, Mother.' His voice was flat and menacing. 'Give it to me.'

'Demetrius, surely you would not harm your own mother?' Helena seemed to blanch a shade whiter at the sight of drawn steel. Good, Demetrius thought. She was afraid.

'Of course not, Mother. These men are here only to protect their emperor. They strike only those who defy me. They would never dream of harming you.'

'Do you swear it?' Helena asked.

'Of course, Mother.' Demetrius had never intended to harm her. Once he had the crown, he would send her to a convent in the country.

'Good,' Helena said. 'Then this audience is at an end.' She nodded her head once, curtly. In an instant the shutters flew back from the windows above them, flooding the hall with light. Archers with bows drawn stood in each opening, their forms black against the white light.

'The doors!' Demetrius shouted. His men rushed to the entrance, but the doors held fast, barred from the other side. What a fool he had been! He looked to the small door at the far side of the room, past the throne. Already, the courtiers had filed out, replaced by guardsmen. The small door closed, and Demetrius heard the thump of the lock bar sliding into place. They were trapped.

Behind Demetrius, the nobles swirled noisily, a panic-stricken mass. Several were feverishly hacking at the thick doors to the hall, doing more damage to their swords than to the wood. Others tried in vain to scale the sheer stone walls and reach the windows. Here and there, Demetrius heard cries of fear rising above the general clamour. 'We're dead men!' 'Charge the door!' 'Take Helena!'

A man charged forward from the crowd, making for Helena. Demetrius heard the twang of bowstrings, and the man fell dead, his body riddled with arrows. A few more men charged, and suddenly the room was filled with the hiss of arrows and the cries of the wounded. A noble, arrows protruding from his chest, lurched towards Helena, and Demetrius himself stepped forward and struck the man down. He had sworn, fool that he was, that no harm would come to his mother.

'Silence!' Helena's voice rang out imperiously above the din. She stood imposingly before the throne, bathed in light, her hand held high in a sign to desist. The arrows stopped, and the hall fell silent.

'Gentlemen,' Helena said. 'You have been deceived. The

man you have sworn to protect is no emperor. No royal blood flows in his veins, for he is not my son. My son, Demetrius, would not bring armed men into this hall. My son would not defy his mother's wish, or his brother's right to rule. This man is no son of mine. He is an impostor.'

Demetrius was dumbfounded. What was she saying? Had his mother lost her mind? Was she disowning him? Would he be blinded? Killed?

'You have sworn allegiance to this impostor, this false emperor,' Helena continued. 'But, since he is not of the royal family, your vows mean nothing. I release you from them. Swear, now, eternal allegiance to the true emperor, Constantine, and as sign of your allegiance, leave your swords here before me.'

'We swear eternal allegiance to Constantine!' the nobles chorused. One by one, they stepped forward to deposit their weapons at Helena's feet. So that was her game, Demetrius thought. Helena could never have let the nobles live had they knowingly sided with him against Constantine. But, if she killed them, then the rest of the nobility would be embittered against Constantine; he would have no peace with them as long as he ruled. So she was granting them clemency in the only way she could: by denying that he was Demetrius and thus invalidating their oaths. Despite himself, Demetrius had to admit that it was brilliant. She had taken Constantine's worst enemies and forced them to swear allegiance to him.

The doors to the hall swung open and the nobles began to file out. 'You, impostor,' Helena called to Demetrius. 'Come with me.' She led Demetrius through the small door behind the throne. At the door two guardsmen took his sword and then fell into step behind them. Demetrius followed Helena through twisting hallways to a tower, where they climbed the stairs to the highest room, a small chamber containing only a bed and a single chair. Once they were inside, the guardsmen closed the heavy door behind them. Helena motioned for Demetrius to sit. She remained standing.

'If I were not your mother, you would already be dead.'

'Mother, I . . .'

'Silence,' Helena snapped. 'I do not wish to hear my son beg. Now, who aided you in this treason?'

'No one, Mother.'

'I know you, son. You did not plan this treachery; it is beyond you. Who then? Gennadius?'

'No.' Demetrius did not trust himself to say more. He swallowed. Helena was watching him closely, her face only inches from his own.

'Notaras?'

'No,' Demetrius said again.

Helena turned away from him, her head nodding slowly. 'They were wise to keep their distance.' She sighed, and her shoulders slumped, making her look suddenly old and tired. 'Why must our best men be always pitted against us?' Then, she straightened, and when she turned back to Demetrius, Helena was once more regal, in command. Her voice was like ice. 'Swear upon your life that when your brother arrives, you will hail him as emperor.'

'I swear it.'

'Good. I will hold you to your oath. In the meantime, you will be confined to this room. If you attempt to escape, I will have your tongue and eyes removed, and you will spend the rest of your life locked away in a monastery. Do you understand?'

'Yes, Mother.'

'Good.' Helena stepped forward and took Demetrius's head in her hands. She kissed him softly on the forehead. 'Welcome home, my son.'

Helena moved to the door and knocked softly. It swung open and she left. The door closed behind her with a thud, and Demetrius heard a metallic rasp as the bolt slid to. He turned and stared out the window, watching the rain pool in the streets. His short reign was over.

JANUARY 1449: MISTRA

On 6 January, the eve of the Orthodox Christmas, Longo stood at the front of the Church of Saint Demetrius in Mistra, capital of the Morea, and waited for the entrance of the man who was to be crowned Constantine XI, Emperor of the Romans. A vast crowd of nobles and dignitaries had filled the church. Longo was on the first row, squeezed shoulder to shoulder between the emperor's bodyguard, John Dalmata, and a short, portly Greek official who kept elbowing him in the ribs. The rich dress of the crowd – a profusion of silk *dalmatics*, belted robes with wide sleeves and collars embroidered with gold – was in sharp contrast to the rank odour that came from so many overheated men and women in close proximity. The smell was made even worse by the attempt of some to mask their stink with cloying perfumes. Longo breathed shallowly and reminded himself that it was a great honour to have been invited to the coronation.

A muffled roar, as of waves crashing on a nearby shore,

came from outside the church as the crowd of commoners surrounding the building caught sight of Constantine. Longo turned with the rest of the crowd to face the church doors. He was curious to see this new emperor, the man who would be responsible for defending Constantinople against the Turks. Outside, the roar of the crowd grew louder and louder, and then the doors of the church swung inward. The sweet smell of incense filled the air as two rows of young men swinging silver censers on long chains passed through the doors. Constantine followed, wearing plain white garments, white shoes and white gloves. He was tall and thin, with tanned skin and a strong, handsome face. His hair and beard were both neatly cut and startlingly white, but Constantine was no old man. At forty-four, he had maintained much of his youthful vigour, and he walked down the central aisle with a determined stride and his head held high. He mounted the steps leading up to the dais that had been erected before the altar, and turned to face the crowd. Close up, Longo could see that he had kind, grey eyes.

'I swear to uphold the one true, unified Church and to protect the faith,' Constantine said, his deep voice steady and solemn.

'God will preserve a Christian emperor!' the crowd responded in unison, although Longo noted that some around him kept silent. Constantine's policy of union between the Catholic and Orthodox churches was not popular.

'I swear to defend, with my blood and my life, the empire that God has granted me.'

'Lord help the pious!' the people replied. 'Holy Lord uplift Thy world!'

'I swear to rule justly, the shepherd of my people,' Constantine concluded.

'These are common prayers. God be with you!' the crowd chanted.

Constantine turned his back to the crowd and knelt before a frail old priest dressed in scarlet robes – the metropolitan of Mistra. The metropolitan held his hand over Constantine and began to speak: 'O Lord, Our God, the King of Kings and Lord of Lords, behold from Thy dwelling place Thy faithful servant Constantine, whom Thou hast been pleased to set as king over Thy holy nation, which Thou didst purchase with the precious blood of Thine only begotten Son.' At this point, two dignitaries draped a scarlet silk mantle over Constantine's shoulders. 'Vouchsafe to anoint him with the oil of gladness and endue him with power from on high,' the metropolitan continued as he anointed Constantine with oil, making the sign of the cross on his forehead.

'Put upon his head a crown of pure gold and grant him long life,' the metropolitan concluded. A young acolyte brought forth the crown of the empire – a thick band of jewel-encrusted gold, topped by a lattice-work of gold filled with whitest ermine. The metropolitan reached to take the crown from the acolyte, but he was old and the crown heavy. As the crowd watched in horror, the metropolitan fumbled and then dropped the crown, which rolled down the steps to the foot of the dais.

'God save us!' the fat official next to Longo gasped. 'A terrible omen!' The metropolitan had frozen, his face pale. People began to whisper, and someone cried out that this foretold the fall of the empire. He was immediately silenced, but the whispering grew louder.

64

Constantine stood and turned to face the crowd, which fell silent. He descended the steps and picked up the crown, lifting it high for all to see. 'I place my trust in God and steel, not in omens,' he declared and placed the crown upon his own head. 'May God grant me the wisdom to rule with justice and the strength to guard with steel the empire of my fathers!' The crowd cheered, and Longo with them. Any doubts that he had had regarding Constantine were gone. This was an emperor for whom Longo would be happy to fight.

Gradually, the cheering resolved into the ritual words that greeted the crowning of each new Roman emperor: 'Holy, holy, holy! Glory to God in the highest and on earth, peace!' The standards of the many nobles in the hall dipped in honour of the new emperor, and the gathered nobles and priests knelt and then prostrated themselves. Longo knelt, but he did not prostrate himself. He was a lord of Genoa, and while he honoured Constantine, he would not grovel on his belly for any man. His head held high, Longo caught the emperor's eye. Constantine nodded solemnly in Longo's direction, and then strode from the church, followed by the metropolitan and the incense bearers. Constantine Dragases was now Constantine XI, Caesar Augustus, king faithful in Christ, Emperor of the Romans.

Outside the church, Longo followed the shuffling crowd back to the courtyard of the palace. Through the thick crowd he could just make out Constantine, sitting on a throne placed in the centre of the courtyard. He sat straight-backed, smiling often, as a continual stream of men passed before him, kissing his knees and pledging their fealty. Longo joined the procession, and soon he stood before Constantine. He stepped forward and bowed low before the emperor. 'Congratulations, Emperor Constantine. On behalf of the people of Genoa, allow me to be the first to offer our friendship and goodwill.'

'Thank you, Signor Longo. Your presence honours me,' Constantine replied. 'And thank you for transporting the crown and my mother's ambassadors aboard your ship. Without you, I would not have been crowned today. You will be my guest at the feast tonight. I shall set a place at my table for you.'

'You are too kind, Emperor,' Longo said. 'But I must decline. I have been too long gone from Genoa, and I am eager to return. I will start back this very day.'

'Well then, I wish you well on your voyage. You will always be welcome at my court.'

'Thank you, Emperor,' Longo replied, bowing low again. 'My sword will always be at your service. If you are ever in need, I will hasten to you call.'

'Godspeed, Signor Longo.'

'And may God protect you, Emperor Constantine.'

JANUARY 1449: NEAR EDIRNE

The Turkish army was on the march, a long, thick column of men that snaked for miles alongside the Maritza river. Mehmed, flanked by Ulu and surrounded by his private guard, rode near the head of the column. It was a glorious, clear winter day, and Mehmed's spirits were high. After weeks of drilling, of gathering men and supplies, he now rode at the head of over sixty thousand well-equipped men. And it was his army.

His father, Murad, travelled with them for now, sitting

in a litter at the heart of the army, but the next day, when they left the Maritza valley and headed east, Murad would return to Edirne. It would be Mehmed alone who conquered Constantinople. After that, there would be no more whispered jibes about 'Mehmed the Scholar', no more months spent wasting away in far-off Manisa. He would take his rightful place as the ruling sultan, whether his father agreed or not. With a triumphant army at his back, and Constantinople under his control, no one would be able to stop him. He smiled just to think of it.

The smile turned into a frown as ahead the front ranks stopped suddenly, bringing the entire army to a halt. 'Ulu, see what has happened,' Mehmed ordered. Ulu galloped away and returned a moment later, followed by a squat Greek who sat uncomfortably in the saddle. Mehmed examined him carefully. The Greek's eyes were intelligent and probing, but guarded. Judging from the deep blue, heavily jewelled caftan and thick gold necklace that he wore, he was some sort of councillor, a political creature, and Mehmed held a deep suspicion of all political men.

'He says he is an ambassador from Constantinople, one Lord Sphrantzes,' Ulu reported. 'He rode at the head of a small troop of armed men. He says that he has an urgent message for the sultan.'

'I am the sultan,' Mehmed said to Sphrantzes in Greek. 'You may give me your message.'

Sphrantzes eyed Mehmed sceptically. 'Very well,' he said at last. 'My name is George Sphrantzes, *praepositus sauri cubiculi* of Constantine Dragases, and ambassador of the Roman Empire. I come with a message from the emperor.'

'The emperor is dead,' Mehmed replied.

'True, John VIII, our emperor and your loyal ally, is no more,' Sphrantzes agreed. 'I come on behalf of his brother, who has been crowned Constantine XI, successor to the imperial throne.'

'And what of his two younger brothers?' Mehmed asked. 'Will they not challenge for the throne?'

'Demetrius and Thomas Dragases have both sworn oaths of allegiance to Constantine,' Sphrantzes said, a bit too smugly for Mehmed's liking. 'They are to rule in the Morea, Demetrius from Clarenza and Thomas from Mistra.'

Mehmed could hardly believe the news. The last he had heard, Constantine was in Mistra, a good month's travel from Constantinople. How had he managed to be crowned so quickly? Mehmed's spies had assured him that the brothers would contest the throne. He vowed silently to have every last one of them beheaded. 'And what is this message that your emperor sends?'

'He has sent me with a tribute of one thousand silver stavratons as a token of his goodwill and desire for continued peace between our nations.'

'Peace?' Mehmed laughed. He gestured to the army stretching away behind him. 'As you can see, it is too late for peace.' The Greeks might be united, but that would not stop Mehmed's plans. 'I have a message of my own for your emperor. Ulu, cut off his head and send it to Constantinople on a platter.'

'You speak out of turn, Prince Mehmed.' It was Murad. He was on horseback behind Mehmed, sitting stiffly in the saddle. Mehmed wondered how long he had been there. 'One should always treat ambassadors with courtesy,'

Murad continued as he urged his horse alongside Mehmed's. 'We are not savages, to ignore all laws of civility.' He turned towards Sphrantzes. 'Greetings, Lord Sphrantzes. You are welcome in the lands of Osman.'

'Many thanks, honoured Sultan,' Sphrantzes replied with feeling and bowed. 'I bring you greetings from My Lord Constantine, newly crowned Emperor of the Romans, who offers you a gift as token of his goodwill.'

'This is joyous news indeed,' Murad said. 'I approve of Constantine's coronation and thank him for his gift. I, of course, desire nothing but peace between our two great empires. Tonight I shall hold a feast at my palace in honour of the new emperor, and you shall be our guest of honour.'

'You are most kind, Your Highness.'

'Now, Lord Sphrantzes, I beg your leave. I shall see you tonight.'

Sphrantzes bowed and was led away. 'But what of our army?' Mehmed asked as soon as he was gone. 'We should strike now, while we are ready.'

'Silence, my son,' Murad replied. 'My decision is made, and I will not be swayed. A wise sultan knows the value of peace.'

'And a wise sultan is not afraid to strike when the time is right,' Mehmed insisted. 'They will not expect our attack, even less so now that an emperor has been crowned, and you have promised peace.'

'I will not attack after I have given my word. Striking now would be foolish. I had hoped for a swift campaign, to take advantage of the fighting amongst the Greeks. Our army is not strong enough to take a united Constantinople, nor is it prepared for a long winter siege.

This campaign is over, Prince Mehmed. Disband the army. You may return to Manisa.'

'Yes, Father,' Mehmed said, his voice thick with disappointment. He sat dejected as the long column of the army reversed direction and began the short march back to Edirne. Silently, he cursed his father's cowardice. He cursed the new emperor as well. They had ruined his plans, taken his army from him. They had stolen his chance for glory, his chance to be the true sultan once more. Mehmed spurred his horse to a gallop, streaking past the long line of troops, flying back towards Edirne as if he could outrun his disappointment. But he could not, and as he rode his eyes stung with bitter tears.

Chapter 4

La Fortuna arrived in Genoa in the evening, gliding across the smooth waters of the bay and tying up at one of the Giustiniani family piers. Beyond the pier, the city rose before Longo, densely packed buildings huddled beneath the steep hills. The tops of the hills were lightly dusted with snow, glowing crimson in the evening light. Longo left his men to unload the ship while he, Tristo and William walked through the city's narrow, winding streets and to the nearby Giustiniani palace. In the courtyard of the *palazzo*, the steward of the house greeted Longo with a mixture of joy and surprise.

'Welcome home, Master Longo – praise God that you are alive! We had feared the worst after your long absence. Will you be staying the night? May I bring you food, wine?'

'No, Jacomo, thank you,' Longo said. 'Bring me a horse, and two more for Tristo and William. We will be riding on to the villa immediately.'

'To the villa!' Jacomo's eyebrows rose in alarm. 'Shall I send a messenger ahead of you so that all will be ready when you arrive?'

'That will not be necessary. I expect we will ride faster than any messenger.' Jacomo wrung his hands. He was obviously anxious to warn the villa chamberlain, Nicolo, of Longo's arrival. Longo wondered what Nicolo was up to. Making trouble as usual, no doubt.

The villa lay just three miles outside the city, set in the foothills overlooking Genoa and surrounded by fields and vineyards. They reached Longo's lands shortly after nightfall and tied their horses off in the vineyards behind the villa. The vines, to Longo's satisfaction, had thrived while he was away, but they occupied only a small portion of his mind now. 'Quiet,' Longo warned Tristo and William. 'Let us see what my good chamberlain Nicolo has been up to in my absence. Tristo, I give you leave to stay in your cottage tonight. I will see you on the morrow.' Tristo moved away quietly towards his cottage, while Longo and William proceeded on foot towards the villa.

The villa was well lit, and as they approached, Longo and William could hear laughter and music. They saw no one as they crept through the vineyard, save for one drunken reveller stumbling off into the vines to urinate and singing loudly:

> Give me a girl to call my own,
> Yes give me a girl I pray.
> Give me a wench to ply my bone,
> For which I'll gladly pay!

The villa was surrounded by a wall some six feet high. Longo mounted it and pulled William up after him. From there, they could see the run of the gardens: fountains, carefully tended paths, hedges and people everywhere.

Longo's servants were stumbling about the grounds, singing bawdy songs and entertaining a host of overly made-up, buxom women in garish clothes – many of them whores, no doubt. Here and there men were slinking off into the hedges, pulling women after them. The festivities extended to the villa proper, where Longo's personal musicians had been recruited to provide music and were busy churning out local folk tunes on their viols, lutes and recorders.

Longo and William dropped to the ground, and Longo led the way through the drunken revellers. At the steps of the villa, one of the musicians recognized Longo and, turning palest white, dropped his instrument and hurried off into the darkness. One by one, the other musicians also stopped playing, and as the music faded, all eyes turned to Longo. Gasps filled the silence. One of the more drunk men bent over and vomited. A portly man carrying a bottle of wine exited the villa singing and, upon seeing Longo, froze. '*Merda*!'

'Good-evening, Anselmo. I see you are having quite a celebration.'

'Yes, My Lord,' Anselmo mumbled. 'It is Candlemas, My Lord. And, and . . .' A flash of inspiration came into the drunken man's eye. 'And, we were drinking to your safe return!'

'Of course. Where is Nicolo?'

Anselmo swallowed hard. 'I believe he's in your bedroom, My Lord.'

Longo nodded. 'Anselmo, clean this mess up. William, stay here and keep an eye on him and the others. Don't let them drink any more wine. Feel free to carve up any man who disobeys you.' William drew his dagger and leered wickedly at Anselmo. Longo strode into the villa entrance hall, up the curving marble staircase and into his bedroom. He found Nicolo in bed, naked, with two equally naked, voluptuous young women feeding him grapes.

'Who dares disturb me!' Nicolo roared as he sat up. Then, upon seeing Longo, he swallowed a grape whole and choked on it. The women took one glance at Longo's glowering face and sword and hurried from the room. Longo remained silent while Nicolo struggled with the grape, his face turning first red, then faintly purple. Finally, the chamberlain coughed out the grape and immediately burst into speech, forcing words out between giant, heaving breaths. 'So good to see you, My Lord . . .' *Gasp*. 'Had feared you dead . . .' *Gasp*. 'Apologize for the mess . . .' *Gasp*. 'Such an unexpected pleasure . . .'

'I see you have been taking good care of my home,' Longo interrupted. 'Tell me, was the wine good this year?' He picked up one of a score of empty bottles at the foot of the bed and sniffed at the dregs. 'Surely you must be thoroughly familiar with last year's vintage. Did the nebbiolo take?'

'Yes, My Lord, most magnificently. You must have a taste.' Nicolo looked about him for a full bottle, but finding none, continued, 'The harvest was excellent. I doubled the size of the herd and have acquired an adjoining vineyard from . . . my good God!' Nicolo was cut short in his account by the distant, wailing scream of a woman who was either terribly frightened or extremely happy. The scream rose to an unbelievably high pitch and then stopped abruptly.

'You were saying?' Longo prompted.

'Yes, a vineyard,' Nicolo mumbled. 'It was from a merchant. Ridolfi was the name.'

'Was it?'

'Yes. But you have said nothing of these, uh, these festivities. You are not angry with me, My Lord?'

'Why would I be angry with you, Nicolo?' Longo asked. He tossed the bottle he held aside, and Nicolo jumped as it shattered on the floor. 'You seem to have everything well in hand. Now come, you must show me the grounds. I am particularly interested to see the fields. I noticed they have not yet been ploughed. We shall see to that tomorrow.'

The scream Longo and Nicolo had heard had come from Tristo's cottage, where his wife, Maria, was both terribly frightened and extremely happy. Tristo had crept silently to the door of the tiny, one-room dwelling, and pausing there, he was not surprised to hear two voices inside instead of one. A man was saying soft and low, 'Magnificent, beautiful. I shall buy you ten more,' while a woman answered with delighted laughter. Tristo screwed his face up into an expression of righteous indignation. He tested the latch, and finding the door unlocked, allowed it to swing open. On the table before him lay a partially eaten feast: a roasted pheasant, various cheeses and three bottles of wine. A fire was crackling in the hearth. And there on the bed lay his wife, partially dressed in a frilly, silken dress, and laying *in flagrante delicto* with a half-naked man that Tristo had never seen before. It was upon seeing Tristo looming in the doorway, his face a mask of outrage and anger, that Maria had begun to scream. Taking her outburst as a sign of unparalleled delight, the strange man, his back to Tristo, increased his efforts with renewed vigour.

Maria was still screaming when Tristo grabbed the man by the nape, lifted him clear off the bed, and sent him flying out the open door. At once, the scream ceased. 'Thank God you're here,' Maria cried to Tristo. 'That vile man was having his way with me!'

The man rose as quickly as he could with his breeches still around his ankles, and hobbled to the door, outraged. 'Having my way with you! What are you talking about, Maria? Who is this man?' Tristo slammed the door shut in the man's face, bringing an abrupt end to his tirade.

'Having his way with you, eh? Who was he?' Tristo sat down at the table and helped himself to a glass of wine. The look of outrage had vanished from his face, replaced by a cheerful smile. He paused to take in the lacy dress his wife was wearing. 'Nice dress.'

'You like it?' Maria smiled and adjusted her dishevelled clothes. She was a big-boned, well-endowed woman, pretty rather than beautiful, with long black hair and a mischievous smile. 'He was nobody. Just some merchant from town. You can hardly expect me to defend myself when you're away, Tristo. Especially for two years! And you could at least have the courtesy to knock. Christ, you scared the liver out of me. I thought you were a ghost, standing there in the doorway looking like Lucifer himself.'

'Well, I'm alive and well,' Tristo said, finishing the wine and moving on to the half-eaten pheasant. 'Now come here and give your husband a kiss.' Maria rose and kissed Tristo full on the lips, while he gave her a sharp slap on the bottom. 'That's for infidelity, you naughty wench,' he said. 'There'll be none of that now that I'm home.' Maria returned the blow, slapping Tristo hard across the face. 'Well what was that for, woman?'

'That was for infidelity, and for daring to strike your wife,' Maria replied tartly.

Tristo jumped from his chair and gave Maria another slap on the bottom. 'Then that,' he said, 'is for not knowing your place, woman.'

She slapped him back. 'And that is for daring to strike a lady.'

'A lady?' Tristo roared, chasing Maria around the table, one hand swinging for her bottom. He caught her, and after a brief tussle, the slapping became hugging, then kissing, and then they were on the bed, holding each other tight.

'Welcome home, Tristo,' Maria said, laughing. 'Oh, how I missed you.'

True to his word, Longo saw to the ploughing of his fields the next morning. He sat in the shade of an olive tree, taking a breakfast of bread and cheese while he watched Nicolo struggle to pull a plough through the cold, hard ground. Longo had strapped Nicolo to the harness himself, and although the chamberlain had been wrestling for nearly half an hour, he had moved no more than a few feet. When he had finished his breakfast, Longo went down to where Nicolo was straining at the harness. The sun had risen and, although the air still retained the chill of winter, Nicolo was dripping in sweat. He sank to his knees in exhaustion as Longo approached.

'Nicolo, you have only ploughed six feet,' Longo said with mock severity. He poked at the dirt with his foot.

'And poorly turned at that. You will be out ploughing every day until summer at this rate.'

Nicolo looked up in alarm. 'Please, My Lord, no more ploughing, I beg you. I will do anything you ask.'

'Very well.' The punishment had been mostly for the benefit of the other servants. Nicolo was valuable enough that Longo would put up with his occasional transgressions. Longo pulled his chamberlain to his feet and helped him from the harness. 'You may start by running to the villa. I am going to take a tour of the vineyards, and when I return, I want horses saddled for myself, Tristo and three men. I must go to a council meeting in Genoa, and I will spend tonight in town. Please send a man to the *palazzo* to make the necessary arrangements.'

'Yes, My Lord. Immediately, My Lord,' Nicolo said, hurrying away despite his weariness.

'And have somebody look at your back, Nicolo,' Longo called after him. 'I'm sure the harness has left its mark.'

'Of course. Thank you for your consideration, My Lord.' Nicolo jogged on up the hill towards the villa, paused to catch his breath at the olive tree where Longo had breakfasted, and then lumbered over the hill and out of view.

When Longo arrived at the villa, he found Nicolo holding the bridle of his horse. Tristo and three armed men stood ready to escort Longo to the city, and with them was William, who rushed forward as soon as he caught sight of Longo. 'Longo,' he cried. 'May I ride with you to the city? I will be no trouble.'

'We are not in the East any longer, William. You must address me as "My Lord",' Longo admonished, although he accompanied his words with a smile. William had spoken in English, and none except for Longo and Tristo had understood. 'You may not accompany me this time,' Longo continued. 'You do not know our ways, and I do not want you getting into trouble. Once you know something of Italian, then you may enter Genoa. Not before.'

'But I will be no trouble,' William protested.

'I am sure,' Longo said, swinging himself into the saddle. 'But you must stay nevertheless. Nicolo,' he said, switching to Italian, 'find something to occupy William. Teach him some Italian.'

Longo spurred away. He and his men rode at a trot through vineyards and fields, down through the tall eastern gate of Genoa – the Porta Soprana – and into the city. As they wound through the narrow streets, the buildings close on either side, Longo caught sight of William running after them, attempting unsuccessfully to stay out of sight. Longo shook his head. The boy would have to learn discipline if he wished to stay in Longo's household.

By the time he arrived at the Ducal Palace, Longo had put William out of his mind. The palace was a tall building, with white marble columns fronting the street and a tall tower rising above the whole. Longo dismounted, handed his reins to Tristo, and entered. The palace was the centre of power in Genoa. The city was ruled exclusively by a few great merchant families: the Grimaldi, Cassello, Boccanegra, Spinola, Adorno, Fregoso, Doria, Fieschi and Giustiniani. They met in council once a month, presided over by the Doge, who they elected for life.

Longo entered the council hall – a long, high-ceilinged room dominated by a massive oval table. He took his place as head of the Giustiniani family, and waited while the table slowly filled. The Doge, Ludovico Fregoso, entered last, a tall, long-nosed man with the pleasant, unexceptional features of his family. He called the council to order, and the talk turned immediately to questions of trade – the anticipated arrival of several caravans from the East, the persistent rumours of a sea passage to the Indies, and the advisability of financing exploration of the passage. From trade, the talk turned to politics: Genoa's great rival, Venice, was expanding its lands in the eastern Mediterranean. Longo sat quietly until the discussion turned to Pera – the Genoese trading colony just across the Golden Horn from Constantinople.

'Signor Giustiniani,' Fregoso addressed him. 'You have recently returned from Constantinople. What news do you bring?'

'The news is not good,' Longo began. 'King Ladislas of Poland was killed at the Battle of Kossova, and John Hunyadi's army was destroyed. The Greeks do not have enough men to fight the sultan's armies. If the Turks attack, then I fear Constantinople will fall unless the Greeks have outside aid.'

The table was quiet. Finally, Niccolò Grimaldi, a soft-spoken, elderly man known for his shrewd business dealings, broke the silence. 'If Constantinople falls, then Pera will be lost. Our trade with the East would be ruined.'

'We would be left with nothing, easy pickings for the Venetians,' agreed Umberto Spinola.

'What course of action do you suggest, Signor Giustiniani?' Fregoso asked.

'We have two choices. We can send an ambassador to the sultan and arrange a treaty guaranteeing the sanctity of Pera. Murad may be an infidel, but he is a man of his word. However, he is said to be in poor health, and I know little of his son, the heir. Moreover, it pains me to go begging to the Turks. Instead, I propose that we arrange a treaty with the Greek emperor. In return for trading concessions, we should begin sending ships and men to Constantinople to fortify the city. I believe that a strong sign of Western support is the only thing that can deter the Turks. Whatever we do, we must act quickly. Only Murad's goodwill has preserved peace thus far. I fear it will not last for long.'

Longo sat back. Spinola, an extremely religious man who could not abide the Turks, responded first. 'I agree with Signor Giustiniani. We must enter no negotiations with the heathen sultan.'

'Fine words,' Giovanni Adorno retorted. He was a plump man, whose merry face and twinkling eyes belied a ruthless intelligence. 'But your religion, Signor Spinola, has not stopped your agents from signing contracts with Turkish warlords or purchasing millions of soldi worth of spices from Muslim traders.'

'You question my faith, Signor?' Spinola bristled.

'Not at all,' Adorno soothed. 'I merely wish to point out that even the most righteous among us have made deals with the heathens. Indeed, our livelihoods depend on it.'

'There are other concerns,' Longo pointed out. 'A deal with the sultan will create anger in Constantinople. We cannot risk losing our docks and warehouses there.'

'Exactly,' Spinola agreed. 'That is why we must aid Constantinople.'

'Forgive me for asking,' Grimaldi said. 'But what would this cost? Financing troops at such a distance is no small matter. I do not wish to bankrupt our city to fight a war that has not yet begun.' Several men nodded or thumped the table in agreement. 'And what if we support Constantinople, and the city falls regardless?' Grimaldi continued. 'We will lose everything.'

'A small sacrifice to defend our faith,' Spinola insisted. 'Or have we all forgotten that we are Christians, that we have a duty to our Lord?'

'I am sure none of us has forgotten, Signor, but we also have a duty to our city and our people,' Fregoso said. 'I propose that we make contact with the sultan . . .'

'But Signor!' Longo interrupted. 'We cannot abandon Constantinople.'

'We will not,' Fregoso assured him. 'We will seek to learn the sultan's mind, but will enter into no official agreement. Meanwhile, the Emperor Constantine will be given assurances of aid, to be delivered when and if an attack occurs.' In short, Fregoso was proposing that they do nothing. 'All in favour?' the Doge asked. A chorus of *ayes* settled the matter. Only Longo and Spinola had abstained. 'Very well,' Fregoso concluded, 'the matter is settled and this meeting is at an end.'

Longo rose and marched from the palace without a word to the others. The decision had not surprised him, but he was upset nonetheless. He sent Tristo and his men on ahead to the *palazzo*. Longo followed on foot, striding ahead as if to outpace his disappointment.

William stood in a shadowy alleyway and watched as Longo exited the Ducal Palace and headed on foot towards the centre of town. He followed at a distance. A dense crowd filled the narrow street, circulating between the shops that lined both sides of the road. Above, covered balconies projecting from the buildings nearly met overhead, leaving only a narrow gap for the pale January sunshine. William watched as a house servant came to the window of one of the balconies and dumped a chamber-pot into the street below. William jumped back, narrowly avoiding being doused with filth.

He turned to find Longo standing before him. William froze, his face flushing crimson. 'I didn't mean to disobey, sir,' he explained. 'But I wanted to see the city – it was dark when we arrived, and I didn't think it would do any harm . . .'

'I am not angry with you,' Longo said, cutting William short. 'I could use your company. We will stop by the market on the way to the *palazzo*. As long as you are out, I might as well buy you something to wear. Those rags barely cover you.'

They walked through the maze of narrow streets and down to the market. It filled the Piazza San Giorgio, only a few blocks from the port, and overflowed into the surrounding streets. The periphery of the square was lined with booths selling a dazzling array of goods – oriental silks, Indian spices, exotic animals, swords, flowers. Milling between the booths was a thick crowd of people, cut occasionally by a noble on horseback. William stopped and gaped, dazzled by the brightly painted buildings that lined the square, the outlandishly dressed street performers and the sheer liveliness of it all. Longo waded into the crowd, and William hurried after him.

They stopped in front of a stall selling bolts of cloth and well-worked leather in long strips. Longo patted the leather appreciatively, then spoke briefly with the merchant, who offered two long lengths of the leather for Longo's

83

closer inspection. Longo nodded his approval and then moved on to examine a bolt of white cotton.

'But I thought we were buying clothes,' William interrupted.

'These are your clothes: leather breeches and a cotton shirt. Tristo will show you how to sew them. Now come. You look half-starved. I will buy you something to eat. You have never had a fig, I'd wager.'

William had never tasted anything quite so wonderful as a fig. It was so sweet it hurt his mouth, but it also had an exotic, earthy flavour that undercut the sweetness. As he and Longo chewed, they wandered over to watch a fire-eater in one of the streets on the edge of the square. The fire-eater took a flaming sword and slowly inserted the blade – all two feet of it – into his mouth so that only the hilt protruded. When he withdrew the sword, the blade was still burning.

'How does he do that?' William wondered.

Longo reflected, chewing on a fig. 'Maybe he drinks something special to protect him. Or maybe it does burn him, but he has grown used to the pain.'

But William was no longer listening. All his attention was focused beyond the fire-eater, to where an Italian noble was approaching on horseback. He was a thin man, whose otherwise handsome face was marred by a perpetual sneer. William recognized that face; indeed, he would never forget it. It was the face of Carlo Grimaldi, the man who had betrayed William and his crewmates to the Turks.

William surged forward, stepping in front of Carlo's horse. 'It is you, you bastard!' he screamed. 'I am going to kill you!'

The horse reared, almost unseating Carlo. He recovered

and stared contemptuously at William. 'You seem to have lost your wits, boy,' he said in accented English. 'I have never seen you before in my life. Now get out of my way.' He slashed his riding whip across William's face, drawing blood.

William drew his dagger and stood his ground. 'You are a murderer,' he spat. 'You stabbed my uncle in the back. You betrayed us to the Turks.'

'I do not take kindly to being insulted, especially by common English scum like you,' Carlo snarled and again sent his riding whip slashing towards William's face. William raised his dagger and sliced the whip neatly in two. 'I will have your head for that!' Carlo roared, drawing his sword.

Longo stepped between Carlo and William. 'I am Longo Giustiniani, and this boy is under my protection. If you have a quarrel with him, then you have a quarrel with me.'

Carlo went white at the mention of Longo's name. 'I did not know the boy was in your service, Signor Giustiniani. But he has insulted me and drawn on me. I demand justice.'

'If you want justice, then you will have to take it from me,' Longo said.

Carlo hesitated. His honour had been challenged, but clearly he did not wish to fight Longo. Finally he nodded. 'So be it. I shall send someone to arrange the details.'

'No,' William insisted. 'I will fight for myself.'

'Quiet, William,' Longo ordered. 'You do not know what you are doing.'

William ignored him. Carlo had killed his friends, and William had sworn to make him pay. He turned to Carlo and said in broken Italian, 'I you fight. I.'

Carlo smirked. 'I would as soon wipe my boots with him as fight this commoner,' he said. 'But the boy seems to need a lesson in manners. I will meet him tomorrow. My man will be at your house presently. Good-day, Signor Giustiniani.'

Carlo's second, his portly brother Paolo, arrived at the *palazzo* no more than an hour later and met with Longo. They quickly agreed to terms: first light, the Piazza di Sarzano, to the death.

Longo found William and Tristo eating at a table in the courtyard, and he stopped to watch them. Tristo was tucking into a heaping plate of vermicelli covered in butter, while William held up a long thin noodle, eyeing it sceptically. 'Looks like a worm,' he noted. 'What do you call it again?'

'*La pasta.*'

'*La pasta*,' William repeated and ate the noodle, chewing carefully. 'Not bad.' He reached for a cup and sniffed at the contents.

'*Il vino*,' Tristo told him.

William took a sip and grimaced. 'Haven't you got any beer?'

Tristo laughed. 'You'll learn to like it, boy. Believe me.' William took another sip and grimaced again.

'Don't go getting him drunk, Tristo. He'll need a clear head tomorrow,' Longo called as he approached. 'William, we have agreed to terms. The duel will be to the death.' Longo studied William's face for any sign of fear, but saw none. 'Have you ever fought with a short sword?' Longo asked him.

'Just daggers, mostly.'

'Take a hold of this, then,' Longo said. He handed William a short sword – a three-foot thin blade with shallow edges, a light sword more for stabbing than for cutting. William took it and slashed the air before him.

'It's so long. Why do they call it a short sword?'

'The sword is named by the length of its handle,' Longo told him.

'Well, so long as it's sharp.' William practised another attack, ducking low and raking his sword through the air, where his foe's knees would be. The boy used the sword like a huge dagger. He had no idea of formal sword fighting.

'I have seen Carlo fight,' Tristo said grimly. 'He's a deadly hand with a sword. I watched him make short work of the youngest Spinola brother some years ago.'

'He has a reputation,' Longo agreed with a nod. What's more, William had to be giving away at least sixty pounds to Carlo. 'If you wish, William, I can put you on a ship tonight. You would be in Chios in a few months' time. There would be no shame in it. Carlo is a nobleman, and he was wrong to accept a commoner's challenge.'

William ran his hand along his cheek, feeling the fresh cut that Grimaldi's whip had left. 'I will fight him. I am not afraid.'

'Very well,' Longo said. 'I suggest you get some sleep. I will see you in the morning.'

Sunrise found Longo and William already at the Piazza di Sarzano, their horses tethered out of the chill wind, in the lee of the old city wall. They stood in the centre of the cobbled square, their breath steaming and their cloaks wrapped tightly about them. Behind them rose the Church of San Salvatore, its facade marked by four towering columns, numerous frescos and an odd stained-glass window shaped like an enormous hat.

The two Grimaldi brothers arrived on horseback and tethered their horses in the shelter of the wall. All four men met in the centre of the square. The air was thick with moisture off the nearby sea and the light was still dim. The city was quiet, still sleeping. They spoke softly, as if afraid to upset the calm.

'Choose your sword,' Longo said, handing Paolo the two blades. He hefted them, and finding them equal, handed one of them to Carlo, who took it and slashed at the air several times to judge the sword's balance. Carlo nodded his satisfaction. Longo handed the other sword to William. 'You each know the terms,' Longo said. 'To the death. No quarter will be sought or given.' William and Carlo each nodded. 'You may take your places, then.' Longo turned to William. 'Keep your guard up, and God save you.' Longo and Paolo stepped away to the edge of the square, while William and Carlo squared off some ten feet apart. William looked pitifully thin and young across from the much taller, stronger Carlo.

'Not much of a contest, I'm afraid,' Paolo said. Then, as if aware that his words might cause offence, he added in a conciliatory tone: 'Still, it should be over quickly. The boy won't suffer.' Longo ignored him.

'Are you ready for your lesson, cur?' Carlo spoke sharply in Italian.

'Go to hell, you son of a Turkish whore,' William spat back in English.

'Very well, then.' Carlo bowed and assumed his fighting stance, his body sideways, his right foot forward and pointed at William, and his sword held lightly, following the point of his foot. William dropped to a low crouch, his entire body facing Carlo, his sword held out sideways before him. The two combatants stood still, gauging one another.

Paolo chuckled. 'The boy looks something like a lobster, does he not?' he said. Longo watched on in silence, and Paolo added: 'I mean no offence, of course. I quite like lobsters. Delicious creatures.'

Suddenly, Carlo sprang forward, bounding towards William in a few short steps and lunging at the boy's chest. William anticipated the attack, and he spun out of the way long before Carlo reached him, slashing in vain at Carlo's heels and then skipping to safety. Carlo continued to press the attack, lunging repeatedly with wicked thrusts. Each time, William spun clear, moving in a large circle around the square. Their fighting styles could not have been more different: Carlo always attacking on a line, moving back and forward only, while William moved constantly sideways, spinning and ducking. William was quicker than Carlo, but he was having a difficult time attacking against the Italian's much longer reach.

Beside Longo, Paolo sensed that the fight would not go as easily as anticipated. 'The boy is a slippery devil,' he remarked. 'No doubt learned it picking pockets.'

Another attack by Carlo, and this time William only narrowly avoided the blow, the sword ripping through the fabric of his shirt. Encouraged, Carlo pressed his attack, trying to close with William. William was on his heels now, no longer circling. He backed away, twisting from side to side and barely avoiding a handful of thrusts.

His shirt showed several new tears, and now blood was trickling down his side. Still, William danced backwards, and Carlo pressed on, lunging again and again, his sword passing within inches of William's twisting body.

A final lunge, and this time William was a step slow. He twisted into the blow, and the sword skewered his left side, just beneath the ribs. William stumbled, but before Carlo could withdraw his sword for another blow, William rose and drove his sword up through Carlo's throat and out the back of his head. Carlo fell instantly, a pool of blood spreading out around his dead body. William staggered backwards, Carlo's sword still lodged in his side. He looked down at the sword for a moment, then collapsed to his knees.

'William!' Longo rushed to the boy's side. To his surprise, the wound did not look to be a mortal one. It bled little, and the sword seemed to have passed through cleanly, damaging neither the lungs nor the intestines. 'You were lucky, boy,' Longo told him. 'But this sword will have to come out now. Brace yourself.'

'It wasn't luck, My Lord,' William replied, gasping as Longo withdrew the sword. 'I couldn't get close enough unless I took a blow. The pig-faced bastard had damned long arms.'

Longo laid William down, and then poured a flask of brandy into the wound. He tore two lengths of cloth from William's new shirt, wadded the first into a ball, and pressed it against the wound. 'Hold that,' he ordered. Longo pressed the other strip against the wound in William's back. He then took a long strip of linen that he had brought with him and wrapped it tightly around William's mid-section several times.

'That should hold you for now, but we had best get you inside,' Longo said. 'The cold won't do you any good, and neither will the Grimaldi men. The duel was honourably fought, but they'll be in a foul mood when they arrive. Paolo,' he called to the heavy-set young man, who was kneeling in shock over his brother's body. 'I trust this puts a satisfactory end to this disagreement? There will be no acts of vengeance?' Paolo gazed at him dumbly. 'Very well then,' Longo continued, 'I suggest you send for some of your men as soon as you can. The dogs will be at the body soon enough if you wait.'

They left the stupefied Paolo still kneeling beside Carlo. Longo helped William into the saddle, then mounted behind him. They rode back to the Palazzo dei Giustiniani, the bells of San Salvatore ringing out behind them to welcome the new day.

The next morning it was clear from the sickening smell of the bandages that William's wound was festering, and later that day the boy contracted a raging fever that left him incoherent, talking to those around him as if he were at home in England with his mother. A doctor was summoned, and he bled William to reduce his bad humours and relieve the fever. Still, the boy continued to burn, and none of the doctor's efforts succeeded in relieving the delirium. Two days passed with no sign of improvement, after which the doctor offered only the direst of forecasts: even if he survived, the doctor assured them, the boy would be an idiot, all his wits burned away by the fever.

Longo could not bear to watch William wasting away. Leaving Tristo with orders to alert him of any change in the boy's condition, he returned to his villa and busied himself with the tending of his vines. The very night of his return there was a frost, and Longo and his serfs spent a busy night lighting pots filled with pitch all along the rows of vines, fighting to keep the killing chill from the young leaves. The next morning, as Longo walked his vineyards to inspect the damage, he was surprised to see Tristo on horseback, galloping down from the villa to meet him.

As Tristo came closer, Longo could see that the huge man was struggling to stay upright in the saddle, and that he favoured his right arm, keeping it pinned to his side. What in God's name had happened to him?

'My Lord,' Tristo said with a wince as he reined in his horse and slid from the saddle. 'I bring news from town.' Tristo's right arm was in a sling, and blood showed through a heavy bandage wrapped around his head.

'What has happened?' Longo asked.

'There was a fight with some of the Grimaldi men. I only happened across it at the last, and I set about trying to separate the men. I had my arm broken by the mace of one of our own men – the cursed idiot – and got a nasty gash on my head for my troubles. Still, the rest had it much worse. Gucio and Piero are killed. Four others are laid up with various injuries. One Grimaldi man is dead, and the rest are pretty badly off.'

The news was not surprising – duels started more feuds than they ended – but it was not welcome either. The Grimaldi were a powerful family, and Longo did not fancy having them as an enemy. Much less did he fancy watching his back each time he rode through the streets of Genoa, or sending his servants to market with armed escort. He would have to act fast. Now that men on both sides had lost friends, the matter needed only a small push – the death of another noble from one of the two families – to evolve into a blood feud.

'Who started the fight?' Longo asked.

'Our men had been to the dock, and most likely to the tavern as well. On returning, they met six Grimaldi men in the street. Probably they were waiting for our men. Insults were exchanged, a Grimaldi man drew, and that was that. From what our men tell me, the Grimaldi men seem bent on revenge for what William did to Carlo. They seem to think the boy is some kind of assassin.'

'And what of William?' Longo asked.

'The same. Only he stopped talking last night. Hasn't said a word since. Loretta, the midwife, says that is a good sign. She says the fever will break now.'

'And what does the doctor say?'

'The doctor says that this is the beginning of the end. The no-good bastard seems to think that William is as good as dead.'

'Then we shall have to hope that the midwife is in the right,' Longo said. 'You will stay here at the villa until you are healed. Have Maria look after you. I will return to Genoa to see to William and take care of this Grimaldi mess.'

Shortly after Longo's arrival, William's fever finally broke, and the boy woke from his long delirium with his senses intact. Longo watched him consume enough pasta to feed ten men, and then left for the Grimaldi *palazzo* to make his peace.

Despite the hostility between the families, Longo was

greeted politely and presented immediately to Niccolò Grimaldi – the father of the recently deceased Carlo and the head of the family. The elder Grimaldi was a small man. Despite his sixty years, his lean, tan face was hardly wrinkled, though his hair was a wild mix of grey and black, like the ash from recently burned wood. He was seated on a balcony overlooking the courtyard, drinking a thick black liquid that Longo recognized as coffee, an eastern delicacy. Grimaldi motioned for Longo to sit. Once the formalities were ended, Grimaldi moved right to the point.

'You have come to make peace between our families,' he said. 'I am an old man. I treasure peace, but it is hard-bought after so much blood.'

'Surely more blood is not the answer,' Longo replied. 'I am a warrior, Signor Grimaldi. I have fought more battles than most men have seen years. I do not fear bloodshed, but I have no quarrel with your family, nor with you. Your son was killed fairly, honourably. Let that be an end to it.'

Grimaldi nodded and took a long sip of coffee before he spoke again. 'No doubt you are right. Still, I have lost a son, Signor Giustiniani. Nothing can replace him. Nothing can repay that loss. But perhaps if I were to find a new son, then I could forgive. By joining our families, we might end this bloodshed. You are not married, I recollect?' Longo nodded. 'Very well, shall I introduce my daughter, Julia?'

'I would be delighted,' Longo replied. Julia was ushered in and introduced, a shy girl of twelve. It was clear that she had been preparing for this meeting from the moment Longo entered the courtyard, for she was dressed in her very best – a flowing gown of white silk embroidered with interlacing red roses – and her hair was braided with ribbons and twisted into an intricate knot atop her head. She was thin and still flat-chested, but she had delicate features and looked likely to grow into a beautiful woman. She curtsied, blushed demurely as Longo complimented her fine dress, and was dismissed.

'She is fertile, no doubt, like her mother,' Grimaldi said. 'And a beauty as well, yes?'

'Indeed, signor,' Longo replied.

'Good. Then you do not object to marrying her?'

Longo paused. As his chamberlain Nicolo often reminded him, none of Longo's properties would be secure until he produced an heir. Julia was young, fertile and certainly attractive enough. A female touch would be welcome in his household, not to mention in his bed. Most importantly, the marriage would transform the budding feud into an alliance with a powerful family. Longo's feelings were beside the point. It was his duty to marry Julia Grimaldi. 'You honour me, Signor Grimaldi,' Longo said at last. 'I would be overjoyed to marry your daughter.'

'Very well,' Grimaldi said, rising. 'Let me embrace you as my new son. But I am not one of these Turks, you understand, to send my daughter away so young. I trust you will not object to a delay in the marriage until she is more of a woman?'

'I am very much of your mind on the matter, signor. I would be happy to wait.'

'Then it is settled,' Grimaldi said, returning to his coffee. 'We shall work out the details in time. I thank you for your visit, Signor Giustiniani.'

'And I for you kindness, Signor Grimaldi,' Longo replied. He bowed and left.

So I am to be married, he reflected as a servant led him back to his horse. Nicolo, at the very least, would be overjoyed.

Chapter 5

Sofia, dressed in a tight-waisted, rust-red caftan with billowing sleeves, followed Constantine, Helena and the other members of the royal family into the great hall of the Blachernae Palace. Constantine had arrived in Constantinople the previous day, and a great feast had been prepared to celebrate his new reign. Sofia passed between long tables heaped with roasted meats, candied fruits and still-steaming bread. Nobles lined the tables, their gold- and jewel-embroidered caftans lending some splendour to an otherwise rather shabby scene. The imperial family had been desperate for money for decades, and the golden plates, goblets and candelabra that once graced the tables of the palace had long since been melted down for coin. Simple pewter plates and wooden cups now adorned the tables, and while candles burned on the emperor's table, the rest of the hall was lit by torches set in the walls.

Sofia was surprised to find herself seated at the emperor's table between Lucas Notaras and the dull but very talkative Grand Logothete, George Metochites. As a woman, it was not Sofia's place to speak unless directly questioned, and so she listened politely to Metochites, stifling yawns while he alternated between his two favourite subjects – the glories of his learned great-grandfather Theodore Metochites, and the dangers of union with the Catholic Church. All the time he managed to eat at a fascinating rate, far outpacing the constant stream of dishes, and shortly a trail of half-chewed food began to form, leading down his shirt and under the table. Oblivious, Metochites prated on and on.

'Did you know that my great-grandfather was something of a scholar?' Metochites asked in a dull monotone. He continued without waiting for an answer. 'Oh yes, he was. Quite the scholar. His studies of Aristotle and of astronomy are simply marvellous. Astronomy is certainly superior to mathematics. Most certainly superior, epistemologically speaking, for astronomy assumes the proper functioning of mathematics, does it not? Even without our understanding of the golden mean or arcs or circles, the sun would still travel around the earth. Of course, our Latin friends don't think so. To them, the sun revolves solely around the pope, with never so much as a nod to any bishops or councils. Did you know that they use unleavened bread in their communion? They might as well be Jews . . .'

Sofia had already met her other dinner companion, Notaras, on several occasions. She found him arrogant, very handsome, and very aware of it. He spent the meal locked in conversation with the royal councillor Sphrantzes and hardly glanced at Sofia. From what she could gather, they were arguing over the possibility of union with the Catholic Church. Only near the end of the meal, after his conversation with Sphrantzes had ended in frustration, did Notaras finally turn to her.

'The damn fool,' Notaras muttered. 'He would have us go begging cap in hand to the Latins.' He glanced at Sofia as if noticing her for the first time, and his gaze lingered. 'I understand that you know something of politics, Princess. Tell me, what do you think of this talk of union?'

Sofia lowered her eyes. 'I am sure that I could tell you little you do not already know,' she replied. She might study politics and philosophy in the privacy of her quarters, but she knew her public limits well enough.

Notaras's eyes narrowed. 'Sphrantzes has told me that you are not so modest behind closed doors. Come now, Princess. You may speak freely.'

'Very well,' Sofia said, raising her eyes to meet Notaras's gaze. 'When help is there, I believe that one should take it. And, I believe that it is not piety that makes us spurn such help, but pride.'

'Hear, hear!' Sphrantzes cried from down the table. Notaras ignored him.

'Perhaps you are right, Princess,' he said, his voice rising. 'Perhaps it is pride that motivates me. But I am not ashamed to say that I am too proud to submit to the rule of the pope; just as I am too proud to see our patriarch dethroned, or to see Latin soldiers walking our walls in place of their rightful defenders. I am proud, Princess, and I hope to God that all the men of this city are just as proud.'

'Your pride will count for very little if the city falls, if our homes and churches are looted and our women raped,' Sofia replied, rather more loudly than she had intended. Around her, the table had gone quiet as people turned to listen, but Sofia continued regardless. 'I do not see the honour in sacrificing an entire city to your finer feelings.'

'You are a woman,' Notaras snorted. 'You could hardly understand such things as honour, could you?'

'It seems you understand little else,' Sofia murmured.

'What was that?'

'I said you are right. I do not understand the honour of which you speak.'

'That is enough, Princess,' Constantine called from the centre of the table. 'We are not here to bicker, but to celebrate. Come, let us all drink to the continued glory and prosperity of our empire.' He quaffed his glass, and the rest of the guests followed suit. A long round of toasts followed: to Constantine; to the empire; and to continued peace and friendship between the Turks and Constantinople. When the toasting was done, Constantine left the table, signalling that the feast was over. Sofia left her place without even a glance at Notaras. She hurried from the great hall and was surprised to find Constantine waiting for her in the corridor.

'Niece,' he said. 'What did you think of the megadux, Lucas Notaras? A fine man, is he not?'

'Yes, sire,' she replied, although in truth she thought him a prideful buffoon. She could not, however, contradict the emperor. 'He is a very fine man, certainly.'

'Good,' Constantine said, smiling. 'Perhaps you shall not believe it, but it would pain me to upset you. I am very glad you enjoy Notaras's company, for he has agreed to marry you. He will be your husband before the year is through.'

Sofia felt suddenly sick. She put her hand to her stomach and lowered her head, breathing deep as she struggled to control her shock and disappointment. 'Yes, sire,' she managed to say in a dead voice. 'I am overjoyed.' She bowed and hurried away before Constantine could see the tears in her eyes.

'On guard!' Sofia cried and lashed out with her sword, swinging for the head of Dalmata, the head of the imperial guard and her fencing instructor. Dalmata gave ground, and Sofia pressed her attack, driving him across the floor of her apartments. Dalmata was much larger than Sofia, but she compensated with exceptional quickness and lightning reflexes. She swung high, then sidestepped a blow from Dalmata before swinging down hard and giving him a cruel rap on the knuckles of his sword hand. The blow stung, despite the leather glove that Dalmata wore and the dulled blade of the practice sword. Dalmata cursed and dropped his sword.

'Well done,' he said, rubbing his hand. After much convincing, Dalmata had agreed to teach her the fundamentals of swordplay, and Sofia had proved an apt pupil. They practised in her quarters, the only place in the palace where such outlandish behaviour on the part of a royal princess could pass unremarked. 'But be careful not to overextend yourself,' Dalmata warned.

Sofia nodded her understanding. She was breathing hard after nearly an hour of practice, but she did not wish to stop. 'Shall we continue?' she asked.

'Very well, one more pass,' Dalmata said. 'But I warn you, I shall not spare you this time.' And with that, he attacked, slashing at Sofia's waist. She parried the blow and spun away, but Dalmata was on her immediately. He swung hard, and Sofia's hand stung as she parried the heavy blow. The pain only made her angry. She ducked another blow and then went on the offensive, attacking with a ferocity that surprised even herself. She drove Dalmata back until he was against the wall, and then their swords crossed and locked. Dalmata shoved hard, and Sofia fell and rolled away.

'Are you injured?' Dalmata asked. Sofia sprang to her feet and shook her head. She would have a bruise on her hip, but she did not want to give in now. She attacked again, pressing Dalmata back against the wall. Again, their swords locked, but this time when Dalmata tried to push her away, she was ready. As he pushed, she gave way and dropped to a crouch, kicking out and knocking Dalmata off his feet. She rose quickly and struck the back of his sword hand hard with the flat of her blade. Dalmata threw his sword aside in frustration.

'Good Lord, child!' he exclaimed. 'You have fought these last days as if you wished me dead. What has come over you?'

Sofia lowered her sword, embarrassed. She was breathing hard, furious still, but certainly not at Dalmata. 'I am sorry, *filos*. Are you hurt?' Dalmata waived away her concern. 'I have not been myself, of late,' Sofia confessed. 'I certainly have no idea why.'

'Do not be coy with me, child,' Dalmata said as he took a seat. 'I have known you too long. It is this talk of marriage that troubles you, is it not?'

Sofia looked away, embarrassed that Dalmata had read her so easily, and then sighed and turned to face him. 'Marriage will be like death to me. I was not raised to spend my days hidden away, ordering about servants and nursing children. I cannot bear it.'

'There is iron in you, Sofia,' Dalmata said. 'I believe you can bear anything. And besides, you must marry some day. You could do far worse than Notaras. At least he is a Greek, not some foreign potentate.'

'You do not understand,' Sofia insisted. 'Once I marry him, everything will end. There will be no more lessons in swordplay, no more studies with Sphrantzes, no more politics.'

'Marriage is not all bad. You will see,' Dalmata comforted her. 'And, you are not married yet. It might interest you to know that there will be a meeting in the council room tonight at which Constantine will decide what message to send the pope regarding union.'

'Tonight? Thank you, *filos*,' Sofia kissed Dalmata on the cheek. He was right. There were more important matters than her marriage. She had taken an oath before the Emperor John to defend Constantinople, and she would keep her word, marriage or no.

That night found Sofia creeping through a dark, narrow passage, her lamp covered so as to throw only a tiny ray of light at her bare feet. The palace was riddled with hidden passages and secret chambers. Few now knew that they existed, and even fewer could find their way through the maze of identical dark hallways. But Sofia was one of the few. She had often played in these passages as a young girl; now she used them to gather information.

She came to the end of the passage and mounted spiralling stairs, moving confidently in the dark. At the top of the stairs she stepped into a small alcove, covering her light completely as she did so. In the total darkness she could make out a tiny prick of light shining through the wall before her. She put an eye to the hole, and there was the council room before her. Six people were seated at a round table. To Sofia's left sat Constantine. Across the table from him were Sphrantzes and Dalmata. Helena, the empress-mother, sat with her back to Sofia, and on the far side of the table were Mammas and Notaras, Sofia's betrothed. Sofia turned her attention to Constantine, who was speaking. Through a trick of acoustics, Constantine's voice came to her clearly, as if she were standing in the same room with him.

'The Turkish threat is very real,' he was saying. 'Murad may have declared peace, but I fear an attack will come soon enough. Sphrantzes saw their army and says that it numbers over sixty thousand men. We will need help to defeat such a force. I shall send an ambassador to Venice and Genoa to request troops. But this creates as many problems as it solves, for we cannot very well send an ambassador to Italy without him paying his respects to the pope.' He paused and looked around the table. 'Of course, the message that we send to the pope is of the utmost importance.'

Of the utmost importance indeed; the approach taken with the pope now would define Constantine's policy on the Union of the Catholic and Orthodox churches, which had been divided for over four hundred years. The Catholics insisted on the primacy of the pope and the *filioque* doctrine, which held that the Holy Spirit flowed from both the Son and the Father. The Greeks, on the other hand, insisted that all bishops were equal and that the Holy Spirit flowed only from God the Father. The doctrinal issues seemed small enough, but they were reinforced by decades of mistrust and anger, culminating in 1204, when the Latins had sacked Constantinople.

The last two emperors had supported union for political reasons: they longed for western aid against the Turkish threat. The clergy, nobles and most of the people, however, were vehemently opposed. Sofia was no friend of the Catholic Church, but she was sure that union was the only way to persuade the Latins to come to the aid of Constantinople.

Mammas spoke first, and his words were no surprise. After publicly championing Demetrius's failed bid for the throne, he had lost the faith of the emperor, and the Catholics were now his only allies. He had little choice but to support union. 'Cardinal Bessarion has written to me from Rome,' Mammas said. 'He tells me that the new pope longs to raise troops for Constantinople. He only awaits a decree of union.'

Sphrantzes nodded. 'I have heard the same. However, with Hunyadi's army in tatters, I do not know how much the pope's support is worth. If Venice and Genoa agree to send troops, then what more can the pope do? He could call for a crusade, but I do not believe that the French would honour it. Resentment over the Avignon Papacy is still strong. As we all know, union would create great anger at home' – a nod towards Notaras – 'and might do more harm than good.'

'Hear, hear!' Notaras agreed, pounding the table for emphasis. 'If we accept the articles of union then we will lose ourselves just as surely as if the Turks take our city. We do not need to go begging to the Latins. We can protect our city ourselves. We have done so for over a thousand years.' Sofia grimaced. It was the sort of prideful idiocy that might well doom them all. Nevertheless, the sentiment around the table seemed to be on Notaras's side. Dalmata nodded sternly in approval, as did Constantine. Even Mammas looked inclined to agree. Only Helena seemed opposed. Sofia could not see her face, but the set of the empress-mother's shoulders told Sofia that she was not pleased. Thank God there was at least one woman at the table to check all this foolish masculine pride.

Constantine noticed Helena's reserve. 'What is your council, Mother?'

'When I was young, our empire was powerful,' Helena began, her voice firm and authoritative. 'We could stand on our own against the Turks then, but not now.' Notaras tried to speak, but Helena cut him off. 'No, Notaras, do not contradict me. I was here when Murad laid siege to the city. If he had not been forced to withdraw in order to deal with rebellions in his own lands, our city would have fallen. We are weaker now and the Turks are stronger. Without Latin help, our city will fall. I would agree to a thousand unions to prevent that.'

'The city will fall?' Notaras asked. 'Who, then, will take it? We have been at peace with the Turks for years. Murad does not want war, and his son is a weakling: he lasted but a few months on the throne after Murad abdicated.'

'If Mehmed is weak, as you say, then that is all the more reason to seek union and to seek it now,' Helena insisted. 'If we can rally the Latins to our cause, then when Mehmed takes the throne, we can strike while he is still young. We could be rid of the Turkish threat once and for all. Is that not worth the price of union?'

'But surely we cannot simply accept the demands of the Latins?' Notaras cried. 'I would never bow before the primacy of the pope, and I know few men who would.'

'Of course,' Constantine agreed, eager to make a conciliatory gesture. He needed Notaras's support. 'The Union is vital, but we must not compromise ourselves. What do you suggest, Notaras?'

'If there is to be union, then it must be on our terms. I propose a letter to the pope, to be written by the Synaxis of bishops. The bishops can lay out the position of the Orthodox clergy, so that we may present a plan for union that meets the full support of the people of Constantinople.'

'The Synaxis?' Mammas sputtered. The Synaxis was a group of bishops who ardently opposed the Union and who refused to recognize Mammas as patriarch. 'But they have no authority.'

'They have the trust of the people,' Notaras replied.

'But not of God!' Mammas retorted.

'And was it God who told you to crown my brother Demetrius as emperor?' Constantine asked.

The blood drained from Mammas's face, and a tense silence settled around the table. Finally, Mammas pushed his chair back and stood. 'I have sworn loyalty to you, Constantine,' he said. 'But if you do not have faith in me, then I will resign and leave now.'

'No, stay. Tell me what you propose.'

'Very well,' Mammas said, sitting. 'I agree with Notaras that a letter should be written, but as the patriarch, I should be the one to write it. Who better to express the views of the clergy?'

'But most of the clergy reject Mammas,' Notaras

insisted. 'They will never accept union unless it is of their own making.'

'We shall send two letters, then,' Constantine said. 'You, Mammas, shall write one, and the Synaxis the other. When confronted with such unified support for union, the pope will surely be willing to concede some minor points.'

'But My Lord!' Mammas protested. 'The Synaxis is not a legally constituted body. If they are to send a letter to the pope, then I want no part of it. I would resign my post before I allowed myself to be associated with those heretics.'

'You speak in haste, Patriarch,' Constantine said.

'No, I assure you,' Mammas insisted. 'If the Synaxis letter is sent, then you will have to find a new patriarch.' The room fell silent.

Constantine frowned. 'The Synaxis will send their letter,' he said at last. 'I beg you to also write to the pope, Mammas, and to reconsider your decision.'

Mammas shook his head grimly and rose from the table. 'I will not stand for this,' he said and stormed from the room. His grating voice could be heard as he stomped down the stairs. 'Let it be on your own heads!' he shrieked. 'On your own heads!' His voice echoed in the stairwell and then faded to nothing.

'I shall send Andronicus Bryennius Leontarsis as our ambassador,' Constantine said, breaking the silence. 'Are there any objections?' There were not. 'Good. Sphrantzes, you will brief him on the position of the Venetians and Genoese. That is all.'

Before Constantine had finished speaking, Sofia was already creeping away. She had heard what she had come for. Constantine would push for union, and that was all that truly mattered. Still, Mammas's outburst worried her, as did the letter of the Synaxis: it was sure to anger the pope. Sofia doubted that simple old Leontarsis would be able to handle the situation. If only she could be there in Rome, then she would be able to soften the words of the letter, to make the pope understand the need for union. But that was not to be. In only a few months, she would be married to Notaras. 'God curse the day that I was born a woman,' she silently swore, and not for the first time.

The monk Gennadius sat behind the broad desk in his cell at Saint Saviour Pantocrator and held up a tiny vial filled with a golden liquid. He watched as the candlelight refracted through the liquid and then unstopped the vial and sniffed. There was almost no odour, only the faint smell of almonds. He was told that many could not smell even that. The liquid had been sent to Gennadius by a friend at the Ottoman court, and it was a most deadly poison. The full dose would kill in a matter of seconds, but in smaller amounts, the poison would take months to do its work and leave no trace. It would be perfect for Gennadius's plans.

There was a knock at the door, and Gennadius placed the vial aside on his desk. 'Enter,' he called. The door opened to reveal the monk Eugenius and behind him, Notaras. 'Welcome, Notaras,' Gennadius said. 'You have come at just the right time. Please sit.' He waved Notaras to an empty chair, and Eugenius withdrew, closing the door behind him. 'You have been at the palace?'

'Yes,' Notaras replied. 'Constantine is committed to union, as we both feared. He is sending Leontarsis to

Rome to discuss terms with the pope. I did as you suggested and supported the entire enterprise, with the condition that a letter to the pope should be drawn up by the Synaxis.'

'And here is the very letter.' Gennadius handed a piece of parchment across the desk to Notaras, whose eyebrows shot up as he read.

'The rejection of the *filioque* doctrine . . . the recognition of councils as superior to the pope . . . the use of leavened bread in the communion . . . such demands!' Notaras said, handing the letter back. 'The pope will be furious.'

'Indeed,' Gennadius agreed. 'I expect he will send us his own set of demands in short order, and, God willing, they will be even more insolent than ours. Not even Constantine will be able to stomach such an affront, and that will be an end to this talk of union.'

'I fear not,' Notaras said. 'The empress-mother has Constantine's ear, and she is committed to union at any cost.'

'The empress-mother?' Gennadius's lips curled back in his predatory smile. 'Never fear. She will not trouble our plans for much longer.'

Notaras's eyes narrowed as they focused on the vial on Gennadius's desk. 'Surely you do not mean to . . .'

'No, no, of course not,' Gennadius lied as he placed the vial in a drawer of his desk. 'I only meant that she is old, very old, and that the end of her time must be near.' He could tell that Notaras was not entirely convinced. 'What of Patriarch Mammas?' he changed the subject. 'How did he react?'

'As you expected. He refused to be involved. He even

went so far as to claim that if the letter were sent, he would resign as patriarch.'

'Good,' Gennadius said, rubbing his hands in pleasure. 'With a little push, perhaps we can convince him to leave Constantinople altogether. I shall have to make sure that a copy of this letter finds its way to him. Can you imagine what a scene he would make were he to run to Rome, telling the pope of how he has been mistreated? He would do more to poison the pope against Union than a thousand of these letters.'

'Indeed,' Notaras murmured. 'Now if you please, Gennadius, I will take my leave. I must rise early tomorrow to inspect the walls.'

'Very well. God keep you, Notaras.' Gennadius called Eugenius and watched him lead Notaras away. Then he opened his desk and once more removed the vial of poison. It was time to deal with Helena Dragases.

'You may enter,' the guard whispered and waved Sofia into Helena's darkened room. After the sunny brightness of the hallway, the darkness was impenetrable at first, and Sofia paused to allow her eyes to adjust. The scene brought back painful memories of the death of her uncle, Emperor John VIII. A stick of incense burned on a table near the door, filling the air with its heady smell. Next to it were two votive candles, their small flames the room's only source of light. They illuminated heavy curtains hung over the windows and an enormous bed, its four posts reaching up into the darkness. Helena lay on the bed, her eyes closed. She had become ill two weeks ago. The court physicians were at a complete loss and could recommend only rest and an occasional bleeding to rectify her humours. Despite all their care, Helena's condition had steadily worsened.

Sofia walked quietly across the deep carpet and knelt beside Helena's bed. This was the first time that she had seen the empress-mother since her illness began, and Sofia was surprised at how frail she was. Her skin looked brittle – papery and white – and she shuddered as she breathed. Helena's eyes opened a crack, and upon seeing Sofia, she smiled, a smile that looked more like a grimace on her gaunt face. Sofia helped as Helena pushed herself up, propping herself with pillows.

Helena turned to Sofia. 'You wished to see me, my dear?' she said, her voice a harsh whisper.

'Yes, *Mamme*, but I do not wish to trouble you.'

Helena waved away her concern. 'This is only a passing indisposition. I will be better soon enough. Indeed, I feel greatly recovered over the past few days. But what of you, my dear? I am told that you have not been sleeping well. Are you ill?' Sofia shook her head. 'Well then, tell me.'

Sofia lowered her eyes from Helena's searching gaze and took a deep breath. 'It is my marriage, *Mamme*,' she murmured.

'Are you fearful of the wedding night?' Helena asked. Sofia blushed and shook her head. 'Perhaps you do not approve of your husband-to-be, Notaras?'

'It is more than that, *Mamme*,' Sofia said, looking up. She paused, and Helena nodded encouragingly. 'It is marriage itself.' The words – so long kept to herself – spilled out now. 'I am every bit as capable as Notaras, and yet as his wife, I will be nothing. Notaras will not allow me to step outside the home, much less take part in councils or handle a sword. The second I marry him, my life will be over. I will be just another pretty thing, good only for bearing children. I cannot submit to it, *Mamme*.'

Helena nodded. 'I once felt as you do, child. After my marriage, I did not emerge from my quarters for months, except on direct summons. But marriage is not the end. I never learned to love Manuel, but my marriage to him gave me far more power than I ever would have had otherwise. Notaras is a powerful man, and if you can control him, then you will have a great say in our empire.'

Sofia was shaking her head. 'But you married the emperor. Notaras is only a noble. And besides, he will not listen to me. He is too proud, too arrogant.'

'I see.' Helena closed her eyes and lay back. She sat unmoving for some time, and Sofia began to fear that she had fallen asleep. Just as Sofia began to rise, however, Helena opened her eyes. 'You will not marry Lucas Notaras,' she said. 'No, do not speak. Let me explain. You know that we are sending an ambassador, Andronicus Leontarsis, to Italy?'

'Yes, *Mamme*.' Sofia blushed. How did Helena know?

'As a young woman, I too sat behind that wall, listening to secrets that I should not have heard,' Helena said. 'Leontarsis is a good man, but his is not the most subtle mind. In dealing with the pope, great tact and intelligence will be required, perhaps more than Leontarsis is capable of. I have persuaded Constantine that we should send another ambassador to second Leontarsis. You shall be that ambassador, Sofia. You are politically able, of the royal household, and most importantly, a woman. The Italians are easily moved by beauty. Perhaps you can convince them to send aid where men would fail.'

Sofia nodded. 'I will not fail you,' she promised. 'But how will this prevent my marriage?'

'The trip to Italy will take months, perhaps years. In the meantime, I will persuade Constantine that Notaras's loyalty is of too great importance to wait for your return before he is joined to our household. Another princess of the royal family will be married to him, and you will be released from your betrothal. In the meantime, I suggest that you find a man that you *can* live with. You cannot avoid marriage forever; it is your duty as a princess.'

Sofia stood and kissed Helena on the cheek. 'Thank you, *Mamme*,' she said. 'Thank you.'

Across the room, the door opened and a tall, spare man in priest's robes entered. He carried a tray with the bread and wine of the Holy Communion on it. 'Here is my priest, Neophytus. You must go,' Helena said to Sofia. 'I may not be long for this world, but at least I shan't roast in hell.'

Sofia kissed Helena again and left, passing the priest on her way. There was something distasteful about the man, but Sofia did not dwell on it. Her mind was elsewhere, already in Italy. She stepped into the bright hallway, a smile on her face. She was free again. Thank God, she was free!

Chapter 6

Mehmed guided his horse out from the cool shade of the forest and on to the baked dust of the road leading to Manisa, the city of princes. Behind him came the hunting party: horsemen, a pack of hounds with tongues lolling after the day's long chase, and the two deer that they had run down in the forests of Mount Sipylus. Mehmed and his party were on the lower slopes of the mountain now, but were still much higher than the city, which spread out on the plain before them, a maze of twisting streets and dusty bazaars broken only by the towering height of the main mosque and by the brilliant green gardens and cool white walls of the newly built palace. The caravanserai on the outskirts of town was crowded with merchants, guards and wandering camels, all taking their ease before continuing the trek to Smyrna or Constantinople. The whole – caravanserai and city alike – was baked by a brilliant late summer sun sitting in a pure blue sky, and heat rose from the ground below, causing the city to shimmer and shift like some fabulous mirage. It was a magnificent sight, but Mehmed gave the city only a glance before spurring his horse down the road at a gallop. The heat from the city was engulfing him already, and he was eager to reach the cool comforts of the palace.

There was no formal business waiting for Mehmed at the palace, which was not a surprise. Although he governed the province of Sarakhan from the palace in Manisa, there was little to do in the way of ruling other than to police and tax the caravanserai, and Mehmed left that task to the able eunuchs who administered the city. He spent his days hunting, practising swordplay and reading. He read mostly military texts – accounts of battles, writings of famous generals, books of strategy – but he was currently reading an account of Constantinople written in the thirteenth century by a Russian visitor to the Greek court. Upon reaching his suites, Mehmed bathed, changed into cool, cotton robes and took the book into the gardens.

Cushions were laid out for him under a lemon tree, and there he reclined, reading amidst the pleasant scent of lemons. He was attended by three *gedikli* – beautiful female slaves, trained from youth to serve him – who fanned him and fed him honeyed dates and wine, but Mehmed's attention was entirely taken up with his book. The Russian author, named Alexandre, described the city in detail, and Mehmed took careful notes as he read, filling a battered old scroll with sketches and ideas. The current section discussed the numerous underground passages in and out of the city – a topic of particular interest to Mehmed – and as he read, his mind drifted, turning to stratagems and plans of attack against the great city. If he could only find those passages, then he might sneak his troops into the city by night and have them open the gates. Or, perhaps he could fill the passages with gunpowder, and thus bring down the walls above them. But Constantinople was only a dream for now. In distant Manisa, Mehmed had little news of the court in Edirne and even less influence there. I cannot even command my own *kadin*, he reflected bitterly, much less an army.

Murad had insisted that Mehmed leave Gülbehar behind at the Royal Harem in Edirne. Mehmed missed her, but even more he regretted having been absent for the birth of his son, Bayezid. The boy was still only a babe – too young to be poisoned against his father – but nevertheless, Mehmed would rather have kept him near. Murad had made it clear that he disapproved of both Gülbehar and Bayezid, and Mehmed feared that his father might take advantage of Mehmed's absence to eliminate them. There was no sense in dwelling on the matter, though; he would have to be patient. And, in the meantime, there were his *gedikli* to keep him occupied. The girl holding the fan was particularly exquisite. She had a broad, oval face and red hair. Mehmed thought she looked Russian and would thus offer a perfect compliment to his book. He made a note in the margin to tell his *haznedar*, the keeper of the calendar of royal nights, to schedule the girl.

A black eunuch approached Mehmed across the garden. He was from Abyssinia, clean-shaven and rather heavy-set. Like most black eunuchs, he was also a *sandali*. Before they reached puberty, the *sandali* had their testicles and penis removed with a single cut of a razor, a wooden tube set in their urethra, and the wound cauterized with boiling oil. Afterwards, they were buried up to the chin in a mound of fresh manure and fed only milk for one week. If they survived, which they did surprisingly often, they were taken into service at the royal court. This particular *sandali* was named Salim, and as he drew closer, Mehmed saw that his brow was knit in irritation.

Salim bowed low before Mehmed, and spoke in a high, distraught voice. 'Forgive me for disturbing you, most gracious Lord,' he said. 'There is a man to see you, a merchant from one of the caravans. He must be very wealthy, for he bribed every guard and eunuch in sight to obtain an audience with me.' Mehmed smiled at this, for the man had no doubt bribed Salim as well. 'I told him that Your Excellency is occupied, but he insists upon seeing you. He says that you know him. He introduced himself as Isa of Attalia.'

Isa. Mehmed did indeed know a man of that name, but he had thought him dead for many years now. When Mehmed was still a child, still third in line to the throne, there had been a doctor of Asian origin named Isa who came to live in his household at Manisa. Isa knew much about herbs, both beneficent and poisonous, and in return for sizeable fees, he had poisoned Mehmed's two older brothers. Afterwards, Mehmed and his mother had concluded that Isa was a liability. Mehmed had dismissed him from his household and then sent a detachment of janissaries to track him down and kill him. The janissaries had reported Isa's death, and Mehmed had put them to death in turn. He had supposed that all knowledge of Isa had died with them. Yet here was a merchant, some six years later, claiming to be this same man.

'Show the man to my private audience chamber,' Mehmed ordered. 'Be certain that he is not armed. I wish to meet with this Isa alone. Only Ulu is to be present.' Salim bowed and hurried away.

Mehmed dismissed the *gedikli* and walked to his suites. Before entering his private audience chamber, he stepped into a small adjoining room and peered through a spyhole. There was Ulu, standing grim and stern next to Mehmed's throne, and there, in the middle of the chamber, stood the very same Isa that Mehmed had known as a child. Indeed, the man seemed hardly to have aged at all, even though he must now be near fifty. His gentle, yellow face was still smooth, his head shaved clean and he had the same lively, slanted eyes that Mehmed remembered so well. Mehmed observed Isa for a few minutes – he insisted on making all visitors wait for an audience – but he learned nothing from the man's impassive face. The Asian was carrying some sort of package: perhaps the reason for his presence lay there. After a last glance, Mehmed entered the audience chamber and seated himself on the throne.

Isa bowed low, his forehead touching the ground. 'You may rise,' Mehmed said, filling his young voice with as much authority as he could muster. He wanted Isa to understand from the start that he was a man now, not the boy that Isa had known years ago. 'It pleases me to see that you are well, Isa. I had feared that you were dead these many years.'

'Many thanks for your generous welcome. I am delighted to see that the years have treated you well,' Isa began. 'As for thinking me dead: I do not wonder that you thought so. I am certain that the janissaries you sent to murder me were quite persuasive when they returned.'

'They told me you were dead,' Mehmed said. 'Were

they still alive, I would have them put to death. Did you bribe them?'

'No. There was no need. I entered a tavern, and your janissaries lay in wait for me outside. I sent the tavern owner out with drink, to ease their wait. When I came out, I told them that the drink had been poisoned, and that they would only have the antidote if they did exactly as I said. They were to return and tell you that I had been killed. After that, I would have the antidote delivered to them. Of course, they were not poisoned at all, but that hardly mattered. I knew that you would have them put to death as soon as they reported back.'

'I see.' Mehmed was impressed. Isa would have to be handled with care. 'And what brings you to my palace after so many years?'

'I come on behalf of another, bearing a gift and an offer.' Isa unwrapped his burden, revealing a finely crafted mahogany box the size of a large book. He stepped forward and held out the box. Mehmed reached for it, but then hesitated.

'Gifts from you often prove poisonous, Isa. Perhaps I should refuse this one.'

'It is only a box,' Isa said. 'But if you wish to refuse it, that is your choice.'

'And what of the offer you spoke of?'

'The offer and the gift are one and the same. You must accept the gift before I can reveal the offer.'

'Very well,' Mehmed said and took the box. Then he reconsidered and handed it back to Isa. 'You open it,' he ordered. Isa gently opened the lid. It swung back on hinges to reveal a brilliant, crystal vial containing an amber liquid. Isa presented the opened box again, and

Mehmed took it. He held the vial up to the light. 'What is it? Poison?'

'A very powerful poison, and untraceable,' Isa said. 'It acts on contact with the skin and can kill in a matter of hours. Swallowed in small doses, the poison works more slowly. Depending on the strength of the victim, death can take days, or even months.'

'On whose behalf have you brought me this mighty poison?' Mehmed asked. 'And what would they have me do with it?'

'A friend from Edirne has sent it. I can tell you no more. As for its use, I wonder that you have not divined it already. After all, we both know that you are not afraid to call on poison when necessary to clear your path to the throne.'

'Are you suggesting that I would assassinate my own father?' Mehmed asked, his voice rising. 'I will have your head for this, Isa. Ulu,' he barked, and the burly janissary stepped forward, drawing his long, curved *yatağan*.

Isa did not so much as blink. 'If you kill me, then you will die before the day is out,' he said in a calm voice. Ulu hesitated, his sword hanging in the air.

'Ulu, desist,' Mehmed ordered. 'What do you mean, I will die?'

'Did you think that I would walk into your palace without taking precautions? The box you are holding is coated with the same poison that is in the flask. You should already be feeling its effects – a drying of your throat, a sudden tendency to sweat.' Mehmed gulped and wiped sweat from his forehead. Isa continued. 'Yes, I held the box too, so we are both poisoned. But there is an antidote. If it is administered soon, we may both live.'

'How do I know that you are not lying?'

'You do not.'

'Give me the antidote,' Mehmed ordered.

'I do not have it with me. It is in my tent at the cara-vanserai. Only I know where it is kept, or, indeed, what it even looks like.'

'Go then, and hurry,' Mehmed said. 'Ulu, do not let him out of your sight. If you make one false move, Isa, I swear that Ulu will kill you.'

'I understand. You should know that I have more than a hundred men in my service at the caravanserai. I will give the antidote to Ulu, but if he or anyone else makes an attempt on my life, then he will die, and you will never see the antidote.'

'Understood. Ulu will allow no harm to come to you.'

'Very well,' Isa said. 'Many thanks for this audience, Prince Mehmed. Your friend in Edirne will be most disap-pointed that you did not accept his offer, but I was told that you are to keep his gift regardless. May it profit you.' Isa bowed, and followed by Ulu, left the audience chamber.

Mehmed remained on his throne, clutching the box. Who was this mysterious friend in Edirne who wanted his father dead? And did they really think that Mehmed would be fool enough to accept their offer? Had he actu-ally been poisoned or was this all a game on Isa's part? Mehmed shook his head, trying to clear his thoughts. He would have spies follow Isa. In the meantime, there was this box and the poison it carried.

Mehmed rose from the throne and passed into his private chambers. He opened a cabinet on the wall, revealing a copy of the Koran in a golden case. He removed the Koran and reached into the back of the cabinet, pressing a hidden latch. The back of the cabinet swung open, revealing a small space containing stacks of gold coins, several bottles of wine and various private papers. Mehmed placed the box inside and then closed the hidden compartment and replaced the Koran. No, he would not be fool enough to poison his father. But, he would keep the poison all the same. One day, perhaps, it would prove useful.

SEPTEMBER 1449: EDIRNE

Halil stood behind a beaded curtain, his arms crossed and his fingers drumming impatiently as he waited for Isa to arrive. Halil had little time to himself, and any absence from the palace of more than an hour was sure to be noticed. He had already been waiting for Isa here, in the back rooms of the rug merchant Farzam's shop, for over fifteen minutes, and he could not wait much longer. To pass the time, he had been imagining devious means of punishing Isa for his tardiness – scalding his eyes with hot irons, drawing his fingernails, dipping his toes in acid. Halil was on the point of leaving and ordering one of these cruel tortures carried out when Isa stepped into the room across the curtain, slapping his clothes to remove the layers of dust that had settled on them during the long ride from Manisa. Isa looked tired and worn, but he did not look afraid. That was good: it meant that he must have succeeded. Halil stepped through the beaded curtain.

'You are late, and you have been followed,' Halil snapped. 'Mehmed's spies were seen riding behind you as you entered town. No doubt they are waiting outside even now. If they see us together, it will mean my head.'

123

'My apologies, Halil,' Isa replied. 'I had no idea that I was followed, else I would never have led the men here.'

'I am sure,' Halil muttered. 'But no matter. You will leave first, from the front, and I will use the hidden door. There is little danger that Mehmed's spies will see me. For your family's sake, I hope that they do not.' Isa's jaw clenched at this, and his eyes narrowed dangerously. 'I trust your journey was a success,' Halil continued. 'The Greek monk seems to have received his drug. My spies in Constantinople report that the empress-mother has taken ill.'

'Yes, I delivered the drug into his hands myself.'

'And what of Mehmed? How did he respond to my proposal?'

'Much as you anticipated: he refused your offer, but he kept the poison.'

'Very good,' Halil replied, stroking his beard. 'Mehmed will use the poison against his father soon enough. I will see to that. You have done well, Isa. Here is your reward.' Halil tossed Isa a small silk bag. He opened it and poured half a dozen small diamonds into his hand. 'I trust it is adequate?'

'Yes, it will do.'

'Good. You are free to go.'

Isa made no move to leave. 'And what of my family?' he demanded. 'You said that you would release them if I did what you asked of me.'

'And I will,' Halil said. 'I will release them when you have done *all* that I ask of you. For now, however, you may see them. You know the house where they are kept. The guards have been told to expect you. You will have one hour, and you will be searched before you enter.'

Isa left without another word. Halil was glad that he had found him. When Mehmed's oldest brother, Ahmet, had been poisoned, Halil had of course looked into the matter. After several years and many, many bribes, he had traced the source of the poison to Isa, then a servant in Mehmed's household, but not before Mehmed's other brother, Ala ed-Din, had also been killed. Shortly thereafter, Isa had disappeared. Halil had thought him dead until last year when, in search of a particularly rare poison, he had visited a caravanserai outside of Edirne. He was led into the tent of one of the merchants, a man who went by the name of Amir, and was surprised to find himself face to face with Isa. Isa had been living as the prosperous merchant Amir for years, always moving with the caravan, at first staying far from the major Turkish cities. But time had dulled his sense of fear, and for some years he had been following caravans to Edirne and even to Manisa, where Mehmed lived. No one recognized him, and Isa had grown more and more confident. He returned to his earlier calling as a dealer in potions and poisons. Three years ago he had felt secure enough to marry, and now he already had two children. Halil had taken Isa's family into his protection – meaning that if Isa did not do exactly as Halil said, they would be killed. Isa was a strong man. He had not even blinked when Halil told him that he knew that it was he who had poisoned Prince Ahmet, nor had he shown any sign of fear at threats of torture or death. He did, however, have a surprising weakness for his family. After Halil had them seized, Isa had proved most cooperative.

Yes, Halil was glad that he had found Isa. Thanks to his efforts, Murad would soon be dead and Mehmed on the throne. He would be much easier to control than his father, and if he were not, then there was always Sitt Hatun. Halil knew that the sultan's wife was a proud woman and resented her low status next to Mehmed's new *kadin*, Gülbehar. Halil had offered her a position of power and respect as mother of the reigning sultan. All he asked in return was that she lie with him so that the prince that was born to her, the prince who would be sultan after Halil eliminated Mehmed, would in fact be Halil's son. Sitt Hatun would have what she wanted, and Halil would be regent and the father of the empire. Sitt Hatun had not accepted his offer yet, but that, Halil hoped, was only a matter of time.

Sitt Hatun sat beside the carp pool in the harem garden, daydreaming as her maidservant Cicek read aloud to her from a book of poetry. The morning air in the garden was warm and relaxing, scented with the perfume of thousands of flowers. Sitt Hatun trailed her hand in the water and felt the carp nibble gently at her fingers. She closed her eyes and exhaled. The months since Mehmed left for Manisa had been peaceful, despite Gülbehar's frequent slights. And lately, Sitt Hatun had hardly seen Gülbehar, who had kept to her apartments since the birth of her son, Bayezid.

At times like this, Sitt Hatun could almost convince herself that the harem was what the common people thought it to be: *dâr-üs-saâde*, the place of happiness. Sitt Hatun, however, knew better. The harem was indeed a place of unparalleled luxury, but it was also rife with treachery and intrigue. It was a world apart, set aside from the rest of the palace grounds. It had its own gardens, its own mosque, its own kitchen and laundries. The harem even had its own people; except for the wives of the sultan and their offspring, none of the inhabitants of the harem was a Turk, for according to law, Muslims could not be made slaves. The women of the harem were sent by foreign rulers eager to establish good relations with the sultan, or else they were captured in war or taken as tribute from neighbouring peoples. They were Greek, Bosnian, Wallachian, Bulgarian, Russian, Polish, Italian and even French. The eunuchs were much the same; they were mostly taken as prisoners of war or rounded up in the *devshirme*, which exacted a tribute of children from all non-Muslims living within the Ottoman Empire.

Friendships rarely lasted amongst this mixed assortment of peoples, not with so many strange tongues and cultures lumped together, joined only by their desire to rise within the ranks of the harem, from slave-girl *jariye* to *odalisque* at the court of one of the sultan's favourites, to concubine and perhaps even to wife or *kadin*. Everybody spied on everybody, eager to commit small betrayals in return for power. Sitt Hatun's one friend, her ally in this pit of vipers, was her cousin and childhood companion, Cicek. After Cicek's parents died, she and Sitt Hatun had grown up together. They had become inseparable, and when Sitt Hatun had married Mehmed, Cicek had chosen to join her in the harem, even though it meant the loss of her freedom. Now, Cicek was Sitt Hatun's constant companion.

'My Lady.' It was Cicek. She had stopped reading and was gently shaking Sitt Hatun's shoulder. 'My Lady!' she whispered again. '*Yilan* is in the garden.' Sitt Hatun opened her eyes and sat up. *Yilan*: the snake. It was what she and Cicek called Gülbehar, on account of her venomous tongue and the sinuous, swaying way she walked – like the undulating body of a charmed cobra. Sitt Hatun located her on the portico at the other end of the garden, her head held high as she stepped on to the lawn. Behind her came no less than ten *odalisques*, each dressed in red silk caftans embroidered with swirling patterns in gold – greater finery than Sitt Hatun herself could afford. But they looked drab beside Gülbehar, who was dressed like a princess from the *Arabian Nights*. She wore a tight, sleeveless silk robe of the deepest red, embroidered with gold and pearls. On her bare arms hung dozens of jewelled bracelets, and her long blonde hair was woven around a diadem of bright gold, set with diamonds. Certainly, Gülbehar did not lack for wealth; Mehmed showered her with gifts. But Sitt Hatun had never before seen her dressed so ostentatiously. She looked more like the wife of Sultan Murad than the *kadin* of a prince, even of the crown prince.

'Greetings, sister,' Gülbehar said. Her Turkish was laced with a strong Albanian accent, yet another thing that Sitt Hatun hated about her. 'It is such a lovely day. I thought that I would join you.' Gülbehar motioned to her servants, and they placed cushions on the ground near Sitt Hatun. Gülbehar sat, and two more servants stepped forward to fan her.

'I am pleased to see you,' Sitt Hatun lied. 'I have seen little of you since our husband left. You have not been feeling ill, I hope.'

'No, I have not been ill,' Gülbehar said and smiled to herself. What did that smile mean? Sitt Hatun wondered. 'Little Bayezid has kept me busy, that is all.'

The words were like a slap. Bayezid was Gülbehar's pride and joy, as well as her favourite tool for torturing

Sitt Hatun. It was because of Bayezid that Gülbehar enjoyed the title of *bas haseki* – mother of the heir – and the privileges that went with it. It was because of Bayezid that Sitt Hatun was wife in name only.

'Yes, your son must be quite a handful,' Sitt Hatun said. 'Do the doctors still fear that he is an idiot?' Gülbehar flushed crimson. Bayezid had been dropped when he was still a newborn, and although he had shown no adverse effects, there was a persistent palace rumour that his wits were addled. It was a silly rumour, but it was the best that Sitt Hatun could do.

'No,' Gülbehar replied. 'He is well. In fact, he looks more like his father every day.' As if on cue, the unseen Bayezid began bawling, his loud cries descending from Gülbehar's quarters and echoing throughout the gardens. 'Such a strong voice, like his father's,' she said. 'I suppose that he should be seen to.'

Sitt Hatun nodded, hoping that she might soon be rid of Gülbehar. 'Yes, no doubt he cries for his mother.'

'No doubt,' Gülbehar agreed. She looked around, as if she were searching for something. 'But all of my servants are busy. No matter. You,' she called, pointing to Cicek. 'Bring me my child.' Sitt Hatun's eyes widened. To order another's servants was to take charge of them, but surely Gülbehar would not dare to steal away Sitt Hatun's favourite. Murad would never allow it.

Cicek did not move. 'Do you hear me, girl? Bring me my son,' Gülbehar repeated. Cicek looked to Sitt Hatun, who nodded and looked away as Cicek rose and left. 'You do not mind, do you, sister?' Gülbehar asked Sitt Hatun. 'I will send you a replacement tomorrow. Anyone you wish.'

But this was too much for Sitt Hatun. 'I do not need a replacement,' she spat back as she rose to her feet. 'The Sultan will not permit this.' Sitt Hatun hurried away to her apartments, struggling to hold back her tears. 'This cannot be,' she repeated to herself again and again. Murad will not allow it. He cannot.

But Murad did allow it. In response to Sitt Hatun's angry plea that Cicek be returned to her, he told her that harem politics were not his affair and ordered her to take one of Gülbehar's *odalisques* in exchange. Sitt Hatun stormed away, furious. She was too angry to even think about letting one of Gülbehar's women, no doubt a spy, into her household. She shut herself in her bedroom and took up her sitar, picking out a nursery song from her childhood in an effort to calm herself. But peace would not come, only fat tears that splashed silently on the finished wood of the sitar. She had no friends in her household now. She was alone.

Alone perhaps, but she was not weak. Sitt Hatun set the sitar aside and angrily wiped the tears from her eyes. She could not afford to indulge in sorrow. She did not have the money or the servants that were showered on Gülbehar. But she had her wits, and she would have to use them. Gülbehar had taken Cicek, but perhaps Sitt Hatun could turn this to her own advantage. Cicek would always be faithful to her, and a spy in Gülbehar's household could prove useful. Very useful, if Sitt Hatun's growing suspicions concerning Gülbehar's sudden wealth proved accurate. Sitt Hatun thought once more of Gülbehar's strange half-smile. Perhaps she would now be able to solve the riddle behind that smile.

*

A week passed before Sitt Hatun saw Cicek again. Returning from evening prayers in the harem mosque, she found Cicek in her bedroom, waiting for her. Sitt Hatun moved to embrace her, but Cicek motioned for her to stop.

'I must be quick, My Lady,' Cicek whispered. 'If *Yilan* learns that I have come to visit you, then there will be trouble for us both.' Sitt Hatun nodded. 'There is a girl outside waiting to speak to you, an *odalisque* from Gülbehar's household. She has asked for your protection in return for information about Gülbehar. She will not tell me her secret, but I believe that it is important. Will you speak to her?'

'Of course. But what of you?' Sitt Hatun asked. 'Does *Yilan* treat you well?'

'I have seen nothing of her,' Cicek replied, her voice tired. 'She has placed me among the lowest *jariye*. I spend my days embroidering and doing laundry. I am not allowed to wait on Gülbehar.' There were tears in Cicek's eyes, and Sitt Hatun could tell that she was sparing her the worst. 'I must go, My Lady.'

Sitt Hatun embraced Cicek, and they clung to one another. 'Thank you, my friend,' Sitt Hatun whispered. 'Now go, and may Allah protect you.'

Cicek left, and seconds later a Polish girl no older than fifteen entered. She wore the same scarlet and gold robes that Sitt Hatun had seen on Gülbehar's *odalisques* in the garden. This meant that she was a member of Gülbehar's inner household. The girl was beautiful, in her own way. She was long and thin, as if she had been stretched. Her slender arms ended in graceful fingers. Her neck was elongated, and her blonde hair hung nearly to her waist.

Her wide eyes were blue, innocent and afraid. She bowed low when she saw Sitt Hatun and did not rise.

'Stand up, girl,' Sitt Hatun ordered, but gently. 'What is it that you have to tell me? Speak freely. You need fear no spies here.'

The girl remained silent, and Sitt Hatun feared she would not speak. But, then she opened her mouth, and the words gushed forth in a torrent. 'Please protect me, My Lady,' the girl began. 'Cicek has told me so many good things about you. She said that I could trust you. Still, I would not ask your protection, but I know that you hate Gülbehar. She would kill me if she knew I had come to you, but I will die anyway without your help. I will tell you my secret, but first, promise to protect me.'

'Protect you from what? From Gülbehar?' The girl nodded vigorously. 'And why should Gülbehar wish you any harm?' The servant girl blushed and lowered her eyes. 'Have you stolen from her?'

'Of course not, My Lady,' the girl protested. 'She is jealous of me.'

'Jealous? I see.' Sitt Hatun was not surprised to hear it. She had experienced Gülbehar's jealousy first hand. But if she was jealous, then it could only mean that this girl had come between Gülbehar and a lover. Who? Surely not Mehmed, far away in Manisa. Sitt Hatun suspected that she knew the answer, but she wanted to hear it from the girl. 'Do not fear,' Sitt Hatun told her. 'I will protect you. Now, tell me why Gülbehar would be jealous of an *odalisque*?'

'Because I am *gözde*,' the girl replied, blushing. To be *gözde* meant literally to be 'in the eye' of the sultan. It meant that Murad had taken note of the girl, and perhaps even ordered his *haznedar* to schedule a night with her.

'And how did you, a servant of Gülbehar, come to be *gözde*?'

'Murad visits Gülbehar's apartments to be with her,' the girl said, her cheeks burning and her eyes fixed on the floor. 'Gülbehar makes us wear masks so that we will not catch Murad's eye, but he took note of me nonetheless. It was not my fault. I did nothing, and yet a friend has told me that the *haznedar* has placed my name on the calendar of royal nights. Gülbehar is a jealous woman. If I lie with the sultan, she will have me killed. My friend tells me that I am scheduled for next week.'

'And what would you have me do?' Sitt Hatun asked. 'I have no power with the *haznedar*. Once a name is written, it is beyond my power to change it.'

'Take me into your household,' the girl said. 'I was there in the garden when Gülbehar took Cicek from you. She offered you a servant to replace Cicek. Ask for me. She cannot refuse you.'

Sitt Hatun was inclined to grant the girl's request. It was the least she could do in return for the information the girl had given her. When Sitt Hatun told Mehmed that his beloved Gülbehar was unfaithful – and with his father no less! – then Mehmed would surely reward her. Perhaps he would even lie with her. But then again, this girl could be lying. She could be a spy sent by Gülbehar. Even if she did speak the truth, Sitt Hatun would need more than this girl's word if she were to accuse Gülbehar.

'I will take you into my household, but first I need proof of what you say,' Sitt Hatun told her.

The girl produced a golden chain, from which dangled a huge ruby that flashed a brilliant red, like the final blaze of the setting sun. There was no mistaking the gem. It was the *kumru kalp*, the dove's heart, and Sitt Hatun had never seen Murad without it. 'Murad gave it to Gülbehar. I took it from her quarters. Do you believe me now?' the girl asked.

'I believe you, girl, but I need to see this with my own eyes. When will the sultan next visit Gülbehar?'

'Tonight.'

'Then tonight you will show me.'

'But that is impossible,' the girl stammered. 'I could · never sneak you into Gülbehar's apartments. Certainly not while Murad was there.'

'If you cannot bring me with you, then there is only one solution,' Sitt Hatun said. 'What is your name, girl?'

'Anna, My Lady.'

'Anna, take off your clothes.'

Dressed in Anna's clothes, Sitt Hatun hurried through the palace and slipped inside Gülbehar's apartments. Although she wore the mask that Anna had given her, Sitt Hatun did not want to take any chances. Her disguise might fool the casual observer, but her clothes – clearly too long in the arms and legs – would not stand up to close scrutiny. She dreaded what would happen if she were found out. It would be easy enough for Gülbehar to have her murdered and then claim ignorance. When a woman left her place within the harem, she had very few protections indeed.

Sitt Hatun entered her old apartments, now Gülbehar's, and took the servants' passage that left the entryway and skirted a reception room covered in pillows and filled with the smoke of a *hookah*. She came out of the passage into the interior garden, bathed in golden light that shone through the open roof. Moving quickly to the far corner of the room, she slipped behind a potted palm and gently pressed one of the cool tiles on the wall, triggering a hidden door. Sitt Hatun slipped through and into another servants' passageway, this one leading past Gülbehar's bedroom and to the apartment's private kitchen.

The passage was dark, save for the pinpricks of light that shone through the wall from small spyholes. They were there so that servants could watch their mistress and respond instantly to her every whim. No one stood at the peepholes now. No doubt Gülbehar kept this passageway empty during her meetings with Murad. Sitt Hatun put her eye to one of the holes and saw Gülbehar's candlelit bedroom before her. Gülbehar had made many changes. The glory of the room still lay in the huge, floor-to-ceiling windows that ran along two sides, showing a spectacular view of the imperial palace stretching away to the river. But the windows were half-hidden now behind screens of woven gold. The rest of the walls were covered with silk tapestries, shimmering with gold and silver thread. The tile floor was now covered with deep rugs. Altogether, the décor gave the impression of a richly decorated tent, an impression that was contradicted only by the enormous bed that dominated the centre of the room. The bed, hung with yellow silk curtains, was easily ten feet wide. And there, nude on the bed, were Gülbehar and Murad.

Gülbehar lay on her back, her head hanging over the edge of the bed so that Sitt Hatun could see her face, contorted in ecstasy. Gülbehar's long legs were wrapped around the waist of Murad, who lay atop her, grunting as he thrust. Gülbehar cried out in Albanian as he moved faster and faster. Finally, Murad moaned with pleasure and collapsed. After a moment, he rolled off and stood. A long scar marked his right shoulder, and there were several more on his thin legs. His sunken chest and large belly were covered with fine grey hair. Gülbehar remained on the bed, naked and covered in sweat, while he began to dress.

'Must you go so soon?' Gülbehar pouted.

'Ibrahim Bey is making trouble again in Karamania. I must write to the loyal beys there,' he told her. 'I spend too much time in your quarters as it is. Even loyal tongues will wag if the price is right. Mehmed is a rash young man. He must not know about us.'

Gülbehar rose and helped Murad to tie the sash around his caftan. 'Mehmed is nothing,' she purred. 'You are the sultan, and you have another heir now – my son.'

The sound of approaching footsteps drew Sitt Hatun's attention from the room. She looked away from the spyhole and saw a light approaching down the passageway from the kitchen. She quickly retreated in the other direction, out into the garden. There was no place to hide, so she passed through it and into the reception room, where she came face to face with Murad. Immediately, Sitt Hatun bowed low, keeping her face to the floor. She backed away, but Murad gestured for her to stop.

'Stand up straight, girl,' he commanded. Sitt Hatun did as she was told. She could see a gleam in Murad's eyes. Was that recognition or simply desire? 'I haven't seen you here before,' Murad continued after looking Sitt Hatun up and down. 'Are you new to Gülbehar's court?'

Sitt Hatun nodded and mumbled in a *basso profundo* that she hoped adequately disguised her voice, 'I must attend to her, My Lord.' She moved to go, but Murad took her arm, holding her back.

'You certainly are in a hurry,' Murad laughed. 'You should not be so eager to escape the honour of the sultan's gaze.' He turned Sitt Hatun toward him, stroking her arm. 'Take your mask off, girl. Let me see your face.'

Sitt Hatun froze, her mind seeking desperately for some means of escape. She could call out, but what would be the use? She could not run, Murad was holding her arm. And now, he was touching her hair. His hand was playing with the knot that held her mask, slowly loosening it. A few seconds now and she would be revealed. Sitt Hatun closed her eyes, her breath caught in her throat.

'Murad!' It was Gülbehar, still nude and standing in the doorway to the reception room, her hands on her hips. Stepping past Sitt Hatun, she pressed herself against the sultan and purred into his ear: 'Leave my servant alone.' Murad released Sitt Hatun, and Gülbehar kissed him voraciously. Sitt Hatun slipped towards the exit.

'Stop!' Gülbehar snapped, and Sitt Hatun froze. Gülbehar's eyes narrowed as she examined Sitt Hatun. 'What is your name, girl?'

What could she say? She could not claim to be Anna. The deception would be too obvious. Only one other name came to her. 'Cicek, My Lady,' she said and bowed low, hiding her face.

'Be gone, girl,' Gülbehar ordered. 'There's work for you in the kitchen.' She paused, and then added: 'And take off those clothes. You are not an *odalisque* in my court!'

Sitt Hatun hurried to the harem kitchens. From there, she took a servant's passage that led to her own apartments.

She collapsed on her bed, shaking as the fear that she had held inside spread throughout her body. After only a moment, though, she steeled herself, forcing herself to lie still. The danger had passed, and now was no time for weakness. What the girl Anna had told her was true. Gülbehar and Murad were lovers. Soon enough, she vowed, it would be Gülbehar who would have reason to fear.

Sitt Hatun spent the next day dreaming of her revenge: how she would tell Mehmed; what Mehmed would do to Gülbehar; how she, Sitt Hatun, would mock her fallen rival. She dreamed, but she did not plan, not yet. After all, there was no hurry. She could not tell Mehmed until he returned from Manisa; there was no messenger that she would trust. And she had decided not to tell Halil. She did not need the vizier and his plan now that she had evidence of Gülbehar's infidelity. Sitt Hatun could look after herself.

That evening she sent a note to Gülbehar requesting that Anna be sent to serve her, and content with Gülbehar's reply that Anna would be sent over the next morning, Sitt Hatun lay down to sleep, looking forward to dreams of vengeance and glory. She awoke with a start at midnight to the sound of a long, terrified scream, cut suddenly short. It had been a woman's voice, and it was strangely familiar. Hearing it, Sitt Hatun's blood ran cold. She listened for a long time, but there was no further sound. Eventually she sank into a troubled sleep.

When she awoke the next morning the day was bright and fair, and the scream seemed distant and unreal – a nightmare better forgotten. Sitt Hatun allowed her *odalisques* to dress her, took a light breakfast of bread and olives, and then went down to the harem garden to read. She had hardly settled down when Anna arrived. From the moment that Sitt Hatun saw the girl's face, she knew that something was wrong. Anna bowed low. 'Gülbehar has sent me to serve you, My Lady. Do you find me to your liking?'

Sitt Hatun nodded. 'You shall have a place in my household. Come, we shall retire to my apartment, and I will show you where you are to live.' Once they reached Sitt Hatun's apartments, she took Anna aside in her private chamber. 'Tell me,' Sitt Hatun commanded, whispering so as not to be overheard, 'is something wrong?'

Anna nodded, her eyes downcast. 'Your friend, Cicek, is dead.'

'How? What happened?'

'Gülbehar accused Cicek of spying and thieving. Last night, men came and took her. She screamed for help, but they cut out her tongue. They tied her in a bag and threw her in the river.' Sitt Hatun could only nod her understanding as tears filled her eyes. Cicek had paid the price for her own foolishness. She dug her nails into her palms and clenched her jaw tight to prevent herself from sobbing.

'There is more,' Anna continued. 'Gülbehar is furious over the disappearance of the *kumru kalp*. She suspects that Cicek gave it to you, and that you know about her and Murad. You are in grave danger, My Lady. I know Gülbehar. She will not rest until you are dead.'

Chapter 7

The sun had long since set on a cold January day when Longo arrived at the *palazzo* of Signor Grimaldi to attend the feast being held in honour of the ambassadors from Constantinople. At the gate he dismounted and handed his horse over to William. He watched as the boy hurried off to the stables, no doubt eager to gamble away his few coins with the other squires. William disappeared into the stables, and Longo entered the grand hall of the *palazzo* Grimaldi.

An enormous chandelier bedecked with innumerable tiny crystals hung from the ceiling, its many flickering candles shedding a glittering light. Candelabras lined the walls, adding to the bright glow. A long table ran down the centre of the room, and around it sat the chiefs of the great families of Genoa. At the top of the table, Grimaldi sat beside his eldest son, Paolo, and they both nodded in greeting as Longo's eyes met theirs. The foot of the table was reserved for the Greek ambassadors, and it was still empty.

Longo spoke to a few men with whom he was on good terms and then took his seat beside his future father-in-law, Grimaldi. 'How are your vineyards?' Grimaldi's son Paolo asked, a trace of a smirk around his lips. Yesterday, someone had set fire to the dry winter vines in Longo's vineyards, forcing Longo to miss the council meeting called to discuss the Greeks' request for troops. Longo suspected that the fire had been set precisely to keep him absent.

'The fire damaged some of my newer nebbiolo plantings – a great blow,' Longo replied. He locked eyes with Paolo before continuing. 'But do not worry on my account, Paolo. I will find who set the fire soon enough, and they will answer for it. As they say, those who play with fire are apt to get burned.'

The moment of tension was interrupted by a blast of trumpets. The men around the table stood as the double doors leading to the hall from the palazzo were opened. The first ambassador to walk through was an elderly man, well preserved, with a long, white beard. 'Andronicus Bryennius Leontarsis,' the herald announced.

Leontarsis moved into the hall, and following him, to Longo's great surprise, came the enchanting young woman he had met at the emperor's palace in Constantinople. 'Princess Sofia Dragases,' the herald intoned. She was elegantly dressed in a tight-waisted caftan of buttery-yellow silk and wore a thin golden tiara woven into her long black hair. What was she doing here? Longo wondered.

Leontarsis and Sofia sat, and the Genoese followed suit. Immediately, servants stepped forth carrying an enormous platter on which sat a whole roasted boar. A low buzz of conversation sprang up around the table. Longo half-listened to the talk around him, while keeping his eyes on Sofia at the far end of the table. Finally, after the last course had been served, the room quieted. The real purpose of the gathering had arrived.

Ludovico Fregoso, the Doge of Genoa, stood and raised his glass. 'To our honoured guests and to the prosperity of their fair city,' he toasted, and the assembled company drank.

Fregoso sat, and Leontarsis rose in turn. 'To our Genoese allies, we thank you for your friendship and support,' he toasted. There was some grumbling when he said 'allies', and not all of those at the table drank the toast.

'Your words are kind,' Fregoso said to Leontarsis, speaking in a voice loud enough so that all could hear. 'We have always prized the friendship of the Roman emperor, and I am sure that many Genoese will rush to your aid if ever there is need.'

'Many Genoese?' Leontarsis asked. 'And what of Genoa herself? Will the republic stand beside Constantinople?'

'*If* the Turks attack,' Fregoso replied, 'then the Republic of Genoa will offer the services of a ship and crew to Constantinople, to serve as a link to the world and as a scourge upon the Turks.' One ship. Longo was not surprised, but he was still disappointed.

'We thank you for your promise of help,' Leontarsis said, 'and if the day comes when the Turks attack, we hope that many brave Genoese will rally around this one ship.'

That seemed to settle the matter. The men around the table had gone back to their food and private conversations when Sofia spoke out loudly. 'I should think that the Genoese would leap at the chance to defend Constantinople,' she said. 'After all, you would be defending not just the Empire of the Romans, but your colony of Pera as well. Surely you would not want to lose your door to the East?'

'What do you know of such matters, woman?' Paolo snorted and took a long drink of wine. 'You should save your talk for the bedroom.' Sofia flushed crimson as quiet laughter spread around the table.

'That is quite enough, Paolo,' Grimaldi said. 'I apologize for my son's lack of courtesy, Princess. But he is right. Fighting the Turks will only antagonize them. I regret to say it, but Pera will perhaps be more secure if the Turks take Constantinople. They at least have the strength to protect our interests there.'

'You truly believe your colonies will be safe in the hands of the Turks?' Sofia demanded. 'The Venetians thought the same of Salonika, but the Turks took it all the same. No, signor, you should not be so fast to trust the Turks.'

'Hear, hear!' Umberto Spinola shouted from the centre of the table. 'The Turks are heathens!' he slurred, obviously drunk. 'We should not deal with the devil.'

'The Turks may be heathens, but no more so than the people of Constantinople,' replied the powerful Signor Adorno. 'They have rejected union with the one true Church for years now. Why should we fight and die for men that spit on our religion?' There was mumbled assent at this remark.

Longo stood. 'Enough! I have fought the Turks. I have stood face to face with them, and I know the difference between a Turk and a Greek. I have already pledged my sword to Emperor Constantine's service. If Constantinople is attacked, then I will defend its walls.' He drew his sword and laid it on the table. 'Who will stand beside me?' He looked at the men around the table and then at Sofia. She nodded her thanks.

There was silence as men shifted in their seats. Finally a young noble, Maurizio Cattaneo, stood. He was followed by a few others – the two di Langasco brothers and the three Bocchiardo brothers. They were all young men with little in the way of inheritance, who had nothing to lose by selling their lives in foreign lands. None of them would bring many troops to the battle, but Longo was glad for their support nevertheless. One by one, they drew their swords and laid them on the table.

'On behalf of the emperor, I thank you all for your courageous offer,' Leontarsis told them. 'But please, keep your swords for now. You may have need of them.' The men sheathed their swords and sat. 'I would also like to thank Signor Grimaldi, our host tonight, and all of those who have made us feel welcome in this city. Our emperor will be most pleased, and Constantinople will always have a place in its heart for Genoa. To Genoa!' he concluded, raising his glass.

'To Genoa!' the assembled men replied in chorus as they stood and drained their glasses. The toast marked a fitting conclusion to the dinner, and afterwards Grimaldi led them outside to the gardens behind the *palazzo*, where his private musicians played by torchlight under a star-strewn sky. Braziers filled with warm coals had been set up at frequent intervals to ward off the night chill, and the guests moved amongst them in the shadows, discussing politics and drinking chilled sweet wine.

Longo had hardly stepped outside when he was cornered by Leontarsis. 'Signor Giustiniani, allow me to again express my thanks for your offer of aid.'

144

'No thanks are needed,' Longo replied. 'My fellow Genoese may not see it, but the fight against the Turks is our fight as much as it is yours. Either we fight them now, or we fight them later; but fight them we will.'

'I agree entirely,' Leontarsis said. 'If you could only persuade a few of your more powerful countrymen to join you, then the emperor would be most appreciative. He would compensate you accordingly.'

'If I could persuade them, then I would, with or without compensation. Besides, I do not need your money. Nor do many of the men here.'

'Money is not what I offer.' Leontarsis pointed to Sofia, who stood nearby in earnest conversation with several men. 'You have surely noticed the Princess Sofia. She is beautiful, is she not?'

'What are you saying?'

'The emperor feels that the Princess Sofia would make an appropriate match for a man who truly helped our city in its time of need.'

'I see,' Longo replied. He knew that this was how marriages were arranged, but still, he felt a stab of jealousy at the thought of this woman being sold off to one of his countrymen. 'And what does the princess think of such an arrangement?'

'What the princess thinks is of no importance,' Leontarsis replied.

'Indeed?' It was Sofia. Neither Leontarsis nor Longo had noticed her approach. 'Is that why you thought not to tell me that I have been placed on the market for the highest bidder?'

'I was only following the emperor's orders, Princess,' Leontarsis said. Then, recovering himself, he added more confidently, 'Why do you think that he agreed to allow a woman on this trip in the first place? Surely you did not think that it was your political skills that were desired?'

'As you said, what I think is of no importance,' Sofia replied, her voice quiet but hard. 'But I will tell you what I know, Leontarsis. I am a princess of the royal family, not a slave to be sold, not by you. If you offer me up as a prize again, you will regret it.' She turned and strode away into the darkness.

'I am sorry you had to witness that, signor,' Leontarsis said. 'But my offer stands.'

'I am not a mercenary to be bought,' Longo replied curtly. 'Good-night, Ambassador.'

Longo walked away, looking for Sofia. He found her alone, nearly hidden in the shadows at the edge of the torchlight.

'Have you come to inspect your merchandise?' Sofia asked, her eyes flashing with anger.

'I am engaged to marry another, but even if I were not, my sword is not for sale, even for so high a price,' Longo told her. 'If my presence grieves you, I will withdraw.'

'No, stay,' Sofia replied more softly. 'It is not you that I am angry with, Signor Giustiniani. Indeed, I should be thanking you for what you did tonight. I apologize for my rudeness.'

'You have no need to apologize. I understand that it is not an easy thing to be married against one's will.'

'You are a man, signor. What can you know of such things?'

'Sometimes men are not so free to choose. We are all of us compelled by duty.'

Before Sofia could reply, Grimaldi appeared, seeming

to materialize out of the darkness. 'There you are, Signor Giustiniani,' he said. Turning to Sofia, he bowed low. 'Princess Sofia. It is an honour to meet you face to face.'

'Princess, this is Signor Grimaldi, the father of my intended,' Longo told Sofia, who curtsied.

'I am sorry, Princess,' Grimaldi said, 'but the evening is nearly over and I must take Longo away from you. He must rise early tomorrow to wait on my daughter. He is taking her on a voyage to my family's home in Bastia, on Corsica. Longo has business there.'

'Corsica is near Rome, is it not?' Sofia asked.

Longo nodded. 'With a favourable wind, it is only a half-day's sail from Corsica to Ostia, the port of Rome.'

'Then if it is not too much of an imposition, I wonder if you could carry me, Leontarsis, and our servants to Rome when you sail for Corsica. We travelled overland from Venice, and our ship is meeting us in Rome. I am eager to arrive there as soon as possible, and I do not relish the prospect of another overland trip. I am told that the roads to Rome are thick with bandits.'

Longo looked to Grimaldi.

'Of course,' Grimaldi said. 'I am sure Longo would be delighted to be of service, and my daughter will be honoured to meet you. Now, if you will excuse us, Princess.'

'It was a pleasure meeting you, Signor Grimaldi,' Sofia said. 'Until tomorrow, Signor Giustiniani.'

Sofia moved away, rejoining the party. Longo turned in the opposite direction, towards the stables, but Grimaldi held him back. 'A moment, signor,' he said. The old man looked hard into Longo's eyes. 'Be careful, Signor

Giustiniani. It would be wise to watch your step around the princess during your voyage to Rome.'

'Surely you do not doubt my intentions, nor the honour of the princess.'

'I do not doubt your honour; but I saw you with the princess, and I do not doubt my eyes, either,' Grimaldi replied. 'Good-night, signor. I will see you tomorrow.'

The pre-dawn air was thick with chill fog when Longo rode into the courtyard of the *palazzo* Grimaldi the next morning. His stomach – usually so calm, even on the eve of battle – was knotted tight. It twisted still further when he saw Julia – thin and frail, dressed in a tightly corseted blue velvet dress that emphasized her budding breasts – and helped her into her carriage. The tension in his belly seized his throat when he arrived in the courtyard of the Fregoso palace and saw Sofia emerge, ravishing in a green cloak, a long divided skirt and high riding boots. Longo got down from his horse and offered Sofia a hand into the carriage, but she only laughed. 'I wish to ride,' she told him. 'I have yet to see much of the city.' And with that, she swung herself into the saddle of one of the horses that had been prepared for the Greek ambassador's retinue. Leontarsis, grumbling about how his old joints hurt in the morning damp, gladly took Sofia's place in the carriage.

The sun rose above the hills behind them, burning off the morning mist and warming the chill air as they rode the short distance to the docks. Sofia smiled and laughed, asking the names of buildings and plazas. She seemed more alive than she had the night before, totally at ease in the saddle. Her buoyant spirits lifted Longo's mood, and soon he too was smiling, the knots in his stomach loosening. By the time they reached the docks and loaded all of the baggage aboard *la Fortuna*, the chilly dawn had transformed into a glorious winter morning. Longo gave the order to make way and left one of his men at the wheel, while he went forward to stand at the rail with Sofia, Julia and Leontarsis. They glided across the bay of Genoa under a favourable wind, the ship cutting confidently through the short, choppy waves.

'The trip should be a quick one with this following wind,' Longo told them. 'We will sail down the Genoese coast, past the Arno river in Florence, and should reach Corsica well before nightfall. We will stay at my family home in Bastia and then sail on to Ostia the next day. You should be in Rome by tomorrow afternoon.'

'I have never heard of Bastia,' Sofia said. 'What is it like?'

'It is a small town, built on the steep, rocky coast of Corsica. The island itself is under the control of a group of Genoese traders called the Maona, and each of the great Genoese families has representatives amongst them. Corsica has been Genoese for almost two hundred years, although you would never know it. The people are still as desperate for independence as ever.'

'My father says that the Corsicans are like animals,' Julia said. 'They must be domesticated to be of any use.' Her face was beginning to take on a greenish cast.

'He would no doubt speak differently if it were his country that were occupied,' Sofia replied. 'I admire these Corsicans. It requires great bravery to fight a battle that nobody believes can be won.'

'Or great foolishness,' Leontarsis mused. 'Sometimes I

fear that we are all of us only playing the fool on this mission.'

'On the contrary, Leontarsis,' Longo said. 'A fool fights when he has no chance. A brave man fights when he has no choice. No, the only fools are those who do not come to your aid. As for the Corsicans, only time will tell whether they are fools or not. I for one cannot blame them for wishing to be free.'

'I did not mean to cause offence,' Julia said, blushing. 'I know little of these matters and . . . If you'll excuse me, My Lord . . .' Julia bowed and, covering her mouth with one hand, made a quick retreat from the rail. Her maid joined her as she hurried below to her cabin.

'I will take my leave as well,' Leontarsis said. 'The air on deck does not appear to agree with me.' He turned and followed Julia below.

Sofia shook her head. 'Seasickness must be terrible,' she said. 'I love the ocean, the feeling of freedom that comes from slicing through the waves, the wind in my hair.'

'You are a sailor, then?' Longo asked.

'Hardly,' Sofia said, laughing as the prow of *la Fortuna* struck a wave head on, spraying both of them with water. 'I had been on ships within the Golden Horn, but my trip to Venice was my first true encounter with the sea. I love it. How lucky you are to have a ship of your own, the freedom to go wherever you wish.'

'I am not so free,' Longo replied. They stood quietly for some time, enjoying the sunshine and the unending rush of the sea under the prow. Longo had canvas chairs rigged for them on the foredeck, and they sat, watching the coast of Italy roll by. The mountainous Republic of

Genoa was ending now, the high hills tapering into the gentler landscape of the central Italian states of Modena and Florence. Other ships began to appear on the horizon. Longo pointed to an inlet on the coast.

'The mouth of the river Arno,' he told Sofia. 'There is a port there that serves Pisa and Florence.'

Sofia nodded. 'I have heard of it,' she murmured. Then, turning to look Longo in the eyes, she asked: 'If you were free to do as you wished, then what would you do?'

Longo paused. What would life even mean without duty to guide him? 'I do not suppose that I would do very much differently,' he said at last.

'And her?' Sofia asked, nodding towards the cabin.

'What? You do not think that she is a good match?'

'She is beautiful, like a delicate flower, but she is so young.'

'She is the daughter of one of the most powerful families in Genoa, and beautiful as you say,' Longo replied. 'She is all that could be asked for in a wife.' He paused, considering. 'But what of you? What would you do if you were free?'

'I would fight to defend Constantinople,' Sofia replied without hesitation. 'And I would travel. I have seen so little of the world, and books can only teach so much.'

'Fighting and travelling are not as glorious as they sound,' Longo said. 'One grows tired of both.'

'Are you tired of fighting, Signor Giustiniani?'

'You may call me Longo, Princess. And yes, I am weary of war. I used to desire nothing more than battle against the Turks, but lately . . .'

Sofia nodded, but did not speak. Longo wondered if she understood him. He felt, somehow, that she did. They sat in silence until the distant smudge that would become Corsica appeared on the horizon. 'We will be landing soon,' Longo told her as he rose from his chair. 'I must make preparations. Until tonight, Princess.'

Longo had Sofia and Julia escorted to their rooms in his family's villa, high in the hills above Bastia, while he spent the rest of the afternoon at the docks, busy reviewing accounts with the factor who oversaw his fishing and shipping interests on the island. It was dark when he finally arrived at the villa. He had ordered a lavish meal for his guests, but when he arrived, Longo found that only Sofia had come to take part in the feast. 'Ambassador Leontarsis and Lady Julia beg your pardon,' the house steward told him. 'They requested that you be informed that neither of them is hungry, and that they will see you tomorrow.'

'I see,' Longo said and sat at the table across from Sofia. 'Julian, see to it that Leontarsis and Julia are taken soup and bread, and have someone find a physician to provide something to calm their stomachs.'

'Very thoughtful of you,' Sofia said.

Longo smiled. 'I was thinking more of my own welfare than theirs. I would prefer that Leontarsis have his wits about him when he reaches Rome. And Julia is to be my wife; I know enough of women to know that the more she suffers now, the more I will suffer in the future.'

'Indeed,' Sofia replied, smiling back. They both busied themselves eating, and the conversation lulled. They moved through the courses – sautéed skate, roast pheasant stuffed with goat's cheese and achingly sweet Corsican oranges – while the candles burned low. Longo watched

Sofia between bites. She was beautiful, but not like Julia. Sofia was no fragile flower; she was more like a finely crafted sword. But she was a bit dull at present, subdued and distracted.

'Is the food to your liking?' Longo asked.

'It is delicious.'

'I ask only because you seem troubled, Princess. Perhaps you are worried about your reception in Rome?'

Longo caught her eyes, and to his surprise, she blushed. 'Yes, that is it,' she agreed. 'The pope's support is vital.'

Longo nodded as he studied her, trying to read her face. When she caught him staring, this time he blushed. He was acting like a fool, Longo thought. Still, he could not take his eyes off her.

'It is growing late, and I understand that we must depart early tomorrow,' Sofia said. 'I should retire.'

Longo took a candle from the table and led her out of the dining room, into the open courtyard at the heart of the villa, and up a set of stairs. He stopped before a room overlooking the courtyard and opened the door.

'Good-night, Princess,' he said, but neither of them moved. They stood facing one another, silhouetted in the doorway. Their eyes met, and this time neither of them looked away. Suddenly Sofia stepped forward and kissed him. Her lips were soft and warm. Longo kissed her back, hard, but then she pulled away. Her cheeks and neck were flushed. She opened her mouth to speak, but no words came. Longo looked into her eyes and saw confusion and panic. He took a step back, putting more distance between them.

'Forgive me,' Sofia said at last. 'That was wrong of me.' Longo said nothing, waiting for her to finish. 'I . . .

Perhaps I should take another ship to Ostia tomorrow, if that is possible.'

Longo nodded. 'There is a ship sailing for Rome before sunrise tomorrow. I will see that you and Leontarsis are safely aboard.'

'Thank you, Signor Giustiniani,' Sofia said. Their eyes met again, and she looked away. 'And thank you for your kindness. Good-night, and God be with you.'

She slipped into her room and closed the door behind her. Longo stood there for several minutes until finally, he turned and walked slowly away.

Longo returned to Genoa two days later. Julia was quiet and brooding throughout the trip and only answered his questions with curt replies. Longo guessed that she was still suffering from seasickness.

When they reached the Grimaldi *palazzo*, Julia hurried inside with hardly a word to Longo. He mounted his horse, but just before he rode out of the courtyard Grimaldi called out for him to wait. Longo turned to find him striding out of the *palazzo*, and Julia standing in the doorway, watching. Longo dismounted and clasped hands with Grimaldi.

'Did you have a good trip?' Grimaldi studied Longo.

'The sea was calm, and business is well.'

'Julia tells me that you spent a great deal of time alone with Princess Sofia. I trust that nothing untoward happened between you.'

'Of course not,' Longo said. But an image of Sofia kissing him burned in his mind, and he looked away.

'Good,' Grimaldi replied, 'because the time has come: Julia is ready to wed.'

'But she is young yet, is she not?'

'She is fourteen, old enough to bear children,' Grimaldi said. 'In two weeks' time, you will marry.' Longo did not reply. He thought of Sofia, laughing aboard *la Fortuna* as the sea spray hit her. 'It is not a suggestion, signor,' Grimaldi insisted.

'I will be honoured to marry her,' Longo replied.

Chapter 8

Sofia stood before the tall, bronze doors of the pope's court, biting her lip as she waited for her first audience with Pope Nicholas. Leontarsis stood to her right, tugging at the jewelled collar of his ceremonial caftan, the letter from the Synaxis gripped tightly in his other hand. They had arrived in Rome a week earlier to find the pope gone, meeting with the German king Frederick III somewhere to the north. The delay had given Sofia time to explore the city. It was a marvel unlike any she had ever seen. Genoa, with its close-packed buildings perched over the bay, had impressed her, and she had been awed by Venice, a city magically built upon water. But Rome tugged at her heart in a way that those cities had not, perhaps because it was so very much like Constantinople. Rome, too, was filled with the ruins left by centuries of empire – the baths of Caracalla, the Colosseum and the forum – but unlike Constantinople, it was a bustling city, vibrant again after centuries of decay. New buildings were rising everywhere, many built from the very stones of ancient Rome. The old Roman forum had come to life once more, holding a daily market.

Everywhere there were signs of prosperity. Constantinople was still the capital of the Roman Empire, but Rome was now the glory of Christendom.

And at the root of it all was Pope Nicholas. Sofia had learned all she could about him over the past week. Although only the son of a physician, he had risen quickly through the ranks of the church due to a prodigious memory and an insatiable love of learning. Elected a little under three years ago, he had already overseen the end of the Avignon Papacy and brokered an agreement with Frederick III that restored the rights of the pope vis-à-vis the German king. Now, he had turned his attention to the East. He wished to aid the Greeks, but he was firmly against any union that did not place him at the head of a unified church. He would not react well to the Synaxis' letter. Still, he loved Greek scholarship, and perhaps Sofia could use that to her advantage.

The doors before Sofia swung inward, revealing a long hall illuminated by rows of windows on either side and filled with expensively dressed courtiers and more humbly dressed religious men. As a herald announced them, Leontarsis and Sofia strode through the crowd, Sofia looking past the finery around her to the pope. She had expected an older man, grey-haired and emanating beatific authority, but Pope Nicholas V proved to be a handsome, polished man in his early fifties. He had sharp Italian features and deep, intelligent eyes ringed with black, the eyes of a man who read much and slept little. He was seated on a small throne in full papal regalia – white robes, a conical hat and a staff in his hand. When Leontarsis reached the foot of the throne, he knelt and kissed the pope's ring. Sofia followed suit. The pope bid them rise and welcomed them in Greek.

'Andronicus Bryennius Leontarsis, Princess Sofia, you are both welcome,' he began, his accent flawless. 'We are honoured by the presence of such illustrious ambassadors. I hope and pray that your stay will be a fruitful one.'

Leontarsis bowed again. 'Your Holiness, it is we who are honoured by your most gracious reception. On behalf of my lord, the emperor Constantine, I must express our thanks for your wise leadership of the unified Church and your constant friendship towards us. He offers his friendship in return and begs that you consider this letter from the Synaxis of Eastern bishops.'

'Ah yes, the unified Church,' Nicholas said as he took the letter and set it aside, unopened. 'I am sure that we will have much to discuss concerning the unified Church. But what of you, Princess Sofia? Do you also bring a message from your emperor? Or shall you allow your beauty to speak for you?'

So he was charming as well as handsome, Sofia thought. 'I never allow my beauty to speak for me,' she replied in Latin. And then in Italian, 'I find words to be much more eloquent.'

'Indeed, as the Bible says, "Speech finely framed delighteth the ears",' Nicholas quoted. 'But I am amazed. You are a linguist, then, as well as a beauty.'

'The two are not mutually exclusive, Your Holiness, although it has been truly said, "Men trust their ears less then their eyes".'

'Herodotus!' Nicholas exclaimed, clapping his hands together. 'You are a scholar then as well. All the better.

I greatly prize scholarship. As you have no doubt read, "There is only one good – knowledge – and one evil – ignorance".'

'Surely, Socrates believed so,' Sofia said, and Nicholas beamed with pleasure. 'But scholarship alone is a poor teacher. Was it not Heraclitus who wrote, "Much learning does not teach understanding"?'

'Yes indeed,' Nicholas agreed. 'And you might have added, "there is nothing so ridiculous but some philosopher has said it".' He arched his eyebrows questioningly.

'Cicero, Your Holiness.'

Nicholas nodded his satisfaction. 'Your learning does you honour, Princess Sofia. I must introduce you to one of your learned countrymen who has done me the honour of residing at my court: the Cardinal Bessarion. He is a wise man, who has taught me much.'

'I shall be glad to meet him,' Sofia replied. And indeed, she would, particularly if Bessarion had the ear of the pope. 'But I do not believe that he could have much to teach Your Holiness.'

The pope smiled. 'Your words are kind, but, as pride is the downfall of man, I shall be forced to disagree.' He picked up the letter from the Synaxis and tapped it nonchalantly against the arm of his throne. 'Princess, Leontarsis, the friendship of the Greek emperor is most welcome, as are you both. You will join me for dinner tonight, when we will discuss this letter of the Synaxis. Until then, I must ask that you excuse me.' The pope rose and left the room amidst respectful silence. As soon as the door closed behind him, the room burst into noisy life, courtiers grouping in clumps to gossip and politic. Leontarsis went straight to a chamber-pot in the corner to relieve himself.

'I thought that went well,' Sofia said to him when he returned. 'The pope seems well disposed towards us.'

Leontarsis merely grunted his affirmation. No doubt he was already preoccupied with that night's dinner, where he would bear the brunt of the pope's outrage over the letter of the Synaxis. Sofia hoped that he would not say anything foolish. Constantine had instructed Leontarsis that he was not to support union unless the pope agreed to all the demands of the Synaxis. The pope would not react kindly to such an intransigent stance, and Leontarsis had little skill for sweetening harsh words. Indeed, it might be better if Leontarsis were not present at the dinner.

'Leontarsis, are you feeling quite well?' Sofia asked him.

'Much better now, yes,' he responded absently.

'I rejoice to hear it, because if you fell ill before this evening's meal,' she suggested, 'you would not be present tonight when the pope discusses the letter of the Synaxis. You would have to postpone your meeting with him until he has had more time to reflect.'

'What? Sick?' Leontarsis asked. His confusion vanished. 'Yes, I am feeling rather poorly. I am not sure that my seasickness has quite passed. Would you do me the honour of representing me at the pope's table tonight and expressing my regrets?'

'Of course,' Sofia replied. That was one problem solved. But there was still the letter to deal with. How to make the pope understand that the only way to deal with the Synaxis was to call their bluff? Perhaps Cardinal Bessarion could be of help. Indeed, he looked like the only hope that she had.

*

A little over an hour later Sofia followed a young priest into Bessarion's study, a square room occupying one of the upper floors of the papal palace's south tower. Books filled the room, overflowing the bookshelves and covering much of the floor as well. In the centre of the room a desk floated amongst the sea of books, and seated at the desk was Bessarion. The ageing scholar's appearance contrasted sharply with the clutter of his study. He was immaculately dressed in the red robes of a cardinal, his white hair cut short beneath a red skullcap and his white beard neatly trimmed. He looked up from the manuscript laid out before him, and his face brightened. 'Princess Sofia, you are most welcome,' he said, his voice quiet and deep. 'I have heard great things of you.'

Sofia curtsied. 'Thank you for seeing me at such short notice, Your Eminence. You do me great honour.'

'Please, call me Bessarion. "Your Eminence" is far too lofty a title for an old man such as me,' he replied with a smile. 'Now, Princess, I presume that it is not questions of scholarship that have brought you to me. You wish to discuss union and support for Constantinople, I have no doubt. Of course, you know that the pope wishes to give what aid he can, so long as the Union is enforced. But I must warn you, this letter of the Synaxis has not helped your cause.'

'You have read the letter, then?'

'Yes. The pope summoned me to him as soon as he left his audience with you. The letter left him quite upset. He is very clear where he stands. The pope will never agree to another council, nor will he agree to a union in which he is not the absolute head of the Church.'

'And what do you think?' Sofia asked.

Bessarion shrugged his shoulders. 'Me? What does it matter what an old fool like me thinks?' It mattered very much indeed, Sofia thought. Bessarion was the only person with enough influence to convince the pope to support Constantinople. After a pause, Bessarion continued. 'I think that union is good for the faith and good for the empire. I have always believed that. That is why I am here in Rome. That is why I am a cardinal. I also believe that Constantinople must be helped. It is not so very far, after all, from Constantinople to Vienna, or from Vienna to Rome. If we could have aid for Constantinople without union, then I would be for that. But that is not to be, and I understand the pope's reluctance. Nicholas is more concerned with the Church than with Constantinople. If he could be convinced that the Union will be implemented, then he might act. But after this letter from the Synaxis, I fear he will be very hard to convince.'

'But not impossible?'

'Nothing is impossible with God's help, my child,' Bessarion replied. 'But God will have to work a small miracle to change the pope's mind. I am not so sure, however, that the pope is wrong. My fellow bishops ran me out of Constantinople for supporting the Union, and just look at how they have treated poor Patriarch Mammas. I do not believe that union is possible as long as such men control the Orthodox Church.'

'I agree,' Sofia concurred. 'But what if these men were not in power? What if we could break the Synaxis?'

Bessarion nodded. 'Go on, Princess. You have my attention.'

'Give the Synaxis what they want,' Sofia said. 'That is the way to break them.'

Bessarion frowned. 'I'm not quite sure I follow you.'

'The bishops of the Synaxis draw all of their strength from their opposition to the Union,' Sofia explained. 'Agree with them on the small issues, and they will be forced to agree with the Union. Once they do, they will lose all of their power with the people.'

'But these are hardly small issues. Surely you are not suggesting that the pope agree to the doctrine of the equality of all bishops, or that he deny one thousand years of teaching and accept that the Holy Spirit proceeds only from God?'

Sofia nodded emphatically. 'That is exactly what I am suggesting. The pope must condone the Greek liturgy, overlook any theological differences, and at least formally accept the equality of all bishops. If he does all of this, then the Synaxis will have no choice but to embrace the Union.'

'But what you ask for is nothing less than a complete renunciation of the Roman Catholic position!'

'Not a renunciation, Bessarion,' Sofia insisted. 'A compromise, and a temporary one at that. The important thing is that the pope will retain real control of the Church. In a few years time, once the people have grown used to the Union, then he can reverse his decrees and slowly bring the Orthodox Church into line with the Latin Church. This is the only way that union can be achieved – slowly, or not at all.'

'There are others who have thought as you do,' Bessarion mused. 'But you ask much of the pope. I know what Nicholas will say to this. Is not protecting the truth of God to be placed above whatever secular gains the Union might bring about? I wonder the same.'

'But what does the truth matter, if there is no one left to teach it to?' Sofia replied. 'If Constantinople falls to the Turks, then any chance to save the Greeks will be lost. Surely it is better for the pope to bring the Orthodox Church into the fold, however imperfectly, than to leave it outside true salvation forever.'

'Enough, enough,' Bessarion said. 'You have made your point, Princess. I will discuss what you have told me with the pope.'

'And?'

'And,' Bessarion smiled, 'I will do my utmost to ensure that he finds your arguments convincing.'

Dinner that night was held in the pope's private dining room around a table that accommodated only ten guests. The room was decorated on three sides with frescos depicting the deaths of saints, and the paintings seemed to come alive under the flickering candlelight. The fourth side of the room was lined with arched windows looking out on the lights of Rome, burning brightly in the clear February sky.

The pope sat at the head of the table, with Sofia and Bessarion to his right and left. The rest of the guests were cardinals and bishops who Sofia did not recognize. The table was set with silver, gold and crystal – a sharp contrast to the plain wooden dishes that served the Greek court. Each course was more delicious than the last: a *tartara* of egg, cheese and ground almonds, spiced with cinnamon and served with sweet white wine; fried sardines stuffed with marjoram, sage, rosemary and saffron, accompanied with a sparkling Lambrusco; hare with a fennel and almond sauce and a full-bodied red from Montepulciano.

While the assembled cardinals and bishops gorged themselves, Pope Nicholas ate little and spoke much, engaging Sofia and Bessarion in philosophical debate upon the merits of Saint Augustine and the brilliance of Averoës.

As the evening dragged on with no mention of union or the Synaxis' letter, Sofia's mind drifted away from the conversation, which currently focused on the question of free will. She found herself thinking of Longo, of their kiss. She wondered what he was doing now, if he thought of her, and at the same time wondered why she should care so much.

She was brought back to the present by a tap on the shoulder from Pope Nicholas. To her embarrassment, she realized that he had just asked her a question. 'I fear you were somewhere else for a while, Princess,' Nicholas said, smiling. 'Perhaps you were contemplating the beautiful logic of Aquinas.'

Sofia blushed. 'Something very like, yes Your Holiness,' she murmured.

'I was asking what you think of the basilica of Saint Peter,' Nicholas said. 'I am contemplating tearing it down and replacing it with a grander structure.'

Sofia was surprised at this. The basilica was a spectacular building. Its towering entrance – massive columns leading to two tiers of arches that held up a peaked roof – was justly famous around the world as a symbol of the papacy. 'Saint Peter's has stood for over a thousand years,' she said. 'I would hesitate to destroy something so ancient.'

'The laws and beliefs of the Catholic Church are also ancient, Princess, yet the Synaxis would have me cast them aside. They claim it is to build a greater, unified Church, but just as you say, I am reluctant to destroy something so ancient, so beautiful.' The Synaxis at last, Sofia thought. The other guests fell silent and leaned forward to hear her reply.

'You would not be destroying the beliefs of the Church,' Sofia countered. 'You would only be adding to them.'

'And what if I grant the Synaxis' requests and they still refuse union? I will have humbled the Church for nothing, and perhaps ruined any chance of ever achieving a true union.' Assent echoed down the table. Only Bessarion kept quiet.

'What you say is true,' Sofia replied. 'The Synaxis might still reject union, even if you accept all their demands. But then the emperor will be free to force the Union through, even if he has to remove every bishop in the Synaxis. They will be unable to stop him, for they have already agreed to union on these terms by signing the letter.'

'If only I could be as sure as you are, Princess, that Emperor Constantine would indeed enforce the Union even over the complaints of his clergy.'

'If Leontarsis were not ill, I am certain that he would be here to pledge the emperor's word. But, since he is not, I will pledge it myself as ambassador of Constantinople.' Sofia offered a silent prayer of thanks for Leontarsis's absence. He would have promised no such thing, and in doing so would have ruined all of her hard work.

Nicholas nodded. 'Very well then,' he said. 'I believe that this matter is settled. After the details are attended to, I shall hold an audience where I will recognize the desires of the Eastern bishops, as a prelude to a true union of the Church. I do hope that Leontarsis will be well enough to attend that meeting.' Nicholas winked. 'In the meantime, let us begin dessert, and there is a question that I have for you, Princess, concerning our friend Aquinas . . .'

The audience the pope had promised came sooner than Sofia had expected, only three days later. Sofia was visiting the studio of the famed painter Vittore Pisano when a messenger entered and told her that she was to come to the pope's audience chamber immediately.

Sofia found Leontarsis wringing his hands as he waited for her outside. 'Do you know why we were summoned so suddenly?' Sofia asked. 'Is the pope ready to officially recognize the Synaxis' demands?'

Leontarsis shook his head. 'I thought we were still weeks away from any declaration. Yesterday, we were still working out the exact language of how the pope would be referred to in the unified Church.'

Far above, in the tall square tower of St Peter's basilica, the bells began to toll the hour of noon, and the doors swung open before them. Sofia's eyes went first to the pope, sombre on his throne, and then to the man standing beside him, the man whose presence explained the suddenness of this audience: Gregory Mammas, Patriarch of Constantinople.

Sofia and Leontarsis reached the throne together and made their obeisances before the pope. Nicholas gave them a brief, strained smile, and then bid them rise. 'Leontarsis, Princess Sofia,' he began. 'Your presence at our court has been most welcome, as have been the kind words that you have brought from Emperor Constantine. Know that you will both always be welcome in Rome.' Both Leontarsis and Sofia bowed in recognition.

'You have offered wise council, and we have had much to reflect on,' Nicholas continued. 'In light of all that we have heard and learned, both from you and from the recently arrived Patriarch of Constantinople himself, we declare and decree, in the name of God the Father, the following response to Constantine, Emperor of the Romans.'

A tonsured priest stepped forward and began to read from a sheet of parchment: 'If you, with your nobles and the people of Constantinople, accept the decree of union, you will find Us and Our venerable brothers, the cardinals of the holy Roman Church, ever eager to support your honour and your empire. But if you and your people refuse to accept the decree, you will force Us to take such measures as are necessary for your salvation and Our honour.'

Sofia frowned. The pope's declaration was even worse than she had feared. It was a wholesale rejection of the Synaxis and all they had asked for. 'But Your Holiness,' Sofia protested, 'this will only strengthen the Synaxis. What of your decision to accept their demands?'

The pope only shook his head; it was Mammas who answered her. 'The Synaxis and the people who follow them are fools and heretics. They will never agree to union. Giving in to their demands will only make them bold and sanction their unholy attempts to usurp the power of the patriarch. If they will not willingly join the Union, then they must be made to join. There can be no compromise with such people.'

Sofia ignored him and addressed the pope again. 'You

would turn your back on Constantinople then? You are abandoning us to the Turks!'

'No,' Nicholas sighed. 'You yourself said that Constantine has the power to force the bishops to adhere to the Union. I agree with Mammas. It is not reason that prevents the Greeks from accepting the Union, but stubborn pride. Let Constantine force their adherence, and then we will send what aid we can to your city. Until that time, we cannot help those who lie outside of the Church. The fate of Constantinople is in God's hands.' Nicholas paused, and when he spoke again his voice was softer. 'I am sorry, Princess, but I cannot place even your advice over the word of the patriarch. He knows his flock better than you or I ever could.'

Sofia nodded, not trusting herself to speak. She bowed and strode from the room, not even waiting for the pope's dismissal. Once outside the audience chamber, she leaned against the wall and sank to the floor, her head in her hands. She had failed. This entire trip had been for nothing. One ship each from the Venetians and Genoese, and now no help from Rome. They might as well have never come.

'Princess?'

Sofia looked up to see Mammas standing above her, shifting awkwardly. 'What do you want?' she snapped.

'I see you are upset with the pope's decree,' Mammas said. 'You must forgive me, then, for bringing yet more bad news. I know that you were close to the empress-mother. She died just before I left Constantinople.'

'What?' Sofia asked. How could this have happened? With Helena gone, there was no telling what Constantine would do, whose influence he would fall under. Sofia stood to look Mammas in the eyes. 'How did she die?'

'Shortly after you left, her illness worsened. The empress-mother dismissed her doctors and confided herself wholly in God. She refused to receive anyone other than Constantine and her confessor. Unfortunately, her condition worsened rapidly. I understand that she was rarely lucid over the last few weeks, but she received extreme unction before she passed.'

Sofia could only nod as tears filled her eyes. She had lost Helena, her friend and protector, and Constantinople had lost the pope's blessing. The palace around her and the city outside suddenly seemed painful and foreign. Whatever awaited her in Constantinople, Sofia was ready to return home.

Chapter 9

Sitt Hatun sat cross-legged amidst a profusion of cushions, surrounded by an evening meal fit for a sultan. Low stools were arranged in a semicircle before her, and on each sat a copper dish heaped with food. To begin, there were roasted almonds, dried apricots and tangy *dolma* – vine leaves stuffed with onions, rice, dill and mint, all mixed in lemon juice. Then there were the side dishes that formed the backbone of any Turkish meal, prepared in the harem kitchen with unparalleled skill: a cool, creamy yoghurt dip; a basket of freshly baked *girde*, a crisp flatbread that melted in the mouth; and a huge platter of boiled rice drizzled with olive oil and sprinkled with black pepper. The main dishes were a whole roasted chicken, with golden skin and tender meat falling from the bone, and Sitt Hatun's favourite, *nirbach* – a rich stew of diced lamb and carrots flavoured with coriander, ginger, cinnamon and pomegranate syrup. To drink, she had a pitcher of refreshing *ayran*, a mix of yoghurt and water flavoured with salt and mint. The mix of pungent smells made her stomach rumble, but she did not eat.

Anna sat across from Sitt Hatun. The Polish girl was even thinner than when Sitt Hatun had taken her into her service months ago. They always dined together, and Anna always ate first. For although Sitt Hatun had official tasters to check for poison, she did not trust them. They had already failed her twice, and both times Anna had come close to death. While Anna lay sick, Sitt Hatun ate nothing but fruit that she herself picked from the harem garden. Anna had just now recovered from the last poisoning, and Sitt Hatun was looking forward to her first full meal in weeks.

Before eating anything, Anna sniffed carefully at each of the dishes. 'I do not recommend the *dolma*,' she said as she put the dish aside. 'Nor do I trust the *nirbach*. It is richly spiced, perhaps to cover a poison.'

Sitt Hatun signalled for a servant to take the offending dishes away. She would take no chances. 'At least we shall not go hungry,' she said. There had been times when all of their food was tainted. On those days, her entire court went hungry, for they dined on whatever Sitt Hatun did not eat. Sitt Hatun would order the food sent back to the kitchen and force her servants to watch while her *as ∈ ibas i*, or head chef, was forced to eat from every dish. It was an instructive lesson for the others in her court.

Anna now began to taste the food. She ate a few almonds, and they both waited while their stomachs twisted from tension and hunger. After several minutes, Anna handed the plate to Sitt Hatun. 'You may eat,' Anna told her. While Sitt Hatun ate the nuts, Anna tasted the rest of the food, pausing for several minutes between each dish. By the time she passed the chicken to Sitt Hatun, more than an hour had passed.

Sitt Hatun scooped up some of the thick yoghurt dip with a piece of flatbread and ate it with a morsel of chicken. She closed her eyes to savour the taste. When she opened them she found a eunuch standing at the doorway to her chamber. She recognized him as Davarnza, one of the secretaries to the grand vizier, Halil.

'I bring a message, My Lady,' Davarnza said. He bowed low and presented a folded piece of paper. Sitt Hatun took it and read quickly: '*Gülbehar has hired assassins to murder you this very night. The sultan himself has given his consent, and your guards have been bribed to let the assassins do their work. I will help you escape the palace, if you accept my offer.*' The letter was unsigned.

'I am to wait for a response,' Davarnza told her. Sitt Hatun had no doubt as to the truth of what Halil wrote. She could try to flee on her own, but she would be lucky to escape the palace, much less the city. She could beg Murad for mercy, but this tactic was even less likely to succeed. Halil was the only person who could help her. Much as she dreaded the prospect of giving herself to him, Sitt Hatun knew that she had little choice.

'My answer is "yes",' she said.

'Then you are to have this.' Davarnza handed her another note. It read: '*My man, Isa, will come for you tonight. Pack nothing; he will provide. He will bring you to me. Afterwards, you will travel to Manisa and tell Mehmed what Gülbehar has done in his absence.*'

Sitt Hatun dismissed Davarnza, and then tore the two notes into tiny pieces. She ate the pieces one by one, washing them down with the cool *ayran*. When she was done, she ordered all of her servants but Anna away, and then tried to sleep. She needed her rest. It would be a long night.

Sitt Hatun woke shortly after nightfall. She armed herself and Anna with daggers, and they arranged pillows in Sitt Hatun's bed to mimic her sleeping form, before moving quietly into the adjoining room. They shut the door behind them and sat down on Anna's bed to wait. There was no moon, and the night settled thick and dark, so that Sitt Hatun could barely make out Anna sitting mere inches away. The busy noises of the harem slowly faded until Sitt Hatun could hear nothing but her own breathing and the racing of her heart. She sat wide awake, straining to hear the slightest noise. Outside, she heard the night watch change – the distant sound of laughing voices and tramping boots. That meant that it was midnight, and still no sign of Isa. Sitt Hatun began to have doubts. What if Halil had betrayed her?

At last, a noise – a boot scuffing against the floor – came from the hallway. Then, there was silence. Sitt Hatun and Anna looked at one another. 'Check the hallway,' Sitt Hatun whispered. 'It may be Isa.'

Anna rose in the darkness, and drawing her long, thin knife, moved to the door that opened to the hallway and peered through a spyhole. She turned back to Sitt Hatun and shook her head. There was no one there. Then another noise: the rustling of fabric from Sitt Hatun's bedchamber. Anna crossed to the door that led to the chamber. She looked through the spyhole for only a second before hurrying back to Sitt Hatun's side. 'Isa?' Sitt Hatun whispered. Anna shook her head, no. A voice barked out in the adjoining room – a harsh exclamation in a language that Sitt Hatun did not understand. 'The servants' passage,' Sitt Hatun whispered and rose, taking Anna by the arm. She led her to the wall, pressed a lever, and a small portion of the wall swung inward, revealing a narrow, inky-black passageway. They slipped inside and pushed the door shut. Sitt Hatun pulled Anna down the passage as behind them, she heard the door connecting her and Anna's rooms crash open.

Sitt Hatun quickened her step, moving by memory in the darkness. They reached a stairwell that led down to the main harem kitchen and hurried down it. Sitt Hatun froze just before she reached the bottom. A man was standing there, dressed in black and lit red by the banked fires in the kitchen. He wore a black scarf across his face and held a long knife in his hand. He had heard them and was peering up the dark stairs towards them. '*Chi va là?*' he called out. Sitt Hatun did not move. '*Chi va là?*' he asked again and took a step up the stairs towards them.

Sitt Hatun turned to run, but Anna stopped her. 'Wait here,' Anna whispered. She slipped by Sitt Hatun and down the stairs. When the man saw her approaching he stopped, but Anna only sped up. She met the man at a run, ducking under his thrusting knife and bowling him over. They tumbled over one another and into the kitchen, where the man landed with a thud, Anna sitting astride him, her knife plunged into his chest. She removed her knife, cut the man's throat to make sure that he was dead, and then rose and motioned for Sitt Hatun to join her.

Sitt Hatun led them down a side passage from the kitchen to the harem's central courtyard. She paused before entering the courtyard to make sure that it was empty, but when she stepped forward, a man's hand grabbed her, covering her mouth and pulling her close. She bit his hand and tried to scream. 'Silence,' the man whispered in her ear. 'It is I, Isa.' He let her go, and she turned to face him. His broad Asian face was smooth and his movements graceful and self-assured. He carried a small pack and wore nondescript brown robes. 'The assassins arrived early at your chambers,' he told her. 'We haven't much time. Follow me.'

He led the way down the side of the courtyard, through a door back into the harem, and through a series of storerooms until they came to a windowless room with a rug crumpled against the wall and an open trapdoor in the floor. Isa took a burning torch from the wall and motioned for them to climb down. 'Hurry,' he said. 'This is the way the assassins entered the harem – the only way out not guarded by the janissary. We must move quickly before they return.'

Once inside the tunnel, Isa removed his pack and produced two more brown tunics of the same type he wore. He handed them to the women and ordered them to put them on over their clothes. Then he led them down the tunnel at a jog, his torch guttering in the damp breeze that blew in their faces. The walls of the tunnel were rough-hewn, dripping with moisture, and the floor sloped gently downwards. Sitt Hatun guessed that they were headed towards the river.

They had travelled only a few hundred yards when they heard voices and footsteps echoing down the passage behind them. Isa dropped his torch, and they stumbled on in the darkness. The steps behind them grew louder, and soon they could see the faint glow of advancing torch-light behind them. Sitt Hatun felt something brush by her side, and then heard it skitter along the floor ahead in the darkness. 'Arrows,' Isa hissed. 'Stay close to the walls.' Ahead, Sitt Hatun could see a break in the darkness, a relative brightness that marked the end of the tunnel. A few seconds later they were through, running down a sandy slope towards the banks of the river.

On the shore sat a small boat, guarded by two men holding swords. Isa rushed straight towards the men. He stopped just short of them and flung a white powder into their faces. The men collapsed, clawing at their throats and eyes, and Isa stepped over them and into the boat, waving for Sitt Hatun and Anna to follow. They clambered in, and Isa shoved off. Sitt Hatun glanced behind her and saw five black-clad men rush out of the tunnel, gesturing and yelling. She was still watching them when an arrow sank into the prow just in front of her. 'Stay down,' Isa barked, as more arrows whizzed past. He took a few strokes at the oars and the current caught the boat, pushing it faster and faster down the river. Isa abandoned the oars and joined them in the bottom of the boat. After a minute, the arrows stopped, and slowly they all rose from their cramped positions. Isa took up the oars again, while Sitt Hatun and Anna moved into the prow.

'You are hurt!' Sitt Hatun cried, as she noticed that Anna's clothes were covered with blood.

'It is not mine, My Lady.'

'That man you killed . . .' Sitt Hatun said. 'Where did you learn to fight like that?'

Anna shrugged. 'My parents died when I was young, and I had to fend for myself.'

It was a cold spring night, and the two of them huddled together in the prow of the boat, looking back on the sprawling imperial palace, the white stone walls lit by hundreds of winking torches. 'The next time we see those walls,' Sitt Hatun swore softly, 'we shall enter in glory, and Gülbehar shall tremble in fear.'

They had been on the river no more than a few minutes when Isa began to row for the shore. He docked the boat at a small pier in Manisa's river port. Then, once they were out of the boat, he pushed it back out into the river, letting it drift away. 'Come, we haven't much time,' he told them and led them into the dark, narrow streets of the city. Their short trip ended at the gate of an innocuous white house in the merchant's district. Isa unlocked the gate and led them through a small courtyard and into the home. They emerged into a round common room with several more passageways branching off from it. A low table sat in the middle of the room, lit by candles and set with food and drink. Halil, wearing a green satin robe with swirling patterns in gold, was seated on a cushion beside the table. It was the first time that Sitt Hatun had seen him in person. He was tall and spare, with long delicate fingers that had clearly never seen battle. His olive-skinned face was thin, but still relatively smooth despite his forty-eight years. He wore a well-trimmed moustache that curved downward into a tiny grey-flecked beard. He might have been called handsome but for the jagged scar stretching down from his right temple to his jaw, and his unnerving eyes. Large and palest grey, they were cold and unblinking, like the eyes of a dead man.

Halil rose and bowed as Sitt Hatun entered. 'Welcome,

sultana,' he said. His smile – thin lips stretched back over sharp teeth – made him look like a wolf at hunt. 'I am so glad that you arrived safely. Your servant can make herself comfortable in there.' He gestured to a side passage. Anna squeezed Sitt Hatun's hand and left. Halil turned to Isa. 'Isa, you may go,' he said, and Isa retreated quietly. Halil motioned for Sitt Hatun to be seated at the table. 'Some refreshments for you? You must be famished after your adventures.'

Sitt Hatun shook her head. She was nervous, and her stomach rebelled at the sight of food. 'Excellent,' Halil said. 'We have little time to spare anyway. The assassins will be looking for you, and you had best be gone before sunrise. Come, follow me.' He took a candle and led her down a side passage to a small room that was dominated by a large, canopied bed. He set the candle on a table beside the bed, and then untied his robe and allowed it to slip to the floor. He was entirely naked, thin and lacking in muscle. He gestured for her to undress, but Sitt Hatun did not move. 'You understand the particulars of our agreement?' Halil asked.

'I do,' Sitt Hatun said. She chided herself for her squeamishness. Any sacrifice was worth making if it meant that her child would be heir to the throne. She could then deal with Gülbehar as she saw fit. Keeping that in mind, Sitt Hatun turned her back to Halil and methodically undressed. When she was naked, she stepped carefully past Halil and blew out the candle. The room went black.

Sitt Hatun suppressed a shudder of disgust as she felt Halil's cold hand on her shoulder. 'Do what must be done,' she whispered.

Sitt Hatun reached Manisa at dusk, eight days after her night with Halil. Halil had entrusted her and Anna to a Greek eunuch named Erzinjan, who had taken them on a merchant ship down the Maritza river and across the Aegean. Their voyage had been blessed with perfect weather, but it was a tense journey. Sitt Hatun had no illusions as to her ability to elude the assassins. If Mehmed did not protect her in Manisa, then they would find her and kill her.

That is, if Mehmed did not kill her first. Sitt Hatun was not sure that Mehmed would protect her, even after she told him of Gülbehar's infidelity. The news might well drive him over the edge. After all, now that she had fled the harem she had no protection, no rights. All she had was the *kumru kalp*, sewn into the folds of her silk caftan. Sitt Hatun prayed to Allah that it would be enough.

Veiled to avoid prying eyes, Sitt Hatun and Anna made their way through the sun-baked streets of Manisa to the palace. Sitt Hatun led Anna around to the side, where a small door protected by eunuch guards gave servants access to the harem complex. She walked straight to one of the guards. 'We wish to present ourselves to the stewardess of the harem,' she told him. 'We desire to serve the sultan.'

The guard examined them both closely. 'Let me see your faces,' he said at last.

Sitt Hatun shook her head. 'We show our faces to no man, only to the stewardess.'

'Very well,' the guard grumbled. 'Wait here.'

Sitt Hatun and Anna stood in the shade of the palace wall as the sun inched across the sky and their patch of shade shrank to nothing. Finally, the stewardess appeared. She was an older woman, but still striking despite the faint wrinkles at the corner of her eyes and the grey in her long black hair. As stewardess of the harem, it was her task to recruit and train the women who would serve the sultan. 'These are the ones?' she asked the guard, who nodded. 'Come with me,' she told Sitt Hatun and Anna.

They followed her down a short passage and into a round room, where the stewardess stopped and turned to face them. 'This is as far as you go until I get a good look at you,' she said. 'Take off your veils.' Sitt Hatun removed her veil, and the stewardess gasped. 'Sultana! What are you doing here?'

'Quiet,' Sitt Hatun ordered as she replaced her veil. 'I do not wish my presence to be known by any but the sultan Mehmed. You will tell him that I have arrived yourself. But first, prepare a bath for me and my servant in a private room. And bring me new clothes. I wish to refresh myself before I see the sultan.'

'Yes, Sultana,' the stewardess said. She led Sitt Hatun and Anna to a large chamber with a steaming bath set into the floor. Sitt Hatun undressed and lowered herself into the water, where Anna gently washed away the grime from her travels. Sitt Hatun dressed with care, slipping into a revealing gold silk robe, which looked as if it could fall off at a mere thought, and a matching veil. Yet, when the stewardess of the harem led her into Mehmed's reading-room, he did not even glance up from the book he held before him. Only when she had removed her veil and settled on the floor across from him did Mehmed look at her. 'Why have you come here, wife?' he began abruptly. 'Is it at my father's bidding?'

She shook her head. 'He does not know that I am here.'
Mehmed set his book aside, his eyebrows raised. Sitt Hatun
was glad to have surprised him; she had the advantage.
'I have come on my own. I bring news of your father.'

'Indeed?' Mehmed replied. 'The news must be quite
important. You know what the punishment is for leaving
the harem without the consent of the sultan?'

'I know, My Lord.' The punishment was death, just as
it was death for those who entered the harem uninvited.
'But *you* are the sultan, My Lord. It is for you to decide
my fate. Once you have heard my message, you will understand that I have only done a wife's duty in coming to
warn you.'

'Warn me?' Mehmed asked. 'My father would not dare
to move against me. I am the heir to the throne.'

'No, My Lord,' Sitt Hatun agreed. 'He would never
raise his hand against his son. But he might place his
hands upon his son's favourite wife.'

Mehmed's eyes narrowed. 'Careful, woman,' he said,
his voice hard and dangerous. 'I will have your tongue if
you speak false of Gülbehar.'

Sitt Hatun felt the blood drain from her face, but she
did not hesitate. 'I do not speak false, husband. I have
seen your father in the bedchamber of Gülbehar with my
own eyes. But I do not expect you to believe me, though
I swear four times by Allah. I have brought proof.' She
took the *kumru kalp* from her robes and placed it before
Mehmed.

Mehmed's jaw tightened when he saw the ruby. He
picked it up and his hand clenched white-knuckled around
the stone. Mehmed stood suddenly, and Sitt Hatun feared
that he might strike her. But instead he strode to his writing

desk and placed the *kumru kalp* there. When he returned, his features were calm once more.

'You are sure that my father does not know you are here?' Mehmed asked. 'He does not know that you have brought me the *kumru kalp*?'

'Nobody knows,' Sitt Hatun told him. 'Only your stewardess of the harem.'

'Good, then we shall keep it that way. You will stay in seclusion so long as you are here, served only by your maidservant and the stewardess.' Sitt Hatun nodded. 'You have performed a great service,' Mehmed continued. 'You have my thanks, Sitt Hatun. How may I repay your loyalty?'

'I have only done my duty as a wife, My Lord,' Sitt Hatun replied. 'And I only ask for my due as your wife.'

Mehmed studied her for a long time while Sitt Hatun sat breathless. Finally, he nodded his head. 'Very well,' he said. 'Come.' Mehmed took her hand and led her into the bedroom.

Moonlight filtered through the curtains of Mehmed's bed, highlighting the sleeping face of Sitt Hatun. She looked peaceful, a faint smile curling her lips. Gazing on her, Mehmed almost felt sorry for his long-neglected wife. Almost. For although he had enjoyed making love to Sitt Hatun, he already regretted lying with her. He had done so not just to reward her, but out of anger and spite, directed both at his father and at Gülbehar. He had allowed his passions to rule him, and he knew that there would be a price to pay. But there were other things on Mehmed's mind as he rose from bed and padded across the soft carpet to his study. He picked up the *kumru kalp* by its golden chain and then hung it around his neck. He would wear the gem as a reminder of Gülbehar's betrayal, a reminder never to trust his heart again.

There was little doubt in Mehmed's mind that Sitt Hatun's accusation was true. The *kumru kalp* never left Murad's neck. It was one of his greatest treasures, a jewel that was said to have been worn by the Roman Empress Anna Comnena herself. Murad had seized it when he conquered Edirne and wore it always as a reminder of his greatest victory. He would never have given it to Sitt Hatun, much less to a mere *gedikli*. Only one woman could have led him to part with it: Gülbehar. Mehmed knew all too well the wild passions that she could spark. Besides, Sitt Hatun's story only confirmed a hundred suspicions of Mehmed's own. So this, he thought, was why his father had been so eager to send him away, why he had objected so strongly to Mehmed's relationship with Gülbehar, why he had insisted that she stay in Edirne. Anger flared up inside Mehmed, and he gripped the gem so tightly that its sharp edges cut into his hand. The old fool; did he really think that he could steal Mehmed's own *kadin*? It was time that he taught his ageing father a lesson. It was time that he resumed his rightful place on the throne of the Ottoman Empire.

Mehmed moved from behind his desk to the cabinet on the wall. He opened it and removed the Koran. It fell open in his hands, and Mehmed read: '*Believers, vengeance is decreed for you in bloodshed: a free man for a free man, a slave for a slave, and a female for a female.*' Surely a god that counselled a man for a man would also approve of a sultan for a sultana.

Mehmed placed the Koran aside and pressed the hidden latch that revealed the cabinet's secret compartment. He slipped on a pair of tight leather gloves and then removed the box that Isa had brought him. He opened the box and took out the vial of poison. The liquid inside was slightly viscous, pale amber in the moonlight. Mehmed still did not know who had sent the poison, but he would deal with that detail later. For now, it only mattered what the poison could do. He would have his vengeance.

Chapter 10

The ringing of church bells reached Sofia faintly as she strode through the palace to Constantine's private audience chambers. The sombre tolling marked the end of mourning for the Empress-Mother Helena. Sofia wished that Helena were with her now, to stand by her as she faced Constantine. She had been expecting his summons since she returned to Constantinople the day before, and she dreaded what he would tell her. Was she still to be married, or would she be free?

Sofia entered the audience chamber to find Constantine seated on his throne, a neutral expression on his face. In his right hand he grasped a crumpled copy of the pope's decree. Sofia curtsied before him, and he bid her rise.

'Welcome home, Princess Sofia,' Constantine said. 'I have asked you here to discuss your mission to Italy. Leontarsis has told me that you were very much involved in the negotiations with the pope. Is this true?'

Sofia nodded. 'Forgive me, My Lord, but Leontarsis is a clumsy politician. I thought that I might be more effective.'

'Leontarsis was my appointed ambassador,' Constantine said, his voice rising.

'Even so, I was nearly successful,' Sofia protested. 'And I believe that we can still turn the situation to our advantage, if you only . . .'

Constantine gestured for her to be silent. 'Your involvement has already led to this!' he roared, holding up the pope's decree. 'I promised my mother on her death-bed that I would enact union, but how can I now? Tell me: how can I!' Then, recovering himself, he continued in an even tone. 'You were sent to Italy to be seen, not heard, Sofia. I had hoped that Leontarsis would find you a husband who could offer us military support, but even that hope is gone.'

How could he reprimand her after all that she had done in Italy? Sofia bit back her anger. 'I did my best to serve you faithfully, My Lord.'

'You serve me best, Sofia, by playing the role of a princess, not a politician. You are lucky that Megadux Notaras is still willing to marry you. I have spoken to him about a date this summer. Until that time, you will do as I say. You are a lady, Sofia. You must behave like one. There will be no more swordplay and no more politicking. If you wish to study, then learn something pleasing: how to sing or play an instrument.'

'Yes, My Lord,' she said in a dead voice.

Constantine frowned. 'I understand that you expressed a wish to visit Father Neophytus, the empress-mother's confessor.' Sofia nodded. 'You have my permission to visit him at the Haghia Sofia. I will send an escort of guardsmen to take you.'

'Thank you, My Lord,' Sofia said. The words tasted

bitter in her mouth. She curtsied once more and departed. She was to be married after all. With Helena gone, there was no one left to prevent it.

Sofia went to visit Neophytus at the Haghia Sofia on a wet, dreary spring morning that matched the sad spectacle of the once great church, the sight of which always saddened her. It was magnificent even now, but its glory had faded. Although the western facade had been kept in decent repair, the statuary on the side walls was crumbling, and many of the windows that lined the walls of the nave and encircled the building's grand domes were broken. Inside the narthex, the decay was even more obvious. Huge chandeliers bare of candles hovered overhead, suspended from a distant ceiling that was lost in the gloom. Candles were a luxury that had been spared for some time now. The rush torches that had replaced them stood in brackets on the walls, guttering in the draughts from the broken windows above and adding their sooty smoke to the general gloom. The only sound other than the crackling of the torches was the loud drip of water from the high ceiling. The church seemed deserted.

One of the guardsmen who had escorted her to the church stepped forward and rang a small brass bell that hung on the far wall. The loud clanging reverberated off the narrow walls before being swallowed up again by the heavy silence. Sofia heard the sound of approaching footsteps – sandals slapping against smooth stone. At the distant southern end of the narthex a door opened, and a pinpoint of light appeared amidst the gloom. The light came closer, resolving itself into a candle held by a tonsured acolyte in monk's robes.

The acolyte, who looked no older than thirteen, bowed when he saw Sofia. 'My Lady,' he said in a cracking voice. 'How may I help you?'

'I am the Princess Sofia. I have come to see Father Neophytus.'

'Princess Sofia!' the boy squeaked, and then continued in a lower voice. 'Father Neophytus is not expecting you. He is . . .'

'I apologize for not requesting a formal meeting, but I do not expect a special reception,' Sofia said. 'I merely wish to speak to Father Neophytus regarding the empress-mother. Take me to him.'

'Y-yes, of course,' the boy stuttered. 'Follow me.' Sofia wondered why he seemed so nervous. He was probably unused to women and awed by royalty. He led her through one of the doors and into the nave, with its grand, domed ceiling more than one hundred and fifty feet above the floor – the mightiest structure in all of Constantinople. They crossed the nave and entered the maze of hallways leading to the priests' quarters, finally coming to a stop at a simple wooden door. The boy knocked and called out, 'Father Neophytus, there is a . . .'

'Halias? Is that you?' Neophytus's voice came from the other side of the door. 'Come in.' Halias opened the door and stepped in, followed by Sofia. Neophytus's cell was small and sparsely appointed. The stone floor and walls were bare of decoration. A low bed covered with a single, coarse linen sheet sat against the wall to the right and a simple oak desk to the left. A small chest in the corner was the only other piece of furniture. Neophytus was at the far wall with his back to them. He was tending the fireplace and looked to be burning something. Sofia caught a glimpse of parchment curling in the flame.

'I have a letter for you to deliver,' Neophytus began as he turned to face Halias, then stopped short when he saw Sofia. He recovered after only a moment's pause. 'Ah, Princess Sofia, what an unexpected pleasure,' he said with a forced smile. 'Perhaps we could speak somewhere where you would be more comfortable.' He gestured towards the door. 'My cell is all that I need, but it is not furnished for a princess.'

'No, you do not need to stand on ceremony,' Sofia insisted. 'I only wish to talk, and this room will serve that purpose.'

'Very well,' Neophytus said, wringing his hands. 'Halias, you may wait outside. Princess, please take a seat.' He pulled his one chair out from the desk. He sat on the bed. 'How can I help you, Princess?'

'It is the empress-mother,' Sofia began. 'You were with her a great deal towards the end. I would like to know if she spoke of me, or if she perhaps left anything for me.'

'I am sorry, but she did not leave anything,' he said. His eyes left her briefly, flicking over to the desk. Sofia glanced that way as he continued talking, but saw nothing unusual: an inkwell, a small vial, a pair of gloves, a hunk of bread and a cup. 'But she did speak of you often. She said – and I hope that I do not offend you – she said that she wished you had been born a man.'

Sofia nodded. That sounded like Helena, but it was not what Sofia wanted to hear. 'Did she say anything else? Did she mention my marriage?'

'I am sorry, Princess, but I do not recall that she said anything about your marriage,' Neophytus said. Sofia frowned. 'Wait, now I remember.' Neophytus paused. 'She wished you great happiness. Just before she died, she said that she wished she could have lived to see you married.' Sofia saw his eyes nervously flick to the side. He was not, she noticed, a very good liar. What was he so nervous about?

Then, she saw it. The cup on the table was not just any cup. The small, solid gold cup with scenes from the Passion engraved on the outside had belonged to Helena. She had used it for her private communion. What was Neophytus doing with it? Had he stolen it? That would explain why he was so nervous, but why, then, had he not already sold it? Why steal the cup and then keep it? There was some mystery here.

'Thank you for your kind words,' Sofia told Neophytus as she rose. 'I see that you have the empress-mother's communion cup.' She took it from the desk, and Neophytus put out a hand as if to stop her. 'It was one of her favourite possessions, a gift from her father,' Sofia continued. 'Did the empress-mother ask you to keep it for me?'

'The empress . . .' Neophytus began, haltingly. 'That is she . . . After she died she . . .'

'No matter,' Sofia said. 'I am glad to find it here. It will be a precious keepsake for me. Had you not protected it, it would no doubt have been melted down for the imperial coffers by now. Thank you.' Sofia headed for the door, taking the cup with her. Neophytus jumped up and followed her. He looked ready to wrest the cup from her hand. 'And thank you for all of your kindness, to myself and to Helena. I will leave you in peace now.'

'But you cannot, the cup is . . .' Neophytus began, and

then stopped. 'That is, I hope the cup brings you some comfort, Princess.'

'God keep you, Neophytus.'

'And you, Princess,' Neophytus replied, making the sign of the cross. 'Halias will show you out.'

The acolyte was waiting for her in the hallway. 'Halias,' Sofia enquired as they walked side by side back to the narthex, 'do you often deliver letters for Father Neophytus?'

'Yes.' The boy nodded.

'Might I ask to whom?' Halias hesitated. 'I am simply curious,' Sofia said, stepping close as she put her hand on the boy's arm.

Halias flushed red. 'M-many people,' he managed. 'The empress-mother, Patriarch Mammas, Father Gennadius.'

Gennadius. Sofia had not known that Neophytus was connected to the monk. 'Thank you, Halias,' Sofia said, releasing the boy's arm.

As she rode back to the palace in her carriage, Sofia raised Helena's cup to her nose. It smelled of almonds. Odd, she thought. She ran a finger along the bottom of the cup and placed it in her mouth, but she tasted nothing unusual, only the faint bittersweet tang of wine residue.

That evening Sofia grew nauseous and then vomited repeatedly late into the night, long after her stomach had emptied out all its contents. Finally, exhausted, she lapsed into a fevered sleep. She dreamed of Helena's golden communion cup, its rim blazing red. In the dream, she took the cup and drank from it, only to find that it was filled with blood. Neophytus appeared and told her to drink her fill. The dream ended as she drained the cup, blood spilling down her cheeks. When she awoke, the cup sat on her bedside table, where she had left it. She fumbled for the cup, knocking it over. To her relief, it was empty. Sofia shuddered and turned away, but the dream stayed with her.

The next morning she awoke with a thundering headache, her limbs heavy and tired. She felt certain that her dream had been a message and that she knew its meaning: the cup was poisoned. That was the explanation for her illness and for Helena's untimely death. And if Helena had been poisoned, then there could be only one man responsible. Not Neophytus: he had nothing to gain from Helena's death. No, it had to have been Gennadius.

Confirming her suspicions would not be easy. She would have to blackmail Neophytus to get to Gennadius, and she could not do that on her own. There was only one person to whom she could turn: Lucas Notaras, her husband-to-be. Constantine had decreed that they would marry in September, and as her fiancé, Notaras was the only man other than her confessor that Sofia was allowed to receive. She wrote a quick message, requesting that he present himself at her quarters the following morning. Involving Notaras was risky, she knew. He was a proud opponent of union and an ally of Gennadius. Still, he was her only hope if she were to avenge Helena's death.

The next day Notaras arrived punctually at her chambers. 'Princess Sofia, I am pleasantly surprised by your invitation,' he said with a bow. 'To what do I owe this honour?'

'I must speak with you about matters of some importance,' she told him. 'We must speak in private.'

'In private, Princess?' Notaras asked with a rakish smile.

'Yes, we will speak in the garden.' Notaras nodded and followed her to a small rose garden in the palace court-yard. There they could talk in private under the watchful eyes of Sofia's maid. They began to walk the gravel path around the garden, and when Sofia was certain that no one was within earshot, she spoke in a low voice. 'I need your help.'

'By all means, Princess.'

'I know that you are supporting Gennadius's bid to replace Mammas as patriarch,' Sofia said. 'You must cut whatever ties you have with him. Gennadius is dangerous.'

'What do you mean, dangerous?'

Sofia stopped. 'What I tell you now, you must swear to tell no one,' she said. Notaras hesitated. 'I promise that it will not compromise your honour.'

'Very well then, I swear it.'

'Good. I believe that I have discovered the cause of the empress-mother's death.'

'The empress-mother? She was sick for months. She died of old age.'

'No, she was poisoned,' Sofia said and continued walking.

'Who told you that?' Notaras demanded as he caught up to her. He did not express surprise.

'No one told me.' Sophia took the golden communion cup from a small bag that she was carrying and handed it to him. 'This was Helena's communion cup. I believe that her confessor, Father Neophytus, used it to poison her.'

Notaras was wary. 'What makes you think that?'

'Smell it.'

'It smells of almonds.'

'Why would a cup that has held only wine smell of almonds?' she asked. 'I merely tasted the residue left in the bottom of the cup and became violently ill.'

'But why would Neophytus want Helena dead?'

'He would not, but Gennadius would. Neophytus is in contact with him, and Gennadius would do anything to stop the Union, even kill.'

'I see,' Notaras murmured as he examined the cup. 'What would you have me do?'

'Tomorrow, we will confront Neophytus together,' Sofia replied. 'You will do whatever is necessary – threaten, bribe or torture – to persuade him to turn on Gennadius. When he does so, we will go to Constantine. You will turn Gennadius over and tell Constantine that you no longer oppose the Union.' Notaras began to protest, but she cut him off. 'I do not ask you to accept the pope's decree, but at the very least work for compromise. You have given your oath to Constantine. If you truly believe in honour, then keep your oath. Rally the nobles behind your emperor.'

'And if I refuse?'

Sofia stopped and met Notaras's gaze. 'Your friendship with Gennadius is widely known. If you support the practices of those who fight the Union, then you will share in their punishments as well.'

'Is that a threat, Princess?'

'Yes, Megadux, it is.'

Notaras paused for some time, staring silently at the cup. 'I will do as you ask, Princess,' he said at last. 'And if what you say is true, then I will turn Gennadius over to Constantine and give my support to the Union. But know that I do so only because I believe it to be best for Constantinople. I do not take kindly to threats.'

'So long as you help me, your reasons are your own concern,' Sofia said. 'Until tomorrow, then. Good-day, Notaras.' She turned and walked away, leaving him holding the cup.

Sofia and Notaras left for the Haghia Sofia early the next morning, accompanied by Sofia's maid. Notaras did not wait for someone to greet them in the narthex. He headed straight into the great hall of the church, and Sofia followed, her maid trailing. They crossed the nave and emerged into a dining hall, where Notaras grabbed a young acolyte and ordered him to guide them to Neophytus's chamber.

When they arrived, Notaras tried the door but found it locked. He pounded on the door and called out in a loud voice, 'Father Neophytus? It is the megadux, Lucas Notaras!' There was no response. Notaras called again, then turned to the acolyte. 'Are you sure that Father Neophytus is in there?'

'Yes, My Lord,' the acolyte said. 'He has not left his cell since the visit of Father Gennadius, last night.'

Notaras reared back and kicked the door hard. The wood around the lock splintered, and the door swung open. The cell, dimly lit by one guttering lamp, appeared to be empty. 'Father Neophytus,' Notaras called out. 'Are you here?' Again, there was no response. Sofia stepped into the chamber and, peering into the dimness, she saw Neophytus.

'There,' she said and pointed to where Neophytus sat with his head on his desk, unmoving. He appeared to be sleeping.

'Father Neophytus,' Notaras called loudly, but the priest did not move. While Sofia tended to the lamp, Notaras went to the priest and shook him. Neophytus slumped and then fell from his chair, landing with his face towards Sofia. As the room brightened, she saw that his lips were black and his eyes were rolled back into his head. Sofia's maid gasped. Neophytus was clearly dead.

Notaras bent down to inspect him. 'The body is still warm.' He shook his head. 'Why would he kill himself?'

'Perhaps he didn't,' Sofia replied. 'Look, he is holding something in his hand.'

Notaras prised Neophytus's hand open and held up a small, empty vial. He held it to his nose. 'Almonds. I think you are right, Princess. Helena was poisoned. I have seen this vial before in Gennadius's study.'

'If Gennadius knew enough to dispose of Neophytus, then he will also know that I took Helena's cup,' Sofia speculated.

'Then you are in great danger, Princess,' Notaras warned. 'You have seen what Gennadius is capable of.'

'But without Neophytus, we cannot accuse Gennadius.'

'There are other ways,' Notaras said, touching his sword.

'No.' Sofia shook her head. 'I do not wish to make a martyr of him. That would only strengthen his cause.'

'Then I will have my men watch the church of Saint Pantocrator,' Notaras said. 'If Gennadius attempts some treachery, then I will know of it.'

'Thank you.'

'It is the least that I can do for my betrothed.'

Sofia frowned at the word. She looked Notaras in the eye. 'You know that I did not choose to become your wife, Notaras,' she began. 'And I have made no secret of the fact that I do not look forward to our marriage. Perhaps I was wrong to judge you so harshly.'

'I did not choose to be your husband either, Princess,' Notaras replied. 'The emperor offered you to me in marriage. It is an honour that I could not refuse, but it was never my desire to marry you against your will. Believe me, if I had my choice, I would not have chosen a woman with such a sharp tongue.' He smiled. 'Nevertheless, we will be married, whether we like it or not. I would like to have your consent, if not your love. I am willing to wait until I have it.'

'Help to make union a reality, and you will have earned my consent,' Sofia told him. 'Perhaps then, you can win my love as well.'

'I ask for nothing more,' Notaras said and bowed low. 'Until union is complete, then, no more talk of marriage. Agreed?'

'Agreed.'

Constantine stood at the window of his audience chamber and looked out on the evening sky while folding and unfolding the letter that he had received earlier in the day from Lucas Notaras. After weeks of worry and un-answered prayer, Notaras's letter had finally eased his mind. The megadux had written that he would support union, so long as it was achieved in accordance with certain compromises. With the backing of Notaras, Constantine could accept the Union without worrying about facing down a rebellion the next day. It was the miracle that he had been hoping for. He could keep his promise to Helena, and more importantly, keep the support of the Latins.

Constantine wondered what had made Notaras change his mind. Perhaps, Constantine reflected, his prayers had not gone unanswered after all.

He opened the letter again and looked to the second part of the message. It seemed that Notaras had also had a change of heart regarding Gennadius. He insisted that the monk was not a proper choice for the patriarchy. However, even though Notaras might have turned against Gennadius, Constantine would not dismiss him so readily. If he could win Gennadius's support for union by offering him the patriarchy, then it would be a small price to pay. With both Gennadius and Notaras in support, Constantine was sure that he would have little trouble with the remaining bishops and nobles.

The tolling of bells told Constantine that it was eight o'clock. Gennadius would be here soon. Constantine had summoned him to the palace that very night to offer him the patriarchy. He folded the letter one last time, slipped it into a pocket, and then took his place on the throne. 'Please, Lord God,' he prayed quietly. 'Grant me one last miracle today.'

Gennadius arrived at the palace in a festive mood. He was sure he knew what the summons meant: finally after years of waiting, he would be Patriarch of the Orthodox Church, with no one over him but God. He hurried to the audience chamber and found Constantine seated upon the throne. Gennadius approached and bowed low. 'Welcome, Gennadius,' Constantine said.

'I am honoured that you would call a humble monk such as myself into your august presence,' Gennadius replied.

'I have called you here to discuss the situation of our Church,' Constantine told him. 'As you know, Patriarch Mammas is in Rome. Our Church is without a head. This situation cannot last.' Constantine paused, as if searching for a way forward. 'The Union has been a source of bitter disagreement between us, Gennadius, but we are not enemies. I have brought you here to ask for your help.'

'I will do all that I can.'

'Good. The Synaxis looks to you as its leader,' Constantine said. 'If anybody can unite them behind my rule, it is you.' Gennadius bowed his head graciously, thinking it best not to reply. 'Would you be willing to lead the Church, Gennadius?'

'I am but a monk. But I feel it is my duty to undertake whatever task God calls me to in the service of our Church.'

'Good. Then I offer you the patriarchy, provided that you use your influence to persuade the bishops to support union with Rome.'

The words 'if the Lord wills it, then let it be so' froze on Gennadius lips as he realized what Constantine was saying. If he accepted Constantine's terms, then he would be nothing more than a puppet of the emperor and a stooge of the pope, like Mammas. 'But My Lord, the bishops will never support union,' Gennadius replied. 'Nor will the nobility.'

'You are wrong, Gennadius. Megadux Notaras has decided to support union. Even he realizes that it is our only hope.'

Gennadius shook his head. So, Notaras had betrayed him. No doubt this was the doing of the meddling Princess Sofia. He would have to deal with her. 'Notaras is a soldier, not a man of God,' Gennadius said at last. 'The Synaxis will not be so easily swayed. There can be no compromise when souls are at stake.'

'They might accept union if you were the one to declare it,' Constantine insisted. 'I know that union means acknowledging the primacy of the pope, but it is better than being forced to bow before the sultan.'

'Is it?' Gennadius replied. 'I am not so sure.'

Constantine's face hardened. 'You dare speak treason to my face, monk?'

'Of course not, Emperor,' Gennadius said and bowed low. 'God willing, I shall bow before neither the pope nor the sultan. But I must always bow before the will of God. I have already renounced a bishopric to better serve Him as a monk. It is His will that I serve Him humbly. I must refuse the patriarchy.' The words were bitter, but he would rather be a monk than a hollow patriarch without power.

'Very well,' Constantine said and sighed. 'I understand your opposition to union, but I meant what I said. We are not enemies, Gennadius. Remember that. You may leave.'

Gennadius bowed and departed. Constantine was a fool. Gennadius would bring him down and union with him, but he could not do it alone. As he rode back to Saint Pantocrator, Gennadius began composing a letter in his head, a letter to the grand vizier of the Ottoman court, Halil Pasha.

Chapter 11

Mehmed rode through the gate into Edirne, his back straight and his head held high. A crowd had turned out to watch him and his household enter the city, but the atmosphere was far from festive. Murad, Sultan of the Ottoman Empire, was dying, and his poor health was no secret. The faces of the people were grim and unsmiling. There were no cheers for Mehmed.

The people's dark mood mirrored Mehmed's own grim thoughts. Only two weeks ago, Sitt Hatun had given him a son, Selim, and Mehmed knew that any child of his could be a rival in the hands of a cunning mother. But that was not the true reason that he disliked Selim. The child raised painful memories of his other son, Bayezid, and of Gülbehar. Even though the *kumru kalp* lay against Mehmed's heart, a reminder of Gülbehar's infidelity, Mehmed still longed for her. The thought of her in his father's arms was a nagging pain that not even Murad's impending death could remove.

Mehmed reached the Eski Serai palace and dismounted in the courtyard. Halil waited on the palace steps along with a crowd of important ministers, eunuchs and viziers.

The entire group bowed low as Mehmed approached. 'Greetings, Your Highness. Allah be praised for your safe journey,' Halil said. Mehmed motioned for him and the other men to rise, and Halil straightened and stepped closer. 'I have a great deal of news for you, but first, the sultan is eager to see you.'

'I will wait on my father shortly,' Mehmed said. 'I have other business to attend to first.' Mehmed turned to Sitt Hatun, who was just emerging from her covered litter. 'Wife, you will come with me. Bring your child.'

Mehmed led them to Gülbehar's apartments in the harem and pushed the doors open without knocking. A *jariye* servant girl was standing in the entrance room, watering plants. She dropped her watering tin at the sight of Mehmed glowering at the threshold. 'Where is she?' Mehmed roared. The *jariye* bowed low and backed away.

'I . . . I will bring her to you, My Lord,' she stuttered and disappeared into the servant's passage. A moment later, Gülbehar appeared with her son Bayezid, who was now two and a half years old. Her eyes narrowed when she saw Sitt Hatun holding the infant Selim, and then she bowed gracefully before Mehmed. Bayezid also bowed. Mehmed could not help but notice that the boy had Murad's golden eyes. His jaw tightened as he felt a fresh surge of anger well up in him.

'And whose child is this?' he demanded. 'Is he my son, or my brother?'

Gülbehar flushed crimson. 'I do not understand, My Lord. He is your son. Bayezid, go to your father.'

The boy took a step forward and then froze, frightened by Mehmed's menacing scowl. 'My son? *My* son!' Mehmed said, his voice rising. He stepped forward and slapped Gülbehar hard. 'Are you sure it is not my father's bastard?' Bayezid was crying now, and Gülbehar pulled him to her, holding him tightly as if for protection. 'Answer me, woman!' Mehmed demanded.

Gülbehar lowered her head. 'I had no choice,' she whispered. 'He is the sultan.'

'*I* am your sultan!' Mehmed roared. He raised his hand to slap her again, but then restrained himself. When he spoke again, his voice was quiet but hard. 'You will leave here and go to your apartments. You are not to leave them. I will post a guard outside, since it is clear that you cannot be trusted.'

'But My Lord, these are my apartments,' Gülbehar protested.

'They were. They are Sitt Hatun's now. You will take her old quarters.'

'But what of my court? Those apartments are too small for them.'

'You have no court,' Mehmed replied. 'You will have your maidservants and a few *jariye* to look after your household. That is more than you deserve.' He turned to go, but Gülbehar stopped him, pleading one last time.

'What of your son, Bayezid?' she asked, tears in her eyes. 'Surely he deserves better.'

'As you see, I have another son now.' Mehmed turned and left, leaving Sitt Hatun alone with Gülbehar. Her gloating would be a more insufferable punishment for Gülbehar than any he could devise.

Mehmed was still angry when he reached his father's chambers, but more at himself now than at Gülbehar. He should not have lost control of himself; it was unbecoming of a prince. It was even worse in a sultan. He would have to rule his emotions more closely now that the throne was practically his. While the Master of the Sultan's Chambers announced Mehmed's presence to his father, Mehmed took the time to compose himself.

Murad did not move when Mehmed entered. The sultan had aged greatly in the almost two years since Mehmed had last seen him. His thin, wasted body looked tiny amidst the pillows that propped him up. Despite the wintry weather and the noticeable chill in the palace, his robes were soaked with a fevered sweat, and two slave girls fanned him vigorously. His hair, flecked with grey before, was now almost totally white. The biggest change, however, was in the sultan's face. Murad's strong, tanned face had become thin and wasted, with dark hollows under his eyes. The scar on his cheek stood out bright red against the sickly pallor of his skin. His father was a pitiable sight, but Mehmed was in no mood for pity. He knew that Murad deserved his fate, and he felt no remorse, only an emptiness.

Mehmed knelt beside his father. 'Leave us,' he ordered the slave girls. 'I wish to speak with my father alone.' He thought that his father might be asleep, or even already dead, but then Murad's eyes opened, the same bright, intelligent eyes that Mehmed remembered. They, at least, had not changed.

'So, you have come to see me die,' Murad croaked, his voice so weak that Mehmed had to lean close to hear him.

'I have come to speak with you, Father.'

'You had best talk quickly then.' Murad managed a short, wheezing laugh. 'I am not long for this world. The throne will be yours again soon, Mehmed. I pray that you use it better this time.'

'I am no longer a child, Father,' Mehmed snapped. 'I will rule wisely, and I will succeed where you have failed. I will make Constantinople the capital of our empire.'

Murad shook his head. 'You are still young, my son. Do not seek to be great so soon. Constantinople has stood for more than a thousand years. Let it wait a few more. You must learn to rule in peace before you can rule in war.'

'I have learned enough, Father. The Greeks are weak. They have no allies. When I strike, they will fall.'

'You have always been too eager. Why will you not do as I say, boy?' Murad said in a louder voice, his eyes flashing. For a second, Mehmed thought that his father might reach out and slap him. But instead Murad collapsed back against his cushions, consumed by a fit of coughing. 'Ah well, you are not the sultan yet,' Murad said when he had recovered. 'Perhaps I will disappoint you and cheat death.'

'No, you will not recover, Father.'

'And why is that?'

Mehmed pulled the *kumru kalp* out from under his caftan, and Murad's eyes locked upon the jewel. Mehmed leaned closer to his father. 'I know what you have done,' Mehmed whispered. 'And I have taken my revenge. You have been poisoned. The drug acts slowly, but it is fatal.'

Murad's eyes opened wide, and Mehmed was pleased to think that he had been able to surprise his father, at least this once. 'It is you,' Murad said, his voice barely above a whisper. 'I have been killed by my own son.'

'No, Father. You poisoned yourself the day you took

Gülbehar to bed.' Murad's eyes were even wider now, practically bulging out of his head, but he did not speak. 'Did you think that you could lie with Gülbehar without my knowledge?' Mehmed demanded. 'With my own favourite?'

Still, Murad did not reply, and Mehmed realized that it was not surprise, but an attack of apoplexy that had distorted his father's features. Murad's jaws were clenched now and his lips trembling. Spittle had collected at the corners of his mouth, and the veins at his temples were bulging. His body began to convulse, and his eyes rolled back in his head.

Mehmed drew back from his father's contorted body and waited until Murad had ceased his shaking and lay still. Then, Mehmed rose and called loudly: 'A doctor! Bring the sultan's doctor, quickly!' The doctor put his head to Murad's chest and then looked to Mehmed. When he spoke, he only confirmed what Mehmed knew to be true.

'He is dead,' he told Mehmed. 'You are the sultan now, My Lord.'

Two weeks later, Mehmed was girded for the second time in his life with the great sword in the mosque of Eyub and proclaimed Mehmed Khan II, Seventh Sovereign of the House of Osman, Khan of Khans, Grand Sultan of Anatolia and Rumelia, Emperor of the Two Cities of Adrianople and Brusa, Lord of the Two Lands and the Two Seas. Afterwards, he rode to the palace for his first official audience as sultan. Before making his entrance, he paused and watched his subjects through a curtain. Emirs, beys and pashas from every corner of the empire stood in the grand hall of the palace, waiting to pay homage to him and to take his measure. To Mehmed's right, Murad's ministers stood wringing their hands; to his left, Murad and Mehmed's wives stood veiled and quiet. A dozen janissaries surrounded the imperial divan, separating it from the mass of people. Mehmed took one last look and then stepped through the curtain and into the hall. At once, the assembled men and women fell silent. The only noise was the whisper of silk as the crowd filling the hall bowed low before their new sultan.

Mehmed's heart beat violently, but he kept his head held high and his pace measured as he walked to the imperial divan, knowing that hundreds of pairs of eyes were watching his every step. He wore a white turban and robes of rose-red silk decorated with intricate patterns in gold. His black beard had been cut short, and he looked in every respect the sultan as he reclined upon the divan, propping himself up on his left elbow. Mehmed knew that many in the audience had not seen him since the last time he took the throne, seven years ago as a beardless child of twelve. He would show them all that he was no longer a child. He would show them that he knew how to rule as a sultan must.

He motioned for the crowd to rise and then turned first to his father's ministers. 'You may take your usual places,' he told them, motioning for them to be seated. Their collective sigh of relief was almost audible as they sat on a row of cushions, each cushion indicating their respective place as minister within the sultan's *divan*. They need not have worried. They had served his father well, and Mehmed had need of their experience. He would allow them to prove their loyalty. And, if any proved unfaithful, then Mehmed's spies would inform him, and the traitors would be beheaded. Mehmed doubted that more than one minister would conspire against him. A beheading was a most instructive example.

Next, Mehmed named the viziers of the empire, calling them before the throne one by one. As they were called, each man stepped forward in turn and bowed low. 'Halil Pasha, Grand Vizier of the Ottoman Empire,' Mehmed began, confirming Halil in his place. Mehmed still resented Halil's role in calling Murad back to the throne years ago, but there was no doubting the grand vizier's usefulness. To moderate Halil's influence, Mehmed named two of his rivals, Saruja Pasha and Zaganos Pasha, as assistant viziers. Finally, he confirmed as Chief Eunuch and Assistant Vizier Shehab ed-Din, his one remaining confidant from his earlier brief rule.

Mehmed turned now to the women of the harem and beckoned them to step forward. Sitt Hatun came first, offering her condolences for his father's death and congratulating him on his ascendance to the throne. Gülbehar followed, and Mehmed had to concentrate to keep the impassive face of a sultan when greeting her. After his own wives, came the widows of Murad: first his newest wife, the childless Christian Mara of Serbia, whom Mehmed ordered sent back to her father; and then Hadije, Murad's favourite and the mother of his youngest son. She was young, younger even than Mehmed, and she cried as she spoke, her voice trembling and broken. Mehmed wondered if the tears were for her deceased husband, or if she already knew the fate of her son. For even as he accepted Hadije's condolences and compliments, Mehmed's servants were in the harem, drowning her young son Ahmet in his bath. Mehmed bore the boy no hatred, but he was a possible rival for the throne, and as such, had to die.

Finally, Mehmed turned to the mass of nobles in the hall. 'Emirs, beys, pashas – lords of the empire, you have my thanks for your presence here today,' he began. 'You served my father well, and I too will have need of your service soon enough. For I swear to you now on the holy Koran that as your sultan, I will not rest until the city of Constantinople falls before me. There will be riches and glory for all who fight beside me. Together, we will grind to dust those who have defied us for far too long. Together, we shall conquer for ourselves a new capital for a new, golden age!'

Murmurs of approval ran through the crowd. A few voices, then dozens, and finally all the hundreds present joined together to shout again and again: 'Hail Mehmed, Sultan of the Ottoman Empire!'

Sitt Hatun sat in the harem garden, enjoying the sunshine on an unseasonably warm late winter day. Anna was with her and between them lay Sitt Hatun's one-month-old son, Selim. Sitt Hatun cooed at the child, who giggled back. She could still hardly believe that less than a year earlier she had left Edirne as an outcast, fleeing for her life. Now she was an *ikbal* – mother to a male heir. No matter that Sitt Hatun did not know if Selim's father was Mehmed or Halil. Selim was hers, and one day he would be sultan.

Loud shouting echoed down from Gülbehar's apartments above the garden, and Sitt Hatun smiled. Gülbehar was not dealing with her fall from favour well, and her distress was another source of contentment for Sitt Hatun. Just now, Gülbehar was screaming furiously, and Sitt Hatun could make out a few words here and there: 'Incompetence! Spoiled brat!' and then a climactic, 'Get out, all of you!' There was a series of slamming doors, and then silence.

A moment later, one of Gülbehar's *odalisques* appeared in the garden, carrying a bawling Bayezid. The *odalisque* looked Russian: a pale girl, no older than fourteen, with dark auburn hair. She went to a row of evergreen bushes not far from Sitt Hatun and sat behind them. After a moment, Bayezid's crying stopped and was replaced by the muffled sobbing of the Russian girl. Sitt Hatun felt for the girl, and for Bayezid, who bore the brunt of Gülbehar's disappointment. Perhaps by befriending them, Sitt Hatun reflected, she could help both them and herself. It would be useful to have allies in Gülbehar's household.

Sitt Hatun motioned for her servants to remain where they were, then rose and went to the *odalisque*, who looked away as she wiped at her tears. Bayezid was nearby, huddled in a small space between two bushes. Sitt Hatun sat down on the grass near the nurse. Bayezid peeked out furtively. He was a precious child, with the fair skin and light hair of his mother and the distinctive nose of his father. His left cheek was bruised bluish-black.

'Hello, young prince,' Sitt Hatun said.

'Hello,' the boy replied.

'You are not to speak to him,' the boy's nurse warned Sitt Hatun. She glanced towards Gülbehar's apartments. 'I should not be seen with you. Please go!'

Sitt Hatun remained seated. 'Gülbehar does not treat you well, does she?' Sitt Hatun asked. She reached out and gently touched the nurse's arm. 'You or the boy?'

The nurse turned away, fresh tears in her eyes. 'I am her servant. I cannot speak ill of her. I should not speak to you at all. My Lady says you are dangerous.'

'Do I look dangerous?' Sitt Hatun asked softly. The young nurse shook her head. 'I am a mother, too,' Sitt Hatun told her. 'It pains me to see young Bayezid suffer.'

'My Lady says that if Selim becomes sultan, you will send men to kill Bayezid.'

'That is nonsense,' Sitt Hatun assured the girl. Bayezid would indeed probably be killed when Selim took the throne, but Sitt Hatun would have little to do with it. 'I swear to you that I will never harm the child. Not everyone in the harem is as heartless as Gülbehar.'

'She is a monster,' the girl spat with surprising vehemence. 'She hits Bayezid and treats her servants even worse. I can live with the beatings, but Bayezid is only a child.' A door slammed in Gülbehar's apartments, and the Russian girl froze. 'You must go,' she whispered. 'I must not be seen with you.'

'I understand,' Sitt Hatun told her. 'But first, tell me: what is your name, girl?'

'Kacha, My Lady.'

'I know how hard it must be for you, Kacha. If you ever have need of a friend, then my quarters are always open to you. Bayezid will be welcome, too. The boy should have a place where he feels safe from his mother.'

'But how, My Lady?' Kacha asked. 'Gülbehar would never allow it.'

'She need never know. There is a secret passage that connects your apartments to mine. Tell me, which room is Bayezid's?' Kacha pointed to a window above them.

'That is perfect,' Sitt Hatun said. 'Here is what you must do. Go to the wall of his room away from the window. The wall is decorated with animals carved from wood. Find the lion and press its head. A door will open.' Kacha nodded. 'Be sure to close the door behind you, so that you are not followed. The passage will be dark. Follow it until you come to a flight of stairs. They will take you down to the harem kitchen. Cross the kitchen and take the central passage on the far wall. It leads directly to my bedroom. Knock like this when you reach the end.' Sitt Hatun mimed two knocks, a pause, and then three knocks.

'I understand,' Kacha said. 'Thank you, My Lady.'

'It is nothing. You may be a slave here, but that does not mean that you should not be treated with kindness.' Sitt Hatun squeezed Kacha's shoulder, then rose and returned to Selim and Anna. A moment later, Gülbehar stormed into the garden.

'Kacha! What are you doing here?' she demanded. 'Bring Bayezid here at once!' Gülbehar gave Sitt Hatun a venomous look and then turned and strode away, followed by Kacha with Bayezid. Sitt Hatun gathered up Selim and also left.

She entered her apartments to find Halil's secretary, Davarnza, waiting for her. He produced a folded piece of paper and handed it to Sitt Hatun. It was a note from Halil. He was coming to the harem to meet with her, tonight.

Sitt Hatun sat on her bed, watching the full moon reflect off the Maritza river as it flowed past the palace. She had sent her servants to their quarters hours earlier, keeping only Anna by her side. They sat waiting for Halil, and

Sitt Hatun thought back to that other night when they had sat together in the dark, waiting for Isa to come and rescue them. She thought of Cicek's death and of her night with Halil. She shuddered as she remembered the cold touch of his hand.

There was a quiet knocking on the hidden door that led to the servants' walkway and down into the harem kitchen. Two knocks, and that was all. Anna rose and opened the door. Halil stepped through into the chamber. He was wrapped in women's clothing and his face was veiled, but Sitt Hatun recognized him immediately from his pale-grey eyes.

'Good evening, Sitt Hatun,' Halil said in his smooth, oily voice as he removed the veil. 'Thank you for agreeing to meet me. We have much to talk about.' He nodded towards Anna. 'I would prefer to speak in private.'

'I have no secrets from her,' Sitt Hatun said. 'Say what you have come to say, Halil, and be gone.'

'Straight to business: a trait I remember all too well from our last encounter,' Halil said. 'Very well then. I wish to discuss our son's future. You know that Mehmed is preparing to besiege Constantinople. Warfare is a dangerous business, and if the sultan were to die, then the succession would be disputed between Bayezid and our Selim. I am sure you realize that if Bayezid were to become sultan, then our precious child would be murdered.'

'But Gülbehar is out of favour, and you are the grand vizier,' Sitt Hatun said. 'Surely it would be Selim who takes the throne.'

'Yes, but I cannot be sure. We would be more secure if there were no disputed succession, if Bayezid were removed beforehand.'

'You mean murdered,' Sitt Hatun accused. 'He is only a boy.'

'But he is a dangerous boy. And after all, when Selim becomes sultan, Bayezid will be killed anyway as a matter of course. Why not act now? It would be an easy enough matter for you or your servants. I could provide you with certain poisons that would make it painless.'

Sitt Hatun thought of young Bayezid, his trusting golden eyes, and shook her head. 'No, I will not have any part in the child's death, and I want no more of your plotting, Halil.' She would deal with Bayezid in her own way. 'We had an agreement, and that agreement is over,' Sitt Hatun continued. 'I have done my part. I will have nothing more to do with this intrigue, or with you.' She turned her back to him. 'You may go now.'

'But think, Sitt Hatun,' Halil said, moving forward and placing his hand on her shoulder. He had no sooner touched her, however, than Anna stepped behind him and pulled his arm away while with her other hand she brought a knife to Halil's throat.

'My Lady asked you to leave,' Anna said. 'I suggest that you do so.'

'You would not dare,' Halil hissed. His free hand went to a dagger at his belt, but Anna pressed her knife more closely to his throat. Halil released the dagger. 'Unhand me,' he ordered.

'I would only be obeying the law,' Anna replied. 'You must know that the punishment is death for any man not of the royal family found in the harem. Unless, of course, that man is a eunuch.' She moved her knife down to Halil's groin. 'If you wish to stay, I can do you that service.'

'No, no, I will leave,' Halil said. Anna withdrew her

knife and stepped away. Halil bowed stiffly to the sultana and moved to the secret door, where he paused and turned. 'Think well on what I have said, Sitt Hatun. You will see that it is for the best.' With that, he left.

Not two minutes later, there was another faint knocking – two knocks, a pause, and three more. Anna opened the secret door and Kacha stepped out, holding Bayezid. 'I am sorry to come so late, My Lady,' Kacha said. 'But I had to get away. Just look at what Gülbehar has done to her own child.' The boy had a fresh mark on his forearm – the angry red imprint of a hand – and he was sobbing quietly. 'I hate her!' Kacha said.

Sitt Hatun took Bayezid and held the boy close. 'There, there. All will be well,' she soothed and then turned to Kacha. 'Did you see anybody on your way here? Were you seen?'

'There was an old woman in the kitchen, but she did not see us.'

'Good,' Sitt Hatun said. 'I am glad you came, Kacha. You and Bayezid will always have friends here.' Sitt Hatun stroked Bayezid's head and thought of Halil's words: for Selim to become sultan, this boy must die.

Several nights later, Halil, his face hidden in the folds of a hooded cloak, emerged from a small side door of the palace and slipped into a curtained litter. Four burly slaves lifted the litter and set off into the heart of the dark city. It was less than a month since Mehmed had taken the throne, and Halil was already chafing under the new sultan's reign. Mehmed was as headstrong as ever and as hard to control as Halil had feared. Halil had spent years helping Murad to craft a peace with the Christians, and already Mehmed was eager to wreck it. He ignored Halil's advice and insisted on giving him the most thankless of tasks. It was almost as degrading as the time many years ago when Murad had given him the loathsome job of rounding up Christian children for the *devshirme*, to provide soldiers for the janissaries. Only then Halil had been a mere *kaziasker*, a military judge in the new province of Salonika, and not the grand vizier.

Halil's litter was set down in an alley behind Ishak Pasha's grand Edirne residence. Halil had been surprised at how readily Ishak had agreed to this late night meeting, but then, Ishak had his reasons. After the battle of Kossova, Murad had appointed him second vizier of the empire. Now Mehmed had passed over Ishak without mention, not reconfirming his post as vizier or as head of the Anatolian cavalry. There were few more loyal to the empire than Ishak, but if his loyalty were to ever waver, now was surely the time.

One of Ishak's servants was waiting beside a small door, and Halil left the litter and followed him into the house. The servant led him up a flight of stairs and into a small room, bare but for a thick carpet, a few cushions and a low table on which was set a tea kettle and two small ceramic cups. Ishak stood there waiting, his hands clasped behind his back. He looked the same as ever – steel-grey hair and a handsome, weathered face. The servant left, closing the thick door behind him, and Ishak stepped forward and embraced Halil. 'Welcome, old friend.'

'Thank you for meeting me,' Halil said as they both sat down on the cushions.

'You said that it was important, and to speak truly, I

am eager for any information that you can give me,' Ishak said. He poured two cups of steaming tea and handed one to Halil. 'What news do you bring from the palace? Has the sultan spoken of me?'

Halil shook his head, and Ishak's shoulders slumped. Clearly, Ishak had been hoping that Halil brought news of an appointment. 'I bring only bad news from the palace, I am afraid,' Halil said. He gestured to the room. 'May I speak freely here?'

'The walls of this room are thick. No one will overhear us.'

Halil nodded, but he lowered his voice nevertheless. 'It is of the sultan that I must speak. I fear that he may not be fit to rule. He speaks only of plots against him. He fears your power and plans to strip you of your rank and exile you to the provinces, where you will be of no threat to him. He is treating all of the able men in the empire likewise. I fear that my turn will come soon enough.'

'This is bad news indeed,' Ishak mused as he sipped at his tea. 'I had hoped that age would make Mehmed wiser.'

'Alas, he has not changed. He surrounds himself with fools and sycophants, just as he did during his first reign. He ignores me and openly scorns his father's ministers, preferring to listen to any who will flatter his vanity. I fear he will lead our great empire to ruin.'

'Do not be melodramatic, Halil. Mehmed is young still. In time he will gain wisdom.'

'In time? When? After we are long dead?' Halil set his tea down untasted and met Ishak's eyes. 'I am not willing to wait that long, Ishak. Are you?'

'What are you suggesting, Halil?'

'Perhaps we would do better to serve a different sultan,' Halil said. Ishak's eyes narrowed, but he said nothing, so Halil continued. 'Mehmed's child Selim is still only a babe. Until he is grown, the empire would be in the hands of those wise enough to rule it properly.'

'Rebellion then,' Ishak said, a trace of disgust in his voice. 'This is your counsel? And what of Mehmed?'

'Mehmed is young and weak. The army bears no love for him, but they will follow you. Raise the army and take the palace. I will see to it that you meet little resistance. Within a month from now Selim could be on the throne with you and I as his viziers, ruling the empire as it should be ruled.'

Ishak did not reply. He finished his tea and then rose and began to pace the room. Finally he stopped, rubbing his hands as if to wash them. 'Why have you come here?' he asked. 'We are old friends, Halil. You know that I would never betray the sultan.'

'But Mehmed is no sultan!' Halil insisted, also rising. 'You remember his first reign: consorting with that half-mad Persian heretic and ignoring the army while the Christians marched on our lands. He is no different today. Now he dreams of conquering Constantinople, this after he almost lost the battle of Kossova despite having more than twice as many men as the Christians. You were there, Ishak. You saw. Are you willing to give your life to satisfy his foolish vanity?'

'He may be a fool, but he is a brave fool,' Ishak replied. 'He led the final charge at Kossova himself and against great odds. But I would follow him were he a fool and a coward, for the choice is not mine. Allah has chosen

Mehmed to be the sultan, and that is an end to the matter.'

'Even if that means that you are passed over and ignored, exiled and left to rot while men like Saruja Pasha take the place that is rightfully yours?'

'I will never raise my hand against the sultan, Halil,' Ishak said with finality. 'Never.'

Halil nodded. He had suspected as much. Still, he had one card left to play. 'This is not merely a question of your loyalty to the sultan. This is not a game that I am playing, Ishak. I know that you despise such plotting, but you cannot hold yourself aloof from this. You must choose a side. Either you are with me, or you are against me.'

Ishak turned his back on Halil. 'Then I am against you, old friend,' he said with a sigh. 'You may leave now. My servant will show you out. Allah go with you.'

'And with you,' Halil said as he left. He had expected no less. Ishak Pasha had always been a man of unshakeable integrity, a soldier with little stomach for the ugly side of politics. No, Halil was not surprised, nor was he upset. His midnight errand had ended exactly as he had hoped it would.

Mehmed had hardly awakened when the chief eunuch appeared and told him that Ishak Pasha requested a private audience with him. The old soldier had arrived at sunrise and had been waiting ever since; he was adamant that he would not leave until he had seen the sultan. Mehmed hurried to dress. This promised to be a most interesting meeting.

As always, Mehmed paused at a spyhole before entering his audience chamber, and took a few seconds to examine

Ishak. He stood stiff and stern, his beard neatly trimmed and his clothes the simple garb of a soldier. Even standing alone, Ishak emanated authority. He was a man that Mehmed would not want against him. After a final look, Mehmed entered the chamber and seated himself on the throne, acknowledging Ishak's bow with a wave of his hand.

'I am pleased to see you, Ishak Pasha,' Mehmed began. 'Now, what is so important that you come before me at this early hour?'

'I have learned of a plot to kill you and place your youngest son on the throne, My Lord. Last night, I was approached and asked to join the conspiracy. Of course, I felt it was my duty to inform you at once of this treason.'

'Treason?' Mehmed frowned. 'This is most serious then. Who has committed this treason?'

Ishak hesitated, and Mehmed could tell that the next words were hard for him. 'I regret to inform you that the traitor is the grand vizier, Halil Pasha.'

Mehmed nodded in satisfaction. 'I am most pleased by your loyalty, Ishak Pasha,' he said. 'It is no easy task to accuse one's friend, even though it be to protect the sultan. I see that my father was right to value you so highly. You are a man who can be trusted, and your loyalty will be rewarded.'

'Thank you, My Lord,' Ishak said and bowed.

'As for Halil, do not fear,' Mehmed continued. 'I already know everything that he said to you last night.'

'You do, My Lord? But how?'

'Because I am the one who sent him.'

'I do not understand, My Lord.'

'I will be moving against Constantinople soon, Ishak

Pasha, and I need commanders who I can trust,' Mehmed explained. 'I needed to be sure of your loyalty before granting you your post. You are to be the Governor of Anatolia, and you shall remain the commander of the Anatolian Cavalry.'

'I am most grateful, My Lord,' Ishak said.

'And I am most grateful for your loyalty, Ishak Pasha. As for the conspiracy that Halil told you of, never fear: it does not exist.'

That night, Halil sat alone, reading by candlelight in his private study – a secure, thick-walled room for which only he had the key. He held in his hands a coded letter from the Greek monk Gennadius. The letter represented the opportunity that Halil had been waiting for. The relationship that he had been cultivating with the rebellious monk had now paid off twofold. Originally, Halil had sent his poisons to Gennadius merely to facilitate the death of the Greek Empress-Mother Helena, and he had expected nothing more. But now Gennadius was offering up Constantinople to him on a platter, going so far as to guarantee the fall of the city so long as Halil assured Gennadius that he would be made patriarch and there would be no union between the Orthodox and Catholic churches.

The offer was too good to pass up. With Gennadius's assistance, perhaps conquering Constantinople would be possible after all. Yes, Halil decided, he would agree to Gennadius's proposal, but on one condition: the monk must see to it that Mehmed died during the siege. The task would not be too difficult for a man of Gennadius's cunning. Mehmed's spies, careful as they were, would not be able to watch over the monk. And Halil would provide Gennadius with enough information to ensure his success. Once Mehmed was dead and Constantinople had fallen, it would be Halil, as grand vizier and regent, who would rule the greatest empire in all the world. He would then gladly turn over the patriarchy to Gennadius.

His decision made, Halil burned Gennadius's letter, stamping the ashes out on the stone floor, and then took up a quill to write his coded response. He would have Isa deliver the letter to Gennadius, along with enough gold to facilitate Mehmed's death. Halil grinned wickedly to himself. How amusing, he mused, that Mehmed's dream to conquer Constantinople would actually succeed, and the success would cost the sultan his life.

Chapter 12

*L*ongo stood at the pier as the ship that bore Sofia glided to a stop before him. He did not know why she had returned to Genoa, nor did he care. She was here now, beautiful in a simple white cotton robe as she stepped off the ship. He hurried to greet her, and to his surprise, she threw her arms around him.

'I am so glad you have returned,' he told her. 'But why are you here? Are you not needed in Constantinople?'

'I came for you,' Sofia told him.

'You are too late,' Longo said, pulling away. 'I am married.'

'No, it is never too late.' Sofia kissed him and her mouth opened to his. 'Come with me.' She led him to his palazzo and then to his chambers, stopping before his bed and turning to face him. 'I've been thinking of you, of our kiss,' she told him.

'As have I. It is foolish, I know.'

'No, it is not.' She untied her robes and they slipped to the floor, leaving her naked. Longo's eyes moved down from the curve of her delicate collarbone, to her small but firm breasts, to the nest of auburn hair that began below her flat stomach.

He shook his head. 'But I am married. We cannot.'

'We can,' Sofia said. She stepped towards him, and Longo pulled her into his arms, kissing her hard. But something was wrong. A *thin layer of smoke had filled the room. Through the window beyond Sofia, he could see that the city was aflame, overrun by the Turks. The room was filling with smoke and fire, and suddenly the scarfaced Turk who had killed his parents was there. He pointed at Sofia and ordered his men to gut her. Longo drew her to him, ready to defend her with his life, but Sofia dissolved into flames, her mouth open in a silent scream as she vanished from his arms. The flames spread over him and the air filled with choking smoke . . .*

Longo awoke to the sweet, acrid scent of burning grapevines. He rubbed his face and looked about him. He was in his villa, and the woman lying next to him was not Sofia but Julia, his wife of nearly two years. He had been dreaming, another nightmare. Longo rose and went to the window that looked out over his vineyards. The sun had risen, and his men were already busy, pruning the leafless vines. The cuttings were being burned in small piles. Behind him, Julia stirred in bed.

'Come back to bed,' she pleaded. 'I'm cold.'

'There is work to be done,' he replied.

'Let Tristo and William deal with it. That is what servants are for,' Julia whined. 'Don't leave.' She sat up in bed, her swollen, pregnant belly extending before her. 'Come. Feel this,' she said, placing her hand on her stomach. 'He's kicking.'

Longo sat on the edge of the bed and placed his hand gently on his wife's stomach. His eyes widened as he felt a slight movement. He took Julia's hand. 'I must go,' he told her. 'Your brother Paolo has invited me to a reading this evening, and I have much to do first. After the pruning, I have a new horse to break.' In truth, Longo was happy for an excuse to be away from his young wife. She was spoiled, moody and demanding, and had become more so since the start of her pregnancy.

'A reading?' Julia asked, brightening. 'I want to come.'

'You know you cannot travel,' Longo said. Julia pouted. 'And anyway, you could not come. The piece is by a young Neapolitan named Guardarti, and apparently it is not appropriate for ladies.' Longo was not particularly interested either. However, Paolo had remained aloof, even hostile, since Longo's marriage to Julia, and Longo was eager to repair their relationship.

'But I want to come,' Julia insisted, frowning in a manner that portended a tantrum. 'I am so *bored* here in the country.'

'You will give birth soon enough. You can visit your family in town then.' Julia's frown deepened. She turned her back to him and pulled the covers over herself without speaking. Longo breathed a guilty sigh of relief. He knew that some servant would bear the brunt of her frustration later that day. 'I will return late tonight,' he told her and left.

Longo was in a foul mood when he reached the Grimaldi *palazzo* that evening. Just before he had left his estate, a fire had begun in his vineyards, spreading from one of the piles of cuttings to the rows of vines. Longo had left William and Tristo to handle it while he rode into Genoa accompanied by six of his men. He would have liked to stay and deal with the fire himself, but he did not wish to spurn Paolo's invitation.

He was soon glad that he had come. Paolo greeted him warmly, embracing him and calling him brother, and throughout the evening he treated Longo with unusual courtesy. Longo also found the proceedings more interesting than he had anticipated. A Spanish noble, one Carlos de Sevilla, was present. He was an elegant man, short and spare with close-cropped black hair and darkly tanned skin, and after the reading he discussed the recent Portuguese discoveries in Africa and the possibility of reaching the Indies by sailing west. As the guests began to depart, Paolo took Longo aside to speak with him.

'I wish to be frank,' he told Longo. 'I regret if I have been less than welcoming since you joined my family. There are those in my father's household who blame you for my brother's death. I fear that I listened too closely to their complaints, and I wish to apologize. There should be no grudge between us.'

'I am glad to hear you speak so,' Longo said. 'And there is no need to apologize. Your goodwill is all I ask.'

'Excellent,' Paolo said, smiling broadly. 'Now come. It is nearly midnight, high time that you return to my sister.'

Longo entered the Grimaldi stables to find his men hopelessly drunk. Judging by the number of empty wine bottles lying about, it looked as if Paolo's men had treated them to free wine, and they had drunk more than their fill. Two were slumped unconscious over a table, a forgotten game of cards between them. Three more lay on the floor, snoring loudly. Only one was awake, lying in a pool of his own vomit. He tried to rise, swayed unsteadily and then collapsed. Longo vowed to have words with his men, when they were sober enough to understand him. Paolo offered to let Longo's men sleep off their debauchery at the Grimaldi *palazzo*, and Longo accepted. He would ride to his *palazzo*, he decided, instead of his country estate.

Longo kept one hand on his sword as he rode through the narrow, dark streets of Genoa. It was not uncommon to come across thieves or bands of cutthroats late at night. He passed through a shadowy square dominated by a large oak, its leaves silvery in the moonlight, and entered a particularly narrow alleyway that wound its way towards his *palazzo*. Halfway down the alley his path was blocked by a hunched beggar, noisily rattling his tin cup. 'Help a man to eat?' the beggar asked.

Longo had slowed his horse and reached for his purse when he noticed a glint of steel from under the beggar's cloak. He was carrying a sword. Longo drew his sword and backed his horse away from the beggar, but it was too late to retreat. Six men, swords in hand and wearing black masks, had stepped into the alley behind him. Ahead, the beggar had been joined by four more masked men.

'Help! Assassins!' Longo shouted, although he knew better than to hope that anyone would intervene. He would have to save himself. He spurred forward, running over one attacker with his horse and striking down another with his sword. But the alley was too narrow to avoid the other men. Longo's horse reared suddenly as one of them slashed it across the chest. Longo fell backwards, tumbling out of the saddle. He rose immediately and found himself attacked by three men. He cut one of them down, ducked a swiping blow from the second and rammed his shoulder into the third, knocking him aside. He sprinted past them, but as he did so, one of the men slashed him across the thigh. Longo gritted his teeth and ran on, limping slightly. Behind him, he could hear the footsteps of his attackers gaining on him.

Longo left the alley and crossed another square. He hurried up a short flight of steps, and a dagger flashed by his head just before he took a sharp right into a shadowy side passage. He turned and waited. The first of the masked men came charging around the corner and ran straight on to Longo's sword. The others pulled up short as Longo retreated into the alleyway. The walls were close enough here that his attackers would only be able to come at him two at a time, and none of the remaining seven men seemed eager to test his blade.

'He is only one man!' one of the masked men shouted at the others in accented Italian. 'Kill him or you will answer to me.' Three of the men inched reluctantly into the alleyway. The rest departed, no doubt circling around the block to attack Longo from behind.

The three men approached, not attacking but staying close enough that if Longo turned to run, they could strike. Longo gave ground, exaggerating his limp. When one of the men came too close, he sprang forward. The man hardly had time to raise his sword before he was skewered through the chest. The other two backed away, swords at the ready. Then, Longo heard the sound of footsteps approaching him from behind. He glanced over his shoulder to see that the other men had entered the alley. He was trapped.

He lunged forward, driving his attackers back a step, and then turned and ran. He spotted a door halfway down the alley and headed for it, but one of the masked men coming from the other direction reached it first. Longo parried the man's thrust and punched him hard in the face. He then grabbed the dazed man, spun and hurled him face first into the door, which banged open. The man landed unconscious on the floor, and Longo followed him into a dark room crowded with vats of tallow. He slammed the door shut behind him. The bolt that locked the door had been broken, so Longo held it with his shoulder.

A second later, someone rammed the door from the other side. Longo staggered back but managed to hold it closed. Again someone rammed the door, and this time Longo stepped away and allowed it to swing open. A surprised attacker stumbled into the room. Longo cut him down and then slammed the door closed again. He could hear the remaining four men outside, discussing what to do next. Longo waited a second, then pulled the door open and rushed out.

He dropped two of the men immediately, stabbing one in the gut and then spinning and slashing the other across the face. A third man lunged for his chest, and Longo just managed to twist out of the way. He hacked down at his attacker's arm, and the man dropped his sword and fell to his knees, holding his bloody arm and crying out in pain before fainting.

Longo turned to face the last man, who had backed well away. 'We shall meet again, signor,' the man said.

'Who are you?' Longo demanded. 'Who sent you?'

The man turned and ran. Longo slumped against the wall of the alleyway, his thigh burning with pain now that the fury of battle had left him. Beside him, the man clutched his bleeding arm and began to moan. Longo rolled him on to his back and knelt down, one knee on the man's chest. He pulled the man's mask aside and slapped him. The man's eyes fluttered open. Longo drew his dagger and held it close to the man's face.

'Who sent you?' he growled. The man did not respond. His eyes closed as he began to lose consciousness. 'Tell me!' Longo insisted, pressing the knife against the man's nose.

'Paolo,' the man croaked, and then he lost consciousness.

Longo stumbled into the courtyard of the Grimaldi *palazzo* with the unconscious man slung over his shoulder. 'Paolo!' he roared as he dumped the man unceremoniously on the ground. 'Where are you? Paolo!'

Paolo, his face pale and eyes wide, came down the steps of the *palazzo*. 'What has happened?' he asked. 'Who is that?'

'You tell me,' Longo snarled. He grabbed Paolo by the collar of his shirt and slammed him against the wall. 'He and ten other men attacked me shortly after I left you tonight.'

'H-how did you escape?' Paolo managed.

Longo ignored the question. 'You are my kinsman, else you would be dead now,' he hissed. 'I know you sent them.'

'You sent that English brat to kill my brother,' Paolo spat back. 'You are a murderer.'

Before he could even think, Longo had his knife at Paolo's throat.

'Longo! What is this?' the elder Grimaldi called out as he descended the *palazzo* steps. He gestured to Longo's blood-stained clothes. 'What has happened?'

Longo released Paolo and turned to Grimaldi. 'Your son hired men to kill me.'

'Paolo, is this true?' Grimaldi demanded. Paolo looked

away. 'I'm sorry, signor,' Grimaldi sighed, turning back to Longo. 'I knew that Paolo was upset over his brother's death, but I never thought he would go so far.'

'Something must be done,' Longo said. 'I will duel him, tomorrow.'

'I cannot allow it,' Grimaldi replied. 'Paolo is my only son. If you strike him, then you strike me. I do not wish to be your enemy, signor.'

'Nor I yours,' Longo said. He turned to Paolo and spat at his feet. 'Count yourself lucky,' he said, then turned and strode away.

'This is not over,' Paolo called out after him. 'Carlos is not done with you. That English bastard of yours is as good as dead!'

'William,' Longo whispered and broke into a run.

'William!' Portia giggled. 'Your beard, it tickles!'

He stopped kissing her ear. 'But you think me very handsome with it?' he asked with a grin. Now eighteen, William was inordinately proud of his short, reddish-brown beard.

'I find you . . . acceptable,' she teased.

'Acceptable?' William asked, kissing her neck. His hand moved slowly up her leg.

'William!' Portia gasped, pushing his hand away from her inner thigh. He moved his hand to her back and pulled her down into the straw of the hayloft, kissing her passionately. She opened her mouth and pressed herself against him. His hand slid down her side to her hip, and then between her legs. 'Stop!' she exclaimed and pulled away. She was breathtaking, her long black hair tousled, her dress half undone and her dark eyes lit by the low flame of the lamp William had brought. 'You do not love me,' she pouted.

'Why do you say such things?' William asked.

'You know why,' she said. She turned her back to him and pulled her knees up to her chest. 'You are the same as all the others. You only want one thing.'

'You know that is not true,' William said, placing his hand on her shoulder. She shrugged it off.

William had met Portia two years ago, a few weeks before the Genoese ambassadors came. She was fifteen then, the daughter of a leather worker in a nearby village. Word of her beauty had spread throughout the region, and more than one prosperous merchant had already approached her father with talk of marriage. The boys of the village followed her in an adoring crowd, but Portia would have nothing to do with them. Later, she had confessed to William that the boys had terrified her. Her wet-nurse – a bitter widow who had lost her husband and child to the plague before taking in Portia – had told her horror stories about what men would do if they ever got their hands on a woman, and Portia had believed her.

William had wooed her for weeks before Portia had even spoken to him. Even then, communication was slow at first, constrained by Portia's shyness and William's halting, broken Italian. Eventually, Portia had grown appreciative of his constant attention. With William around, she no longer had to worry about the groups of boys who whistled and leered at her when she went about town, at least not after he single-handedly chased off a gang of would-be lovers, slapping their backsides with his sword and threatening in English to cut out their tongues and stuff them up their arses. Portia had begun to look on William as a friend, and then as something more.

Portia's father did not approve of William. He did not want his daughter married to a soldier. So they met in secret, spending long afternoons walking the countryside and magical nights here in this barn behind a farmhouse just off the main road. It was the only place in the countryside they could find that was safe, private and reasonably warm, even if it did smell of chickens and cow manure.

'What do you want me to say?' William asked her.

'You know what I want.'

William swallowed hard. 'Will you marry me?'

Portia turned, a smile lighting up her face, and threw herself upon William. 'Yes,' she whispered between kisses. 'Yes, yes.'

The stable door creaked open and they both froze. 'My father!' Portia whispered. 'He'll kill us!' She rolled off William and began to lace up her dress.

William crawled to the edge of the hayloft and peeked down. It was not Portia's father. A man dressed in black stood in the shadowy light, a sword hanging from his waist. He was small with dark features. He looked up, and his eyes met William's. William caught a flash of steel and a second later a dagger embedded itself in the wood of the loft just in front of his face. He scrambled back.

'Stay here!' he told Portia. He grabbed his sword and swung over the edge of the loft, dropping to the stable floor below. He rolled as he landed and sprang to his feet just in time to parry a sword thrust aimed at his heart.

His attacker lunged again, his movements quick and graceful, and William skipped away backwards, stepping behind one of the wooden posts that held up the loft. 'Who are you?' he asked.

'I am Carlos, and I am the last man you will ever meet,' the man said in Italian with a heavy Spanish accent.

The man lunged past the post, forcing William back. He pressed the attack, and William gave ground as he struggled to parry the Spaniard's lightning moves. William had received endless hours of sword lessons from Longo, but he was no match for this man. Carlos swung high, and as William ducked, Carlos's knees came up to catch him in the chin. William stumbled backwards and his back slammed into the wall of the barn. He parried a blow from Carlos, and their swords locked, bringing them close together. Carlos head-butted William, stunning him, and then slashed across his sword arm. William dropped his sword. There was nowhere for him to retreat.

Carlos lunged, and his sword dug into the wall as William twisted out of the way. Then the Spaniard stumbled back cursing as something made of glass shattered against his head with a flash of light. William swung out, catching his adversary in the chin and dropping him. He looked up and could make out Portia standing in the loft. She had thrown the lamp at Carlos, but the burning oil had sprayed across the floor, and the trampled straw had caught flame. Chickens in their coops began to squawk and the cows snorted and rolled their eyes. The fire was spreading quickly, filling the barn with smoke. Flames began to run up the wall of the barn towards the loft.

'Jump!' William called to Portia. She leapt from the loft, and he caught her, falling as he did so. They scrambled to their feet and ran out leaving the prone form of Carlos behind.

William put his arm around Portia and pulled her close to him as they stood in the cold night, watching as the flames engulfed the building. Behind him, William heard the thunder of hooves and turned. It was Longo and Tristo. They reined in, and Longo leapt from the saddle. 'Are you all right?' he asked. 'Both of you?'

William nodded. 'There was a man, Carlos. He tried to kill me,' William said. He pointed to the barn. 'He's in there.' Just then, the roof of the burning structure gave way and collapsed, sending a shower of sparks into the sky. 'Do you know why?'

'Paolo,' Longo explained. 'I fear we have not seen the end of this.'

A long wail of pain reached Longo where he stood at the low wall that surrounded his villa, waiting for the birth of his child. Julia's birth pains had started the previous night, shortly after Longo had returned with Tristo and William. After hours of waiting, Longo had finally fled his quarters to the wall, where the cold rain was preferable to Julia's terrible screaming.

The news of Paolo's betrayal had upset her, and she had entered labour early. Longo was worried for her, but even more for the child she carried. Ever since his childhood, he had been tormented by dreams of the scar-faced Turk who had murdered his family, but now when he dreamt, he often dreamt of a son. He knew that his child might well be a girl, but in his dreams the child was always a boy. Longo would teach him to read or to ride, or they would fish or walk the vineyards together. The boy would have a good life, the life that Longo had not had.

A particularly loud, anguished cry from Julia drew Longo from his thoughts. And then there was silence, broken almost immediately by the loud bawling of an infant. A moment later, Tristo's wife Maria and the midwife emerged from the villa. The midwife was covered in blood; she cradled a wailing infant in her arms. There were tears in her eyes.

'What has happened? Is it a boy?' Longo asked.

The midwife nodded, and showed Longo the bundle she held. It was a boy, with fine blond hair and Longo's blue eyes. The child cried in the cold, and Longo took him and held him close.

'Julia asked that he be called Carlo, after her brother,' Maria said.

Longo nodded. 'How is Julia?'

The midwife turned away, choking back tears. Maria placed her hand on Longo's shoulder. 'I am sorry. She died giving birth.'

Longo held his child closer as he turned away and looked out over the rows of pruned vines. He had not loved Julia, but he had grown fond of her, and he felt for his newborn child, who would never know his mother. Carlo was only a babe, and already his life was marked by loss.

'We are in mourning,' Longo said. 'Cover all the mirrors and close up the shutters of the house. I will ride to town to inform her father.'

Longo rode into the Grimaldi *palazzo* and was shown immediately to Grimaldi's private quarters. Grimaldi sat at a small table, drinking coffee. He rose when Longo entered. 'If you have come about Paolo,' Grimaldi began, 'then I must again apologize for my son.'

'It is not that,' Longo told him. 'Julia has given birth.'

Grimaldi's face lit up. 'A son?'

Longo nodded. 'That is not all. She died in childbirth.'

Grimaldi sank back into his chair. 'I see,' he said, his head down. 'I am sorry, Longo. She was a lovely child.'

'She was,' Longo agreed. He sat across from Grimaldi. 'I have a request to ask of you.'

'What is it?' Grimaldi asked, looking up.

'I want you to take my son. His name is Carlo.' Grimaldi's eyes went wide. 'I have no reason to remain in Genoa,' Longo explained. 'Julia is dead, and I fear there will be more bloodshed between our families if I stay. I am leaving for my lands on Chios. The East is no place for a child. Our merchants returning from Constantinople say that the sultan is preparing for war, building castles and forging cannons. He will strike soon, if not this year then the next. Carlo will be better off here.'

'You are sure of this?' Grimaldi asked. 'You are his father.'

Longo looked away, fighting to keep tears from his eyes. 'Yes,' he said. 'And I will do what is best for my child. The boy has already lost his mother. He should not have to watch his father die as well.'

Grimaldi nodded. 'I will raise him as my own son, signor.'

'Thank you,' Longo said. 'I will return for him once the war is over. If I die . . .'

'I will see to it that he inherits your lands,' Grimaldi

promised. Longo nodded his thanks. 'When do you leave?' Grimaldi asked.

'After the funeral,' Longo said. 'As soon as my household is in order.'

Longo scanned the horizon as he paced the deck of *la Fortuna*, which swayed gently beside the pier, riding low with the ebbing morning tide. All was ready for departure. The ships were loaded, and Longo's men were all aboard with him or on a sister ship, *la Speranza*. A few wives had joined them, including, to Tristo's chagrin, his wife Maria. Nicolo was on *la Fortuna*, complaining already of seasickness. The one person who was not yet on board was William. The night before he had gone to bid farewell to Portia. Longo half hoped that he would stay with her. William had grown into a capable young man, and Longo had come to rely on him. But if William stayed in Italy, he could have a better life than that of a soldier. He would be wise to choose love over revenge.

The sun was only minutes from cresting the distant hills. Soon the tide would set against them, trapping them in the harbour. It was time to depart, William or no. Tristo had been standing at the crosstrees, watching the horizon for William, and now he slid down a backstay and on to the deck. 'We can wait a bit longer, I think,' Tristo said.

'No.' Longo turned from the shore to face the sea. 'We should be underway before we miss our tide. Give the orders to cast off and make sail.'

The orders were given, and *la Fortuna* drifted away from the dock and slowly gathered way. They were gliding towards the centre of the harbor, followed by *la Speranza*, when the lookout caught sight of a horse charging into the dockyard. He hailed the deck, and Longo turned to look. Two people dismounted, and an argument ensued with a group of sailors on the dock. Finally, a boat shoved off with the two riders in it, rowed by four sailors. Longo ordered the sails slackened, and the boat quickly gained on them. William was one of the passengers sitting in the stern. The other was cloaked against the spray, and Longo could not make him out.

Within minutes the boat pulled alongside *la Fortuna*. William clambered aboard first. 'Sorry I'm late,' he said.

Tristo laughed and engulfed him in a hug. 'Nonsense. We're just glad you made it.'

'We are indeed,' Longo said, taking William's hand.

'I still have a score to settle with the Turks,' William said. 'When the war comes, I will be there.' He withdrew his hand and turned to help the other passenger into the boat. 'And now, the reason for my tardy arrival. May I present my fiancée, Portia Fiori.' Portia stepped on to the deck and pushed back the hood of her cloak, freeing her hair to stream in the gusting wind. A few low whistles of appreciation were heard from the hands on deck. Portia blushed.

Longo bowed. 'My Lady,' he said, 'you are most welcome aboard my ship.' Portia blushed an even deeper shade of crimson and curtsied. 'William, show her to her quarters. She can sleep with Maria and the other women. Tristo, give the order to make all sail. Let's take advantage of what little tide remains while we can.'

The ship moved ahead once more, and Longo walked aft to stand at the rail. The sun finally crept over the mountains, transforming the sea into molten gold. The wind teased his hair, and Longo breathed deeply of the tangy ocean air. For the first time since Julia's death, he permitted himself to smile. Love and revenge. There was, Longo supposed, room in the world for both after all.

Part II

Chapter 13

Sofia prayed silently as she knelt on the stone floor of the Haghia Sofia. It was Easter but the great church was not even half full. Ever since Union had been declared the previous December, the Haghia Sofia had been avoided by the populace. Few had come today to listen to the mass performed by the official papal delegate, Archbishop Leonard. Sofia was not listening either. In her late-night snooping about the palace, she had heard reports of tens of thousands of Turkish soldiers massing on the Bosphorus. She had also seen the official estimate of soldiers in Constantinople. They numbered less than seven thousand. A few Italians and Spanish had come to defend the city, but no new troops had arrived for weeks. Despite his promise to Constantine, Longo had not come. So while Leonard preached, Sofia prayed for Western aid.

Archbishop Leonard began the Easter communion and Sofia stepped forward to receive the sacrament. She had just knelt before the altar when a dust-covered messenger entered the sanctuary and hurried to Constantine's side. The messenger whispered in Constantine's ear, and the emperor rose immediately. 'My apologies, Archbishop,' he said, before striding from the church. As he went, he called to Dalmata: 'Send messengers to the other commanders. Have them meet me at the gate of Charisius.'

The service faltered as rumours spread like a wildfire through the congregation. Cries of 'The Turks are here!' were heard, and men began to leave in ever greater numbers. Sofia took advantage of the confusion to slip out of the sanctuary, leaving her escort behind. She caught up to Constantine and followed discreetly behind him. Outside, she took the horse of one of the emperor's guardsmen without asking, simply hauling herself into the saddle and riding away with the emperor's party. The dumbfounded guardsman said nothing. Sometimes, Sofia reflected, royalty had its advantages.

They took Constantinople's main thoroughfare, the Mese, to the gate of Charisius, and climbed to the top of the gate tower, some seventy feet above the surrounding countryside. Notaras was there waiting for them. He noticed Sofia and raised his eyebrows questioningly, but said nothing. Taking care to stay out of Constantine's sight, Sofia got as close to the edge of the tower as she could. She need not have worried: the emperor's attention was fixed elsewhere. He stood gazing into the distance, his knuckles white as he gripped the wall. Sofia followed his eyes but saw nothing, just fields and scattered villages stretching across the rolling hills to the empty horizon.

'Where are they?' Constantine asked.

'They will be here soon enough,' Notaras replied.

As they watched, a thin, dark line appeared on the

horizon and spread quickly, like ink spilled on parchment. Soon, the distant hills were covered with men on horseback – a solid wave of motion that turned the hills black. The line of men stretched for miles across the horizon.

'My God,' Constantine whispered. 'There are so many.'

'That is just the advance guard,' Notaras said. 'The main body is still several days behind them.'

'The time has come, then,' Constantine said. 'Dalmata, have the bridges across the moat burned and close the gates. Notaras, have the great chain put in place to seal off the Golden Horn. No one leaves the city without my permission. Is that understood?' The two men nodded and hurried away. Constantine remained on the wall with a few guards and Sofia. Below them, men set fire to the bridge leading to the gate of Charisius, and the black, acrid smoke reached to the tower, stinging Sofia's eyes. In the distance, men continued to pour over the horizon. 'We are at war,' Constantine murmured. 'God save us.'

Mehmed arrived at Constantinople four days later with the last detachment of the Turkish army. By this time the Turkish camp had already been laid out and the sprawling red and gold tent of the sultan had been erected on a hill beside the Lycus river. From it, Mehmed could see almost the entire stretch of Constantinople's walls, running in an unbroken line for over two miles from the Golden Horn to the Sea of Marmora. The defences were three-tiered. First there was a ditch, or fosse, some sixty feet across and flooded in places, with a low breastwork immediately behind it. Past the fosse, an outer wall rose some twenty-five feet high, studded with towers. Beyond that was the inner wall, which had never been breached. It was forty feet high and up to twenty feet thick in places, with towers reaching as high as seventy feet. The walls had turned back many an invader, including Mehmed's father. But Mehmed was not his father.

Mehmed had spent his entire life preparing for this siege. He knew the walls' weaknesses, and he would exploit them. From his tent he had an excellent view of the Mesoteichion – the weakest part of the walls, where they crossed the Lycus valley. This would be the focus of his attack, and he wanted it constantly under his eye.

He looked away from the walls, allowing his gaze to drift over the field before him. Some two hundred yards from the walls, his men were busy building their own fortifications – a deep ditch backed by an earthen rampart, topped with a wooden palisade. The fortifications would discourage any night-time raids by the Christians, and they would provide a platform for the cannons. Between the fortifications and Mehmed's tent lay the tents of the janissaries. And finally, surrounding Mehmed's tent, were the tents of his own private guard.

Mehmed's generals and advisors were making their way through the tents towards him. Ishak Pasha and Halil were at their head. After them came Baltoghlu, a Bulgarian-born pirate, famed for his raids against Venetian and Genoese merchant ships. Mehmed had appointed him admiral of the Turkish fleet. Next to him waddled the bazibozouks' short, fiery commander, Mahmud Pasha, and Kardja Pasha, the commander of the over ten thousand European troops provided by Mehmed's vassals and allies. Bringing up the rear was the brilliant Hungarian cannon maker, Urban. He had worked for the Greek court until Mehmed had lured him away, offering him four times the pay. Ulu already stood beside Mehmed. The huge supreme *aga* of the janissaries rarely left the sultan's side. When the men reached Mehmed at the entrance to his tent, they all bowed.

'We have much to discuss,' Mehmed said and led the way inside. A table covered with maps, diagrams and lists of figures stood in the centre of the tent. Mehmed shoved these papers aside to reveal a large, detailed map of Constantinople. He pointed to the long line of walls drawn on the map. 'I have heard grumbling in the camp that these walls are impenetrable, that they cannot fall,' he said. 'That is nonsense. I want any man heard to utter such talk punished with a whipping. Each of you, gather your men tonight. Tell them that Allah is on our side, and that their sultan has perfected a plan to bring down the walls of Constantinople. Tell them of the riches and glory that will be theirs, that the first man over the walls will not only win a special place in paradise, but also a fortune to last a lifetime.'

The men around the table nodded, and Mehmed continued. 'You will each move your men into position tomorrow. Baltoghlu, you will bring the fleet here, to block the Bosphorus and to control the entrance to the Golden Horn. You will cut off any ships that try to bring aid to the city. Ulu, you will place the janissaries along the Lycus, across from the Blachernae quarter and the Mesoteichion. Ishak Pasha, you will position your men along the wall to the south. Kardja Pasha, you will place our European allies across the Golden Horn, to cut off any possible Christian retreat. Mahmud Pasha, you will hold your bazibozouks in reserve behind the lines, until such time as they are needed.'

'When do we attack?' Mahmud Pasha asked.

'Soon enough. But first we must weaken the walls. Urban, when will your cannons be in place?'

'I need a few days more,' Urban said. 'The mud has made moving the cannons difficult. When they are in place though, they'll knock down the walls of Babylon itself.'

'You have seven days,' Mehmed told him. 'Take as many men as you need.'

'Yes, My Lord.'

'Seven days?' Mahmud Pasha asked. 'But Sultan, my men have come here to fight. They will not like this standing around.'

'Never fear, Mahmud Pasha. I plan to keep your men quite busy. Take a look at these plans.' Mehmed took up an old, battered scroll and unrolled it across the table.

There was silence as the men took in the detailed, some-times fantastical sketches: ships on land, floating bridges, networks of tunnels. They were all in the sultan's own hand. It was Ishak Pasha who spoke up first. He pointed to the sketch of the ships, apparently sailing across land into the Golden Horn. 'Forgive me, Sultan, but is this even possible?'

'There is no question of possible, Ishak Pasha,' Mehmed said. 'It will be done. You have three weeks to make this happen, no more. I am sure that you will not fail me.'

Gennadius wound his way through the dark catacombs beneath the Church of Saint Saviour Pantocrator, a torch lighting his way amidst the dank crypts. He was wrapped in a black cloak instead of his monk's robes, and he had left behind the conspicuous golden cross that usually hung from his neck. Eugenius followed, dressed much the same except that he wore a sword at his side. If they were seen by the men that Notaras had stationed outside the monastery, Gennadius hoped that they would be taken for a merchant and his bodyguard. But Gennadius did not plan on being seen.

They came to a narrow staircase and followed it down to the edge of a huge underground reservoir with a low ceiling supported by hundreds of pillars. The cistern dated from Roman times, and the monks still drew their drinking water from here. The flame of Gennadius's torch reflected off the water, causing strange lights to play across the many-vaulted ceiling. Before him, wooden walkways wound their way between the pillars and over the water, stretching off into the darkness. The walkways had not been repaired for decades, and the wood was slowly rotting in the damp air. It creaked and groaned under foot as Gennadius set out across the cistern. He had only taken a few steps when he saw something long and scaly move in the dark waters beneath them. Giant fish the size of a man were said to live in the waters, and Gennadius had no desire to discover if the legends were true. He picked his way forward, carefully avoiding the loose planks.

The walkway ended at a heavy wooden door, and Gennadius produced a key and unlocked it. When he pushed the door open, bright morning sunlight poured into the tunnel. He stepped into a shallow cave that had been carved into the side of the hill that the church of

Saint Saviour Pantocrator crowned. Below him, the Golden Horn sparkled in the sun. Christian ships were moored beside the great chain that had been stretched across the mouth of the Horn on wooden floats. Beyond the chain, Gennadius could see the Turkish fleet patrolling the Sea of Marmora.

A path led down from the cave to the sea walls, which ran parallel to the shores of the Golden Horn, separating the port from the city. Although not as imposing as the land walls, they were still massive, rising thirty feet high and studded with towers. And because of their position along the Golden Horn, the sea walls were impossible to take unless an enemy completely controlled the harbour. Although the walls had originally marked the limit of the city, over the centuries warehouses had been built beyond them to service the docks there, and in time taverns, inns, bawdyhouses and churches had sprung up to service the sailors who used the docks and warehouses.

Gennadius and Eugenius took the path down to the sea walls, where a guard loyal to the Synaxis let them through, and then they walked north along the docks to a small Orthodox church. There were no tunnels that Gennadius knew of directly into the city, but this church would do. A tunnel in its crypt led to the basement beneath a monastery in the nearby settlement of Cosmidion, only some two hundred yards north of Constantinople along the Golden Horn. Gennadius and Eugenius entered the church and moved to the back of the sanctuary, where a staircase led down to the crypt. There, behind a row of stone sarcophagi, they located a trapdoor with a ladder leading downwards into the darkness. Eugenius took a torch from the wall and descended first. Gennadius followed, and when he reached the floor of the tunnel he found Isa waiting for him. He held a torch in one hand and a small birdcage containing a pigeon sat at his feet.

'Greetings, Isa,' Gennadius said. 'Do you have what I asked for?'

'I have brought the poison,' Isa confirmed. He took out a small leather pouch and handed it to Gennadius. Gennadius opened it and peered inside. It was filled with white powder.

'What is this?'

'A powerful poison, made from bitter almonds,' Isa explained. 'When inhaled, the powder is fatal. The assassin need only throw it near the sultan.'

'Then it will do perfectly,' Gennadius said, carefully closing the pouch.

'The grand vizier wishes to make it clear that the city is not to fall until the sultan is dead. Those are the terms of the deal. If you fulfil them, then you shall have what you wish.'

'Tell Halil not to worry. The messenger who will bring the key to unlock the city and the assassin who will kill the sultan are one and the same,' Gennadius said. 'I will send him when the time is right, when the siege has grown old and the sultan is desperate enough to listen.'

'What you do is your concern. So long as you succeed, the less that Halil knows, the better. In the meantime, if you should need to communicate with Halil, you will come here.' Isa picked up the birdcage and handed it to Gennadius. 'Use this bird to contact Halil. No message is necessary. Simply release it, and it will fly to Halil. A messenger will meet you here the night that he receives the bird, just after sunset. He will ask you a question to determine your identity. The answer is "Edirne".'

'I understand,' Gennadius said. He was impressed. The bird was an elegant mechanism.

'Then we are done here,' Isa said and turned to go.

'God go with you, my son,' Gennadius called after him.

'God abandoned me long ago,' the man said as he disappeared into the darkness.

Halil sat alone in his luxurious tent, propped up by cushions and with a portable writing desk across his lap. He had been busy writing since early morning, letter after letter to nearby emirs and beys, in which he requested the delivery of food and other supplies. The sultan's army consumed enormous quantities, and even after months of preparation, they would not be able to stay in the field for much over a week without fresh supplies. It was Halil's task to acquire those supplies. The letters he wrote were, of course, a mere formality. If the lords refused to supply the sultan's army at a fair price, then troops would simply take the provisions.

As Halil started yet another letter, Isa stepped into his tent. 'Servants, leave us,' Halil said. 'Isa, you may sit.' He gestured to some cushions on the floor, but Isa remained standing. 'I had expected you back sooner. You delivered the poison and the bird?'

'The monk has them both, and he promises that the city will not fall until Mehmed is dead.'

'Did he say anything else about his plans?'

'No, only that the messenger who brings the secret to

conquering Constantinople will also be the one who brings news of Mehmed's death.'

'A riddle then,' Halil said. 'And one best left unsolved. The less we know of Gennadius's actions the better. I have another task for you.'

Isa held up his hand, cutting the vizier off. 'I grow tired of serving as your messenger. You promised me the release of my family if I did as you asked, and I have done all that you asked and more, these three years past.' He pulled a small pouch from beneath his robes. 'I am done with this. Release my family, or I will kill you here and now.'

A trickle of sweat ran down Halil's spine. 'Do not be rash, Isa,' he said, managing to keep his voice steady. 'If you kill me, then your family will die. You know that. Do not throw their lives away when you are so close to winning their freedom. I have but one more task for you, and then your family will be free.'

Isa hesitated, then finally put the pouch back beneath his robes. 'What would you have me do?'

'Go back to Edirne and kill young Bayezid, the son of the sultan,' Halil told him. 'Make his death look natural, but do it quickly. He must die before this siege is through, before the death of Mehmed.'

'And if I do this, then my family will be freed?'

'When my men hear that Bayezid is dead, then they will turn your family over to you, and you will be well rewarded for your many services.'

'I do not want any more of your money, Halil, only my family.' His hand went back to the pouch of poison. 'Do I have your word that they will be freed?'

'You have my word.'

'Very well. For your sake, you had best keep your promise,' Isa said and left the tent.

Halil watched him go. Isa's family was his weakness, and it would be his undoing. Halil placed the letter to the city of Chorlu aside and began a new one, this time in code, to his agents in Edirne.

Constantine stood at his post at the Fifth Military Gate, near the middle of the Mesoteichion, and squinted against the early morning light as he watched the Turkish army form ranks in the distance. Dalmata stood beside him, and Notaras was not far off at the Blachernae wall. The siege was now ten days old, and not a cannon had fired, not an arrow had flown. While the men of the city waited on the walls day after day with increasing anxiety, the Turkish camp remained unnervingly quiet. Now, the Turkish army had finally sprung to life. Even though he dreaded the carnage to come, Constantine found himself looking forward to the release of the dreadful tension that had hung over the city.

On the far plain, the Turkish army had finished forming ranks. Flags waved over each regiment, identifying the origins of particular units. In the centre of the janissaries, directly across from Constantine, the flag of Mehmed – a white standard covered in ornate Turkish script – waved in the breeze. Horns sounded from the Turkish army, their loud call shattering the silence, and the regiments began to move, marching forward in step to the boom of drums, the clash of cymbals and the ringing of small bells held high on sticks. The sound of the approaching army was deafening after the long silence. 'Prepare to fight!' Constantine shouted over the din. He had no sooner spoken than another blast of horns sounded, and the Turkish army halted.

'What are they waiting for?' Constantine growled. 'Why don't they just attack and be done with it?'

'I do not think that they mean to attack just yet,' Dalmata said. 'Look, heralds.'

All down the Turkish lines, at intervals of a hundred yards, heralds dressed in red caftans stepped forth, accompanied by men carrying white flags of truce that snapped in the wind. They stopped just short of the fosse, where they raised their trumpets and together blew a shattering blast. Before the note had entirely faded, the heralds began to speak in unison, loudly and in Greek.

Where Constantine stood on the wall, the voice of the herald before him came and went as the fitful, swirling breeze pushed his words now towards the walls, now away. Still, the message was clear; it was a call for surrender. 'In accordance . . . law of Islam, the great sultan promises to spare those who voluntarily surrender to him. If any man surrenders . . . family and property will be safeguarded. Those who choose to stay . . . no mercy. You have until sunrise, tomorrow, to decide.' Their message delivered, the heralds returned to the lines. The sultan's army turned and marched back to camp.

'Shall I send a reply, Emperor?' Dalmata asked.

'No reply will be necessary,' Constantine said. 'But let it be known in the city that this gate will be opened for any who desire to leave.'

'But My Lord,' Dalmata protested. 'We are undermanned as it is. We cannot stand to lose any more men.'

'I will not force men to fight who would rather run,' Constantine said. 'Their swords will be of little use anyway.

Open this gate for those who would surrender and let us pray that our people choose honour over the promises of the sultan. And Dalmata, have my supper brought to me here.'

'Here, My Lord?'

'It will be a long night, and I would rather spend it here than pacing the halls of the palace. I trust in my people to stay and fight, but if any of them wish to leave, let them look upon the face of their emperor as they do so.'

As night gave way to morning and the Turkish camp came alive with the innumerable sounds of an army in the field, Mehmed stood atop an earthen rampart and peered out over the palisade towards the imposing walls of Constantinople and the city gate that had been left open all night. In the dim pre-dawn light he could just make out the figure of the emperor standing atop the gate. Ulu told him that Constantine had been there all night. During that time, seven Venetian ships had slipped out of port, but that was all. Not a single person had fled through the open gate, beneath the gaze of the emperor. Now, as the rays of the sun struck the top of the gate, it swung slowly shut. The Greeks had rejected Mehmed's offer. The time for mercy had ended.

'They are brave, there can be no doubt of that,' Mehmed said to Ulu. 'All the better. It will make our victory that much sweeter.' He turned to Urban, who was directing a dozen men as they finished loading a giant cannonball nearly four feet tall into the mouth of the largest cannon that the world had ever seen. The barrel, all twenty-seven feet of it, hung from thick ropes attached to a wooden frame, a system that Urban had devised to absorb the cannon's violent recoil, which would destroy the traditional wooden cradle used for the other cannons. Urban called his monstrous creation *the Dragon*, and Mehmed liked the name. He had had artists paint the barrel with the serpentine shape of a dragon. He wanted the cannon's fearsome voice to be the first thing the Christians heard that morning, telling them that the siege had begun and that the end was near. 'Urban, is the cannon ready?' Mehmed asked.

'As ready as I can make her, My Lord,' Urban replied. 'She's still a little shaky, but she'll hold.'

'Are you certain? You know how much depends on the Dragon.'

'Sure as sure,' Urban said. 'I'd stake my life on it.' Urban froze as the words escaped his lips. A mistake.

'Very well,' Mehmed replied. 'Your life it is, then. As for my part, I will stake your weight in gold. It will be yours if the cannon holds and the cannonball reaches the city. You may fire when ready, Urban.'

'Yes, My Lord,' Urban said. He turned back to his crew and bellowed: 'Open the palisade!' Men tugged at ropes, and the hinged door of the palisade that protected the cannon swung open. Urban was busy at the rear of the cannon. He checked the ropes holding it in place one final time, and then took up a burning slow match. 'You'll want to cover your ears, Sultan,' he said. Mehmed did so, and Urban lowered the slow match to the cannon's touch hole.

Instantly the cannon belched forth a long tongue of fire and jerked violently backwards. Even with his ears covered, the noise set Mehmed's head ringing and shook the platform. He turned to follow the flight of the massive cannonball. It seemed to float in the air for an incredibly long time as it travelled the two hundred yards to the walls. It soared over the fosse and crashed into the outer wall, which was instantly enveloped in a cloud of dust and flying debris. A split second later, the loud report of the impact came to Mehmed, and then, slowly, the dust cleared. The Christians had hung the walls with strips of leather and bales of hay and wool in the hope of absorbing the impact of cannon fire, but their precautions had done little good. The cannon had hit the wall midway up and blasted a hole clean through it. As the wind blew the last traces of dust away, the portion of the wall above the hole collapsed. The Turkish lines erupted in wild cheering.

Mehmed turned to congratulate Urban and saw that the rear of the cannon had fallen from its frame, pinning a man beneath it. Urban and his crew were at work with crowbars, desperately trying to heave the huge weight off the poor man's crushed legs. The man himself was unconscious, or dead.

'Fix it,' Mehmed said. 'I want it firing again before the sun has set.'

'What of our wager?' Urban asked tentatively, scratching his neck.

'The cannonball reached the wall, as I requested. We will call it a draw.' Urban bowed. 'Besides, I need you to get the cannon firing again. Get to it.'

'Yes, My Lord,' Urban said and began barking orders.

'Ulu, tell the other artillery commanders down the line that they may fire when ready,' Mehmed ordered. 'I want cannons firing day and night. Concentrate on the Mesoteichion. Tell the men that every time a section of the wall falls, I will reward the unit that brings it down with one hundred aspers. The walls of Constantinople have stood for more than a thousand years. Let us see how long it takes for us to bring them down.'

Chapter 14

Sofia sat on the floor of the palace library, surrounded by old books and tattered manuscripts, an ancient map spread out before her. The library windows looked out beyond the wall, and when she stood at them, she could see the Turkish batteries pounding away at the city. Her attention, however, was completely taken up with the yellowing map before her. Sofia could not fight at the walls, but that did not mean that she would not do her part to defend Constantinople. She was looking for anything that could be useful, but most of all she was looking for information about tunnels into the city. Despite persistent rumours over the decades, no such tunnels had ever been found. The map before her looked like another dead end. It detailed the cisterns, tunnels and pipes that ran under the city, but it did not show any tunnels leading beneath the walls.

A deafening crash pulled her attention from the map. The floor shook unnervingly, and she stood, prepared to run for cover. But after a few seconds, the shaking stopped.

Over the past three days, Sofia has grown accustomed to the constant booming of the Turkish guns, but the occasional rending crash as a cannonball hit the palace still startled her. Fortunately, the guns firing on the Blachernae quarter were not nearly as imposing as the enormous cannon that had been placed across from the Mesoteichion.

Sofia went to the window, but the portion of the palace that she could see still looked intact in the early morning light. She was about to turn back to her books when she noticed people rushing through the square below, away from the walls. As she watched, more and more people streamed past. Where could they be going? Had the Turks breached the walls? Sofia stepped out of the library to ask a palace guard.

The hallways were empty so she headed to the palace entrance, and finding it unguarded, slipped out into the street amongst the thinning crowd. She stopped a bent old woman who was tottering past. 'Many pardons, *maame*,' Sofia said. 'Where is everybody going?'

'To the Acropolis to watch,' the woman replied. 'Help has come at last! Christian ships have been seen in the Sea of Marmora.' Sofia fell into step beside her.

'When were they seen?' she asked. 'Do you know where they are from?'

'A lookout spotted them at first light. Where they are from, I don't know. So long as they bring help, they could be from Hades and I would bless every one of them.'

'As would I. Thank you, *maame*.' Sofia hurried on past her, following the crowd. She found a spot near the southern edge of the Acropolis, high above the sea below. To the south-west, still small in the distance, she saw four tall ships making their way towards the Golden Horn under full sail, flying before the southerly breeze. Even at this distance, Sofia could make out the large red cross on a white field flying from the mast of the largest ship. But even had she not seen the cross, the response of the Turkish fleet would have been enough to tell her that the approaching ships were Christian. The fleet had left its anchorage at the Double Columns, a quay just north of Pera, and a swarm of galleys and smaller craft were rowing against the wind towards the four Christian ships. The Turkish ships moved slowly, their oars often becoming entangled with one another. Nevertheless, it was clear that they would surround the approaching ships long before the Christians reached the safety of the Golden Horn.

The Christian ships grew steadily in size and clarity, until Sofia could make out the tiny figures of men moving on the decks. She was far too distant to make out faces, but she tried nevertheless, hoping for some sign of Longo. Looking to the advancing Turkish fleet, however, she almost hoped that he had stayed in Italy.

As the sun reached its zenith, the Christian ships met the Turkish fleet off the south-east corner of Constantinople, less than a quarter of a mile from where Sofia stood. The four ships sailed headlong into the wall of advancing boats, shoving some aside and crushing others. The Christian ships towered over the smaller Turkish vessels, and from their high decks the Christian sailors rained down arrows and javelins on the Turks, while the Turks could not effectively fire back. The Turks' only option was to try to board, but they had difficulty hooking on to the swiftly moving Christian ships. The few Turkish boats that did manage to hook on promptly came to regret it. The Christians covered them with Greek fire – a viscous, clinging liquid that continued to burn fiercely even when doused with water. The oily, burning substance coated the vessels, and the Turks' frantic attempts to extinguish the flames only spread them. The Greek fire continued to burn even after the Turkish ships had sunk, leaving small puddles of fire floating amongst the waves.

Within the space of a few minutes the Christian ships had sailed through the Turkish fleet. 'They've done it!' a woman yelled, and Sofia joined in her enthusiastic cheering. The Turkish galleys threw up their sails and turned to give chase, but it seemed only a matter of time now before the Christians reached the safety of the Golden Horn.

And then the wind died.

Longo stood at the wheel of *la Fortuna*, anxiously watching the sails as they shuddered and then fell limp. The wheel died beneath his hand as the ship lost its way and the current gripped it, pulling them back towards the Turkish fleet. He looked behind him. Their oars out again, the Turkish galleys were advancing quickly, cutting through the water. There was no way that the bulkier Christian ships would be able to outrow them. Already the foremost Turkish ship, a low trireme flying the flag of Baltoghlu, the admiral of the Turkish fleet, had reached the grain transport. *La Fortuna* and the other ships would be surrounded soon enough. The safety of the Golden Horn was within sight, but with the wind gone it might as well have been miles away. They would have to fight.

'Axes out, men!' Longo called, as he left the wheel and took up an axe. 'We're going to have to hold our own until the wind returns. Let's give them hell!' The men cheered. Longo had more than six hundred soldiers with him: two hundred and fifty here aboard *la Fortuna* and an additional two hundred each aboard *la Speranza* and *l'Aquila*, a ship that he had picked up in Chios. The fourth ship, a grain transport sent by the pope, was the weakest part of the convoy. The captain, Phlatanelas, was a brave man, but his ship held more grain than men.

The Turkish flagship reached the transport, ramming it across the bow, and a horde of screaming Turks swarmed up the sides, only to be met with a shower of burning Greek fire that swept them into the sea. Longo turned away from the spectacle to shout orders to his crew. 'Tristo, take two companies and man the starboard side. William, take the same and command the port,' Longo ordered. 'Archers, get aloft and begin firing as soon as the Turks are alongside. Firemen, be ready with those buckets.'

'And what about me?' Nicolo asked. Longo's portly chamberlain stood awkwardly in a bulky suit of armour, wringing his hands as he stared at the approaching Turkish ships.

'First of all, take off that armour. You can hardly move in it,' Longo told him. 'Then go below and help the men bring up ballast stones from the hold.'

'But why? Are they not needed for . . . for ballasting?'

'Take them to the rail and drop them on any Turkish ship that comes alongside. Their ships have thin hulls. God willing, the stones will go right through them.'

'How clever,' Nicolo murmured, but Longo was no longer paying attention to him. The first Turkish ships were closing

266

in and had begun firing flaming arrows at the ship. Most of those that hit sputtered out, but a few caught. The firemen hurried about the deck, dousing the flames with buckets of water. Shortly after the arrows hit, the first Turkish boat reached them. It rammed the side of the ship with a solid thump that knocked several of Longo's crew off their feet. The thick sides of *la Fortuna* absorbed the blow with no damage, but the bow of the ramming ship was splintered and crushed on impact. The Turkish soldiers aboard could not swim in their heavy armour. Their panicked cries were drowned out one by one as the ship sank quickly beneath the waves.

Three more Turkish ships came alongside, followed by dozens more. Within seconds *la Fortuna* was surrounded and engulfed in chaos. Turks swarmed the ship from all sides, yelling like demons and fighting desperately to board. Longo's men fought them back, their heavy axes severing the hands and heads of would-be boarders. Tristo wielded a massive axe, protecting a full five feet of railing by himself as he took off head after head. On the opposite side of the ship, William had eschewed an axe for his sword. He slipped in and out of his men, striking where needed and dispatching Turks with ruthless efficiency. Above, the twang of bowstrings could be heard from high in *la Fortuna*'s rigging, and arrows filled the air, whizzing into the Turks below. Nicolo stumbled past Longo carrying a huge ballast stone. The chamberlain dropped it over the side and then clapped his hands with glee as the stone crashed through the deck of a Turkish ship below. Water bubbled through the ragged hole, flooding the deck, and the Turkish soldiers began to strip off their armour and abandon the sinking ship. And all this time, flaming arrows continued to rain down on the deck of *la Fortuna*.

Longo was kept busy, rushing to help wherever one of his men fell or gave ground. He was at the stern, pushing back a fresh wave of attackers when the Turks managed to force their way on deck at *la Fortuna*'s bow. 'To the bow!' Longo yelled to his men as he rushed across the deck to where more than a dozen Turks had already gathered. Moving at a full sprint, Longo hurled his axe at the nearest Turk, catching him square in the chest and knocking him off his feet. Longo drew his sword on the run and slammed into the rest of the Turks. He fought with a savage abandon, spinning, twisting and slashing his way through the boarders, forcing his way to the railing at the bow, where he confronted a final Turk. He parried the attacker's thrust, lowered his shoulder, and slammed into him, knocking him over the rail and into the sea below. More Turks were clambering up the side, and Longo cut the ropes that they were using to climb aboard. As they fell into the sea below, Longo looked around him.

The bow of the ship was clear. His men had followed his charge and had swept the Turks aside. Around them, the sides of the ship were holding, and the initial ferocity of the Turkish attack had abated. Longo looked to the other Christian ships. *La Speranza* was closest and seemed to be holding its own. *L'Aquila* also appeared to have weathered the storm, but the transport, furthest away from Longo, was in trouble. Their small crew was under heavy pressure from more than a dozen Turkish ships. The Turkish flagship was still alongside, and men continued to pour out of it and up the sides of the transport. Without help, the transport would be lost, and with it enough grain to feed all of Constantinople for several days.

Longo looked again at the other Christian ships. The current had brought them closer together, so that there was no more than thirty feet between each of them. Longo realized that with some rope and a little luck, there was still a chance that they could save the transport.

'Rope!' he yelled to his men. 'Bring me four lengths of rope, and grappling hooks. Tristo and William, get over here!' While his men prepared the rope, Longo explained his plan. 'Tristo, do you think that you can reach *la Speranza* with a rope?' Tristo nodded. 'Good. Then I want you to throw three ropes between our two ships. Once they have tied off the ropes on *la Speranza*, the men can pull the two ships together. We'll board *la Speranza*, then pull *l'Aquila* to us, then the transport. William, you'll stay in charge of the ship here. If we act fast, we can still reach the transport in time.'

Longo went to shout his plan to the captain of *la Speranza*, while Tristo took a coil of rope with a hook tied to the end and moved to the rail of the ship. While the other men kept the Turks at bay, Tristo stood on the rail and began to swing the hook, letting out rope until it was swinging in a large circle. Finally, he let it fly. The hook arced through the air as the rope uncoiled by Tristo's side, but it came up short, bouncing off the side of *la Speranza* and sinking into the sea. There was a disappointed silence on the ship, interrupted by Tristo roaring, 'Give me another!' He took another hook, and this time let it go with a slightly higher arc. The hook soared through the air and landed with a thud in the middle of *la Speranza*'s deck. The men on both ships cheered. Tristo threw two more ropes over, and the crews began pulling the ships together. Within a few minutes, they were close enough for Longo and Tristo to leap from *la Fortuna* to the deck of *la Speranza*, and the whole process was started over again, this time with *l'Aquila*.

By the time they latched on to the transport and began to pull it close, the fighting there had become truly desperate. Pockets of Turks had forced themselves on to the transport's deck at various points, and the Christian crew was beginning to give ground. The heavy transport was proving very difficult to pull close, and if help did not come soon, Longo feared that the lines between *l'Aquila* and the transport would be cut and the ship lost. 'There is no time to wait,' Longo told Tristo. 'We must go now.'

Longo swung out on one of the ropes, and hanging by his hands and feet, began to crawl between the ships. 'Crazy bastard!' Tristo called after him, and then turning towards the crew, he shouted: 'Well, come on then!' He swung out on the rope, followed by the rest of Longo's men.

Arrows whizzed past Longo, but he managed to reach the far side unharmed. He was about to clamber on to the deck when there was a skirmish at the railing and a Turk appeared at the side above him. The Turk raised his sword to cut the rope that Longo was hanging from but was struck down from behind. Phlatanelas, the transport's captain, appeared at the side and pulled Longo up. The situation on board was desperate: the crowds of Turks at the bow and stern were growing larger by the second.

'Greek fire?' Longo asked as he pulled a winded Tristo up on to the deck.

'We have only one barrel left.' Phlatanelas pointed to

the squat barrel in the centre of the ship, standing next to a bucket with a burning torch in it.

'I have an idea for that barrel,' Tristo said.

Longo nodded. 'Concentrate your men on the stern of the ship, Phlatanelas. We'll take care of the bow.' Phlatanelas hurried to the stern, while Longo and Tristo went to the barrel. 'Are you sure this will work?' Longo asked.

'No choice,' Tristo replied. Longo hauled down one of the foresails, while Tristo took the stopper from the top of the barrel. Grunting, he lifted the heavy barrel and poured Greek fire over the sail, while Longo used a rag to spread it about. 'All right,' Tristo nodded. 'Here we go.' Tristo and Longo both took hold of a line and hauled the sail upward. When it was some twenty feet above the deck, they stopped. Longo grabbed the torch and drew his sword.

'Are you sure about this?' he asked Tristo. 'Last time we burned the ship down.'

'If she burns, at least the Turks won't take her,' Tristo replied with a grin.

'God save us!' Longo shouted as he slashed through one of the stays holding up the foremast, then another. The mast fell slowly forward and Tristo let go of his line so that the sail swung forward in front of the mast. Longo yelled at his men in the bow: 'Retreat! To me, to me! Retreat!' Longo's men rushed away from the bow, and the Turks came pouring after them. Longo charged towards them, running after the billowing sail. At the last second, he touched the torch to it, and the sail burst into flames as it swung forward and into the Turks, sweeping them off the deck. As the flaming sail followed the last of the Turks over the side, the foremast came down with a crash next to Longo. At the rear of the ship, Phlatanelas and his men were in control again. Perhaps they would survive this after all.

'I told you it would work,' Tristo said, grinning. As he spoke, the sails on the mainmast filled briefly, and then fell limp again. 'Come on, damn wind, blow!' Tristo growled, and as if in response, another strong gust filled the sails, followed by another.

'Cut us off from *l'Aquila*,' Longo ordered. By the time he reached the wheel, the gusts had settled into a constant wind from the north, blowing them towards the mouth of the Golden Horn. The crew cheered as the transport gathered way, crashing through the Turkish ships around it. Their cheers were matched by those from the other Christian ships sailing ahead of them, and by the ringing of bells echoing down from the heights of Constantinople above. The great chain protecting the harbour had been drawn back just enough to allow them to pass. 'Thank God,' Longo murmured as they sailed into the Golden Horn. They had made it to Constantinople at last.

As evening fell, Sofia stood before the mirror in her chambers, appraising herself in yet another caftan, the third she had tried. The close-fitting caftan of gold-embroidered scarlet silk accented her thin waist and pushed up her breasts, emphasizing her cleavage. She nodded, finally satisfied. She began to apply kohl around her wide, hazel eyes, and noted with disappointment that the faintest traces of wrinkles were beginning to form at their edges. At least she was still fit and graceful. Her skin was healthy, even if it did not approach the pale perfection of an ideal lady. But then, Sofia did not suppose that she would ever be anyone's idea of a perfect lady. She was herself, no more and no less.

When she arrived in the great hall the tables were already crowded. Longo and Phlatanelas sat at the table of honour, to the right and left of Constantine. Sphrantzes and Dalmata also sat to the emperor's left, and Notaras and the Archbishop Leonard sat on his right. A steward guided Sofia to her seat to the right of the emperor, between Archbishop Leonard and the dull Grand Logothete, Metochites. Sofia pretended to listen to their discussion – a heated debate regarding the use of unleavened bread for communion – while trying to catch as much as she could of the conversation at the centre of the table. But she could make out little until late in the meal, when the great hall quieted and the toasts began.

Constantine stood first. 'To Signor Giustiniani and his brave men,' he said, raising his glass. 'May the example they have set today inspire us and lead us to victory!' There was much thumping of tables and hearty shouts of 'Hear! Hear!' as the guests downed their drinks.

Longo stood and offered a toast in return: 'To Constantinople, fairest city in the world, and to the people who have so graciously received us. It is an honour to fight beside you.' Again, there was a great deal of table thumping before glasses were drained.

A variety of toasts ensued: 'To the Turks, may they rot in hell!' 'To the Empire of the Romans!' 'To the Emperor!' 'To the Venetians!' 'To the Genoese!'

Archbishop Leonard, clearly far from sober after the rounds of toasting, stood unsteadily and added, 'To the Union and all that it has brought!' There was an uncomfortable silence, and then a round of mumbled voices echoed: 'To Union.' At least half of the guests did not drink the toast, which proved to be the last of the night. A cloud seemed to have come over the party.

'I only meant to point out that Union has already brought us Signor Giustiniani,' Archbishop Leonard grumbled as he sat down. 'More help is no doubt on the way. Surely that should make even the damned Synaxis happy.'

'What have you heard, Signor Giustiniani?' Notaras asked. 'Has the pope kept his word? Is there more help on the way?'

The hall quieted as all attention focused on Longo. 'The pope has called for a crusade,' Longo began.

'Ah, see!' Archbishop Leonard interjected.

'But the French and English kings refuse to fight, and the Hungarian army is bogged down with troubles of its own. I know of no other forces coming from Genoa or Venice.' The hall was silent. 'I could be wrong. My ships have been storm-bound at Chios for weeks, and we have heard little for some time now. Perhaps matters have changed.'

'*Perhaps?*' Notaras asked. 'That is all we have heard for months now. Perhaps the West will rally to our cause. Perhaps Venice will send its fleet. Perhaps the Hungarian army is on the move. Perhaps help is almost here. Meanwhile, there is nothing hypothetical about the sultan's army. It is there, just outside the walls, and promises alone will not defeat it!'

'Enough, Notaras,' Constantine said. 'This is a feast of celebration. Whether or not more help comes, Signor Giustiniani and his men are here now, as is the grain sent by the pope. This is cause for rejoicing! Come; bring more wine. Let us have music and dance. For tonight, at least, let us enjoy ourselves.'

The entrance of the musicians and scantily clad dancers was the signal for the women to leave. Sofia did not envy the men their drunken revelry, but she was sorry to go. She had hoped to speak with Longo, although she was unsure what she would say to him. She rose from the table, bowed to the emperor, and exited via the narrow, torchlit hallway leading to her suites.

'Princess Sofia,' a familiar voice called, and she turned. It was Longo. 'I was sorry to see you leave. I had hoped to speak with you.'

Sofia blushed. 'And what did you wish to speak about, Signor Giustiniani?'

'Please, do not stand on formality. Call me Longo.'

'I should not even be speaking to you here, alone,' Sofia said. 'And besides, you will surely be missed.'

Longo shrugged. 'Nobody will miss me; their eyes are on the dancing girls. But if you do not wish to speak, then I understand. Please, forgive my impertinence.' He turned to go, but Sofia touched his arm, stopping him.

'No, stay,' she said. 'I wished to speak with you as well. And I can surely trust the honour of a married man.'

'You can trust my honour, Princess, but I am not married. Julia died in childbirth more than a year past.'

'I am sorry. She was so young.'

'Too young,' Longo agreed. 'But perhaps it is all part of God's plan. Were it not for her death, I might not be here. She was the last link holding me to Genoa.'

'And now that you are free, you have come to honour your promise to Constantine?'

Longo paused. 'Yes, that is why I am here,' he said finally and looked away. They both fell silent. 'But what of you?' he eventually asked. 'Is one of the men you sat beside your husband-to-be?'

Sofia laughed, thinking of the boorish Metochites and drunk Archbishop Leonard. 'Fortunately, no,' she said. 'I am engaged to Megadux Lucas Notaras.'

'He is a lucky man,' Longo said. He took a step towards her, so that no more than a foot remained between them. Sofia's heart began to pound in her chest and her breathing quickened. 'I wished to speak with you about Corsica,' Longo said. 'I have thought much about that night.'

'As have I,' Sofia replied.

'*Ahem*!' It was Notaras, stepping into the hallway behind them. Longo and Sofia stepped quickly apart. 'Signor Giustiniani, I see that you have met my betrothed, the Princess Sofia. I am the megadux, Lucas Notaras, the commander of the emperor's forces.'

'I am most pleased to meet you, Megadux,' Longo told him, and the two men clasped hands. 'The Princess Sofia spoke well of you.'

'Did she?' Notaras said. 'I was not aware that you two were on familiar terms.'

'We met briefly, in Italy,' Longo explained.

'Ah, very interesting,' Notaras said. 'You will have to tell me all about it, Sofia. Come. I will take you to your quarters. It is not proper for a young princess to walk the halls unescorted.' He took Sofia by the arm. 'Signor Giustiniani, good night.'

The emperor greeted Longo as soon as he stepped back into the great hall. 'Signor Giustiniani,' Constantine said, 'I need to speak with you alone. Come with me.'

Constantine led Longo through the passageway behind the hall and out into an interior garden. The garden was quiet, the many flowers silver in the moonlight, the air filled with their heady perfume. The emperor picked a rose blossom as they walked and examined it. 'It is wonderful, is it not, that flowers know neither peace nor war, only sunshine and rain. An enviable state, no? This rose bush blooms as it has every spring. It would bloom just as beautifully for a sultan as for an emperor.' In the distance, they could hear the occasional boom of Turkish cannons. The emperor dropped the flower and turned to face Longo. 'I have asked you here so that we may talk freely.'

'And what is it that you wish to speak of, Emperor?'

'First, I wish to thank you, man to man, for coming to our aid. The endless bombardment and this infernal waiting have been driving us mad. The soldiers quarrel daily. The Venetians and the Genoese cannot abide one another, and many of my Roman troops refuse to fight beside either of them. Your victory today has lightened our spirits and inspired us all. Romans, Venetians and Genoese were all united in celebration of your arrival. It is truly a blessing.'

'I told you long ago that my sword was at your service should you ever have need of it,' Longo said. 'I am a man of my word. I would not leave you to fight this battle alone.'

'I am glad that you have come, for I do indeed have need of your sword, and your wisdom too, Signor Giustiniani,' Constantine said. 'I understand that you have experience with siege warfare.'

'I was at the siege of Belgrade in 1440, where we held off the armies of the sultan. If you need counsel, then I will be happy to offer it.'

'I need more than your counsel, Signor. I need your leadership. None of my men knows the Turks as you do, nor can they rally men as you did today. I want you to take command of the defence.'

'But My Lord, for all that I love Constantinople, I am foreign to these lands,' Longo protested. 'Surely your people would be more willing to follow one of their own. If none of your men are able, then you should lead them. It is your right and duty as their emperor.'

Constantine shook his head. 'I am a soldier, Longo, but I am no strategist. I will take my place on the wall and lead my men in battle. I will die defending this city if I must. But I am not the one to organize its defence. The one siege that I led was a disaster. My men were slaughtered and I barely escaped with my life. I do not wish to see the same happen to Constantinople.'

'And what of the megadux, Lucas Notaras?' Longo asked.

'Ah yes, Notaras,' Constantine sighed. 'He is brave, it is true, but also rash and headstrong. I fear he would sacrifice this city if it meant saving his own honour.'

'I too am a man of honour, Emperor.'

'Yes, I know, but you understand that sometimes true honour requires sacrificing one's pride for a greater good. I am not sure that Notaras does. And besides, he bears little love for the Latins. They will never follow him the way that they would follow you. You, Longo, are our best hope. God has sent you to us for a reason.'

'If it is truly your will, then I accept,' Longo said.

'It is settled then.' Constantine clapped Longo on the back. 'You will stay nearby, close to the walls. One of the Venetian merchants who fled the city left a fine house.

You shall have it. And once we are victorious, you shall have the island of Lesbos as your reward.'

'Thank you, Emperor.'

'Now come. Let us introduce my people to the new commander of Constantinople.'

Chapter 15

Mehmed stood outside his tent, watching the artillery flash in the pre-dawn light as he did each morning. He saw a cannonball strike the base of a tower along the Mesoteichion. The tower shook, then toppled forward, and Mehmed smiled. He had been to look at the walls the previous day, and the amount of damage was even greater than he had hoped. The outer wall along the Mesoteichion had been almost entirely reduced to rubble. The time to strike had come.

'Your Excellency seems pleased,' Halil remarked, stifling a yawn as he joined Mehmed. 'Is it good news, then, that you wish to discuss with me at this ungodly hour?'

'Very good news, Halil. Tomorrow night, under the cover of darkness, we will attack. You will distribute ladders and torches and make sure that the men have everything they need.'

'Do you think an attack wise, Your Excellency? Perhaps another week of bombardment, as we had agreed, would make success more certain. Patience is, after all, the principal virtue in siege warfare.'

'Patience will not feed my men, Halil,' Mehmed said. 'You know better than anyone how difficult it is to keep an army of this size in the field. I had thought that you would be happy to finish the siege early. It will mean an end to your ceaseless search for supplies.'

'I would be only too happy, your Excellency. But the walls of Constantinople, even weakened, will not be easy to take. We must be patient and allow your other plans to bear fruit. After all, think of what a defeat now might do to the morale of the army.'

'There will be no defeat,' Mehmed said curtly. 'I am not a fool or a child who you need lecture, Halil. The walls of Constantinople are only lightly manned at night. We will strike quickly, sending the bazibozouks north and south to distract the defence while the janissaries focus their attack near the Lycus, where the walls are weakest. They will overrun the defenders before they are able to rally more troops, and Constantinople will be ours.'

'I was here when your father besieged the city. The walls of Constantinople will not fall so easily, I fear,' Halil said. Then, after a long pause, he bowed and added: 'But may it be as you say, great Sultan. I defer to your greater wisdom.'

Mehmed frowned. He did not like Halil's tone, nor did he understand why his grand vizier was so eager to delay the attack.

'Excuse me, Sultan,' Ulu said as he appeared at Mehmed's side. 'Zaganos has come from the mines.'

'Very good, Ulu. Bring him to me.' Zaganos was Mehmed's chief miner. He appeared a few seconds later, his face and clothes black with dirt.

'We found something, Sultan,' Zaganos said. 'A tunnel near the gate of Caligaria, where you directed us to focus our efforts. It leads towards the walls, but it hits a dead end before it reaches them. It appears to have been filled in.'

'Take me to it,' Mehmed ordered. 'I shall see for myself.'

He followed Zaganos towards the rear of camp. Mehmed had ordered the tunnels to be started here, far out of sight of the walls of Constantinople. It had meant a long, laborious dig, but the tunnels were finally nearing the moat beyond the Blachernae walls. Still passing underneath the moat and walls would take several more weeks. It would be much easier if they could find one of the passages that Mehmed had read about in the Russian's description of Constantinople.

They reached the tunnel's entrance – a hole some five feet high, braced with wood and dug into a hillside. 'Are you sure you want to enter?' Zaganos asked. 'The mines aren't entirely stable.'

'I want to see,' Mehmed insisted.

'Very well. Mind your head, Sultan,' Zaganos said as he led the way into the tunnel. The passage was narrow, only slightly broader than Mehmed's shoulders. Frequent wooden braces held up the ceiling, and lamps hanging from some of the braces offered a weak, flickering light. The ceiling was black dirt, as were the walls halfway down. Below that, the rest of the walls and the floor were made of fine grey clay. As they walked, the ceiling grew lower until Mehmed had to walk bent at the waist. Zaganos, a powerfully built but short man, only had to duck his head.

'The tunnel we discovered was beneath where we have

been digging,' Zaganos explained as they walked. 'That is why we didn't find it earlier.' He pointed to a side tunnel as they passed. 'We've run side tunnels like this out to either side of the main tunnel, but we were digging too high. It was only luck that led us to the tunnel. One of our diggers was pushing a cart full of clay through one of these side tunnels when he fell through the floor, and into another tunnel below.' Zaganos stopped before a dark side passage. 'This is it.'

Zaganos took a lamp from the wall and led them into the side tunnel. After about fifteen feet there was an irregular hole in the floor, with a ladder leading down. 'I'll go first to light the way, Your Excellency,' Zaganos said. He clambered down the ladder, and Mehmed followed. When he reached the bottom, Mehmed found that he could stand up straight. The tunnel was at least seven feet tall. The walls were of stone, leading up to an arched ceiling, also of stone. The floor was dirt. The tunnel that the Russian had described was made entirely of stone – ceiling, walls and floor. This must be a different tunnel.

'This way towards the walls,' Zaganos said. They followed the tunnel for some thirty feet before it ended suddenly in a pile of rubble.

'Perhaps this is just a cave-in,' Mehmed suggested. 'Have you tried to dig around it?'

'We have, Your Excellency,' Zaganos said. 'There's no way through. The tunnel has been collapsed for as far as we can see.'

'And what about the other direction? Where does it lead?'

'The tunnel is collapsed in that direction, too. My guess is that somebody used charges to bring the tunnel down.

Somehow, the section that we're standing in escaped the destruction.'

'Well then, let us take advantage of our good fortune,' Mehmed said. 'There are other tunnels here, and we are going to find them. You will have as many men as you need, Zaganos. I want you to dig side passages off this tunnel, stretching the length of the walls if need be, until you find something.'

'I understand, Sultan.'

'Good. Start digging.'

Sofia held an old, tattered book in one hand and a candle in the other as she descended the steps from the palace kitchen to the storerooms below. She had come straight from the library after she had come across a book, written hundreds of years ago by a Russian named Alexandre. He wrote of tunnels beneath the walls, built when the new wall surrounding the Blachernae quarter had been put up in the seventh century. Even more intriguing, the Russian insisted that he himself had passed through one. He said that during the Latin conquest, the emperor had used a tunnel to escape from the city. For a small price, a cook who had served in the Imperial Palace during the conquest had shown the Russian the tunnel. The entrance, Alexandre wrote, was beneath the imperial palace itself.

At the rear of the storerooms she found a stairway leading down into the palace dungeons. She descended the steps, her candle shedding a feeble light in the subterranean gloom. The staircase opened into a large underground room. The floor glistened with what looked like guano. Sofia thought that she could hear the titter of bats overhead, but the light of her candle did not reach to the ceiling. Other than the bats, the dungeon was silent. No prisoners had been kept here for centuries.

Three passages led from the room, and after consulting the book, she took the one on the furthest right. It led through a series of low rooms, and then to a staircase, which led down to a lower level of the dungeon. At the bottom, the stairs opened on to a long hallway. The air was colder here and the walls glistened with moisture. A large rat, startled by the sudden light, scurried away from beneath Sofia's feet, and she inhaled sharply. As she exhaled, she could see her breath in the cold, heavy air.

She pulled her robe more closely around her and walked down the hallway. To her left and right were a series of old prison cells, their doors open. Sofia peered into them as she passed. Manacles hung from the walls, and in one cell she saw an old skeleton. Other than that, the rooms were empty. At the end of the hallway, past the cells, was a large door.

Sofia consulted the book again and then pushed the door open. It swung slowly inward, groaning on rusty hinges, and she stepped into a room cluttered with various instruments of torture, all covered with a thick layer of dust and cobwebs. Set in the wall to her right was a fire pit, and next to it hung branding irons and pincers. On her left was a rack, a device for slowly pulling victims apart until they would confess to anything. Other implements were scattered about: restraints, spikes and wicked-looking knives. She shuddered.

A large tapestry depicting the fall of Constantinople to the Latins in 1203 hung on the far wall. Various scenes from the siege ran around the edges of the tapestry, framing a larger image that depicted the Latin knights breaking through the sea walls and overrunning the city, looting churches and burning homes. There was no door leading from the room. She had reached a dead end.

Sofia moved closer to the tapestry. At the bottom was a series of scenes depicting the emperor's escape. There was the emperor, walking through the palace dungeon, then passing through a long tunnel and finally emerging on a hillside, with Constantinople burning in the distance. Sofia stepped back and paused to consider. Who would hang a tapestry in a torture chamber? She grabbed it and pulled the rotting cloth aside. Behind it was a door. Sofia pulled hard, but it did not budge. She set the book and her candle down and tried again. Nothing. She took one of the branding irons from the wall and wedged its head into the tiny space between the door and the jamb. With all her weight, she pushed on the handle of the iron, using it as a lever, and with a loud crack the door swung open. A cold draught of fresh air rushed from the dark tunnel beyond. The candle guttered and then grew steady again, burning brighter in the fresh air. Sofia picked it up and stepped into the dark passage.

The floor and walls were of rough-hewn stone, damp with moisture. Ahead of Sofia, the tunnel sloped gently downward, stretching away into blackness. She moved slowly forward, and as she walked the draught grew stronger. She had been walking for a few minutes when a particularly strong gust of air blew the candle out. Sofia passed her hand in front of her face and saw nothing; the darkness was absolute.

Panic rose up inside her and she had to force herself to breathe. The passage was straight; she could not get lost. All she had to do was turn and follow the wall, and it would lead her back to the dungeon. But first, she needed to find out where this tunnel led. For if it did indeed lead out of the city, then the Turks could just as easily use it to enter. Sofia took a deep breath and reached out to touch the wall. The stones were cold and slimy. She stepped forward, running her hand along the wall as she continued down the passage.

Eventually, the passage stopped descending and levelled out. Shortly after that, the wall she had been following disappeared from under her hand. She reached in front of her but felt nothing, only empty space. She moved back and found the corner where the wall turned sharply to the right. She turned and followed the wall, running her hand along the cold stones. The wall had begun to curve away from her to the right, and after only a few more steps, it again vanished. She stepped forward a few feet and the wall resumed. She had discovered a side passage. A few feet later, she found another, and then another after that. With excitement, she realized that she knew where she was. The Russian had written about this place: a sort of hub, a round room with passages leading in all directions. According to him, the hub lay halfway between the palace and the exit on the far side of the wall. One of these passages, then, should lead beyond the walls. But which one?

Sofia turned around and counted until she was back to the passage that she had come down. It would be easy to get lost: she imagined herself stumbling about from passage to passage in this darkness, alone, until she died. She wanted to press on, but first she needed to think. She closed her eyes, trying to clear her mind, when she heard a sound: a distant clank, as of metal banging against metal. Then nothing, only her breathing and the loud beating of her heart. Her every instinct told her to turn and run back to the palace, but she would be a fool, she told herself, to run because of a mere sound. Besides, if the Turks were there somewhere in the darkness, they would no doubt have torches, and their eyes would not be adjusted to the darkness. She would see them long before they saw her.

She bent down and placed the book at the mouth of the passage, with her candle on top of it. Then she turned and again followed the curving wall. She paused at every side passage she came to, listening hard for any sound, but heard nothing. The room was immense, and she quickly lost count of the number of side passages. She had begun to fear that she was moving in circles, when finally, she stopped before the mouth of a passage and felt a warm wind ruffle her hair. The draught of fresh air was steady. Somewhere ahead, this passage led to the outside world.

She had only gone a few feet down the tunnel when she heard the clanking again, louder and closer this time. She froze as the hairs on the back of her neck stood up. Sofia listened, holding her breath to hear better. The noise did not repeat itself, and she continued on her way.

The passage began to slope upward. She picked her way forward, pausing frequently to listen, but the clanking noise did not repeat itself. At every step she half-expected a band of Turks to spring forth, but there was nothing, only the continuing darkness. She estimated that she had walked some one hundred feet when she ran into something solid. The sudden impact surprised her, and she jumped backwards, dropping into a defensive crouch. The clanging noise was back, loud and right in front of her. She waited, not daring to breathe, as the clanging slowly faded. When it was gone, she crept forward, her hand stretched out before her. She felt something: a metal bar, stretching from the floor towards the ceiling. Next to it was another, and then another. She grabbed the bars with both of her hands and shook. The clanking returned. She knew now what had caused it: a locked gate, rattling in the wind.

The Russian writer had not mentioned a gate, which meant that either it had been added after his trip through the tunnel, or she was in a different passageway. She felt the bars of the gate again. They had been spaced to keep out men in armour, but she might be able to fit through. She pushed her head through first, and then, turning sideways and holding her breath tight, she just managed to squeeze through. She continued down the tunnel into the darkness. She could hear a new sound now, a deep, repeated booming, which sounded to her like the heartbeat of the earth. It took her a moment to realize what it was: cannons. Eventually, the sound faded away. She could only guess what that meant. Had she passed them? Was she moving away from some exit that she had missed in the dark? Despite her doubts, she kept walking. A weak light began to fill the tunnel, and in the distance she spied a pile of large stones blocking the way ahead.

Sofia hurried forward. It looked as if there had once been a small room here, with stairs leading upwards – just as the Russian had described the exit from the tunnel. She dropped to her knees and moved among the fallen rocks, looking for a way through. Finally, she found it: a narrow passageway that wormed its way up through the rubble to where she saw a thin sliver of blue sky. She wriggled into the passageway, but after several feet, her progress was blocked by a large stone. Sofia shoved against it, and the stone shifted slightly. She braced her legs against the sides of the passage and pushed harder. This time, the stone rolled aside, revealing the blue sky beyond.

Sofia pulled herself upwards until her head poked out of the tunnel. She was on the side of a small hill, hidden by tall grass. The heavy, flat stone that had covered the tunnel entrance lay to the side. She looked about, but saw nobody. She wriggled the rest of the way out of the hole and crouched in the grass. Before her, empty hills rolled away into the distance. To her right was the final stretch of the Golden Horn. She turned around and edged her way up the hill. When she reached the top, she dropped to her stomach in the grass. Only a hundred yards in front of her lay the Turkish encampment, stretching away far into the distance, all the way to the walls of Constantinople.

As the sun reached its zenith overhead Longo walked the walls alongside Dalmata, inspecting the damage wrought by the Turkish cannons. They started at the Blachernae wall, just north of the palace. This was the newest section of the wall, built in the seventh century to enclose the Blachernae quarter. Unlike the rest of the land wall, it was only a single wall, but it was thick and had held up well to the bombardment.

'The walls are stronger than I had imagined,' Longo said.

'Wait until you see the Mesoteichion,' Dalmata told him. 'It is where they have placed their largest cannons.'

They continued and crossed over on to the innermost of the Theodosian walls, built over one thousand years ago, in the early days of the Eastern Roman Empire. At first, the walls looked strong, but as they sloped down towards the Lycus river, gaps began to appear in the outer wall. By the time they reached the Mesoteichion – the area around where the Lycus river passed through the walls – the gaps had become the norm, and stretches of wall the exception. The inner wall was still more or less whole, but the outer wall had been almost completely destroyed. Longo stopped and looked down on the ramshackle stockade that had been built on the rubble. Dirt had been thrown on the debris to create a walkway, and then planks and sacks of earth used to create a low barrier. At the top, barrels filled with dirt formed a battlement, providing the defenders with some cover.

'The stockade cannot hold up to their cannons,' Dalmata said. 'The soldiers draw lots to see who will defend it each day, and who will rebuild it each night.'

Dalmata's words were punctuated by a tremendous boom. A moment later, the stockade below them exploded in a shower of dirt and splintered wood. As the dust settled, Longo saw that a gap five feet wide had been blown in it. In the middle of the gap, an enormous cannon-ball sat buried amidst the wreckage.

Longo shook his head. 'What was that?'

Dalmata pointed to where a huge cannon sat on the Turkish rampart some two hundred yards away. 'The men call it the Big Bastard,' he said. 'The Turks call it the Dragon. Either way, it's a monster. Nothing we build will stand up to it.'

A palace messenger approached them along the wall.

'Signor Giustiniani, I bring a message from the Princess Sofia,' the man said. He handed Longo a folded note. It read: *I have important information. It is urgent that I speak with you. Come to the palace, quickly. – Princess Sofia.*

'I must go,' Longo told Dalmata. 'We can continue this later.' Longo hurried to the palace, where Sofia's maid-servant guided him to the library. Longo found Sofia standing at a table examining a large map. 'Princess Sofia,' he said and bowed.

Sofia looked up from the map. 'Come, look at this,' she told him. Longo moved to stand beside her. She smelled of honeysuckle, and as she leaned forward over the map, she revealed the soft curves of her cleavage. Longo forced himself to look away to the ancient map spread out before him. It was a plan of subterranean Constantinople, detailing cisterns, sewers and underground tunnels. 'This is part of a series of surveys from the twelfth century,' she said. 'Do you see this underground chamber, where the many tunnels come together?'

'What of it?' Longo asked. The chamber in question looked to be near the wall. Tunnels radiated out from it towards the palace and to other parts of the city.

'The map is incomplete,' Sofia said. 'Look at the edge of the chamber here, where these lines are indented. Do you see the smudging? A tunnel has been erased.'

'Are you sure?' Longo asked.

Sofia smiled. 'I found the tunnel myself this morning. It leads out past the walls and beyond the Turkish army. The entrance to the tunnel is beneath this palace.'

'Have you told anyone of this? The emperor? Notaras?'

Sofia shook her head. 'No. Secrets are not easily kept

in this city. If our enemies find out about these tunnels, then we are lost.'

Longo looked back to the map. 'You are right. If the Turks make their way into these tunnels, then they will have access to the entire city.' He looked up from the map, and their eyes met. 'But why tell me and not the emperor?'

Sofia lowered her eyes. 'You are in command of the city's defences,' she said, and then looked back at Longo. 'And I trust you.'

Longo stared into her hazel eyes. 'I will not disappoint you,' he told her. From the doorway the maidservant coughed, and Longo straightened and looked back to the map. 'I will have my men destroy the tunnel. Is it the only one that leads under the walls?'

'It is the only one that I have found,' Sofia said. 'There could be others.'

'Let us hope not. In the meantime, I need to see this tunnel as soon as possible. Can you take me to it?'

'Not now,' Sofia replied, lowering her voice. 'We would draw unwanted attention to the tunnels and ourselves. I do not wish to fuel idle gossip. Meet me at midnight, outside my quarters, and make sure you are not seen.'

Longo consulted with Constantine until late that night. He suspected that more than information on how the siege was progressing, the emperor simply wanted company. He did not blame Constantine. The emperor was battling to prevent the end of an empire that had lasted more than a thousand years.

Longo left the emperor's quarters near midnight but did not leave the palace. Instead, he made his way to Sofia's apartments, sticking close to the shadows. The palace was all but empty at this hour, and he saw no one until he reached Sofia's quarters. She was at the door, waiting for him.

'Come,' she whispered. 'Follow me.' She led him into her apartments. They passed from the waiting room into her bedroom, where Sofia pressed a tile on the wall and a portion of it swung open, revealing a hidden passage. She took a candle and stepped into the darkness. 'This way. We can reach the kitchens without being seen.'

She closed the door behind him. The passage was narrow, and the tiny light of the candle only reached a few feet in front of them. 'I had not heard of these tunnels,' Longo whispered as they walked. 'Are they for servants? Who else knows of them?'

'I do not know why they were originally built,' Sofia said. 'But I have never seen another person in them. I found them as a child.'

'Do they run throughout the palace?'

Sofia nodded. 'Shh,' she added, dropping her voice even lower. 'We must not talk until we reach the kitchen. The walls are thin here. We might be overheard.' They walked on in silence; the only sound the quiet scuffing of their feet. The tunnel branched several times, but Sofia moved on without hesitation. They went down two tight spiral staircases, and then came to a dead end. A tiny spyhole in the wall before them glowed red from the light outside. Sofia put her eye to it. 'We are in luck. No one is here,' she whispered. 'Come. We must hurry before someone returns.'

She pushed on a hidden catch and then pulled. The wall swung open towards them, and the dim red light of a banked fire lit the passage. They stepped out into a little-used corner of the kitchen. Knives and pots hung everywhere, and on the opposite wall was a huge fireplace – twenty feet wide and ten deep – where a banked fire smouldered. Sofia pointed to a torch in a bracket on the wall beside the fireplace.

Longo took the torch, and they hurried through the kitchen to a stairwell leading down to the storage area, where barrels and sacks of grain were stacked to the ceiling. Sofia led Longo to another staircase, and they descended into the damp darkness of the dungeons.

'We can talk freely now,' Sofia said as she led Longo into the high-ceilinged entrance to the dungeons. 'No one will hear us down here.'

'What is this place?'

'These were the palace dungeons, but they have been abandoned for many years now,' Sofia answered as she led Longo to the right down a long passage. 'Now only bones remain.'

They entered another room, startling a group of bats. The bats swooped down from the ceiling, squeaking shrilly and flapping about their heads. Sofia raised her arms to protect her head, and Longo put an arm around her, pulling her close as he waved the torch above them to keep the bats away. When the last of the bats had disappeared, Sofia stiffened and stepped away. Longo could still feel the warmth of her body beside him. They stood still for a second, but the moment passed. She turned and led the way to another stairwell.

'You came all this way by yourself?' Longo asked as they descended. 'In the dark?'

'Does that surprise you?'

'Most ladies are not overly fond of dark dungeons, or

bats for that matter,' Longo said, looking around him. 'In fact, most men would hesitate to come here alone. There is something unnerving about this place.'

'Well then, you are lucky to have me to protect you,' Sofia said with a smile as they came to the end of the hall and stepped into the old torture chamber. Sofia went to the far side of the room, where she had rehung the tapestry as best she could. She pulled it aside and tugged the door open. 'I fear the fall of Constantinople more than bats or darkness.'

'You seem to fear very little, Princess.'

'I fear those things that I cannot control,' she said as she led him into the tunnel. 'The success of our men in battle, the future of our empire, even my own fate. Princess is a pretty title, but I would gladly trade it for a chance to choose my own destiny, to do as I wished, love who I . . .' she cut herself short.

Longo stopped. 'You do not love the megadux, then?'

Sofia turned to look at Longo. 'No, I do not love him.' She moved on ahead, her face lost in the shadows. 'But I speak too much,' she said. 'I am a princess. I cannot choose who I marry.'

They walked in silence until they came to the large, round chamber with tunnels branching out from it. Sofia went from tunnel to tunnel, feeling for the telltale gust of wind that indicated the tunnel led to the outside. 'Do you know where these other tunnels lead?' Longo asked.

'According to the map, they lead to other points in the city,' Sofia replied. 'They are all blocked up now, I suspect, or else the tunnel outside the city would have been discovered long ago.' She stopped before one of the side passages; a gentle breeze was ruffling her hair. 'Come. This is it.'

They did not walk far before they came to the gate blocking the tunnel. 'It is locked,' Sofia said. 'I was able to squeeze through, but I'm afraid that this is as far as you will be able to go.'

'Perhaps,' Longo said, examining the rusty chain and lock. 'Step aside, Princess.' He handed Sofia the torch, and then drew his sword and struck hard at the chain. Sparks flew, and the chain dropped to the ground. The gate swung open, screeching on protesting hinges. 'After you,' he gestured, and they continued down the tunnel.

The ground was sloping upward now, and the torch burned brighter in the fresher air. The boom of the cannons grew louder and then faded again as they walked. 'The Turks,' Sofia said suddenly. 'I heard that you were one of them once, a janissary. What are they like?'

'Ordinary men, for the most part,' Longo said. 'It is not an easy life, that of the janissary. They are taken from their parents as children and forced to serve the sultan. They either learn to love him or to hate him.'

'And you hate him?'

'The janissaries killed my family when I was only a child. I have searched for the man who killed them all my life. For a long time my hatred of him was all that I had.' They both fell silent until they came to the jumble of rocks at the end of the tunnel.

'This is it,' Sofia said. 'The exit has been destroyed, but there is a passage through the rocks, here. I did my best to cover the exit.' Crouching down, Longo could see a sliver of starlit sky at the other end of a narrow passage. He handed the torch to Sofia.

'Go back and tell my men, William and Tristo, what you have found,' he told her. 'If there is no messenger you can trust, then go yourself. Tell them to bring men to guard the tunnel and explosives to destroy it. If I'm not back by noon, then they are to destroy the tunnel.'

'Where are you going?'

'Out there,' Longo said. 'The Turks will not be content to bombard the walls forever. I will never have a better chance to find out what else they are up to.'

'That is mad!' Sofia protested. 'They'll kill you!'

'As you said, I was a janissary once,' Longo told her. 'I know my way around a Turkish camp.'

'Be careful, then.'

'You too, Sofia. And hurry.'

Sofia nodded, but did not move. They stood close together, Longo staring into her eyes. He thought he saw fear there, and love. Finally, Sofia turned to go, then stopped. 'About that night in Corsica . . .' she said, turning to face Longo. 'Perhaps it was wrong, but I do not regret it.'

'Nor do I,' he replied. He stepped forward and kissed her. After a brief pause, she pressed herself against him, and he put his arms around him. Her mouth opened, and Longo felt her tongue slide against his. He pulled her more tightly to him. Finally, she pulled away.

'If I were free to love . . .' she began, but then hesitated. The torch trembled in her hand, and her eyes were wide and shining.

'No one can tell you who to love,' Longo said softly.

Sofia nodded and took a step closer to Longo. 'I know,' she whispered. She kissed him again, quickly, and then, before he could reply, she turned and was gone.

Dawn was still at least three hours away when Longo emerged from the tunnel and on to the hillside beyond the Turkish camp. The darkness was intense, and he slipped unseen up to one of the sentries and dispatched him silently, covering his mouth as he slipped a dagger between his ribs. Longo donned the dead janissary's armour and headed into the Turkish camp, passing hundreds of grazing mules and lowing cattle before entering amongst the tents.

Despite the early hour there was a surprising amount of activity. On the outskirts he saw dozens of carpenters busy making ladders, bow makers stringing weapons and blacksmiths at their forges. As he passed amongst the tents of the janissaries, Longo heard all around him the quiet rasp of weapons being sharpened. He saw many men seated around fires, eating as they prepared their weapons and armour. Here and there he heard the excited clamour of a game of dice.

The janissaries grouped their tents by *orta*, or battalion, and at the centre of each *orta* was a large mess tent that bore the battalion's emblem. Longo walked through the tents until he came to a symbol that he knew well – the double-bladed sword of Ali, embroidered in red on a tent from which flew a triangular green flag. It was the stand-ard of one of the *solak* imperial guard units from Edirne, the elite amongst the janissaries. At the nearest fire several battle-hardened men were eating, using stiff flatbread to scoop a pilaf of boiled wheat and butter from a common pot. Longo took a seat among them, broke off a piece of bread and gestured for someone to pass the food. One of the janissaries began to pass the pot, but another, grey-haired man stopped him. The older man wore a vest lined with fox fur, the mark of a battalion commander, and the double-bladed sword emblem was tattooed on his shoulder. He squinted at Longo. 'I don't recognize you,' he said at last, in Turkish.

'I'm from one of the Salonika *orta*,' Longo explained in perfect Turkish.

'Then why don't you go back there.' It was not a question.

Longo smiled. 'I was a little too lucky at dice tonight,' he said and patted his full purse. 'I'm afraid I'm not exactly welcome in my *orta*. The Saloniki are not good losers.' Longo was taking a risk. While the rule was rarely enforced, gambling was officially forbidden amongst the janissary. The *orta* commander could have Longo caned on the soles of his feet for admitting to luck at dice.

The old janissary's eyes moved from Longo's face to his fat purse, and then the man grinned. 'Those coins of yours sound like a burden. We'd be happy to relieve you of them,' the janissary said. He took out a pair of dice and rattled them in his hand. 'Give us a chance to win some of your purse, and you will be welcome at our fire.'

'Very well,' Longo said. He reached into his purse and then tossed a golden asper before him. 'But I have to warn you: I've been very lucky.'

The old janissary grinned, and the other janissaries chuckled. 'Luck never lasts forever,' the old janissary said, and threw the dice. They landed double sixes – a perfect first roll. Longo went on to lose the game, and after that, he lost repeatedly. He suspected the dice were loaded, but he was happy to lose. Winning made the janissaries more talkative. After a dozen games, they were slapping Longo on the back and treating him like one of their own.

'Easy come, easy go,' Longo said, fingering his now nearly empty purse. 'I suppose I'll have to wait until the city falls to refill it. I hear Constantinople is full of gold.'

'And women,' the janissary next to Longo leered.

'Be the first over the wall, and you will have a thousand such purses,' the old janissary, Qayi, said. 'Not that you will get the chance. I expect the supreme *aga*, Ulu, will claim the prize. I, for one, would not stand in his way.'

'Nor would I,' Longo agreed. He sighed as another bad roll cost him the last contents of his purse. 'I only wish that we could attack now. I could use some of the fabled wealth of Constantinople.'

'Patience, my young friend,' Qayi said. 'Allah willing, the city will fall to us tomorrow night, and you will fill your purse with the wealth of Constantinople. And then,' he added with a smile, 'you can lose it to us again at dice.'

'Agreed,' Longo said. 'After all, luck never lasts forever.'

Qayi chuckled, and then the smile dropped from his face. He scooped up the dice and stood suddenly. The other janissaries followed suit, as did Longo. Walking towards them, not twenty feet away, was Ulu. He had not yet seen Longo. The men saluted as Ulu approached, and Longo took the opportunity to slip quietly away from the fire and into the darkness. As he crept away, he could hear Ulu's deep voice behind him. 'Qayi, you and your men should get some rest. Your regiment will have the honour of leading the charge on the stockade tomorrow night.'

If Ulu saw him, he was lost. Longo crept away. He had more business outside the walls before the sun rose.

*

While Longo was entering the Turkish camp, Sofia returned to her room through the secret passage from the kitchen. She did not trust anyone but herself to deliver the message to William and Tristo. She threw on a long, hooded cloak and buckled a sword around her waist. Then she quietly opened the door to her apartments and slipped out into the dark hallway. She froze instantly, her hand on her sword. A man was standing in the corridor outside her room. He stepped out of the shadows. It was Notaras.

'Megadux, what are you doing here?' Sofia asked.

'I might well ask the same of you, Princess,' Notaras replied. 'I heard a nasty rumour that Signor Giustiniani had entered your apartments and not left.' He looked past her into her apartments. 'I am relieved to see that it does not appear to be true.'

'Of course not!' Sofia said, feigning outrage. She was glad that the shadows hid her scarlet cheeks.

'Still, you will not mind if I take a quick look about your apartments?' Notaras asked.

'There is no man in my quarters,' Sofia replied. 'I should hope that my word will be enough, but you may do as you wish, Megadux.'

'Your word will be quite enough, of course,' Notaras said, although he took one last glance into her room before Sofia shut the door. 'Still, leaving the palace in the early morning hours is hardly proper behaviour for a princess.'

'And is that what you wish for me to be, Notaras? Proper?'

'No, Sofia,' Notaras said. 'But I do wish for you to be careful. You are my betrothed, and my reputation is just as much at stake as yours.'

'Surely you do not suspect me of carrying on some sordid affair by night. You know me better than that.'

'Yes, Princess, I know you very well indeed,' Notaras said. Sofia felt his sharp gaze burrow into her and looked away. 'But not all the citizens of Constantinople know you as well as I do. You must be careful, Sofia. Come, at least let me escort you to wherever you are going.'

'Thank you, Notaras, but I can find my own way. I have business that does not concern you.'

'At this hour? What kind of business could that be?'

'I have an important message to deliver. Trust me, Notaras. The safety of Constantinople depends on it.'

'I do trust you, Sofia,' Notaras replied. 'But you must trust me in turn. Have I ever betrayed your trust? Tell me what you are doing, and I will help as I can.'

Sofia gave Notaras a long look. Perhaps he was right; perhaps she was wrong not to trust him. He was arrogant and prideful, but he would fight to the death for his city.

'Very well, Notaras,' she said. 'I have discovered a tunnel that leads from beneath the palace to beyond the walls. I have told no one but Signor Giustiniani. As the head of the defence, I thought he should be the first to know. He is outside the walls even now, spying in the Turkish camp. I am going to tell his men so that they may prepare to destroy the tunnel.'

'And Signor Giustiniani did not see fit to inform me of this?' Notaras demanded.

'He has just learned of it himself, Notaras. And I advised him to keep quiet. You of all people should know how difficult it is to keep a secret in this city.'

'You are right. Thank you for telling me, Sofia. You

will see that your trust is well placed. Allow me to deliver this message for you. The city streets are no place for a woman at this time of night.'

'I will deliver the message, Notaras, but you may escort me,' Sofia said. 'After all, it appears that I could not stop you from following me even if I wished to.'

'I watch over you only to protect you, Sofia.'

'I can protect myself, Notaras,' Sofia replied, placing her hand on the hilt of her sword. 'Now come. Dawn is close. We must hurry.'

As Longo reached the Turkish ramparts he could hear a mounting commotion coming from the camp behind him. On his way through the camp he had stolen a brand from an untended fire and set a dozen of the gunners' tents ablaze. The fire was spreading quickly amongst the closely pitched tents. All along the ramparts the gun crews had ceased firing and had turned to watch. Some were already leaving their posts to try to put out the flames. Longo stepped up on to the platform where the Dragon stood. The cannon was huge: over twenty feet long and taller than he was. A dozen crewmen stood motionless beside it, gazing at the distant blaze. 'Well, what are you waiting for?' Longo snapped at them. 'Those are your tents on fire, men. Get down there and save them!'

The gunners responded immediately, rushing to save their possessions. Longo watched them go, then he stepped closer to the Dragon, looking for a way to disable it. He ran his hand down the long barrel to the mouth, where the cannonballs were loaded. Perhaps he could plug it, but with what? He turned and went to the back of the cannon. The powder chamber – a smaller barrel some three feet across that was connected to the rest of the barrel by a hinge – was swung open. If he could find some way to damage or remove the powder chamber, then the cannon would be useless. But again, how?

He stepped back and leaned against a wooden barrel, looking about him for something to use. He saw nothing promising: a shovel, several huge cannonballs, the winch for loading them, a bucket with a slow match burning in it, and these barrels. Wait – not just barrels, barrels of gunpowder. Longo had an idea.

Back in the camp, the gunners had begun to pull the intact tents away from the blaze, creating an empty space around the fire. It would burn out soon enough, and then they would return. Longo put his back against one of the heavy barrels of gunpowder and pushed with his legs, toppling it. He rolled the barrel forward until it rested against the side of the Dragon. He rolled another barrel over to the dragon, and then another. He looked back to the camp. The fire was dwindling and men were headed his way. Longo took up the shovel and prised the lid off one of the barrels, spilling black gunpowder on to the ground. He scooped up a double-handful and poured out a trail of gunpowder, leading several feet away. Longo took up the slow match and was just about to light the gunpowder trail when he heard a voice behind him: 'Hey, you! What're you doing?'

Longo turned to find a short, squat man facing him. He was clearly not Turkish. The man's eyes went from the slow match in Longo's hand to the trail of gunpowder leading to the three barrels. His eyes were wide by the time they came to rest on Longo's face. 'Don't you dare,' he growled. 'I'll crucify you.'

Longo did not reply. He touched the slow match to the powder and sprinted down from the rampart and back towards the Turkish camp. The man hesitated for a second and then hurled himself after Longo. Longo had only made it a few steps from the rampart when the gunpowder blew. The deafening explosion knocked him flat on his face, while dirt and spent powder rained down around him.

Longo picked himself up and dusted himself off. Behind him, the frame that had held up the Dragon had been blown to pieces. The cannon lay on the ground, its barrel bent inward in the middle. The powder chamber was nowhere to be seen. It had been blown clean off. The Dragon would roar no more.

At the bottom of the rampart, a few feet away from him, the stubby man lay flat on his back, groaning. All around, men were arriving, rushing towards the smouldering ruins of the Dragon. 'Quick!' Longo yelled at them. 'Get water! And a doctor!' He was dressed as a janissary, and the men obeyed automatically. As they hurried off, Longo walked after them and on through the camp. Men rushed past him to the ramparts, but no one stopped him.

Chapter 16

William paced back and forth at the end of the tunnel. He and twelve of Longo's best men had been waiting there for hours, guarding the tunnel while Longo was gone. The other men, veterans all, lounged about playing dice or even napping, but William could not hold still. He was no longer a boy now, but a man of nineteen, old enough to do more than keep watch in this tunnel. He wanted to be out there with Longo. He glanced at the light that filtered in through the rubble that blocked the tunnel's exit. It was growing brighter by the minute. 'It will be dawn soon,' William said to no one in particular.

'Don't worry yourself, William,' a thin, short man named Benito said from where he sat leaning against the wall of the tunnel. 'Longo's a tough nut. He'll be all right.'

William nodded and kept pacing, his eyes on the light shining into the tunnel. Then the light disappeared and Longo's voice called out in greeting from beyond the rubble. A few seconds later his head poked out from the narrow passage. His hair and face were blackened as if he had rubbed soot all over himself.

'What happened to you?' William asked.

Longo clambered out into the tunnel, then rubbed his cheek and examined his now blackened hand. 'Gunpowder,' he said. 'I paid a visit to the Dragon. It won't fire again.'

'And did you learn anything?'

'The Turks are going to attack tonight,' Longo replied. 'We have much to do. Are you ready to destroy the tunnel?'

William shook his head. 'We need Tristo to set the charges, and he's nowhere to be found.'

'Go to Croton's tavern, just south of the Turkish Quarter. It's Tristo's home from home in Constantinople. Bring him back quickly. I want this passage destroyed before noon.'

William went to the palace stables and took two horses. He reached Croton's before the sun had climbed above the city walls. The tavern was a two-storey building, garlanded with banners of red silk. William tied up the horses and then stepped over a drunken soldier sleeping in the doorway and into the tavern. Two long tables lined with drunken men dominated the dim interior, but Croton's was clearly more than just a tavern. In the corner to William's right, a crowd had gathered around a trio of tables where men were busy gambling at dice. To his left, men sat on the floor, smoking at hookahs. And everywhere, scantily clad, heavily made-up women milled about, offering their favours to the clientele, for a price.

'You're a young one, aren't you,' said a busty prostitute with long black hair in curls. 'Come for a good time?'

'I'm looking for my friend, Tristo.'

'Oh, that one,' the woman chuckled. 'He's been lucky at dice. He just went upstairs. First door on your left.'

William nodded his thanks. He climbed the stairs and pounded on the locked door. 'Go away! I'm busy!' Tristo bellowed from within.

'Longo needs you at the palace!' William shouted back. 'It's important!'

A moment later, the door opened a crack, and Tristo's face appeared. 'Can it wait five minutes?' he asked. William shook his head. 'Curse it!' Tristo exclaimed and slammed the door closed. When he opened it again a moment later, he was buckling on his sword belt. A plump, naked woman lounged on the bed behind him.

'Sorry, love, duty calls,' Tristo told her. He caught William's disapproving glare and spread his hands. 'What? You can play the saint while our wives are back on Chios, but I don't have it in me. Besides, she reminds me of Maria. That means I'm faithful at heart.' William laughed. Shaking his head, he led the way down the stairs.

He was on the final step when he stopped short. A man had just entered the brothel, and there was something familiar about his darkly tanned face. The man stopped just inside the doorway and returned William's stare. It was Carlos, the Spanish assassin that had tried to kill both Longo and William in Genoa.

'Mother of God, I don't believe it,' William whispered to himself. 'He's alive.' He had no sooner spoken than the assassin turned and ran. 'Come on, Tristo!' William yelled, drawing his sword and running after the Spaniard. 'We've got to catch him!' Tristo followed, running as fast as his bulk would allow. William was beginning to gain on the Spaniard when he turned the corner ahead. William rounded the corner after him and stopped. He found himself standing before a street market. Carts full of goods were set up all along either side of the street, and several dozen women and children milled about in the space between. His quarry had disappeared amidst the crowd.

'What now?' Tristo huffed as he caught up to William.

William caught a glimpse of the Spaniard, dodging through the crowd twenty yards ahead. 'There!' he shouted. 'You take the right, I'll take the left.' They split up, and William pushed his way through the crowd on the left-hand side of the street. He was about halfway through the market when he caught the glimmer of a blade out of the corner of his eye. He ducked and rolled just in time as a sword flashed over his head. William sprang to his feet to see the Spaniard hurrying away into the crowd. 'Tristo! Over here!' William shouted as he gave chase.

Ahead of him, the assassin slipped out of the crowd and turned into a narrow alleyway between two buildings. William followed. After only twenty feet the passage ended at a tall wall, but there was no sign of Carlos. There were no doors, nor even any windows in either of the buildings that formed the sides of the passage. There was no way out at all, yet the Spaniard was gone.

Seconds later, Tristo arrived. 'Where did he go?' he panted.

'I don't know.'

'Who was he?'

'The assassin that Paolo Grimaldi hired to kill Longo and me,' William answered. 'Apparently, he has come to finish the job.'

'Well, lucky for him then that he got away.'

'Lucky for him, and bad for us,' William agreed. 'Now come on. We've wasted enough time already.'

Longo was standing on the inner wall at the military gate of Saint Romanus, overseeing the further reinforcement of the Mesoteichion stockade, when he saw William hurrying along the wall towards him. Not ten minutes earlier, Longo had heard the muted rumbling as the charges had gone off, destroying the tunnel beneath the walls. William looked to have come straight from the destruction of the tunnel. He had cleaned his face and hands, but the rest of him was covered in a thick layer of grey stone dust.

'Well met, William,' Longo said. 'The tunnel has been destroyed?'

'Yes,' William replied. 'We brought down the entire stretch from just past the wall to the tunnel's exit.'

'I heard the explosion from up here,' Longo said. 'It caused a great stir in the Turkish camp. Even our own men were unnerved. I heard two Greeks arguing over whether thunder on a clear day was a good or bad omen.'

'And what did they decide?'

Longo smiled. 'I am happy to report that it is a good omen. It means that God is on our side.' A grimace replaced his smile. 'And we shall have need of Him tonight when the Turks attack. It will be all we can do to hold the wall.' Longo glanced up at the sun, estimating the time. 'I must go to the palace to meet with the other commanders.'

'Wait,' William said. 'The Spanish assassin that Paolo sent to kill you lives. Tristo and I saw him while returning to the palace.'

'So much for good omens,' Longo said. He looked again at the sun. 'Nothing can be done now. I must get to the palace. William, stay and watch over the men while I am gone. And watch yourself. The assassin is here for you, too.'

When Longo had arrived at the palace he allowed the other commanders to gather in the council room while he explained his plans to the emperor. When all were present, the two men went to the room, pausing at the closed door before entering. Longo gestured for the emperor to be quiet, and they both put their ears to the door. 'But he's a Latin!' they heard an angry voice say. Longo thought it might be Notaras. 'The city should be commanded by a Roman.'

'He knows more about the Turks than the rest of you combined. He fought at Sofia and Kossova, and . . .'

Another voice, perhaps Archbishop Leonard's, cut him off: 'He knows a bit too much about the Turks, if you ask me. I hear he was raised a janissary. How can we trust him?'

Constantine frowned, looking ready to storm into the room. Longo placed a hand on his shoulder and held him back. 'Let me deal with them,' he said. 'I will report to you after the meeting.' Constantine nodded, and Longo entered the room alone. Notaras was at the head of a large table around which stood Archbishop Leonard, Dalmata, the Venetian bailiff Minotto and a dozen other commanders. The men fell abruptly silent.

'Thank you for coming,' Longo began. 'I know that there are some of you who doubt Constantine's wisdom in appointing me commander. I myself asked him to take charge of the city's defences, but he refused. He has given me the command, and I will not fail him.' He paused, and no one interrupted him. That was a good sign. 'I understand your concerns. I am not a Roman; it is true. But I am Christian, as are you. I will organize the defence, but it is you who must save this city. I cannot do it alone. None of us can. We must fight together, Romans, Venetians, Genoese and even Turks. All who call this city home must defend it as brothers. Are we agreed?'

They all nodded or added their murmured assent. 'Good, then we may begin,' Longo said. 'I have learned that the Turks will attack this very night, as soon as darkness falls.'

'Are you certain?' Notaras asked. 'I have heard nothing of this.'

'I assure you, my information is reliable,' Longo told him. He was reluctant to reveal how he knew of the Turks' plans. The tunnel had been destroyed, but there might be others. The fewer who knew about them, the better.

'What if this information is a ruse?' Notaras insisted.

'A night keeping watch will do our men no harm,' Longo replied. 'The Turks are counting on the element of surprise to overwhelm us. We must be ready for them.' The megadux nodded his head in consent, and Longo continued. 'We will place the majority of our forces along the land walls, keeping only enough men on the sea walls to call for help in the event of trouble. Archbishop Leonard, you will join the Langasco brothers in defending the walls where they run down into the Golden Horn. Minotto, you will defend the Imperial Palace and the Blachernae walls.'

'He spends enough time there, anyway. He's more

interested in courting the palace ladies than fighting, if you ask me,' sniggered one of the Bocchiardo brothers, Troilo. He and his brothers, Paolo and Antonio, had arrived from Genoa several weeks before Longo. Longo had known and respected them for years, but he did not appreciate the interruption. He gave Troilo a cold stare.

Minotto ignored Troilo. 'I will be happy to take the post,' he said.

'Good,' Longo said. 'Bocchiardo brothers, you and your men will take up positions south of Minotto, where the Blachernae and Theodosian walls meet. You will share command of the Blachernae with Minotto.'

'With that Venetian prig?' Troilo objected. 'My men won't fight alongside Venetians!'

'I will have your hide for that,' Minotto said, his hand moving to his sword. 'I demand satisfaction!'

'Silence!' Longo shouted. He drew his sword and laid it on the table. 'I will not have bickering amongst you,' he said, his voice quiet and hard. 'We are here to fight the Turks, not one another. If any of you seek satisfaction, then I will offer it to you myself. Is that understood?' Troilo nodded. 'Minotto?' After a pause, the Venetian nodded.

'Good,' Longo continued. 'Theophilus Palaelogus will command the wall south of the Lycus river to the Pegae Gate. Filippo Contarini and his Venetians will defend the walls from the Pegae Gate to the Golden Gate, which Manuel and his men have volunteered to defend. The Protostrator, Demetrius Cantacuzenus, will defend the southernmost portion of the wall. The Venetians will have command of the fleet and the Golden Horn. The sea walls will be manned by Greek monks and any remaining forces in the city.' Longo was pleased to see each of the commanders nod as he spoke his name. None questioned their assignments. 'My men and I will be stationed south of the Bocchiardo brothers, with the emperor at the Mesoteichion. Prince Orhan and the Turkish troops will join us there.'

'But they are infidels,' Archbishop Leonard protested. 'You cannot use Turks to defend our most vulnerable point. They will betray us to the enemy.' Several other men at the table nodded agreement. Orhan, a Turkish prince who had taken shelter in Constantinople to avoid death at the hands of Mehmed, opened his mouth to speak, but Longo gestured for him to remain silent.

'There are Christians, even Greeks, fighting in the Turkish army. I see no reason why Turks should not fight in ours,' Longo said. 'Constantinople is their home, too, and Orhan's men are some of our strongest fighters. We need their help on the walls.'

'Does the Union mean nothing then?' Leonard asked. 'The pope would never stand for this.'

'The pope is not here, nor are his men. In their absence, we need all the help we can get,' Notaras said firmly. Longo was surprised by Notaras's support. The megadux turned to Longo. 'And what of my post?'

'You will command a reserve force, stationed where the Blachernae wall meets the Theodosian walls. You will offer support wherever there is trouble.'

'My place is on the walls, not cowering behind them,' Notaras said.

'Do not mistake me, Notaras,' Longo said. 'Your post will see no lack of danger. You will be free to seek out battle wherever it offers itself, and you will always find yourself at the centre of the worst fighting. I have offered you this post because I know of your courage and skill as a warrior.'

'If the post is so glorious, then perhaps you should take it.'

'I would be happy to, Megadux, but there is another consideration. I understand that you possess a number of mobile cannons. They will prove vital in turning back the Turks if the wall is breached. I did not think that you would wish for someone else to command your artillery, but if you are willing, then I will gladly take command of the reserve force.'

'No, that will not be necessary,' Notaras said. 'But understand that only I will decide when and how my men and cannons are deployed. I will fight beside you, Signor Giustiniani, but I will not fight under you.'

'So long as you fight, Megadux, I ask for nothing more.' Longo looked around the table, pausing at each of the men in turn. 'I do not ask any of you to fight for me. If you seek a man to fight for, then fight for the emperor.' Longo's gazed settled at last on Notaras. 'And if you do not wish to fight for any man,' Longo concluded, 'then fight for Constantinople.'

'Hear, hear,' Minotto agreed, and one by one, each of the men added their assent. All eyes turned to Notaras, who alone of the men had remained aloof.

'For Constantinople,' he said and nodded his head curtly.

'Very well, then,' Longo said. 'Have your men at the walls well before sunset. Until the fighting starts, keep them busy repairing the walls, making arrows or building mantelets. When the attack comes, we will regret every second wasted. Are there any questions?' No one spoke.

'Good. Then take your posts, and may God protect you all.'

Longo, William and Tristo stood atop the stockade, their battle armour glinting in the torchlight. The sun had long since set and the last colour faded from the sky, swallowed up by inky darkness. Longo watched the Turkish camp for signs of the impending attack, but saw nothing unusual. Cooking fires glimmered in the distance, and the cannons continued to roar.

Longo heard a commotion behind him and turned to see the emperor approaching, dressed in heavy plate armour. 'Greetings, Signor Giustiniani,' Constantine said. He pointed to the distant Turkish camp. 'All looks calm. Perhaps there will be no attack.'

'I hope that you are right,' Longo said. He looked at the numerous holes blasted in the stockade during the day's bombardment and then at the men grouped behind the barrier. Even with Prince Orhan's troops and most of Constantine's personal guard, Longo had less than three thousand men to defend the entire Mesoteichion against at least ten times as many Turks. 'If there is a battle,' he said. 'Then we shall be hard pressed.'

'God will protect us. He will not let the Empire of the Romans fall,' Constantine said. 'I must inspect the other troops. God be with you, Signor Giustiniani.'

The Turkish bombardment stopped soon after the emperor had departed. As the boom of the last gun faded, silence settled over the walls for the first time in weeks. Men rushed forward to place mantelets – portable wooden barriers – across the openings that the cannons had made. Atop the stockade, Longo peered into the darkness. He

317

saw nothing, but the cannons would be quiet for only one reason. 'They're coming,' he said to William and Tristo. 'Go to your posts.' Longo drew his sword and held it aloft. Behind him, he heard the rasp of hundreds of swords being drawn. 'Ready, men!' he shouted.

From the north and south, Longo could now hear the dull roar of fighting elsewhere along the walls, but still he saw nothing in the darkness before him. Then a flare lit the sky over the stockade, then another and another. Beneath their red glare an onrushing horde of janissaries was visible only a hundred yards away, swarming across the fosse and towards the stockade. Ten thousand strong, they let loose a blood-curdling mass scream as the light hit them, and their cry of *Allah! Allah! Allah!* was soon joined by the heavy beat of drums and the eerie wail of bagpipes. It seemed to Longo as if the mouth of hell had opened up before him, and the Turks, lit red by the flares, were screaming demons.

As the Turks scrambled up the far side of the fosse, an arrow thumped into the stockade before Longo. Another slammed into the chest of the soldier beside him, and he dropped, screaming in pain. 'Down, men!' Longo yelled as he crouched behind the stockade, his shield raised over his head. The compact bows of the janissary, made of wood, horn and tendon, could fire arrows with enough velocity to punch through even plate armour. Arrows continued to thud into the stockade and skitter off Longo's shield, and then they stopped. The first Turks had reached the wall. 'Up men!' Longo roared. 'For Constantinople! God is with us!'

Turks placed ladders against the stockade in front of Longo and began to swarm up them, while others threw grappling hooks over the wall and tried to pull down the wooden face of the stockade. Longo moved about the wall, kicking over ladders and cutting the ropes from the grappling hooks. Although the Turks greatly outnumbered them, the defenders were holding up well. Here and there Turks managed to reach the top of the wall, but they were quickly dispatched. The real fighting was taking place in the gaps that had been blasted in the stockade. The janissaries' greater numbers were of no help in the narrow gaps, where the thicker armour of the Christian forces gave them a decided advantage. The fighting was furious, but all down the line the stockade appeared to be holding. Still, for every janissary that was killed there were five more to take his place, and the fury of the attack did not slacken. As the moon crawled across the sky, the Turkish dead piled up before the stockade, until the janissaries could reach the top by climbing upon their fallen comrades.

Longo spotted several janissaries with torches making their way across the fosse, and soon a small portion of the stockade before him was in flames. He had anticipated such an attempt, and his men were prepared. The wall had been wetted earlier that night, and now men rushed forward with buckets of water to douse the few flames that did spread. Further down, however, flames had caught and were spreading. Longo could see Tristo atop the stockade, his huge bulk silhouetted by the fire as he beat at the flames with a wet blanket. Then the portion of the stockade on which he was standing collapsed outward, and Tristo disappeared.

When Tristo came to, he found himself half buried beneath

bags of earth and smouldering timbers. He looked about him, quickly taking stock. The stockade where he had been standing had collapsed outward, opening up a gap some thirty feet wide. All around him janissaries were scrambling over the wreckage. The only Christian soldiers that he could see were unconscious or dead, buried around him in the ruins. Tristo tried to rise, but he was pinned beneath a log. He pushed against the log with all his might. It shifted slightly, but not enough to free him. Nearby, a janissary noticed his efforts and began to climb over the wreckage towards him. Tristo's sword was nowhere in sight. He turned his attention back to the log, but it would not budge. He glanced back. The Turk was almost upon him.

Desperate, Tristo picked up a three-foot piece of wood – a fragment from the collapsed stockade – and swung it at the janissary's legs. The janissary jumped the blow, then kicked the piece of wood out of Tristo's hand. 'Come on then, bastard! Get it over with!' Tristo growled at him. The janissary raised his curved *yatağan* high, but he never completed the blow. He dropped his sword and slumped to his knees, a blade protruding from his chest. William stepped out from behind the fallen Turk.

'What took you so long?' Tristo grumbled.

'Is that any way to thank me for saving your life?' William asked as he pushed bags of dirt off the log that was pinning Tristo.

'I had the situation under control,' Tristo replied. He pushed on the log – now much lighter with the bags of earth removed – and it rolled off of him. Tristo rose, clutching his chest where the log had pinned him.

'Are you well? Can you fight?' William asked as he handed Tristo a sword.

'I'm fine,' Tristo growled. 'Come on, let's get out of here.'

Longo stood in the middle of the wide gap in the stockade, his face set in a snarl as he fought furiously. He had watched Tristo disappear amidst the burning ruins of the stockade and was now filled with a cold fury. He ruthlessly dispatched any Turk unfortunate enough to face him. As he confronted yet another janissary, he sidestepped a spear thrust, chopped the shaft of the spear in two, spun and impaled his attacker, all in one smooth motion. As soon as the janissary fell, another stepped forward to take his place. Despite Longo's furious efforts, he and his men were giving ground. The thin line of Christian soldiers that had filled the broad gap could not defend it indefinitely against the greater Turkish numbers, and if the Turks managed to push through and get inside the stockade, then the outer wall would be lost. After that, it would only be a matter of time before the city fell.

The janissary now facing Longo was a huge man, wielding a curved sword in one hand and a heavy spiked club in the other. Longo parried a sword thrust, ducked under the club and kicked the janissary hard in the knee. The janissary stumbled and then, to Longo's surprise, collapsed dead. Standing in his place was Tristo, bloodied sword in hand. Behind Tristo, Longo could see William, spinning and twisting as he fought off numerous attacks. The two stepped through the Christian line and took up their places on either side of Longo.

'I thought you were dead,' Longo shouted to Tristo.

Longo deflected a sword thrust with his shield, and Tristo finished off the attacker, impaling him though the stomach.

'Buried, but not dead,' Tristo roared back. 'William came and dug me out. A good thing too; it looks like you can use the help.'

'We can't hold out much longer,' Longo said as he inched backwards under the weight of the Turkish attack. 'We need reinforcements.' The janissaries' yelling drowned out Longo's final words as a fresh wave of Turks joined the attack. Here and there, janissaries forced their way through and the Christian line suddenly disintegrated, dissolving into scattered islands of desperate men amidst the sea of janissaries. Longo, Tristo and William found themselves alone, fighting back to back as they were pushed towards the inner wall. 'To me! To me!' Longo yelled to his troops. 'We must reform the line!' Several nearby Christian soldiers joined them, but they were not enough to push back the Turkish tide.

'We must sound the retreat!' Tristo shouted. 'The stockade is lost!'

Longo was about to agree when a series of loud booms cut him short. Nearby, a wave of onrushing janissaries simply vanished. Notaras had arrived with his cannons, rolling them into place around the gap in the stockade. They fired again, and the Turkish charge dissolved in the face of several hundred pounds of shot.

'Come on!' Longo shouted, seizing the opportunity. 'Back to the stockade, men!' He charged back to the gap, and his men followed. They swept aside the few janissaries who had survived the cannon fire and reached the gap in the stockade, where they again formed a line.

The janissaries mounted a final, desperate charge, but

the assault collapsed as Notaras's cannons reached the line and opened fire. Horns sounded in the Turkish camp, calling the retreat, and the men around Longo burst into cheering, calling out taunts after their retreating foes. For tonight, at least, they were victorious.

Mehmed stood on the Turkish ramparts and watched in disbelief as weary, bloodied soldiers streamed past him. Many carried fallen comrades. They had lost hundreds of lives, and for nothing. Mehmed watched until the last of his men had left the field and returned to camp. He remained there until the flares lighting the battlefield had all faded and he stood in the darkness, gazing at the walls that had defied him. He had suffered defeat in battle for the first time, and he did not like the taste of it.

Mehmed was still on the ramparts when Halil and Ulu arrived. He was not pleased to see either of them. Halil's insistence last night that the attack be delayed gnawed at Mehmed. He thought he could detect a certain smugness on the grand vizier's face. As for Ulu, he had failed Mehmed. Ulu had lost the battle for the wall. Mehmed turned to him. 'How many men did we lose?'

'Several hundred of our best, Sultan,' Ulu replied. 'The Edirne *orta* was almost entirely wiped out.'

'And the Christians? What were their losses?'

'Few, My Lord. Perhaps fifty men.'

Mehmed turned away to look at the wall again. 'How did this happen?' he asked. 'We outnumbered them ten to one. The wall is in ruins. Victory should have been ours.'

'They were ready for us, My Lord,' Ulu said. 'The holes opened in the stockade by the cannon were narrow, and our greater numbers useless. They had fully armoured knights and cannons waiting. Surprise was not with us.'

'Spies,' Mehmed hissed. 'I fear that we have a traitor in our midst.'

'Perhaps, Your Excellency,' Halil said and then hesitated before continuing. 'But the janissaries grumble that Allah is against us. The members of the janissary *divan* are waiting for you in your tent. They insist that we raise the siege and return to Edirne.'

'Nonsense,' Mehmed replied. 'We must simply stretch the Christian defences further. I have a surprise for them – one that they will not be prepared for.'

Halil cleared his throat. 'I am afraid that the janissaries are not willing to debate the point. If you do not agree to raise the siege, then they will kill you and proclaim your son, Bayezid, sultan.'

'Rebellion, then,' Mehmed said quietly. The siege had lasted less than a month, and already his dreams of glory were falling to pieces around him. He shook his head, forcing the thought from his mind. His men might run from the Christians, but Mehmed would not give up so easily. He would show his army the fate of those who defied him. 'And you, Ulu?' he asked. 'Are you with them?'

'I serve only you, My Lord,' Ulu replied.

'Good. Then gather a dozen men whose loyalty you trust and bring them to my tent.' As Mehmed strode back through camp, he saw *orta* after *orta* of janissaries, still in their battle armour, standing around the tall copper cooking pots that served both to prepare their meals and as their rallying point in battle. The pots had all been overturned: a declaration of mutiny. Mehmed met the eyes of as many men as he could. Some saluted him, but most of them looked away, embarrassed. A few defiantly returned his gaze. The crowd was thickest near Mehmed's tent. Mehmed walked through the janissaries, some with their swords still in hand, and stopped before the entrance to the tent. He turned and addressed them in a loud voice.

'You have served me loyally in this campaign. You have marched far, from Edirne to Constantinople. You fought bravely tonight before the walls of Constantinople, and although victory was not ours tonight, do not think that I value your service any less. I am a just ruler, and I will always reward faithful service. For your efforts thus far in this campaign, I will increase your pay by fifty aspers each.' Mehmed paused as there was scattered cheering amongst the men. 'For it was neither the walls nor the defenders of Constantinople that defeated you, but traitors in our own midst. Tonight, they stole victory from us, and now they would have us turn tail and flee. They would steal the glory and the spoils that are rightfully yours.

'We will not let them!' Mehmed roared. 'No, we will stay, and we will fight! In the days ahead, there will be glory for the brave and spoils enough to make rich men of you all. All the wealth of Christendom will be laid at your feet. You have but to follow your sultan, and I will lead you to glory!' He paused and turned slowly in a circle, meeting the eyes of the men around him. 'Now,' he continued. 'Who will follow me to glory? Who will serve their sultan, even unto death?'

At first, there was simply frozen silence, and then a janissary near Mehmed knelt and raised his fist in salute. Another followed him and then another, until all around Mehmed the janissaries knelt. Ulu bellowed out 'Hail to the sultan!' and the cry was taken up and repeated. The chant swelled and swept over Mehmed. The men's cheering was intoxicating. For the first time since taking the throne, he truly felt like the sultan. But his work was not done. He had dealt with the janissaries. Now he had to deal with their leaders.

As the chanting and cheering subsided, Mehmed turned and called Ulu to him. 'Enter the tent,' Mehmed told him. 'Seize the commanders, but do not kill them.' Ulu nodded and led his men into the tent, their weapons drawn. When the shouts and clash of arms had faded, Mehmed strode in after them.

He found the leaders of the rebellion, eight janissary commanders, kneeling on the floor of the tent, each with a sword to their throat. 'If I allow you to live,' Mehmed told them, 'then I will never see the end of challenges to my authority. I am a just sultan, and betrayal of this sort demands justice. Ulu, take these men outside and have them beheaded before their men. Be quick about it, and do not let it become a spectacle. Let my men see that I deliver justice swiftly and fairly.'

The commanders begged for mercy, but Mehmed ignored them as they were dragged from the tent. He went to his private quarters and poured himself a cup of wine. He tried to drink as little as possible while in the field. After all, alcohol was forbidden by the Koran, and he did not want his men to think him impious. Still, after the events of the night he felt the need for something stronger than water. As he raised the cup to his lips he heard from outside a strangled cry and the sickening thud of the executioner's sword. He set the cup back down, untasted.

*

After bathing and changing into breeches and a tunic, Longo did not reach the palace until after midnight, but the victory celebration was still in full swing. The palace's great hall was packed with soldiers and women, all drinking toast after toast to victory. Longo paused at the entrance to the hall, and a herald announced him. The crowd cheered and raised their cups in salute. Longo found himself surrounded by well-wishers. As he greeted a succession of men and women, he scanned the hall looking for Sofia. He spied Tristo roaring with laughter and William smiling at his friend's merriment, but Sofia was nowhere to be seen.

'Congratulations, my friend!' Constantine exclaimed as he approached Longo. 'What a glorious victory. God is truly with us! The Turks will never conquer these walls!'

'I hope that you are right, Emperor,' Longo began, but the rest of his remarks were cut short by the herald announcing the arrival of Megadux Lucas Notaras. Longo noticed that the cheering was even louder for Notaras than it had been for him and was pleased. Perhaps this glory would make Notaras more cooperative.

'Ah, the megadux,' Constantine said. 'I must congratulate him as well. Without his cannons, the battle would have been lost.' Constantine moved away, and Longo made his way through the crowded hall looking for Sofia. When he did not see her there, he headed out into the interior garden. It was empty.

'Looking for someone?' Startled, Longo turned to find Notaras standing at the entrance to the hall. The megadux had a dangerous gleam in his eye, and Longo suspected that he had been drinking.

'No,' Longo lied. 'The hall was crowded. I just wanted some fresh air.'

Notaras stepped out of the shadows and into the garden. 'I see,' he said. 'I thought perhaps you might be searching for Princess Sofia. The two of you seem to be very close.'

'I do not like your tone, Notaras,' Longo replied. 'Be careful what you say.'

'No, Signor Giustiniani, it is you who should be careful.' Notaras stepped forward so that he and Longo were face to face. Longo could smell the wine on his breath. 'I know about the tunnels, and I also know about your late-night meeting with Princess Sofia. Mark me well, signor: I will do whatever is necessary to protect her honour and my own.' Notaras stepped past Longo and strode from the garden.

Longo watched him go. Notaras must have surprised Sofia last night when she was returning from the tunnel. Now the megadux was jealous, and jealous men were dangerous. Was that why Sofia was not at the celebration? Had Notaras done something to her? There was only one sure way to find out. Longo headed for the kitchen and the secret passage to Sofia's chambers.

He reached the end of the secret passage and fumbled in the darkness for the mechanism to open the door. When he finally found the catch and pulled the door open, he found Sofia standing before him, dressed in a thin sleeping tunic and holding a sword. She smiled when she saw him and dropped the sword. 'It's you,' she said and stepped into his arms, kissing him. 'Thank God you are all right. I heard news of the battle and feared the worst.' She stepped out of his arms, and suddenly realizing that her tunic was not entirely opaque, went to the bed and threw a blanket over her shoulders.

Longo discreetly turned his head. 'Why did you not come to the celebration?' he asked.

'Constantine has forbidden me from leaving my quarters after sunset. Notaras told him I was roaming the palace late last night.'

'Notaras warned me not to see you,' Longo said.

'He is not a man to be trifled with. You should take his warning seriously.'

'I know.'

'Yet you are here.'

'I wanted to make sure that you were all right. When you did not appear tonight, I feared that something had happened.'

'And is that the only reason you came?' Sofia asked.

'No, no it's not,' Longo said. He pulled her into his arms and kissed her. Her mouth opened to his, and his hands moved down her sides, encircling her thin waist and pulling her into him. Sofia kissed him greedily and began to unbutton his doublet. Longo pulled back. 'Are you sure?'

Sofia stepped back and slipped the blanket from her shoulders, revealing her firm breasts, just visible through her tunic. 'I have never been more sure. I have chosen you to love, Longo.' Then she took his hand and led him to her bed.

Chapter 17

Sunrise was more than an hour away, and Sofia's bedroom was still dark when Longo rose and began to dress. He had come to her chambers each of the past five nights, risking their reputations and perhaps even their lives to be with her. He watched her now as she slept, a strand of her chestnut hair falling over her peaceful face, and decided once more that the risk had been worth it. He buckled on his sword belt and was about to leave when Sofia stirred in bed. 'It is early yet,' she said, sitting up. 'Where are you going?'

'To the walls. The night grows long, and if I am not at my post by dawn, then I will be missed.'

'Will you return tonight?'

'I do not know. We are risking much, Sofia. If we are discovered, then you will be ruined.'

To Longo's surprise, she laughed. 'I would rather be ruined than live out the rest of my life locked up behind doors as a proper lady. Tell me that you will come again tonight.'

Longo looked at her, fiery and beautiful, and felt his resistance crumbling. 'I will come if I am able.'

Sofia rose and kissed him. 'Then go and be safe. I will see you tonight.'

Longo left through the secret passage and emerged into a dark, empty side street next to the palace. He strode towards his post on the wall at the military gate of St Romanus, overlooking the Mesoteichion. Once he thought he heard footsteps behind him, but when he turned he saw nothing. It was not the first time in the last five nights that he had suspected he was being followed. He could not forget what William had told him: the Spanish assassin was here in Constantinople. He tightened his grip on his sword and slowed his pace, listening for footsteps, but he reached the wall without further incident.

Longo stood atop the wall as the sky around him lightened, revealing first the stockade below and then the fields beyond, stretching away to the Turkish ramparts and their camp. There was little movement anywhere – even the air was still – and the occasional boom of the Turkish cannons seemed muffled. Looking out over this sleeping world, Longo felt himself at peace. For the first time that he could remember, he cared about something more than revenge. He was not here simply to defeat the Turks. He was here to save the city, and Sofia.

The sun rose fiery orange over the distant hills, giving a pinkish cast to the world. On the walls of Constantinople the guard changed, the night-watch going home to a well-deserved rest. The morning watch replaced them, still bleary-eyed and yawning. Many of the men had come straight from the fields just within the walls of Constantinople, where they had been up late struggling to bring in the crop of winter wheat and to sow their fields for spring. Tristo and William came with them and joined Longo at the wall.

'You're up early,' Tristo said, grinning at Longo. 'A long night, eh?' Longo gave Tristo a hard look, and Tristo's smile faded. 'Jesus you're a surly bastard in the morning. I was just asking. Anyway, have you heard the commotion coming from the sea walls?'

'The sea walls?' Longo asked. 'What has happened?'

'We're not sure,' William said. 'But when we were coming to the walls, half the city seemed to be headed down to the Golden Horn. We thought that you might know something about it.'

'Perhaps he'll know,' Tristo said, pointing to Dalmata, who was hurrying towards them along the wall.

'Longo, you must come quickly,' Dalmata said as he reached them.

'What is it? What has happened?'

'Something that you must see to believe.'

Longo stood on the sea wall, not far from the Blachernae Palace, and watched in amazement. Dalmata, Constantine, Tristo and William stood with him. To either side of them, the entire length of the sea wall was lined with people, all with their eyes focused across the Golden Horn on the stretch of land beyond the city of Pera. There, a forest of masts was slowly rising over the horizon. The Turkish fleet was sailing towards them, sails billowing in the wind, and it appeared to be sailing over dry land.

'I do not believe my eyes,' Constantine said. 'This is not possible.'

'Is there a river there?' Longo asked. 'An inlet of some sort?'

'There is nothing. Nothing that could explain this,' Dalmata said, shaking his head. 'The land there is unbroken between the Bosphorus and the Golden Horn.'

They watched in silence as the masts rose higher and higher above the hills on the horizon. Finally, the prow of the nearest ship appeared. As the hull rose clear of the horizon, they could see that the oars were out, beating in rhythm against the empty air. Then, as it crested the hill, the ship's mysterious method of progress became clear. It sat suspended above the ground in a huge, wheeled cradle. Teams of oxen were slowly pulling the cradle forward. The enormous wheels of the cradle glinted in the sunlight: they had been cast in bronze to withstand the weight of the ships. Longo and the others stood speechless.

'Unbelievable,' Constantine said at last. 'I would not have thought it possible.'

A huge flag was unfurled from the mast of the ship. Even from this distance, Longo could make it out: golden Turkish lettering on a white-silk background, the standard of the sultan. Now that the ship was heading downhill towards the water of the Horn, it picked up speed. With each passing minute Longo could make out more details. A dais had been erected on the deck and on the dais a throne. Mehmed sat there, fanned by two slaves as he rode regally over the dry earth.

'The bastard looks a little too comfortable,' Tristo growled. 'We have a cannon that will reach that far, don't we?'

Dalmata smiled. 'I think we do.'

333

Longo shook his head. 'We would do better to save the powder. It would take a miracle to strike his ship at this distance, and we're going to need all the gunpowder we have in the days to come. As long as the Turkish fleet is in the Horn, it will be nearly impossible to receive any more supplies from the sea. We will have to fight with what we have.'

'I shall have to decree a rationing system,' Constantine said. 'Without supplies from the outside, food will run short before a month is out.'

'And with those ships in the Horn, we'll have to double the number of troops on the sea walls and in the fleet,' Dalmata added. 'We'll need to take men from the main wall.'

'We have too few men as is, and we'll have fewer once hunger sets in,' Constantine said. 'We must do something about those ships.'

Longo nodded in agreement. 'We must burn them.'

Halil stood on the deck of the sultan's flagship, both hands gripping the rail as he struggled to stand while the ship bounced along, swaying erratically in its huge wooden cradle. Halil would just as soon have stayed in camp, but Mehmed had insisted that he be here, standing next to the throne. 'Look. They are watching us,' Mehmed said, pointing across the Horn to the sea walls of Constantinople. 'I hope they are enjoying the spectacle.'

'I am sure that they find it quite edifying,' Halil said, wiping sweat from his brow. Ahead of him, row upon row of sweating men sat rowing their oars through the air, and on the far end of the boat the stroke was being beaten on a huge drum: *boom, boom, boom*. The constant beating of the drum, combined with the hot sun over-head, was beginning to give Halil a headache. 'But is all of this really necessary?' he asked. 'Perhaps the ships might move faster were they not weighted down with all of the rowers.'

'I wish to let the Christians see that I command the land as well as the sea,' Mehmed replied. 'I will row my ships wherever I please.'

'Such foolishness . . .' Halil muttered under his breath.

'Foolishness?' Mehmed hissed. Halil swallowed, aghast. 'And what else would you have these men do? Would you prefer that they sit around camp, idle and discontented, stirring up another mutiny? This rowing may look foolish to you, Halil, but it keeps the men occupied. So long as they cannot fight, at least they can row.'

'Very wise, My Lord,' Halil said, impressed despite himself. Mehmed was right. Today, at least, these men would be too tired to cause any trouble.

'Yes, it is,' Mehmed agreed. 'And I have more ideas in mind to keep our men busy over the coming days. Tell me what you think of this.' He handed Halil a weath-ered sheet of paper. On the paper was a sketch of some sort, a construction plan complete with measurements. Halil made out what he thought were large barrels tied together, and over them a network of planks and boards. The entire structure seemed to be floating on water.

'What is it?' Halil asked.

'A bridge across the Golden Horn. It will stretch from there' – Mehmed pointed to the shore of the Horn below them – 'to there' – a point just past where the wall of Constantinople ran down into the Horn.

The project was ambitious, but the strategic implications

were obvious enough. A bridge would allow the Turkish army to threaten the sea walls of Constantinople, forcing the Christians to spread their defences even thinner. It was a stroke of genius, and Halil did not like it. He had counted on a long, difficult siege in order to give his plans time to develop.

'A brilliant idea, Sultan,' he said. 'But dangerous, and perhaps impractical. Surely the Christian fleet would never allow this bridge to be built.'

'You are right, Halil. The Christians would do anything to prevent it. That is why I am placing you in charge of moving twelve cannons across the Horn to protect the fleet. The Christians would be fools to attack in the face of both our fleet and our cannons. We will build the bridge, and if the Christian fleet tries to stop us, then we will destroy them.'

'Very clever, My Lord,' Halil murmured. Indeed, too clever. Mehmed could not be allowed to conquer the city before Gennadius could eliminate him. The monk needed to act fast or else Halil would lose all that he had worked for these many years.

Five days later, Halil returned from overseeing the placement of the first of the cannons across the Horn to find a messenger waiting outside his tent. 'What is it?' Halil snapped, irritable after a long day in the burning sun.

'One of your messenger pigeons returned to the coop in camp this afternoon without any message attached to it, Grand Vizier. You told us to inform you if this happened.'

A pigeon without a message: it was the sign that Halil had been waiting for. He called for a horse and rode straight to the imperial pigeon coop. He found the grey-bearded head keeper pottering amidst the many cages, scattering birdseed.

'Keeper,' Halil called. The man turned and upon seeing Halil, dropped his birdseed and prostrated himself on the floor.

'How may I serve you, great Vizier?'

'Get up,' Halil told him. The keeper scrambled to his feet. 'A pigeon returned this afternoon without any message. Do you remember which one it was?' The keeper nodded. 'Good. Take me to it.'

'Yes, Your Excellency.' The keeper showed Halil to a cage where a single pigeon sat. Halil took it from its cage and examined it. Sure enough, there was a dark spot just behind the pigeon's head. There could be no doubt now. There would be a meeting with Gennadius this very night.

Not an hour later, Halil stood in a dark tunnel, fingering the jewelled handle of his sword as he waited impatiently for Gennadius to arrive. After finding the agreed meeting point, Halil had extinguished his torch, and he now stood in absolute darkness, listening keenly for any sound. He was sure that he had not been followed, but nevertheless, he was edgy. He did not like putting himself at risk like this. Still, with Isa gone to Edirne, he did not trust anyone else to meet with Gennadius. And this was a meeting that Halil could not afford to miss.

Footsteps echoed down the dark passage – the sound of sandals slapping against stone. The footsteps grew louder, and then a light came into view – a torch flickering in the distance. Halil studied the monk as he approached. Gennadius was compact and thin. His face was lined, but he walked with the erect, determined stride of a much younger man. He wore the simple black cassock of a monk, garb which matched his tonsured black hair. Gennadius slowed as he reached the meeting point. He still had not seen Halil.

'Where is the answer?' Halil asked, stepping out of the shadows and into the light cast by Gennadius's torch. Surprised, Gennadius took a step backwards, and his hand dropped to the dagger tucked into his belt.

'Who are you?' Gennadius asked. 'Where is Isa?'

'First, answer the question,' Halil insisted. 'Where is the answer?'

'Edirne.'

'Good. Edirne is also the answer to your question. Isa is there.'

'And who are you?'

'I am Halil.'

'Halil?' Gennadius asked, looking more closely at the vizier. 'Why are you here? I thought that we had agreed that the less contact there was between us, the safer we would both be.'

'Yes,' Halil agreed. 'But Isa is gone, and I do not trust anyone else. I am glad that you sent the bird; I need to speak with you. The siege is progressing faster than I had expected. We must act soon, or we will lose our chance.'

'I do not think so,' Gennadius replied. 'Moving a fleet into the Golden Horn is one thing; moving an army over the walls another. Constantinople has not stood for a thousand years only to fall easily now.'

'All the same, the time for action is now,' Halil insisted. 'I have paid you well, Gennadius. I hope for your sake that it was not money wasted.'

'Do not threaten me, Halil. You will find me decidedly harder to dispose of than one of your Turkish lackeys,' Gennadius warned, his voice low and hard. 'But we are not here to waste our breath on threats. In fact, I have information for you: an attack on the Turkish ships in the Golden Horn is planned for tomorrow night, under the darkness of the new moon.'

'Tomorrow night?' Halil's mind was racing. If the Turkish ships were destroyed, then perhaps it would buy him more time. 'What is their plan? How will they attack?'

'A fleet of small ships will sail after nightfall,' Gennadius told him. 'They plan to use Greek fire to burn the Turkish fleet.'

'You have done well, Gennadius. This is valuable information. I will see to it that the Christian fleet succeeds.'

'No, that is not why I have told you this,' Gennadius said. 'You must tell the sultan. In order for my plan to assassinate Mehmed to work, he must know that you have a contact within Constantinople, and he must see that the information from that contact is valuable.'

'I see,' Halil said. He thought he was beginning to understand Gennadius's plan, but Halil knew that the less he knew of the assassination, the safer he would be. 'You need say no more. I will do as you say. Is that all that you have to tell me?'

'That is all.'

'Very well,' Halil said. 'Do not contact me again unless it is absolutely vital. These meetings are too dangerous.'

'Dangerous?' Gennadius snorted. 'I have little enough to fear from my fellow Greeks. The people trust me more than the emperor, and those that oppose me are fools.'

'Let us hope that you are correct,' Halil said. 'Regardless,

I do not wish to risk my life to prove your point. There will be no more meetings. The next time we meet, I expect that the sultan will be dead, and you will be the patriarch of a Turkish Constantinople.'

Gennadius nodded. 'So be it.'

'So be it,' Halil echoed, then he turned and walked away into the darkness.

Gennadius climbed out of the dark tunnel into the church basement, which was lit by the flickering light of a single lamp set on the floor. Eugenius was waiting where Gennadius had left him – kneeling on the floor beside the lamp, his head bent in prayer. Gennadius touched Eugenius's shoulder. 'It is time to go, my friend.'

Eugenius nodded and rose. 'You were gone longer than I expected,' he said. 'Were there any difficulties?'

'Everything is proceeding according to God's plan,' Gennadius said. 'Now, let us return to the monastery before it grows dark.'

They made their way out of the small church and along the docks beyond the sea wall. The gates through the wall were shut by order of the emperor, but several of the guards at the Ispigas gate were loyal to Gennadius, and he had little trouble passing through into the city. From there, he and Eugenius wandered off the road and found the shaded path that sloped up to the cave that they would use to re-enter the monastery. Eventually, the path they were following levelled out. Ahead of them lay the dark entrance to the cave. They entered, but Gennadius had only taken a few steps when Eugenius froze. Gennadius stopped beside him, and as his eyes adjusted to the darkness, he realized that something was amiss. Ahead of them, the door set into the back of the cave was open.

Eugenius bent down and inspected the ground at their feet. 'Somebody has been here,' he said, pointing to the faint outline of footprints in the dirt. He moved forward, tracing the footsteps further. 'And they have not left.' He reached for his sword, but it was too late. From the corner of his eye, Gennadius saw several shadows detach themselves from the walls and surge towards them. Eugenius rose to fight them, but he was swarmed by three men before he could draw his sword.

Gennadius turned to run, but he had taken only a few steps when another man stepped out of the shadows to block his path. Gennadius was reaching for his dagger when he felt a sharp blow to the back of his head. The world spun. He felt himself falling and then, nothing.

Gennadius awoke to the splash of cold water on his face. He quickly took stock of his surroundings. His hands were tied to the arms of a heavy wooden chair and he sat in a dark, luxuriously furnished room: thick Persian carpet, fine paintings on the walls, and a broad desk in front of him. Whoever was with him was not in view. They must now be standing behind him. Gennadius tried to twist his head around, but saw no one. However, from where he sat he could see several tools of torture on the floor nearby: a whip, screws and, most disturbingly of all, a giant metal spike of the sort that traitors were sometimes made to sit on. Gennadius felt panic welling up within him. 'Who's there?' he asked. 'What do you want from me?' There was no answer. Gennadius fought down his panic, forcing himself to breathe evenly. He was still alive, and that was good. Whoever had captured him wanted something from him, or he would be dead already. Or, Gennadius reflected grimly, they wanted him to suffer before he died.

A door opened somewhere behind Gennadius, and he heard footsteps approach. 'Welcome to my home, Gennadius.' The voice was that of Notaras. He strode into view and sat down at the desk, facing Gennadius.

Gennadius managed a weak smile. He glanced significantly at the ropes tying his hands. 'Thank you for your generous hospitality.'

'The ropes are necessary,' Notaras told him. 'I have some questions to ask you. My friend here will make certain that you answer.' Notaras gestured to the man behind Gennadius, who now stepped forward into view. He was tall and dark-skinned, his face lined with scars. He held a wicked-looking curved knife, which he tapped against his hand.

Gennadius ignored the man. He had to keep his conversation with Notaras going. He had information that might save him, if only he could get Notaras to listen. 'I will be more than happy to answer any questions you have for me, Notaras. I have nothing to hide.'

'Odd that a man with nothing to hide would leave his monastery through a secret tunnel. Stranger still that he would leave the city walls.'

'I did nothing of the sort.'

'Do not lie to me, monk,' Notaras snapped. 'The guards at the sea wall are not as loyal to you as you think. I know you left the city. Now I want to know what you are plotting. Consorting with the enemy is treason, Gennadius. The punishment is death. But if you speak truthfully, I might spare your life. Tell me: why did you leave the monastery in secret?'

'I have nothing to hide,' Gennadius replied. 'But I do have good reason to be careful. I took the tunnel to avoid you and your men. You have been poisoned against me, Notaras. I knew that you would not understand what I was doing.'

'And what exactly was that? Arranging another poisoning? Perhaps Sofia this time, or the emperor?'

Gennadius laughed. 'Don't be a fool. It is not the emperor that I wish dead, but the sultan.'

Notaras's eyes narrowed. 'Impossible. You could never get near him. No one can. He is surrounded by dozens of janissaries at all times.'

'No, not impossible, Notaras. Not with your help.'

'And why should I believe you? This is just another one of your tricks.'

'No, Notaras,' Gennadius protested. 'This is no trick. Together we can kill the sultan and save our city. You will be remembered forever as the saviour of the empire.'

Notaras shook his head. 'I do not believe you, Gennadius, and I will not listen to any more of your lies. I have seen enough of your treachery. You had Neophytus poison the empress-mother, and you killed him to save yourself. You would sacrifice anything or anyone to destroy the Union and become patriarch.'

'Would I, Notaras? Did Princess Sofia tell you that? You would be wise not to believe all that she says. I told you before that she could not be trusted. Each night she lies with Giustiniani, the man who has taken your rightful place as defender of the city.'

Notaras did not speak. He gestured and the dark-skinned

343

man stepped forward and put his knife to Gennadius's throat, pressing hard enough to draw a thin trail of blood. 'Careful what you say, monk,' Notaras said. 'I shall lose my patience and have you killed before I am quite done with you.'

'Kill me if you wish, Notaras, but what I say is true,' Gennadius said, struggling to keep his voice from shaking. 'Why else do you think the emperor has confined Princess Sofia to her quarters after sunset? I informed him that something is amiss.'

'I did not know that the emperor had done any such thing.'

'There is much that you do not know, my friend. And I will not always be there to protect your interests. You must look after that woman of yours. She could be dangerous to you . . . to all of us.'

'You lie to save yourself,' Notaras replied coldly.

'Do I? Send your men to Sofia's chambers after night-fall. You will see if I lie.'

Notaras did not reply, but it was clear to Gennadius that he had only confirmed the megadux's fears. And those fears were eating at Notaras, undermining his better judgement, his distrust of Gennadius. Finally, Notaras waved off the dark-skinned man, who removed his knife from Gennadius's throat and used it to cut the ropes that held Gennadius's hands. Gennadius rubbed his wrists and breathed a sigh of relief.

'Very well,' Notaras said. 'I will watch Giustiniani, and if what you say is true, then I will listen to your plan to kill the sultan. But know that if this is a trick, then you will wish that you had never lived. Now come.'

Notaras rose and strode from the chamber, and

Gennadius followed. The dark-skinned man trailed behind Gennadius, staying uncomfortably close. They came to a tight spiral staircase and descended three flights of stairs to a narrow, dimly lit hallway. Notaras led Gennadius to a door halfway down the hall and stopped. He produced a key, unlocked the door and held it open. Gennadius looked inside. It was a small, square cell, the floor covered with straw. Eugenius sat slumped in the corner.

'What is this?' Gennadius asked.

'Your cell,' Notaras replied, and before Gennadius had a chance to protest, the dark-skinned man shoved him from behind and sent him tumbling in. He landed hard on the floor and turned to see the door swing shut behind him. It closed with a clang, and he heard the key turn in the lock. Gennadius scrambled to his feet and rushed to the grill in the door.

'What are you doing?' he cried through the opening. 'You cannot keep me here! I am a man of God!'

'You are alive. Thank God for that,' Notaras replied. 'You will be freed when I know that what you say is true.' With that, he turned and left. Gennadius heard his footsteps retreating down the hallway, and then there was only silence.

'What do we do now?' Eugenius asked.

'Patience, my friend,' Gennadius said. 'Now we wait.'

The next night there was no moon, and William could only just make out the ships closest to him as his boat glided over the dark waters of the Horn towards the Turkish fleet. To his left he could see what he thought was Longo's boat, and to the right loomed a Genoese transport, the dim outline of its huge bulk barely visible. The rest of the Christian fleet was lost in the darkness.

'Quiet now, men,' William whispered to his crew. 'Row gently.' They had wrapped their rowlocks in cloth before they left, and now the only sound was the gentle slap of waves against the side of the boat and the quiet dip of the oars in the water as they pulled away from the rest of the Christian boats and headed for their target: two ships at the far edge of the Turkish fleet. Ahead, the distant shore and Turkish ships were impossible to make out in the darkness.

They had nearly reached the far shore, and still Matthias could not see the two ships they had been assigned to burn. 'Where are they? Are we still on course?' he whispered to the man at the tiller. The man nodded. Then, far to their left, a flare went up from the Turkish shore. The men stopped rowing and turned to watch.

'What in Jesus' name is that?' the coxswain called out.

'Quiet,' William hissed. The flare fell slowly, illuminating the other Christian ships, which were grouped together some two hundred yards to port, ready to attack the heart of the Turkish fleet. William spied Longo's boat in the middle of the fleet. Giacomo Coco – the commander of the expedition – had broken clear of the rest of the ships and had almost reached the Turks. He was standing in the prow, urging his longboat forward. As William watched, a Turkish cannon barked out on the far shore, and a second later Coco's head simply disappeared. His body slumped and fell overboard just as the flare burned out, plunging the scene back into darkness.

The Turkish cannons on the far shore erupted, and the scene descended into chaos. By the intermittent flash of the cannons, William watched cannonballs skip across the water and rip through the Christian fleet, splintering hulls and sweeping sailors from their boats. He thought he saw Longo's ship pulling out of the chaos, but then lost it in the darkness. When the cannons flashed again, Longo's boat was gone.

'What should we do?' one of the men called out. 'Should we turn back?'

'No,' William replied. 'We head for the Christian fleet. The men won't last long in water that cold, and if they swim to the Turkish shore they are as good as dead. We will save as many as we can.'

'But sir,' the coxswain protested. 'The cannons will eat us alive.'

'No – listen. The cannons have stopped.' William pointed to the Turkish fleet, which was now pulling towards the Christians to finish them off. 'They won't risk hitting their own men. Now turn the boat around.'

'Aye, sir,' the coxswain said. 'Right back, left forward. Row!' he called. The boat spun around and then surged forward towards the battle. They had not rowed a hundred yards when a tall Turkish ship loomed up out of the darkness ahead of them, blocking their path to the Christian fleet. The ship was crowded with men, but all were at the far rail, attacking one of the Christian ships. They seemed not to have noticed William's small ship.

'All right, men. Let's do what we came for,' William called to his crew. 'Oars in. Not a sound,' he whispered as his boat glided up next to the Turkish ship. Quietly, they hooked on to the side of the vessel, and pulled themselves close. 'Ready the fire,' William whispered, and one of the sailors lit the fuse to a barrel of Greek fire. William let it sputter for a few seconds. 'Unhook the ship,' he whispered finally. Immediately, the Turkish ship began to drift away. 'Now!' William yelled. The men grabbed the small barrel and hurled it up and on to the neighbouring deck, where it rolled to the middle and burst into flames.

'Row! Row!' William yelled as the fire spread over the Turkish ship, engulfing it. They pulled away to safety, and the burning ship, its tiller aflame and useless, veered into another Turkish ship, setting it afire too. The two ships burned brightly. By their light, William saw the Christian fleet in full retreat and Turkish ships racing out to capture any stragglers. Nearer, just past the burning Turkish ships, William saw a dozen men flailing in the water. A Turkish galley was rowing out to finish them off.

'There!' William told the coxswain. 'Row for those men, and pull hard!' They reached the men and pulled them on board just as arrows from the galley started to fall around them. Longo was not amongst the men. William stood in the stern and scanned the water for him. The coxswain pulled William back down.

'Time to leave, sir!' he shouted, pointing to the approaching galley.

'You're right. Pull for home, men!' William ordered. 'And you,' he said to the rescued men, shivering at the bottom of the boat, 'take the oars. It will warm you.'

They pulled away from the slower galley and were halfway back across the Horn when they came across two men, struggling in the water as they swam towards the Christian shore. A minute later, William helped to haul Tristo and Longo into the boat.

'That's two I owe you,' Tristo said through chattering teeth.

They all three looked across to the far shore where the Turkish harbour lay. The Turkish fleet was almost entirely intact, lit by the light of three burning ships. The Christians had lost at least twice as many ships. The attack had been a disaster. 'They were ready for us,' Longo said.

'Aye,' Tristo agreed. 'There's a rat in this city. Somebody let them know we were coming.'

'We'll never get them out of the harbour now,' Longo said. 'And with the harbour in their hands . . . We don't have enough men to defend the sea walls and the land walls.'

'So what do we do now?' William asked.

'We send for help,' Longo answered. 'And pray that somebody comes.'

Five nights later, *la Fortuna* was ready to sail. William had been eager to join the expedition, and as much as he feared for the young man's safety, Longo had agreed. After all, William had fought bravely during the attack on the Turkish fleet, and he had saved Longo's life. The least Longo could do was give him this chance for glory, and also a chance to visit his young wife on Chios. He would serve as lieutenant to Phlatanelas, who had volunteered to captain the ship.

The ship could be seen docked alongside a pier in the distance. Under the cover of night, the sides of the ship had been lined with shields like a Turkish warship, and the Turkish colours now flew from the mainmast. Longo spotted William on the deck, giving orders to the crew. Like the rest of them, he was dressed like a Turk in baggy pants, a loose red shirt and a turban.

As Longo and Tristo came on board, William hurried to greet them. Tristo engulfed him in a hug. 'Take care of yourself out there, young pup,' he said, lifting William off the ground. He put him back down and clapped him on the back. 'Stay safe, William.'

Longo stepped forward and clasped William's hand. 'I will be fine,' William said before Longo could begin. 'It's the city that you should be worried about, Longo. Keep it safe until I return.'

'Keep yourself safe,' Longo told William. 'Phlatanelas is a good man; do as he says. And remember, if you see a Turkish ship, run. You're going out to find help, not to defeat the Turks single-handedly.'

William nodded. 'I understand.' He looked across the ship to where the one Turkish member of the crew, Turan, was busy tying off the cable from the tugboat. William lowered his voice. 'This Turan, can we trust him?'

'Not all Turks are our enemies, William,' Longo said. 'His family has lived in Constantinople for generations. This is his home, and he will fight for it as hard as you or I. He speaks Turkish, too, and can interpret for you should you need it.'

'Longo!' Phlatanelas called as he crossed the deck to join them. 'Well met. Thank you again for offering your ship.'

'Of course,' Longo said, clasping the captain's arm. 'Keep her safe, and make Chios your first stop. My men there will be able to tell you where the Venetian ships are, if they are out there at all.'

'I will,' Phlatanelas said. 'And you, hold the city until we get back.' He released Longo's arm and went to the wheel.

Longo turned back to William. 'You should get away without trouble,' he said. 'On a night this dark, the Turks should take you for just another of their warships.' Beneath Longo, the ship had started to move forward, towed out into the Golden Horn. Longo grasped William's hand again and held it. 'Come back safe,' he told William.

'I will, and we will not fail you,' William replied. Then, Longo turned and leapt from the ship to the pier. He watched as the vessel made its slow way out into the estuary. William waved once from the poop deck and then turned to face the sea. Longo watched until first William, and then the entire ship, disappeared into the darkness.

'Never fear,' Tristo said, placing his hand on Longo's shoulder. 'He's a tough little bugger, William is. We'll see him again.'

Chapter 18

Sitt Hatun stood at the window of her bedchamber
and looked out over the imperial palace and beyond
to the river. In the hazy morning light she could just
make out the heavily laden boats setting out to resupply
the army at Constantinople. Seeing them, she thought
of her trip to Manisa months ago, but then shook the
thought from her head. There was no sense in dwelling
on past misery. Those times were over. Now she was the
bas haseki, mother of the sultan-to-be, with more money
and more servants than she needed. She had everything
that she desired.

She turned from the window to watch her son. Selim
sat in the corner, playing quietly with Bayezid. The two
young princes were a study in contrasts. Bayezid, now
nearly four years old, was a solidly built, athletic child
with fair skin and sandy brown hair. Already, it was clear
that he would excel as a hunter and a warrior. Selim, one
and a half years Bayezid's junior, was thin and frail, with
olive skin and black hair. His face was gentle, but he had
Mehmed's intelligent, piercing eyes. Although he was small

for his age, Selim already displayed an insatiable curiosity that delighted his tutors.

Sitt Hatun smiled to see them together. Fate worked in strange ways, and none were stranger than this: that the son of Sitt Hatun's most bitter rival should become a regular in her household and the playmate of Selim. Bayezid's visits had grown more and more frequent over the past months, since Sitt Hatun first showed his nurse, Kacha, the secret passage leading from his bedroom to her apartments. Bayezid preferred Sitt Hatun's apartments to those of Gülbehar, and Sitt Hatun could hardly blame him. Kacha told her that Gülbehar often slept until noon, and that she spent much of her day at the *hookah* smoking hashish. And since Mehmed had left for Constantinople, Gülbehar's tirades, which echoed all the way to Sitt Hatun's chambers, had become an almost daily event. Little wonder that young Bayezid was eager to escape his mother's presence.

At first, Bayezid had come only at night when Gülbehar's household was asleep, but lately he had come in the mornings as well. Kacha covered for the young prince in his absence and hurried to inform Sitt Hatun if Bayezid's mother called for him. Despite herself, Sitt Hatun had grown fond of the child. At first, she had seen the boy merely as a tool to be used against Gülbehar, and had cultivated his friendship in order to turn him against his mother. But now she found that she cared for Bayezid almost as if he were her own son.

Sitt Hatun moved to her bed and sat down to watch Bayezid and Selim. They were playing with a set of carved pieces intended to represent the siege at Constantinople. There were towers, gates and sections of the wall, all of which could be fitted together. In addition, there were dozens of tiny figurines of Christian knights and Turkish soldiers. The entire set was carved from ivory, and the workmanship was exquisite. Mehmed had sent the set to Selim so that he could follow the siege and begin to learn military strategy.

Sitt Hatun watched as Bayezid helped Selim to piece together the wall of Constantinople. They had only been playing for a few minutes, but already the miniature wall stretched for four feet across the floor of the room. 'Now we need a tower,' Bayezid said. Selim found the appropriate piece, and Bayezid took it and set it into place. 'Now a gate.'

After Bayezid set the gate into place, Selim took up one of the figurines – a Turkish bey on horseback – and placed it in the gate. He turned and gestured proudly. 'Look, *anne*!' he said. Selim always called her his *anne*, or mamma. 'Father!'

Sitt Hatun smiled. 'That is very good, Selim.'

There was a knock at the door, and Kacha entered through the secret passage. 'Excuse me, My Lady,' she said. 'But Gülbehar has awakened and is calling for her son.' Bayezid pouted at this and sat down, his arms folded across his chest.

'I don't want to go,' he said.

'You must,' Sitt Hatun told him. 'Your mother will be angry if you do not return soon. And if she learns that you are here . . .' Sitt Hatun did not need to finish. Bayezid understood that if his visits were discovered, he would never see Sitt Hatun or Selim again.

The boy frowned, but he rose and went to the secret passage. He stopped at the door. 'I am a prince,' he said.

'Why can't I choose where I live? Why can't I choose my mother?'

Sitt Hatun shook her head sadly. 'There are some things that even princes cannot choose,' she told Bayezid. 'Now go. Farewell, little prince.'

Kacha took Bayezid's hand and led him away. After a moment, Selim came over to Sitt Hatun and placed his hand on his mother's knee. 'What's wrong, mother?'

Sitt Hatun realized that there were tears in her eyes. She had hardened herself against such sentimentality, but Bayezid's words had moved her. The boy deserved better than Gülbehar for a mother. But how could Sitt Hatun play mother to this boy when he would have to die in order for Selim to take the throne? She knew that she should use Bayezid or send him away. Loving him was not an option.

Sitt Hatun wiped her eyes and lifted Selim on to her lap. 'Nothing is wrong, my prince,' she told him. 'Nothing at all.'

Isa stood in the shadowy entrance to a narrow alley and watched as night fell on a busy street in Edirne. Across the street from him stood a row of houses and merchants' shops, crowded close together. In the centre, looking no different from any of the other dingy, stuccoed buildings, was the house where his family was kept prisoner. Isa had not seen his wife and two children for nearly a year, but tonight he would be with them again. And this time, he would take them with him, far away from this accursed place. He had only one task to complete first. Once the young prince Bayezid was dead, Isa and his family would be free.

The shadows deepened around Isa and the crowd thinned until only a few merchants remained, hurrying home down the dark street. The moon would not rise for several hours yet, and in his tight-fitting black clothes, Isa was nearly invisible. It was time. He turned his back on the house and slipped away down the alley. Keeping to the shadows, he made his way to the palace, where he stopped in an alleyway across from the outer wall. All around the palace there was a paved, torchlit space some twenty feet wide. At night the space was forbidden ground. Archers patrolled the walls, and anyone caught trespassing would be shot on sight. Isa would have to cross the open space unseen if he hoped to enter the palace.

From where he stood, he could see two guards talking on the wall above. He waited several minutes, but they did not move away. Isa drew his dagger and prised a stone loose from the wall next to him. He threw it far down the street to his left, and it landed with a loud crack and rolled clattering along the pavement. The guards turned to follow the sound, and Isa took the opportunity to dash across the open space. He flattened himself against the wall and waited, motionless. No alarm was raised. He had not been seen.

Isa crept along the wall and rounded a corner to the side that faced the river. He continued until he came to a rusted metal grate set low into the wall. The grate covered the mouth of a small sewage tunnel, some three feet across. He slipped on a pair of black leather gloves and then drew a pouch from his belt and carefully sprinkled a dark green powder around the edges of the grate where it joined with the stone of the tunnel. He took a leather water skin and splashed the powder with water. There was a hissing sound, and then noxious green smoke rose from the edges of the grate. A few minutes later the grate came loose in Isa's hands. He set it aside and crawled into the tunnel.

The bottom of the tunnel was covered with a slippery, foul-smelling layer of muck – the rotting refuse washed down the kitchen sewer. Isa ignored the smell, thinking of his family's freedom as he wormed his way through the filth. After a hundred feet the tunnel ended beneath another grate. He quietly shoved the grate aside and emerged into the empty, dimly lit harem kitchen. He replaced the grate, crossed the kitchen and entered a narrow spiral stairwell. At the top he emerged into a light-less corridor. He moved slowly down the corridor, feeling the walls with his hands. After a few feet he found a latch and pulled it. The wall swung open before him and he stepped into the reception room of Gülbehar's apartments. The room was dark, which meant that Gülbehar's house-hold was probably asleep. That would make his job easier. With any luck, he could slip in and out without being noticed. Everyone would assume that the boy Bayezid had simply died in his sleep.

Isa slipped silently through the reception room and entered a long hallway that ran the length of the apart-ment. Halil had informed him that the entrance to Bayezid's quarters was at the far end of the hall. The boy's quarters consisted of three rooms: a reception room, a play room and his bedroom. Isa had almost reached the door to the reception room, when it opened and an *odalisque* stepped out. She screamed and turned to run, but Isa lunged for her and grabbed her by her long auburn hair. He yanked her towards him and slit her throat, cutting short her terrified screaming. Isa stepped over her and into the room. He shut the door behind him and locked it, then moved into the play room and again shut and locked the door. There were noises now coming from the hallway behind him. Isa would have to hurry.

He took a small vial from a pocket and kicked open the door to Bayezid's bedroom. The bed was empty. Isa quickly searched the room, but the boy was gone. In the next room, the doors shook as somebody tried to open them. Isa knelt and reached for one of the pouches that hung at his belt. Better to die here than to live and see his family killed for his failure.

Then he saw it: a thin crack running up the otherwise seamless wall on the far side of the room. It was the edge of a secret door, left slightly ajar. All was not lost. Isa slipped through the door and shut it firmly behind him.

Sitt Hatun awoke from a troubled sleep to the sound of loud knocking. She jerked upright, suddenly wide awake. The knocking repeated itself – two knocks, a pause and then three knocks. It was the code that she had worked out with Bayezid and Kacha. She hurried to the door and opened it.

'Bayezid!' Sitt Hatun exclaimed. 'What are you doing here?' She stopped. Bayezid had not moved and his face was ghostly white. 'Are you well?' Sitt Hatun asked. 'What has happened?' Bayezid still did not move. Sitt Hatun crouched down and took the boy's head in her hands so that he was looking her in the eyes. 'Tell me what happened, Bayezid.'

'A man . . .' he began and then started crying. He buried his head in Sitt Hatun's robe. Now that he was talking, he could not stop. 'He killed Kacha. He's going to kill me. I'm going to die. I'm going to die.'

'Shhh, you're not going to die. I will protect you,' Sitt Hatun told Bayezid as she lifted him into her arms. She shut the secret door and turned to call for Anna, but she was already there.

'I heard the knocking,' Anna said. 'What has happened?'

'An assassin,' Sitt Hatun said as she crossed the room. 'He has come for the boy. Take him and keep him safe.' Anna nodded and took Bayezid in her arms. She left the room, and Sitt Hatun shut the door behind her. When she turned, she saw Isa standing in the doorway of the secret passage. 'You!' she exclaimed. 'What are you doing here? Did Halil send you?'

'I have come for the boy, Bayezid,' Isa said quietly. 'Tell me where he is.'

'He is not here,' Sitt Hatun lied. 'And you must leave now before you are discovered.'

'I will not leave without the boy.' Isa drew a small pouch from his belt. 'I do not wish to hurt you. The boy is here. Tell me where he is.' He took a step towards Sitt Hatun.

'Stop!' Sitt Hatun ordered, trying to control the trembling in her voice. 'All I have to do is scream and guards will come. You know the fate of men who are found in the harem. Your genitals will be cut off and stuffed in your mouth, and you will be tied in a bag and thrown into the river to drown.'

Isa took another step towards her. 'If you scream, you will die.'

Sitt Hatun met Isa's gaze and held it. 'Then we will both die,' she said. 'But you will not touch Bayezid.'

'Nor will you touch my mistress,' Anna said as the doors to the room swung open and she stepped through holding a sword. She stepped into the space between Isa and Sitt Hatun.

Isa looked from Sitt Hatun to the sword and back again. 'Do not be a fool, Sitt Hatun,' he said. 'Bayezid must die if your son is to be sultan. Better that it happen now, at my hand. I will be quick. The boy will not suffer. Or would you rather he be drowned in his bath by the palace guards on the day that Selim takes the throne?' Sitt Hatun hesitated, and Isa continued. 'All you have to do is step aside and your place as *valide sultana* will be assured.'

Sitt Hatun was torn. As *valide sultana*, mother of the sultan, she could have all that she wanted, including Gülbehar's head on a platter. And all she had to do was turn her back and let Bayezid die. It would be so easy. And Isa was right: the boy had to die sooner or later if Selim was to be sultan. But then she thought of Bayezid, and of the terror in his eyes as he begged her to protect him. She thought of her own son, Selim, and of what she would do if he were taken from her. 'No,' she said finally. 'I cannot. He is only a child.'

'So be it,' Isa said. He moved with surprising quickness, reaching into the pouch and flinging a cloud of white powder at Anna. But Anna was ready. She dropped to the ground, rolled under the cloud, and sprang to her feet on the far side, slashing at Isa with her sword. Isa managed to parry the blow with a small dagger, then he kicked out, knocking Anna's leg from under her. As he raised his dagger to finish Anna, Sitt Hatun started screaming. She grabbed the only weapon she could find – a heavy golden candlestick – and hurled it at Isa. It caught him

360

square on the forehead, and he staggered backwards, bleeding.

Sitt Hatun stepped forward and helped Anna to her feet. From outside the bedchamber, they heard a crash as the eunuch guards burst through the main doors to the apartment. Isa looked towards the sound, then back at them. He hesitated, then turned and fled through the secret passage. The door had just swung shut behind him when the eunuch guards rushed into the bedchamber.

The guards paused when they saw that Sitt Hatun and Anna were alone, and that Anna was holding a sword. 'What are you doing here, captain?' Sitt Hatun asked calmly. She would not send the guards after Isa. After all, he had saved her life once, and besides, Isa's visit would be difficult to explain without revealing Bayezid's presence in her apartments.

The captain bowed low. 'We heard your screaming, Sultana,' he said. 'We came as quickly as we could. Are you all right?'

'As you can see, I am fine. Thank you for your vigilance, captain, but it was only a dream that startled me. You may go.' The captain looked dubiously from Anna's sword to the bloodied candlestick lying on the ground.

'An *odalisque* was killed tonight in Sultana Gülbehar's quarters, and the prince Bayezid is missing,' he said. 'Are you sure that you have seen nothing? The assassin may still be loose in the harem.'

'Then I suggest that you go and find him, captain.'

'Very well, Sultana. But I will leave a guard outside your quarters.'

'You have my thanks,' Sitt Hatun said. The captain bowed and led his guards from the room.

When they were gone, Bayezid appeared in the doorway. He ran to Sitt Hatun and buried his head in the fold of her dress. 'Is it safe?' he asked. 'I knew that they would come for me, just like my mother said. Are they going to kill me?'

Sitt Hatun gently stroked his head. 'There, there,' she told him. 'No one will harm you, Bayezid. You are safe.'

By the time Isa reached the harem kitchen, the entire palace had been alerted that an assassin was on the loose. He just managed to squeeze into the sewer and pull the grate back over his head before a troop of eunuch guards came marching through the kitchen. Isa squirmed through the tunnel as quickly as he could. He emerged outside the wall and glanced above him. The archers were no doubt on high alert now, but Isa had no time to wait. He sprinted across the open space next to the wall, heading for the mouth of a nearby alley.

Arrows hissed past his head, but Isa reached the alley safely. Still, he did not stop running. The twisting, narrow streets of Edirne were an easy place to lose oneself, and he knew the guards would not catch him now. But it was not the guards that worried him. The news of his failed assassination attempt would travel fast, even at night. If Isa wanted to see his family freed, then he had to reach them before their keeper learned of his failure.

Isa ran without stopping until he reached the quarter where his family was kept. He slowed. The quarter was quiet, all dark streets and windows. There were no soldiers on the street. He had made it in time. He slipped back into the shadows and headed for the house where his family was kept. When he reached it he strode directly to the door and pounded on it. There was no response, so he knocked again. Finally, he heard a noise inside. After a minute, the door opened.

In the doorway stood a tall, well-muscled man with a bushy beard and a large birthmark on his forehead. He wore leather breeches and a close-fitting wool tunic. For three years this man had been the keeper of Isa's family. Isa knew nothing about him, not even his name, but he hated him all the same.

'What are you doing here?' the man asked. 'You were not to come until the prince is dead.'

'The prince is dead,' Isa lied. 'I have come for my family.'

The man's eyes narrowed. 'I have heard nothing of this.'

'I killed Prince Bayezid in his bed, not half an hour ago,' Isa replied. 'His death will not be discovered until morning.'

The scarred man yawned. 'Then come in the morning. Your family will be freed then, not before.'

The man began to shut the door, but Isa blocked it with his foot. 'I am through waiting. I have done all that Halil asked. My family is free now, and I will wait no longer. Take me to them.' He reached for a pouch on his belt. 'I will not ask you again.'

The man at the door took a step backwards at the sight of the pouch. 'Put that away,' he said. 'You will have no need of your poisons here. If you are in such a hurry then come. I will take you to your family.'

He let Isa into the house and led him down a corridor with several rooms opening off it. A dozen men lounged in these rooms – the guards Halil had assigned to keep Isa from his family. His family was confined to the upper floor, where it would be more difficult for them to escape.

They reached the stairs, and the scarred man stopped and motioned for Isa to go first. He stepped past the man and hurried up the narrow staircase. The heavy door at the top of the staircase was unlocked. Isa pushed it open and stepped into the dimly lit hallway, which was a mirror-image of the one on the floor below. 'They are in the second room on the right,' the keeper said from behind. 'The door is unlocked. They are waiting for you.'

Isa needed no further instruction. He hurried down the hall and pulled the door open. The room had no windows, and it was very dark, lit only by the light from the door. Isa could not see his family. 'Jina!' he called. 'Children?' No response. He entered and was immediately assaulted by a powerful odour of decay. Something was very wrong here. 'Jina?' he called again in rising panic. He took a few more steps into the room before he saw his family. His wife and two children were slumped motionless against the far wall. He rushed across the room and knelt beside his wife. Her throat had been slit, as had the throats of his daughter and son. Judging by the decayed state of their bodies, they had been dead for several days.

'Halil told me to thank you for your service,' the keeper said from the door. 'But you are too dangerous to leave alive. As Halil promised, you'll be joining your family now, forever.' Isa ran for the door, but before he was halfway there, it slammed shut. The room went black. Isa heard a deadbolt slide to, and then another.

He stumbled back across the dark room to the door and pounded on it with his fist, but there was no response. 'You will pay for this!' he shouted. 'You will pay!' Still, there was no reply. He yanked on the handle, and then kicked the door hard. It did not budge. The door was made of solid oak. It would take an axe to bring it down. He was trapped.

Isa slumped to the floor and sat still. Despite all that he had done, despite all his years of working for Halil, he had failed his family. His life meant nothing now. But if he could not save his family, he would at least avenge their deaths. 'Halil,' he mumbled to himself. He repeated the name over and over again, like a mantra. It gave him strength. There was purpose in his life yet. He would see to it that Halil suffered as he had suffered.

But first, he would kill his family's keeper. And before he did that, he would have to escape. Isa closed his eyes and cleared his mind, forcing himself to ignore the putrid smell of the corpses of his beloved wife and children. He had time to think. The keeper would most likely leave Isa there to starve, but if Isa was lucky, then the man would come back to kill him. Isa could deal with him then. Even if he had to face every guard in the house, Isa was determined that his life would be dearly sold. If no one came, then Isa would simply have to find another way out.

He closed his eyes and meditated, trying to focus his thoughts on the task at hand. He had been sitting for only a few minutes when sweat began to trickle down his shaved head and he noticed that the door at his back was growing hot. He touched the wall next to the door and then the floor. They were all warm. He put his nose to the crack at the bottom of the door and smelled smoke. With alarm, Isa realized that the house was on fire. The keeper intended to burn him alive.

Isa rose and moved around the room, feeling the walls for any cracks, any weakness that could be exploited. There were none. He moved around the floor, stomping and checking for loose planks, but gave up after only a few seconds. If he did manage to make it through the floor, then he would probably only find himself in the fire. Isa moved back to the walls, coughing as smoke began to fill the space. He had to find a way out soon. He began to circle the room again, this time knocking on the walls. He moved along the wall to the left of the door, then turned the corner and moved to the back of the room. Still nothing. The smoke was thick now, rising up between the floor-boards to sting his eyes and burn his throat. He raised his shirt to cover his mouth, but still he gasped and choked as he started out along the wall where his family lay. Again, he heard only the dull knock of his hand on the hard plaster. He was beginning to lose hope when he heard something different. At waist height, directly over the body of his wife, the wall reverberated with a hollow thumping sound. He put his head to the wall and listened as he struck it again, harder. *Thump*. The wall was not solid. There must have once been a door or a window there that had later been plastered over.

Isa drew his knife and scraped at the wall, but to little effect. A few bits of plaster came away, but nothing more. Desperate, he stood back and then kicked the wall as hard as he could. It trembled slightly. He kicked it again, and the shaking was more pronounced. He was about to kick again, when he turned and saw that the door to the room was on fire and that the flames were spreading to the walls and ceiling around it. He had no more time. He moved to the middle of the room, and then turned and ran towards the wall. He lowered his shoulder and hit the wall moving full speed. He heard a crash, felt the wall give, and the next thing he knew he was flying through empty space. He fell only a few feet before he landed with a painful thud on the roof of a neighbouring, one-storey house. He rose unsteadily, coughing from the smoke he had inhaled. He had separated his shoulder when he hit the wall, and it was pulsing with pain. But he was alive . . .

Isa staggered across the flat roof, away from the burning building. He reached the edge of the roof and dropped into the alley below. Then he leaned his shoulder against the wall of the alley, and with a wrenching motion, popped his shoulder back into its socket, clenching his jaw to keep from crying out. When the wave of agony had passed, he left the alley and circled around until he reached the street that ran towards the burning house. People were hurrying past, carrying buckets of water from the well to throw on the fire. Somewhere, a bell was ringing. At the house itself, a crowd of spectators had gathered to watch the flames. His family's keeper was standing amongst the onlookers.

Isa took a vial filled with a dark, viscous liquid from inside his tunic and carefully poured three drops on to the blade of his knife. He worked his way through the crowd, approaching the keeper from behind. When he reached him, Isa sliced the knife quickly along the back of the man's neck, leaving a small cut. The man grabbed at his neck and turned to face Isa. The man's eyes went wide with surprise. He opened his mouth but could not speak. The poison was acting too fast. Isa grabbed the man and pulled him close. 'The poison you are experiencing is taken from crushed cherry laurel leaves,' he whispered as he wiped his knife on the man's shirt. 'You will be dead in a few seconds. A better fate than you deserve.'

The man began to shake all over as Isa released him and stepped away, slipping back into the crowd. He watched as the keeper collapsed, shaking violently. A veiled woman screamed. The rest of the crowd backed away, frightened. 'What's happening to him?' someone asked. The keeper's entire body was contorted now. Foam ran from his lips. 'He's possessed!' someone shouted. Then the keeper froze, his body rigid, his eyes protruding. He twitched a few final times and then lay still. He was dead.

Two men dragged his body off to the side, where his family, the authorities or the dogs – whichever reached him first – would deal with him. The rest of the crowd turned back to watch the fire. Isa watched with them. Men continued to rush forward with buckets of water. Within an hour it was clear that the fire would not spread, and the crowd began to thin. Isa waited until the crowd had all long gone and the last ember had ceased to burn. Then, he walked over the ashen ruins of the burned house. He scooped up a handful of ash and placed it in one of the pouches that hung from his belt. This was all that he had left of his family. Dawn was breaking as he left the smoking ruin behind him and strode away towards the Maritza river to catch a boat to Constantinople, where he would find Halil.

Chapter 19

Torch in hand, Tristo marched through one of the dark tunnels far beneath the Blachernae Palace, hurrying to finish his midnight inspection so that he could move on to more entertaining pursuits. Although he had destroyed most of the tunnels, he had left some standing, afraid that bringing them down might also bring down the palace and walls that stood above them. These remaining tunnels had been bricked up, and Longo had placed guards at the end of each of them. Tristo had already inspected three of the guard posts and was on his way to the final one. This tunnel, situated under the Gate of Charisius, was the furthest from the palace. He found the two guards – men who had fought beside Longo for years – seated on the floor and leaning against a barrel of gunpowder. A lantern hung from the wall, illuminating a game of dice.

'Benito, Roberto, how goes it?' Tristo asked.

'Well enough,' Roberto replied. 'Considering that I can't seem to win.'

Tristo crouched down and watched as Roberto lost yet

again. 'Never fear,' Tristo told him. 'Bad luck never lasts forever.' Roberto nodded glumly. 'Now, you both know your orders?'

'If we see any sign of the Turks, then blow the tunnel and run for help,' Benito replied.

'Good. Somebody will be here to relieve you at first light.'

Tristo turned and stomped off down the tunnel. As soon as he was out of sight, Roberto and Benito resumed their game. But Roberto's rotten luck did not change, and after only an hour Benito had relieved him of his last few coins. 'Now what?' Roberto grumbled.

'If we can't play, then at least we can get some sleep,' Benito replied. He patted his full purse. 'I'll dream of all the beautiful Greek women that your money will buy me.'

'Fine, but you take first watch as punishment for your cursed good luck. I'll dream of winning my money back.' And with that Roberto lay down on the floor and closed his eyes. Within a few minutes he was snoring loudly.

Benito watched Roberto sleep and wondered if his winnings were enough to afford the fetching, high-priced Greek girl that he had had his eye on. He was entertaining himself with thoughts of his time with her when he heard a faint noise, a scratching sound barely audible over Roberto's snoring. Benito cocked his head, trying to locate the sound, but the noise did not repeat itself. Perhaps it had merely been a rat, scrambling across the floor in the distant darkness. Then Benito heard the sound again; this time it was a clearer, chinking sound. He shook Roberto awake.

'It's not my turn already, is it?' Roberto asked.

'Listen,' Benito told him.

'To what?'

'Just listen.' They waited in silence, and after a few seconds the chinking noise returned, louder this time. 'There! Do you hear that?' Benito asked.

'It sounds like it's coming from over here,' Roberto said as he put his ear to the wall. 'I can hear it better now. It's close. It sounds like a pick, like somebody digging. Wait – I hear a voice. I think it's a Turk!'

The words had no sooner left Roberto's mouth than the blade of a pick smashed through the wall, striking him in the head and killing him instantly. He slumped to the floor, and torchlight poured through the hole where his head had been only a second before. Turkish voices filled the passage.

Benito wasted no time. He took the lantern and lit the fuse to the powder keg that would destroy the tunnel. Then he ran. The fuse was a short one, and he would not have much time to get beyond the range of the blast. After a minute, Benito stopped. The powder should have gone off by now, but he had heard nothing. That meant that the fuse had failed or, worse, the Turks had broken through the wall and extinguished it. And if the Turks were in the tunnel, then Benito had to raise the alarm. He turned to run, but had taken only a few steps when a crossbow bolt slammed into his back, dropping him. Despite the pain, he crawled forward, crying out for help as he went. His voice reverberated down the passage, but there was no answer. Then the Turks reached him, and Benito's cries were silenced with a single blow of a sword. His severed head rolled to the side, his now silent mouth still stretched open to scream. The passage fell silent save for the quiet shuffle of hundreds of Turkish feet.

*

Longo and Sofia sat naked on her bed, a chessboard between them. She watched as he puzzled over his next move, his brow furrowed. Finally, he took her rook with his bishop. Sofia smiled. Longo did not know it yet, but four moves later he would lose his queen and three moves after that the game. 'That was a mistake,' she told him. 'I've got you now.'

Longo looked back at the board and groaned as comprehension dawned. He leaned over and kissed Sofia. 'You are too clever by half,' he told her. 'Perhaps you should be leading the defence of the city.'

'And what would you do then?'

'I would be your second in command. What do you command me to do, great leader?'

'I command you to come over here,' she said, laughing.

A loud knock on the door to Sofia's apartments interrupted them. Longo sprang from the bed and hurriedly pulled on his breeches. 'Who could that be at this hour?' Sofia wondered as she pulled on a robe. The knocking grew louder and more insistent. 'I will take care of it,' she told Longo. 'You stay here.' She left the bedroom but had not yet reached the door to her apartments when it crashed open and Notaras entered at the head of a dozen armed men.

'Where is he?' he demanded.

'Notaras! How dare you!' Sofia exclaimed indignantly.

'Where is he?' Notaras repeated, grabbing Sofia by the arm.

'I don't know who you are talking about,' Sofia said. 'No one is here but myself and my maidservants.

Notaras released her and turned to his men. 'Search the apartments and find him. I'll inspect her bedroom.'

'You cannot!' Sofia protested, stepping in front of Notaras. 'These are my private chambers. You have no right to be here!'

'I am your husband-to-be, I have every right.' He pushed her aside and strode into the bedroom. Sofia followed close behind. To her relief, there was no sign of Longo.

'Are you satisfied?' she asked. 'Now go!'

'Not yet, Princess.' Notaras went to the bed, where the chess pieces lay overturned and scattered amongst the sheets. He picked up a piece and held it out to her. 'What is this?'

'That is a queen,' Sofia replied. 'You are familiar with the game of chess?'

'Do not trifle with me, Sofia, I have no patience for it. What are these pieces doing here in your bed?'

'I was playing against myself. It is all the entertainment that I am allowed since Constantine has had me confined to my chambers.'

'I see.' Notaras continued his tour of the room and then froze. In the corner, propped against the wall, was Longo's sword. Notaras picked it up and drew the sword from its scabbard. There was no mistaking the distinctive curved blade, nor the Asian symbols etched into it. 'And what is this?' he asked, his voice cold.

Sofia flushed scarlet. 'It is . . . I . . .'

Notaras stepped close to her, and their eyes met. 'Tell me true, Princess, and be careful how you answer. On your honour, was Longo here tonight?' Sofia did not speak, but her blush deepened, spreading to her neck. Finally, she lowered her eyes and gave an almost imperceptible nod. 'I see,' Notaras said, the words forced out past his clenched jaw. 'And where is he now?'

Sofia shook her head. 'No, I cannot.'

Notaras grabbed Sofia by the arms, squeezing so hard that she gasped. 'Tell me!' he growled. 'Where is he?'

'He left,' she said. 'I don't know where he is.'

Notaras held her a moment more, then released her. His hands left red imprints on her arms. 'No matter, I will find him.' He strode from the bedroom, and Sofia followed him. Notaras's men had ransacked her apartments, turning over furniture and tearing tapestries from the walls in an effort to find some trace of Longo's presence. 'Men!' Notaras called. 'Signor Giustiniani has left, but he can't have gone far. Search the palace and find him.' The men left, and Notaras began to follow them but then stopped and turned. His eyes were shining, whether with grief or anger Sofia could not tell. 'I will deal with Longo first,' he said. 'But do not worry. I will return to deal with you, Princess.'

'And what will you do to me?' Sofia asked defiantly. 'You do not own me, whatever you may think.' She paused and looked him in the eye. 'I love him, Notaras. Don't you understand?'

Notaras smiled a twisted, painful smile. 'Yes, I do,' he told her. Then he turned and left, slamming the door to her apartments behind him.

Half-dressed, his boots unlaced and his shirt untied, Longo stumbled through one of the many hidden passages that snaked through the walls of the Blachernae Palace. He had not taken a light from Sofia's chambers, and he tripped often in the impenetrable darkness, keeping his hands on the walls to steady himself. He had not gone far when he heard something unexpected: the distant sound of footsteps. Someone was in the tunnel.

Longo quickened his pace, hurrying down a spiral staircase. The sound of steps was growing louder, and when he reached the foot of the stairs, he saw the faint glimmer of a distant torch, headed his way. Longo raced down the corridor away from the light and then into a side passage. A few seconds later, he emerged into an empty side street next to the palace and breathed a sigh of relief. He had made it.

Longo headed away from the palace, towards the nearby house where he was staying. He was just turning into his street when he came face to face with Notaras, whose lips curled back in a wicked smile. Longo hurried by, hoping to avoid a confrontation, but Notaras reached out a hand to stop him. 'And what are you doing out at such a late hour, Signor Giustiniani?' Notaras asked. He pointed to Longo's half-tied shirt. 'And so clumsily dressed?'

'I heard that there was a disturbance at the palace,' Longo lied. 'I came as quickly as I could. I hardly had time to dress.'

'Indeed,' Notaras replied. 'You even seem to have forgotten your sword.' Longo reached for his sword, but it was not there. Notaras patted his belt, and Longo saw that two swords hung there, one of which was his. Notaras unsheathed the sword and held it between them. 'A fine blade. You should be more careful where you leave it.'

'I can explain.'

'And what do you wish to explain to me, Signor Giustiniani?' Notaras spat. 'You stole my post as defender of the city, and now you have stolen Sofia. I understand perfectly.'

'She does not love you, Notaras.'

'So I have heard, but it is not Sofia that you should be worried about.' Notaras slashed Longo's sword from side to side, testing its weight.

'You are an honourable man, Notaras,' Longo said. 'It is beneath you to strike down an unarmed man.'

'Who are you to speak to me of honour?' Notaras roared. 'She was my betrothed!' He swung out, and Longo stumbled backwards, dodging the blow but falling as he did so. Notaras looked down on Longo coldly but did not attack. 'But you are right,' he said at last. 'It would give me no satisfaction to kill you unarmed.' He tossed Longo's sword to the ground and drew his own. 'Come, Signor. Either I shall have my revenge, or you shall have my life as well as my love.'

Longo left his sword lying between them as he rose. 'We should be fighting the Turks, not each other. After the siege, then you may have your duel.' Longo picked up his sword and turned to leave.

'Coward! Fight me now or all of Constantinople shall know of your cowardice and of Sofia's shame.'

Longo paused, then turned and held his sword at the ready. 'Very well then,' he said. 'But let us fight only to first blood.'

'To the death!' Notaras snarled and attacked, slicing at Longo's head and then pressing him with a series of quick thrusts. Longo parried and gave ground. He had expected Notaras to be a skilled swordsman, but he was surprised by the extent of the megadux's control. Despite his anger, Notaras fought with precision and balance.

Longo spun away from Notaras's last thrust and slashed at the megadux's side, but Notaras turned and blocked the blow, then delivered a vicious kick aimed at Longo's knee. Longo sidestepped the kick, but in doing so he lost his balance. Notaras seized the advantage and pressed his attack. He cut at Longo's legs and then shifted the direction of his sword at the last second, thrusting at Longo's chest. Longo narrowly sidestepped the blow, leaving Notaras overextended. Longo stepped in close to finish the matter, but to his surprise, Notaras managed to recover at the last second. Their swords met and locked together at the hilt, each man pushing at the other with all his strength.

Suddenly, a giant explosion shook them apart, and they each stumbled back as the ground trembled beneath their feet. As the tremors faded, they heard shouts coming from the palace. Longo and Notaras's eyes met, and they each lowered their swords.

'What was that?' Notaras asked. 'Cannon fire?'

'No,' Longo replied. 'It was an explosion in one of the tunnels.'

'Tunnels? Then that means . . .'

'The Turks are in the city,' Longo finished for him. 'Come, we must protect the emperor.'

The thick oak door to the emperor's quarters shook in its casings as a heavy blow struck it. The blow was followed by another and then another. The door had been block-aded with tables and chairs, and Constantine, Dalmata and a dozen palace guards stood ready to defend the emperor and his family. Sofia stood towards the back of the room, her sword in hand. She had hardly had time

377

to recover from Notaras's visit when Dalmata had arrived and hurried her here, telling her that Turks were in the palace.

The wood of the door began to splinter as it bent under the weight of repeated blows. One of its iron hinges was ripped from the wall, and the door sagged inwards. Constantine turned to Sofia. 'You should wait in the next room, with Sphrantzes,' he told her. Sofia began to leave but stopped in the doorway. She watched as Constantine drew his sword. 'Ready yourselves, men,' he said. 'If we are to die tonight, then let us sell our lives dearly.'

From the hallway, Sofia heard loud shouting in Turkish and the clash of swords. Then the shouting stopped and the door ceased to shake. In the silence, Sofia could hear her heart hammering in her chest.

Then, the pounding on the door started again, only this time it was less violent. 'Open the door!' a voice shouted from the other side.

'It's Longo!' Sofia cried.

'Let him in,' Constantine ordered, and a few seconds later the door swung open. Longo stepped into the room, followed closely by Notaras. A troop of palace guards stood in the hallway behind them. Notaras caught Sofia's eye, and she lowered her head.

'Thank God you have come,' Constantine said to Notaras and Longo.

'There is no time to rejoice,' Longo replied. 'We have routed the Turks, but we must stop them before they escape. If we capture one of their miners, then he can tell us where the rest of their tunnels are. Otherwise, we are still in danger.'

*

Deep beneath the palace, Notaras followed Longo through a rocky tunnel only dimly lit by their flickering torches. All around him, Notaras could hear the sound of distant footsteps echoing off the tunnel walls. Occasionally, he heard loud Turkish voices. The sounds grew and fell in volume, sometimes sounding louder in one direction and then in the other. Several times Notaras was sure that they would find the Turks around the very next corner, but there was nothing.

Behind Notaras, several hundred palace guards followed, keeping well back so that Notaras and Longo would better be able to listen for the Turks. Notaras looked back, and in the subterranean darkness, the guards appeared as little more than shadows. He could kill Longo now, Notaras realized, and in the darkness, nobody would know what he had done. Notaras would again command the city's defences. Sofia would be his once more. He half raised his sword, but then stopped.

Ahead of him, Longo had paused before a split in the tunnel. 'Do you hear that?' he whispered. There were voices coming from the tunnel to the right, and then footsteps, loud and approaching fast.

Notaras turned and shouted to the guards. 'Men, come forward now!' He swung back to see torches appear in the tunnel ahead. In the darkness he could see the light glinting off approaching swords. Notaras raised his blade and stood ready beside Longo. Then, to Notaras's amazement, Longo sheathed his sword and strode forward to meet the onrushing men.

'Tristo?' Longo called. 'Is that you?'

'Of course it's me,' Tristo replied as he strode forward into the light of Notaras's torch. 'Where are the Turks?'

Longo shook his head. 'We can't find them. It's like chasing shadows.'

'We should split up,' Notaras suggested. 'We'll have a better chance that way.'

'But if we find them, will we have enough men to stop them?' Tristo asked.

'Notaras is right. We have no other choice,' Longo replied. 'We'll divide into three groups. Tristo, you take your men back down the tunnel you came from. Notaras, you take half of the guards to the left. I'll take the other half back to the last side tunnel. Leave a torch at every branch of the tunnel to mark where you have gone. If you find the Turks, call for help. We'll come as fast as we can.'

Notaras took his men and headed down the tunnel at a jog. Now that they had split up, the sound of footsteps was even more confusing. It seemed to be coming from everywhere at once. Still, Notaras tried to follow the sound. After several twists and turns he stopped before a side tunnel. There was something strange here. The air smelled sweet, like earth and grass.

'You three,' he pointed to three of the men, 'go back and find help. The rest of you, follow me. We've got them.' Notaras set off down the tunnel at a run, his men following close behind. The breath of fresh air turned into a breeze as they ran down the tunnel, and their torches flared and guttered in the draught. Notaras could now hear Turkish voices mixed amongst the sound of tramping feet. Ahead, the tunnel turned sharply to the left. Notaras rounded the corner and ran headlong into the back of a Turkish soldier, knocking the man sprawling. The passage ahead was crowded with Turks. Some twenty yards ahead, they were squeezing through a small hole that had been broken through a brick wall.

'Don't let them escape!' Notaras yelled as he led his men into the crowd of Turks. If he could reach and hold the gap in the wall, then the Turks remaining in the tunnel could be trapped and taken prisoner. Notaras was only a dozen yards away from the hole when he noticed a barrel of gunpowder next to it. As he watched, one of the Turks touched a torch to the fuse leading to the barrel. Several of his men saw it too. 'Run! Quick!' someone yelled, and the men around him turned and fled.

'No! Stay and fight!' Notaras yelled as he sprinted in the other direction, towards the barrel. If the tunnel was destroyed, then the Turks would escape. He had to stop the fuse.

There were still five Turks between Notaras and the barrel. Either they did not know what was happening, or they were willing to sacrifice their lives so that their comrades could escape. Notaras crashed into them at a sprint, planting his shoulder into the chest of the first Turk and bowling him over. He spun off the impact, slashing with his sword as he did so and cutting the arm of another Turk, who dropped his weapon. There were still three Turks in the way and more were coming back down the tunnel to help them. The lit fuse was now racing up the side of the barrel. Notaras scooped up the sword that the injured Turk had dropped and charged towards the barrel. As he reached the remaining Turks, he parried a blow, spun to his right, lashed out with both swords, and then charged between two of the Turks, knocking them aside. The fuse was over the side of the barrel and racing towards the powder. Notaras lunged forward and sliced through it, cutting it in half only an inch from where it entered the barrel. The bit of fuse that was still burning landed harmlessly on the tunnel floor.

A second later, a sword slammed into Notaras's side. The blow was deflected by Notaras's chain mail, but it knocked the wind from him and sent him stumbling into the wall. He spun to find himself facing four Turks. Notaras lashed out, driving them back a step, but the numbers against him were too great. A sword snuck through his defences to slice his leg. He dropped to one knee. Another blow struck his arm, and he dropped one of his swords. The world around him seemed to slow. He looked up to see the Turk immediately in front of him raise his sword high to finish him off, but the blow never came. Instead, the Turk dropped his sword and slumped to the side. Standing where the Turk had been was Longo. Behind him, Greek troops were hurrying through the hole in the wall in pursuit of the Turks.

'You,' Notaras mumbled. Longo stuck out his hand and pulled Notaras to his feet. 'But why?'

'Because you would have done the same,' Longo replied. 'Now come.' They stepped through the hole in the wall, but had only gone some thirty yards before they met Tristo coming from the opposite direction, dragging a Turk behind him.

'Look what I found: a Turkish rat!' Tristo rejoiced. 'He's a miner. I found him giving orders to blow up the tunnel further down.'

'Do you know the location of the other tunnels?' Longo asked the man in Turkish.

'Allah curse you, infidel!' the Turk spat back.

'He knows something,' Longo told Tristo. 'Round up

as many prisoners as you can. You know what to do, Tristo.'

Tristo grinned. 'Don't worry, they'll talk.' He dragged the prisoner off down the tunnel, leaving Longo and Notaras alone.

Longo turned to Notaras. 'If you still wish to duel, I suggest that we wait until tomorrow. Now is not the time.'

'There will be no duel,' Notaras responded. 'You saved my life. I will not tarnish my honour by taking yours.'

'And Sofia? What will become of her?'

'I will say nothing. You can have her,' Notaras said and walked away.

Dawn was breaking when Sofia finally returned to her chambers. Constantine had insisted that she stay in his quarters until the palace had been searched, and he was certain that all of the Turks were gone. When Sofia reached her chambers, she found Notaras waiting for her, his face hard and unreadable.

'Notaras, what are you doing here?' Sofia asked.

Notaras did not reply. Instead he strode across the room and slapped her so hard that Sofia tasted blood. She sank to the floor, holding her cheek. Notaras spat at her feet. 'There is nothing between us anymore,' he said. 'You are not worthy of me.' He strode past her to the door.

'Notaras,' Sofia called after him, and he stopped at the doorway. 'I am sorry. I did not mean to hurt you.'

Notaras turned, and Sofia could see that his eyes were shining. 'Then we are both sorry, Princess,' he said and left.

*

Gennadius was awakened before dawn by the sound of a single pair of footsteps approaching down the long stone corridor that led to his prison cell. The footsteps stopped outside his cell, and he heard keys jangling. As the key clanked in the lock, Gennadius sat up, trying to look as composed as possible after ten days without a bath or a change of clothes. The door swung open. Squinting against the sudden brightness from the torchlight that flooded the cell, Gennadius could make out the features of Notaras. The megadux looked far from pleased.

'Good-morning, Notaras,' Gennadius said. 'What brings you to my humble quarters at this early hour?'

'You are free to go, monk.'

'Then what I told you about Sofia was true?'

Notaras nodded. 'Now, Gennadius, tell me of your plan to kill the sultan. I am ready to listen.'

Chapter 20

As the sun rose, Mehmed stood on a hill just out of reach of Constantinople's cannons and watched as the headless bodies of his troops were tossed over the walls, one after another. The bodies would lie at the base of the wall and rot, a grisly barrier intended to dispirit Mehmed's troops when they attacked. Mehmed had been standing there since late the previous night, when he had ordered the attack through the tunnels. He had sworn to himself that he would stay until he had seen every last body come over the wall. That was the punishment for his failure.

An ear-splitting boom caused Mehmed to clap his hands over his ears. There was a loud rumbling and just to his left, a one-hundred-yard long stretch of earth running from the wall towards the Turkish camp collapsed. As the rumbling faded, Mehmed could hear cheering coming from the walls of Constantinople. A few seconds later there was another loud boom, and another long line of earth collapsed in a cloud of dust.

'Great Sultan,' a messenger panted as he arrived at Mehmed's side. 'The Christians have discovered our tunnels.'

'Yes, I can see that,' Mehmed replied. One of the miners that the Christians had captured must have talked. And now, after weeks of digging, all that work was wasted. Over the next hour Mehmed watched as one by one, each of the Turkish mines into the city was destroyed. He consoled himself by imagining that each headless body that fell from the walls of Constantinople was the corpse of one of the miners who had betrayed him. Finally, the last of the Turkish soldiers was cast over the walls. There was renewed cheering from Constantinople, and then nothing.

Mehmed had seen enough. 'Tell my generals and viziers to meet me in my tent,' he told the messenger. But Mehmed did not go immediately to join his generals. Instead he walked through the Turkish camp with Ulu trailing behind. Dressed as a simple janissary, Mehmed drew little attention. After all, most of his troops had never seen him face to face. Everywhere he saw men with pinched faces and vacant eyes, speaking little except to grumble about the interminable siege. Mehmed joined a group of janissaries who were breakfasting before a fire. Ulu stayed out of sight just beyond the ring of firelight.

'I just got off watch,' Mehmed said. 'Spare a bite to eat?'

The grizzled old veteran who was tending the cooking pot gave Mehmed a long look, but then scooped a ladle of some white, runny substance from the pot and poured it into a bowl. He handed it to Mehmed along with a

386

piece of rock-hard *peskimet* biscuit. 'Eat your fill, or as much as you can stomach.'

Mehmed snapped off a piece of the *peskimet* and scooped up some of the concoction. He placed it in his mouth and nearly gagged at the taste. He chewed doggedly and then forced himself to swallow. 'You don't like it?' the veteran asked. 'It's the best I can do with the supplies they give us. Every day the food gets worse. But he doesn't care.' He nodded towards the sultan's tent in the distance and then looking pointedly at Mehmed: 'He eats like a soul in paradise while we're left with this slop.'

Mehmed stubbornly took another bite. 'A small price to pay for the glory and riches that will be ours when the city falls,' he said. The men around the campfire burst into laughter.

'That's rich,' the man next to Mehmed said. 'You sound just like the sultan.'

'The only thing likely to fall around here is us,' another added. 'Just look at what happened last night. The sultan's brilliant plan cost us another hundred of our best men, slaughtered without a chance in those damned tunnels.'

'I fought in his father's army,' the old veteran added. 'If Murad couldn't take the city, then what chance does this boy think he has?'

Mehmed put the bowl aside and stood. 'Thank you for the meal,' he said stiffly.

'Any time,' the old veteran retorted. 'We always have room for a fellow soldier.'

Mehmed strode away, and Ulu joined him. 'Shall I have those men beaten, My Lord?' Ulu asked.

'No. Find out who the old man is. I want him placed in charge of supplies for my troops.'

'Very well, My Lord.'

Mehmed stormed into his tent in a foul mood. Halil and his chief generals – Ishak Pasha and Mahmud Pasha – bowed as he entered. Mehmed marched straight past them and to a low table that had been covered with a lavish spread of food. He swept it on to the floor. Servants stepped forward immediately to remove the mess. 'Leave it!' Mehmed shouted, and then turned to face his advisors. 'What is this, Halil?' he snapped. 'Why am I served fine foods when my men have only filth to eat?'

'I have done my best, Your Highness,' Halil sputtered. 'The army is so large and . . .'

'Enough. You are no longer in charge of supplies.' Halil began to protest, but Mehmed cut him off with a wave of his hand. 'I have another task for you, Halil, something more suited to your talents.' He turned to Ishak Pasha. 'Ishak, what went wrong last night?'

'The tunnels were much more extensive than we anticipated, My Lord. It took the men some time to find their way, and by then the Christians had been alerted.'

Mehmed nodded. 'Do you think that the Christians knew of our plan?'

'No, My Lord,' Ishak replied. 'I believe they were surprised.'

'I see. Halil, have you found any spies in our army?'

'I have uncovered several traitors who have been in communication with the enemy, Your Highness.'

'Have them executed immediately. Let them be an example to all who dare betray me.'

'Excuse me, My Lord, but is that wise?' Ishak asked. 'Morale amongst the men is low. An execution could cause trouble.'

'Very well. Execute them quietly, Halil,' Mehmed ordered.

'I will do so,' Halil said. 'But Ishak Pasha is correct. The men are not happy, Your Highness. They say that this siege is cursed, that Allah does not wish us to succeed.'

'Allah? Allah does not wish it?' Mehmed's voice was rising. '*I* wish it. That is all that matters.'

'Still, Your Highness, the men are tired. They grumble that they came to fight, not to dig tunnels and haul cannons. Perhaps we should pull back for a time?'

'And what do the rest of you think? Do you agree with Halil?' Mehmed asked. Ishak and Mahmud Pasha both nodded yes. 'Very well, I shall allow the men to rest for now. You are all right about one thing, at least. This siege must end, and soon.'

Several days later, not long after sunrise, Longo walked along the top of the inner wall, inspecting the damage done by the Turkish bombardment. The wall was holding up well for the most part, although the outer wall at the Mesoteichion – where the wall dipped down into the Lycus valley – had long since been reduced to rubble. Still, Longo was more worried about the men defending the city than the walls.

Over a week had passed since the Turks' midnight attack on the palace, and other than the continual bombardment and a brief, probing attack by the Turks a few nights ago, the days had passed uneventfully. Life in the city had even taken on a sense of routine as people grew accustomed to the siege. Instead of the Turks, people's worries had turned to food and the coming harvest. The soldiers on the walls were not immune from such worries; every day they looked thinner. Many of the Greek troops at the far south end of the wall had yet to see any fighting, and rather than sit and wait at the walls, they had begun to desert their posts in large numbers. Two days ago, Longo had come across a dozen troops, their armour piled to the side as they worked in the fields just inside the city wall. He had ordered them to return to their posts, but they had refused to go.

'How can I sit on that wall and do nothing when my family is starving?' one of the men had complained. 'The rations that are handed out every day aren't enough to live on.'

'And who knows when this cursed siege will end?' another man had added. 'If we don't get this harvest in and the crops planted for the autumn harvest, then we might as well let the Turks take the city. We'll starve otherwise.'

Longo had responded to their complaints by instituting a rotation system, so that only a third of the men at any given time would leave the walls for the fields. But the problem of supplies could not be solved so easily. Food in the city was growing scarce, and rationing only delayed the inevitable. Each day the troops grew weaker and hungrier. In another two months' time there would be nobody left to defend the walls. The city desperately needed fresh supplies from outside, but each day the lookouts scanned the distant horizon to no avail. No ships had come to relieve them. William had not returned.

Longo stopped on the Blachernae wall where it crested the hill overlooking the Golden Horn. In the middle of the calm waters of the Horn lay another source of worry: a partially completed floating bridge that advanced from the far, Turkish-controlled shore of the Horn towards the sea walls on the Christian side. Built from wide planks lashed over the hulls of ships, with dozens of huge barrels placed in the gaps between, the bridge looked strong enough to support hundreds of men and perhaps even cannons. As of now, it reached only halfway across the waters of the Horn, but once the bridge was completed, the sultan's armies could threaten the sea walls. Longo needed no reminder that when Constantinople had fallen to the Latin crusaders in 1203, the attack had come against the sea walls. He would have to move more men, men he could not spare, to protect those walls.

Longo was distracted from his grim thoughts by Paolo Bocchiardo, the commander of this section of the wall. 'Longo, there you are,' Paolo called. 'Have you noticed the cannons? They've stopped.'

He was right. For the first time since the siege began, the Turkish cannons had fallen silent. 'No cannons, yet there is no sign of an attack. What does this mean?' Longo asked.

'That is what I came to tell you,' Paolo said, grinning. 'There has been a messenger from the Turks. They say that the sultan wants to discuss peace!'

Late the next night, Longo stood at the window of Sofia's bedroom and gazed up at the heavens, where the full moon was slowly disappearing in a spectacular eclipse. The uneclipsed edge seemed to glow brighter as it shrank into a smaller and smaller sliver of light. 'It's beautiful,' he said to Sofia. 'You should come and look.'

Sofia stayed on her bed. 'It is a bad omen,' she said. 'They say that when Constantine the Great first founded the city, there was an eclipse. He predicted that the city would not fall until there was another eclipse to extinguish his glory.'

Longo laughed. 'Surely you do not believe such things.'

'No, but it is an old prophecy, and many people do believe it. They will see only disaster in your pretty moon.'

'Why such dark thoughts?' Longo asked. 'There is hope at last. The siege is going well, and any day now help should arrive from Italy. Mehmed knows this. That is why he is sending his grand vizier to negotiate a peace.'

'Perhaps he only seeks to buy time to prepare for another assault.'

Longo moved to the bed and pulled Sofia close to him. 'Smile,' he said. 'The worst is over. Perhaps this eclipse is a good omen.'

'But you do not believe in omens.' Sofia turned to look Longo in the eyes. 'When the siege is over, what will become of us?'

'What do you mean?'

'The emperor will never agree to our marriage. He values your service, but you are only a minor noble, Longo. And there will be dozens of new alliances that he can cement through my marriage.'

'Do you need his permission?' Longo asked.

'I am a princess, Longo, I too have responsibilities. If I do not fulfil them, then I will be nothing.'

'No, not nothing. You will be my wife, and if that means that we are not welcome in Constantinople, so be it. I swear that I will never leave your side so long as I live. We can live on Chios. It will be a good life.'

'You would save the empire, only to flee it? Protect the emperor, only to steal a princess?'

'If it means winning you, then yes. And you, will you come with me?'

'Of course.' Sofia embraced Longo, and they held each other tight. Finally, Sofia drew away. 'You should go,' she said. 'With the eclipse the streets are dark. There will be no better time to leave.'

Longo sighed and rose from the bed. 'Very well.' He pulled on his boots and then belted his sword around his waist. 'I shall return as soon as I am able.' He kissed Sofia, then headed for the secret passage.

'Longo,' Sofia called, stopping Longo just before he disappeared into the dark passageway. She rose from the bed and went to him. 'There is something that I need to tell you. It is about Notaras.'

'What? I thought that he had agreed to say nothing about us to the emperor.'

'It is not my reputation that I am worried about,' Sofia said. 'You must be careful of Notaras. He came back here the night he found out about us. There's something not right with him now. I fear he will do something foolish.'

'I will keep an eye on him,' Longo said and slipped into the secret passageway.

The streets of Constantinople were so dark that Longo could only dimly make out the outline of the houses around him as he walked the short distance from the palace to his *palazzo*. There was a hush in the air, and he could clearly hear the gentle rustle of leaves coming from a stand of trees in the walled courtyard he was passing. Somewhere ahead of him a dog barked furiously and then suddenly stopped.

Longo was crossing through a small square when he thought he heard footsteps behind him. He turned but saw nothing. Nevertheless, he kept his hand on his sword as he continued. Longo left the square and entered a narrow, dark passageway that wound towards the *palazzo*. He had only gone a dozen feet when he heard a rock bouncing across the street behind him. He drew his sword and turned, but the passage behind him was empty. 'Is anybody there?' he called out. He waited, but there was no answer. Then, behind him, he heard another noise: the almost imperceptible hiss of steel sliding past leather. Longo spun around just as a dagger flashed by his head and embedded itself in the wall behind him. Overhead, the eclipse had begun to pass, and the passageway was now growing lighter. Longo squinted and could just make out the dim outline of a man dressed in black disappearing down the alley. He had not seen the man's face, but he could guess who it was: the Spanish assassin.

Longo pulled the dagger from the wall and then made his way back to the *palazzo* without further incident. Tristo was up late gambling, and he rose in alarm when he saw Longo enter with sword and dagger in hand. 'What happened? Are you all right?'

'Fine . . . just,' Longo replied. 'The Spanish assassin attacked me moments ago. I was lucky not to receive his dagger in my back.' He handed the knife to Tristo, who smelled it.

'The blade is poisoned.'

'It seems this assassin is determined to finish his job.

I wonder how much Paolo Grimaldi is paying him,' Longo said. 'I want guards posted at the *palazzo* at night. And Tristo, keep your ears open. There are not so many Spaniards in the city. See if you can find him.'

The next morning Longo met with Constantine and Sphrantzes in the palace council room. The grand vizier was to come to the city under a flag of truce to discuss the terms of a peace between the Turks and Christians, and Constantine had asked Longo to attend the negotiations. Sphrantzes and Longo sat, while Constantine paced the room.

'Do you believe this talk of peace?' Constantine asked them. 'I fear this may only be another of the sultan's tricks to distract us while he prepares some fresh devilry.'

'Whether the sultan truly seeks peace is beside the point,' Sphrantzes said. 'We must take him at his word. The question is: what are we willing to sacrifice to obtain peace? Increased tribute to the sultan is certain, as is an expanded Turkish quarter. But are we willing to sacrifice our Black Sea provinces? The Morea even?'

'I long for peace, but I do not wish to save Constantinople only to lose my empire,' Constantine said. 'I would rather fight, so long as we stand a chance. What say you, Longo? Can we hold the walls if the sultan's demands are too great?'

'I do not know, My Lord,' Longo replied. 'The men are hungry and tired. Every day they grow weaker. We desperately need reinforcements. If the Turks attack now, it will be a close-fought battle. I cannot predict the outcome, but I will tell you this: no price is too great to pay for peace.'

Constantine nodded. 'Then let us hope that the sultan's offer is not a ruse.'

There was a knock on the door, and it opened. Dalmata stepped through. 'Grand Vizier Halil Pasha,' he pronounced.

Halil entered the council chambers and bowed low before the emperor. 'Thank you for receiving me, Your Excellency,' he said.

'You are most welcome in my city,' Constantine replied. Halil bowed again. Constantine gestured towards Sphrantzes, who rose and bowed. 'This is George Sphrantzes, my most trusted advisor, who I believe you have met.'

'A pleasure to see you again, Vizier,' Sphrantzes said to Halil.

'And this,' Constantine continued, 'is Signor Giustiniani, the commander of the city's defences.'

Longo rose but did not speak. He stood stiffly, jaw clenched and his hand on his sword as his mind filled with painful memories. Standing before him was the man that he had hunted all these years, the man who had murdered his family.

'Signor Giustiniani?' Sphrantzes asked, but Longo barely heard him over the blood pounding in his temples. He felt oddly detached from the world, as if his rage had somehow severed the link between his body and his soul.

When Longo spoke, his voice was quiet and hard. 'It is a pleasure to see you again, Halil Pasha. I have looked forward to this meeting for a long time.'

'My apologies, but I do not recognize you. We have met before?'

'We have indeed.' Longo drew his sword.

'What treachery is this!' Halil exclaimed, backing away into the corner.

'I was only a child, living near Salonika,' Longo continued, ignoring Halil's protest. He took a step towards the grand vizier. 'You burned my home and killed my brother. You took me captive and forced me into the janissaries. You had my parents gutted and left for the wolves.' Longo took another step and raised his sword.

Constantine stepped between the two men. 'Think of what you are doing!' He hissed. 'This is our one chance at peace. If you kill him, then we may well all die.'

Longo paused. He had devoted his life to the death of this one man. How could he simply let him go? What did it matter what happened afterwards so long as Halil was dead? Longo looked at the grand vizier, cringing in the corner. 'You do not understand,' he told Constantine. He pushed past the emperor and strode to Halil, who shrank back and raised his hands in a futile attempt to protect himself.

'He is a madman!' Halil cried. 'Somebody stop him!'

But there was no one to stop him. Longo raised his sword high, but then paused. An image of Sofia had flashed into his mind, an image of her as she had looked last night. He had sworn then that he would never leave her. He had sworn that he would protect her. If he killed Halil, then he would not just be sacrificing Sofia, but all of Constantinople. Longo lowered his sword. 'Count yourself lucky,' he told Halil. 'And pray that we never meet again.' He sheathed his sword and headed for the door.

'I remember you, now,' Halil said, stopping Longo in the doorway. Halil had straightened himself and regained his aloof demeanour. 'Enforcing *devshirme* in Salonika was a nasty business. I made examples of so many people. But I remember you, in particular.' Halil fingered the long scar running down his cheek. 'I could have had you killed for what you did to me that day. You owe me your life.'

Longo stood unmoving in the doorway for a moment, his head bowed. Then he raised his head and looked Halil in the eyes. 'I owe you nothing,' he spat and strode from the room. He left the palace and then kept walking, mounting the land wall and heading south towards the Sea of Marmora, some two miles off. But no matter how fast he walked, he could not outpace the memories that tormented him: his family's home in Greece; the thatch roof on fire; his brother cut down by janissaries as he struggled in vain to defend Longo; and most painful of all, his mother's face as he had last seen her. Despite all her pain, her eyes had still been alert and focused. She had looked right at Longo, silently pleading for help, for vengeance.

Longo came to a halt atop the Golden Gate and turned to face the distant Turkish camp, his hands gripping the rough stone of the tower battlement so hard that it hurt. But he hardly registered the pain; he was thinking of all the years that he had trained, of all the Turks he had killed, all so that he could avenge his parents. Now he had finally found their killer, and he had let him live. There were more important things than revenge. He knew that now.

Longo released the battlement and turned away from the Turkish army, letting his eyes follow the walls as they ran down to the Sea of Marmora, which sparkled under a cloudless sky. As he gazed out at the waters below, he spotted a lone Turkish ship tacking towards the Acropolis and the Golden Horn beyond. Longo looked more closely. He recognized that ship. It was *la Fortuna*!

As *la Fortuna* neared the Acropolis, a pair of Turkish warships set out to intercept it. *La Fortuna* sailed straight for them and then slowed, allowing the Turkish ships to come alongside. Longo expected Turkish sailors to storm aboard *la Fortuna* any second, but after a moment, the ship sailed on, unmolested. Its disguise had worked. William had returned.

Longo was waiting at the dock long before *la Fortuna* arrived. Tristo had joined him, and a crowd had gathered on the sea walls to welcome the ship. The people cheered as the vessel slid into its place alongside the pier. William leaped down from the side of the ship before it was even moored.

Tristo stepped forward and engulfed William in a powerful hug. 'Welcome back, young pup. I knew you'd make it.'

'If you squeeze him any harder, he may not survive the welcome,' Longo said with a smile and stepped forward to embrace William. 'We missed you. Now, what news do you bring?'

'The good news first,' William said. 'Tristo, you are to be a father. Maria is with child.'

Tristo's eyebrows arched. 'A father?' he said softly. Then he grinned and slapped William on the back. 'A father!' he roared. 'I just hope the little bugger is mine.'

Longo laughed. 'Congratulations, old friend.' He turned back to William. 'And your other news?'

'Phlatanelas is dead. On our way out, we had to fight past a Turkish ship blocking the Dardanelles Strait.'

William eyed the crowd. 'The rest of my news is worse still. Perhaps we had best discuss it inside.'

Longo nodded. 'I will take you to the emperor.'

Longo led William to a pair of horses. They mounted and rode for the palace to the renewed cheering of the crowd. They arrived in the great hall to find the emperor waiting for them.

'Thank God you have come,' Constantine said as William and Longo approached. 'What news do you bring? Are there more ships on the way?'

'I am sorry, My Lord, but no more help is coming from the West,' William said. 'The Venetians sit in Crete, but they refuse to move until they receive official orders from Venice. I fear the orders will take months to arrive.'

'But the pope called for a crusade!' Constantine said. 'Surely someone has answered the call.'

'We found no other ships willing to come to our aid,' William said. 'I am sorry, My Lord.'

'And what of my brothers, Demetrius and Thomas?'

William shook his head. 'Demetrius refused to see me. Thomas at least offered grain. I took as much as my ship's hold would carry.'

'You have done well, William,' Constantine said, although his slumping shoulders betrayed his disappointment. 'Now, I must return to my meeting with the vizier. Let us pray for peace, gentlemen.'

Chapter 21

William awoke to the sound of yelling. He rose and went to the window, tiptoeing so as not to wake Tristo, who shared his room. He looked out, and in the pre-dawn light he could see a man running down the street, crying out loudly as he went. All along the street men and women were stepping out of their homes, forming an excited crowd. Some people cried to the heavens, while others began to weep. Several women fainted.

'Tristo!' William shouted. Tristo snorted and rolled away from him. William went to him and shook him awake. 'Come look at this.' Tristo joined him at the window. Just then, bells all over the city began to ring. There were renewed shouts from the crowd in the street.

'The bells . . . it must be an attack!' William said.

'We must get to the walls!' Tristo replied. They rushed downstairs and out into the street. Tristo saw one of Longo's men and grabbed him. 'Where are you going?' he demanded. 'You should be at your post.'

'My post?' the man asked. 'What?'

'Are you daft?' Tristo yelled, struggling to be heard over the noise of the crowd and bells. 'The Turks are attacking. You must get to the walls.'

'The Turks aren't attacking,' the man shouted back. 'It's over! The siege is over!'

'What do you mean, it's over?' William put in. 'What has happened?'

'Haven't you heard? The emperor reached terms with the grand vizier. It's over! We've won!' With that he moved off down the street.

William and Tristo looked at each other, and then embraced, Tristo lifting William clear off the ground. 'Thank God!' he roared. He put William down. 'Let's celebrate! I'm going to get famously drunk!'

'Let's find Longo first,' William said. 'I want to hear this news from him.'

William and Tristo found Longo atop the wall, standing with the emperor and Dalmata. They were looking out at a pavilion that had been erected on the broad field that lay between the city walls and the front lines of sultan's army. 'Is it true?' William asked. 'Will there be peace?'

'Last night the grand vizier and Sphrantzes agreed to terms,' Longo replied. 'This morning Halil returned to request a meeting between the emperor and the sultan. They are each to be accompanied by only one guard. That is all we know.'

'What about the bells?'

'Rumours often travel faster than the truth,' Constantine said. 'And they are more easily believed, I fear.'

'Look, there he is,' Longo said. He pointed to the plain

below where the sultan, accompanied only by Ulu, was riding out to the pavilion.

'Ready my horse,' Constantine said.

'Do not go, My Lord,' Dalmata urged. 'It is a trap.'

'Trap or no, I must go,' Constantine said. 'Look at their numbers.' He pointed to the Turks' endless camp, stretching away to the horizon. 'We cannot hold out forever. I must make peace with the sultan.'

'Then at least let me be the one to accompany you, My Lord.'

'No, Dalmata. I will take Signor Giustiniani.'

'But My Lord, I should be the one,' Dalmata protested.

Constantine placed his hand on Dalmata's shoulder. 'Stay here, old friend. If anything goes wrong, I want you to lead a group of riders to rescue me. And if I die, then you will protect my family.' Dalmata nodded. 'Very well then,' Constantine said. 'Come, Signor Longo. I am eager to meet the sultan face to face.'

Longo and Constantine descended from the wall to find that a crowd had gathered around the Golden Gate. The people knelt when they saw their emperor and scattered cries of 'God be with you!' and 'Bless you Constantine!' accompanied him as he mounted and rode out through the gate. He and Longo passed through the double walls and trotted out to the pavilion, a square, open-sided tent that had been set up over a red carpet. Next to the pavilion, the sultan sat astride his horse, waiting for them. Beside him was Ulu, grim and stone-faced. He showed no sign of recognizing Longo. Longo turned his attention to the sultan.

Mehmed was younger than Longo had expected, twenty or twenty-one years old at the most. He was of average height, with an athletic build and striking features: full lips, a prominent nose and high cheekbones. But Mehmed's eyes were what caught Longo's attention. Intense and penetrating, they seemed to burrow into Longo's very soul.

'Emperor Constantine,' Mehmed said in accented but correct Greek. 'Your presence is most welcome.'

'Sultan Mehmed, I am honoured to meet you,' Constantine replied. 'I hope that we can establish peace between our peoples. This siege has lasted too long.'

'I certainly agree,' Mehmed said. He gestured to Ulu. 'This is Ulubatli Hasan, the supreme *aga* of the janissary and my personal guard. As promised, he is unarmed. And who is this who accompanies you, emperor?'

'Count Giovanni Giustiniani Longo of Genoa and Chios, the commander of my forces,' Constantine replied.

'Ah, the defender of Constantinople,' Mehmed said, regarding Longo with renewed interest. 'You have proven yourself a worthy adversary, signor.'

Longo bowed at the compliment. 'And you, great Sultan, have shown wisdom beyond your years.'

'You flatter me, signor, but it is flattery that I am happy to receive. Now, shall we be seated?' There was a table in the centre of the pavilion, with one chair on either side. Mehmed sat in the seat on the side of the Turkish army; Constantine on the side of Constantinople. Ulu and Longo stood behind the chairs of their respective leaders. 'You have, I believe, discussed terms of a peace with Halil?' Mehmed began.

'The grand vizier and my councillor, Sphrantzes, have agreed upon terms that I am willing to accept,' Constantine replied. 'I will pay an increased tribute for three years, to cover your costs for the siege. And the pretender Orhan will be returned to your court.'

Mehmed waved his hand dismissively. 'There will be no such peace. I have not come for your money or for the head of Orhan. I have come for Constantinople.'

'But this is an outrage!' Constantine protested. 'The grand vizier . . .'

'The grand vizier means nothing,' Mehmed said with finality. 'I am the sultan. My word is the only one that matters. And I tell you that there can be no peace between us so long as you control Constantinople. The city is a thorn in my side and a threat to my empire. As long as it is in Christian hands, my people will never feel secure.'

'Constantinople is not mine to give,' Constantine replied sternly. 'It is the key to an empire that has lasted for over a thousand years. I will die before you set foot within its walls.'

'You are a noble man, Constantine. I expected nothing less. But know that if you choose to fight, then no quarter will be given to you or your people. Your men will be slaughtered; your women raped and sold into slavery. Their blood will be on your hands.'

'No, Sultan. It will be on yours.'

'That may be,' Mehmed agreed. 'But I can live with their blood. Can you?' Constantine made no reply, and Mehmed continued, leaning forward over the table as he spoke. 'Surrender, and your people will be spared. Those who wish to leave Constantinople will be given free passage. And you may keep the Morea to rule over as you see fit. I will also grant you a fiefdom elsewhere in my empire, wherever you desire. But if you choose to fight, then I swear to you, you will die and the streets of Constantinople will run with blood.'

Constantine sat speechless, his head bowed. When he looked up, Longo met his eyes and saw in them anger battling with a hopeless resignation. Finally, Constantine spoke. 'You will have my answer, but not now. I need time.'

'Very well,' Mehmed said, and rose from his chair. 'You have one day to answer, no more. And let me remind you. Our law allows for two days of plunder. If you do not accept my terms, then you and your people can expect no mercy. You have one day. Farewell, Emperor.'

Mehmed turned and went to his horse. Ulu stayed behind. 'Leave this city, Longo,' he said quietly. 'If we meet again, then one of us will die.' Then he turned and followed his master.

'Come, Constantine,' Longo said. 'We must get back to the walls. It is not safe here.'

Constantine rose slowly, his eyes still fixed on the retreating figure of the sultan. 'I am the protector of my people. Shall I allow them to be slaughtered? What should I do?'

'You are the emperor. It is for you to decide.'

'You are right.' Constantine straightened, and his jaw took on a firmer set. 'Come. There is much to decide and not much time. I must speak with the council.'

The council met that evening in the emperor's palace. Sphrantzes, Notaras, Longo, the Archbishop Leonard and the various commanders were all there. When the emperor arrived, he looked as if he had aged years since that morning. His shoulders were slumped, his brow creased and bags had formed under his eyes.

'Thank you for coming,' he began. 'We face a difficult decision. The sultan has offered to spare the lives of my people if I surrender. He will give free passage to any who wish to leave the city, and he has offered me the Morea and a fiefdom in his lands.' Constantine paused and looked at each of the men around the table in turn. 'I will not surrender Constantinople,' he said finally. 'I will stay and fight, to the death if necessary. If we withstand this final assault, then victory will be ours.

'But I will not force you to stand beside me,' Constantine continued. 'If any of you wish to try to escape tonight by sea, then I will understand. You will have my thanks for the sacrifices that you have already made.'

'I will stay by your side to the death, My Lord,' Dalmata said.

'And I,' Longo echoed. One by one, each of the men around the table pledged themselves to stay.

'Thank you all,' Constantine said. 'Tomorrow I will send a messenger to the sultan telling him that I have refused his offer. Whoever delivers the message may not return. I will not order a man to his death. Ask amongst your men for volunteers.'

'I will go,' Notaras said.

Longo had not expected anything like this. 'No, Notaras,' he said. 'We need you here, at the walls. The Greeks look to you as their leader.'

'And if I die, then they will fight to avenge me,' Notaras said. 'But I do not plan to die. I have heard that the sultan is an honourable man. I do not believe that he will dare to put to death the megadux of Constantinople. And if he does, then I will not die without a fight.'

'I thank you for your offer, Notaras,' Constantine said. 'But I forbid it. You are too valuable to risk your life in such a way.'

'You cannot forbid me this,' Notaras replied. 'As megadux it is my right and duty to speak for Constantinople. I will not send another to do my duty.'

'It is not your duty to die like this,' Constantine said.

Notaras met the emperor's eye. 'You said it yourself, My Lord. If I am not willing to give my life, then how can I ask the same of my men?'

'Perhaps Notaras is right,' Sphrantzes added. 'The sultan has killed lesser emissaries, but he will hesitate before putting the megadux to death. Notaras might even be able to persuade the sultan to let us evacuate some of the women and children.'

'Very well,' Constantine said. 'You will deliver my message to the sultan, Notaras. But I expect you to return. Do nothing foolish.'

'I will not, My lord,' Notaras replied. 'I swear it.'

The next morning Notaras stood in the shadow of the Golden Gate, dressed in his finest silver-plated armour in preparation for his visit with the sultan. The armour was for show only. Notaras had no intention of fighting. He had spent the night before at the Haghia Sofia, praying. Now he felt calm and ready. He would do what needed to be done.

The emperor and Longo had come to see him off. Constantine stepped forward and embraced Notaras. 'God give you strength We will be watching and waiting on the walls. I expect you to return.'

'I will do what I must, My Lord,' Notaras replied.

Longo stepped forward and offered Notaras his hand. After a moment's hesitation, Notaras took it.

'It has been an honour to fight beside you,' Longo told him. 'Do return, Notaras. We will need you in the days to come.'

'If I do not return, guard the city well,' Notaras replied.

'I will,' Longo said. He lowered his voice. 'About Sofia . . .'

'You are a good man,' Notaras cut him off. 'I cannot blame you for loving her. I ask only that you protect her.'

Nearby, bells began to ring, signalling a changing of the guard on the walls of Constantinople. 'It is time,' Constantine said. 'God be with you, Notaras.'

Notaras nodded and mounted his horse as the Golden Gate swung open before him. He rode out past the walls and on to the plain beyond. Ahead of him loomed the Turkish fortifications: pointed logs projecting from a rampart of dirt some four feet high. Notaras headed for a low point in the middle of the earthen wall. When he reached it he found a troop of janissaries in their black armour waiting for him. At their head was a giant of a man.

'Dismount and come with us,' the huge janissary said in heavily accented Greek. Notaras dismounted and the troop closed around him, forming a large square with Notaras in the centre. Together, they set off into the middle of the camp. Notaras could see little past the janissaries around him, but from what he did see, the camp appeared to be in a frenzy of activity. He glimpsed several men piecing together wooden ladders, and many others sharpening weapons. Clearly, the sultan anticipated a fight.

The square came to a halt, and the janissaries in front

of Notaras stepped to either side, revealing a large red tent with the sultan's standard flying atop it. Notaras stepped towards the entrance, but a tall, thin man in luxurious robes came out of the tent and stopped him. 'Greetings,' the man said in perfect Greek. 'I am Halil, grand vizier to the sultan. What is your name, and why have you come?'

'I am Lucas Notaras, megadux of Constantinople,' Notaras replied. 'I have come on behalf of the Emperor Constantine to deliver his response to the sultan.'

'Very well,' Halil replied. 'You must remove your weapons.' Notaras unbelted his sword and handed it to the janissary leader. The giant man began to search Notaras, but Halil waived him off. 'I will search him personally, Ulu,' he said. He quickly searched Notaras, patting his sides and feeling under his armour. When he had finished, Halil waved Notaras forward. 'Follow me.'

Notaras followed Halil into the tent. The floor and walls were covered with thick carpets, and the space was well lit with braziers and lanterns. On the far side of the tent the sultan lounged upon a divan, surrounded by generals in dark-grey armour and advisors in robes of gold and scarlet. Janissary guards lined the sides of the tent. Ulu followed Notaras inside and stood directly behind him. Halil motioned for Notaras to stop some twenty feet from the sultan. The grand vizier then spoke to Mehmed loudly in Turkish. Notaras understood nothing but his own name.

When Halil had finished, he turned and addressed Notaras in Greek. 'It is customary to kneel before the sultan.'

Notaras frowned. 'I am megadux of the Roman Empire. I kneel before no man but the emperor.'

There was grumbling from all sides at his response. Ulu leaned forward and growled in Notaras's ear, 'Bow before the sultan, dog.'

Notaras stood his ground. Ulu began to draw his sword, but the sultan waved him back. 'Let him be, Ulu,' Mehmed said in Greek. 'If the megadux will only kneel before his master, then so be it. He shall kneel before me soon enough. Now tell me, what message do you bring from the emperor?'

'The emperor will not surrender,' Notaras said. 'Nor will he ever serve you. He does ask, however, that you give safe passage to any women or children who wish to leave the city.'

Mehmed laughed. 'The emperor refuses my offer, and yet he makes demands.' The smile fell from Mehmed's lips, and when he spoke again his voice was harsh. 'There will be no safe passage. The people of Constantinople have had their chance to flee. When Constantinople falls, my soldiers will be given two days to sack the city. That is our law. I cannot change it. Tell that to your emperor. You may go.'

Notaras did not move. 'I have not finished. There is more that I must tell you, but I must speak to you alone.'

'Alone?' Mehmed retorted. 'Do you think me a fool? Whatever you have to say, you may say it here.'

Notaras glanced around the room at the men lining the walls. He would have preferred to speak to the sultan in private, but what he had to say would become known soon enough. And besides, most of the brutes in the tent probably did not speak Greek. 'I wish to make you an offer, Sultan,' Notaras said. 'You have seen how strong the walls of Constantinople are. The people of Constantinople are equally strong. They will fight to the death, and your army will be broken upon our walls.'

Mehmed sat upright. 'You speak of an offer, and yet I hear only insults,' he snapped. 'What is it that you wish to say? Speak quickly, Megadux, before I lose my patience.'

'I can show you a way into the city.'

'And what do you seek in return?'

'The emperor is a fool to reject your offer,' Notaras said. 'I am no fool. I ask for that which you offered the emperor: the territory of the Morea to rule as emperor.'

'Is that all?'

'I ask also that the Orthodox Church be allowed to remain in Constantinople and that the monk Gennadius be made patriarch. He is a wise man. It is he who showed me the way into the city.'

'A pity that he is not here, then,' Mehmed said. He paused, studying Notaras. The seconds passed, and Notaras could feel sweat beading on his forehead. If the sultan did not accept his offer, then all was lost. Finally, Mehmed spoke, but not to Notaras. 'What do you think of this offer, Halil?'

'I know of this monk, Gennadius. He is the one who warned us of the attempt to burn our fleet,' Halil replied. 'He can be trusted. I think that you should consider the megadux's offer.'

Mehmed nodded and turned back to Notaras. 'I have heard of you, Megadux. You have a reputation.'

'Then you know that you can trust my word.'

'What I have heard,' Mehmed continued, 'is that you would do anything to protect the Roman Empire, even sacrifice your life. Yet now you offer me Constantinople. Why?'

'I fought for the people of Constantinople,' Notaras said. 'They have betrayed their faith. They have betrayed me. There is nobody left there to fight for.'

'Not even the emperor?'

'The city will be better ruled by you than by Constantine,' Notaras replied. 'He turned our defences over to a Latin and sold our city to the pope for nothing. He has sealed his fate. I would rather live under the sultan than under such a man.'

'Very well. Show me the way into the city. If you can offer me Constantinople, then you will have everything you ask for and more.'

Longo and Constantine stood on the wall above the Golden Gate, their eyes fixed upon the distant tent of the sultan. Sphrantzes and Dalmata had joined them, and they all waited in silence. Sphrantzes bit at his thumbnail, while Dalmata fingered the hilt of his sword. Constantine gripped the wall. Longo stood with his hands clasped tight behind his back. Finally, Notaras emerged from the tent. His polished armour flashed in the sun, making him recognizable even at this great distance. His horse was brought to him, and Notaras mounted.

'He is safe,' Constantine said. 'Thank God for that. The megadux is a difficult man. But he is brave, and his men love him. I do not know how we would have replaced him.'

Longo merely nodded. Notaras was not out of danger yet. A dozen mounted janissaries surrounded him and led the megadux some twenty yards from the sultan's tent.

Then they stopped. 'Look,' Longo said. 'The sultan.' Mehmed had emerged from the tent, and all around him Turks were kneeling. A horse was brought to Mehmed, and he mounted and joined the group around Notaras. Together, they all set off at a trot, riding towards the walls of Constantinople.

'Perhaps the sultan is honouring the megadux by escorting him from his camp,' Sphrantzes suggested.

'Or perhaps Notaras is being led to his execution,' Dalmata countered grimly.

The group of horsemen had passed the Turkish fortifications now. They stopped just short of the range of the Christian cannons, turned to their left, and began to ride parallel to the walls. They were close enough now that Longo could make out their gestures. Notaras seemed to be pointing to the walls as he rode.

'What is he doing?' Constantine asked.

Notaras brought his horse to a halt opposite the point where the single Blachernae wall met with the Theodosian double walls. A huge round tower stood at the juncture of the two walls. 'It is there,' Notaras called back to the sultan, who sat astride a horse some ten feet away. He pointed to the dark wedge of space formed where the curve of the tower met the Blachernae wall. 'There is a sally port called the Kerkoporta hidden by the curve of the tower. It allows troops to emerge and surprise anybody who is attacking the Blachernae wall.'

'That is all you have to show me?' Mehmed called back. 'What good will this do?'

'If you attack just before dawn in two day's time, I will see to it that your men find the door unlocked and unguarded,' Notaras replied. 'From there, your men can enter the city. They will attack the defenders from behind, and the city will fall.'

Mehmed rode his horse closer to Notaras. 'How do I know that this is not some trick? I see no door. Perhaps you hope to have my men ride into an ambush.'

'The Kerkoporta is there,' Notaras insisted. 'Come closer and I can point it out to you.' After a pause, Mehmed spurred his horse forward, so that he was now only a few feet from Notaras.

'Where is it?' the sultan asked.

Notaras leaned over and pointed with one hand, while his other hand slipped inside his armour. 'There.'

'Yes, I see it!' Mehmed said. The words had hardly escaped his lips when Notaras pulled a pouch from inside his breastplate and flung the contents at the sultan. A white cloud of powder enveloped Mehmed. He collapsed in his saddle and then fell from his horse, shaking and coughing violently. At the same time Notaras was pulled from his saddle from behind. He landed hard on his back, and before he could move he found Ulu's curved sword inches from his face. Out of the corner of his eye, Notaras could see that Mehmed had stopped moving. Notaras heard cheering coming from the walls of Constantinople. He smiled, then Ulu kicked him hard in the side.

'You will pay for this, dog,' Ulu growled. 'You will wish that you had never lived.'

Halil had watched as Mehmed's motionless body was taken back to the sultan's tent, and then he had called a meeting of the army's generals for that night. Now, he watched from behind a curtain as one by one the generals filed into his tent. Only Ulu was missing. The generals shifted uncertainly and talked in hushed tones. They needed somebody to take command, Halil thought, to tell them what to do. They would be grateful to Halil for seizing power until the next sultan was of age. Halil let them wait a few minutes more and then entered.

'Greetings,' he began. 'I have called you here tonight to discuss what must be done in the wake of the sultan's death. These are dark times, but we cannot let ourselves forget the task at hand. The army is uncertain. We must show the men strength, despite this tragedy.'

'What are you suggesting?' Ishak Pasha asked. 'That we continue the siege even after the sultan's death?' Halil nodded. 'But how will we get the men to fight? Some of my men have already begun to pack.'

'My men have no stomach for a fight either,' added Mahmud Pasha, the bazibozouk commander. 'If I order them to fight, I will have a mutiny on my hands!'

'You are wrong, Mahmud Pasha,' Halil replied. 'If we let the men go, then we will have mutinies and chaos. Think! If we disband the army now and retreat, then we will be weak and defenceless. The Christians armies of Hungary and Poland are waiting for just such an opportunity to strike, and who knows if we can rally men to a child sultan? But if we stay and defeat Constantinople, then all the world will know of our strength.'

'But the men will only fight for a sultan,' Ishak Pasha insisted.

'And they will,' Halil said. 'They will fight for the memory of Mehmed. He began this siege. It was the great work of his reign. He would want us to see it to the end, to take vengeance for his death. Tell that to your men.'

'And who will command the attack without a sultan?' Ishak Pasha asked.

'I am the grand vizier,' Halil replied. 'It is my duty to rule until the next sultan is of age.' He met the eyes of the men around him, challenging them to question him, but none of the generals spoke. 'Very well, then. It is decided. I . . .' Halil was interrupted by the arrival of Ulu. 'What is it?' Halil snapped.

'The sultan wishes to see you, Grand Vizier.'

'The sultan?' Ishak Pasha asked. The other generals began to whisper amongst themselves. The blood drained from Halil's face. He felt as if he might be sick.

'What do you mean? The sultan is dead.'

'No, he lives,' Ulu replied. 'And he requests your presence immediately.'

'Very well. Tell the sultan that I will be there shortly,' Halil said. 'Generals, you may go.' As the generals filed out, Halil hurried into the inner chamber of his tent. He grabbed a sack of gold coins and poured it into a dish. It was customary to bring a gift when called suddenly into the sultan's presence. If the sultan wished merely to speak with you, then the gift would be a welcome reminder of your value. If the sultan was angry, then the gift might save your life. Halil only wished that he had something more lavish to bring.

As he stepped out of his tent, two janissaries grabbed his arms and pinned them behind his back. The dish fell from his hands, spilling coins everywhere. Ulu stepped forward and pulled a black cloth sack over Halil's head. The world went black, and Halil began to scream when a brutal punch to the stomach cut him short. The janissaries dragged him away, limp and unresisting. They were gone before the last of the coins had stopped rolling.

When the sack was removed, Halil found himself face to face with the sultan. Halil was lying on a table, his hands, feet, and head tied down so that he could not move. Mehmed was standing over him. The sultan was pale, but other than that he looked no different than he had that morning. Halil swallowed nervously.

'What is the matter, Halil?' Mehmed asked. 'You look as if you had seen a ghost.'

'The poison,' Halil managed. 'How did you survive?'

'Have you not heard?' Mehmed asked, smiling. 'It is a miracle. Allah favours me. All my men believe it to be so. They are sure that now, with Allah on our side, the walls of Constantinople will fall.'

'But I saw the megadux attack you,' Halil insisted. 'I saw your body. You were dead.'

'Perhaps you only saw what you wished to see, Halil.'

'Me?' Halil protested. 'But surely Your Highness does not believe that . . .'

'Silence!' Mehmed snarled. He then resumed in a more even tone. 'I do not wish to hear any more of your lies, Halil. But you will tell the truth soon enough. You will tell me everything. Isa will see to that.'

'Isa!' Halil exclaimed. He had thought Isa dead. If he were alive and here, then Halil was doomed. Isa would have told Mehmed everything. 'Do not believe anything he says, great Sultan. He is an assassin. You cannot trust him.'

'I trust nobody,' Mehmed said. 'But Isa saved my life. He gave me the antidote even before the megadux tried to kill me. He also told me about you and Sitt Hatun, about your child Selim. No, Isa is not the one who has betrayed me.'

'Lies. I never betrayed you. I swear it,' Halil pleaded. 'I knew nothing of the megadux's plot. I dealt with the monk Gennadius only to defeat Constantinople.'

'No, you plotted with Gennadius to kill me so that your son could rule in my stead. You betrayed me, and you will suffer accordingly.'

'But I have given you the key to the city!'

'Indeed?' Mehmed leaned forward until his face was only inches from Halil's. 'Speak truly now. Is the plot with the monk Gennadius real? Will the Kerkoporta be unlocked and unguarded as the megadux said?'

'Yes,' Halil said. 'I swear it. You may kill me if I lie.'

'The megadux says differently. He says that it was only a lie so that he could get close enough to kill me.'

'The megadux is a fool, Gennadius only used him as a tool.'

'I see. And how do I contact this Gennadius?'

'There are tunnels . . .'

'The tunnels have been destroyed, Halil,' Mehmed said. 'If that is all that you have to tell me, then I have no further use for you.'

'No, please!' Halil begged. 'There is another way. Spare my life, and I will tell you.' Mehmed nodded, and Halil continued. 'The megadux, he can deliver the message.'

'The megadux will be dead before another day passes.'

'Exactly. His dead body will bear the message,' Halil explained. 'Gennadius is a monk. If he performs the burial, then he will find the message.'

'And if someone else finds it?'

'Then you will have lost nothing. But you have everything to gain if Gennadius does help you.'

'Very clever, Halil. We will see if your scheme works.' Mehmed stepped away from the table so that Halil could no longer see him. 'Isa, he is all yours,' Halil heard him say. 'You may do as you wish but do not kill him. I wish to reserve that pleasure for myself.'

'No, wait!' Halil screamed. 'You said you would spare me!'

'You of all people should know better than to be so trusting,' Mehmed said, and Halil heard him walk away. A second later Isa appeared over Halil. He held a bowl in his hand and was slowly stirring something.

'Do you know what this is?' Isa asked.

Halil ignored him. 'Help me, Isa,' he pleaded. 'Set me free. I will give you money, women, lands.'

'This is a special poison,' Isa continued as if he had not heard Halil. 'Eaten, it is fatal . . .'

'Please, Isa, listen to me,' Halil said. 'I can give you anything you want.'

'. . . but placed on the skin, it acts more slowly.'

'Damn you, Isa,' Halil cursed. 'If you will not help me, then you can go to hell. I do not fear your poisons. Death does not frighten me.'

Isa shook his head. 'This poison will not kill you, Halil, but it will make you wish for death.' He took a brush from the bowl and dabbed a small amount of the poison on to Halil's forehead. Halil felt nothing at first, then there was a tingling that grew in intensity until it was a burning pain, a live coal set on his forehead. He began to scream.

420

'Make it stop! Please, Isa! I'll do anything, anything you want!'

'I only wish for you to suffer as my family suffered,' Isa whispered in his ear. 'That, Halil, is all I want from you.'

Chapter 22

As the sun rose the next day, Longo stood on the inner wall of Constantinople and inspected the progress that his men had made reconstructing the rampart before the Mesoteichion. With the sultan's cannons silent, it was the first chance that they had had in weeks to properly address the damage there. Longo had spent a sleepless night at the walls, urging his men to work and keeping an eye on the Turkish camp. The last that he had seen of the sultan, he had appeared dead, killed by Notaras. Rumours were rampant in Constantinople that the siege would now be lifted. Longo was not so sure.

A sound in the distance caught Longo's attention, and he looked out to where a procession was just leaving the Turkish camp, marching to the beat of a drum. At the head of the procession marched a troop of around fifty janissaries. Bringing up the rear was a regiment of Anatolian cavalry some one hundred strong. Between them rode a single rider in distinctive red and black armour. Two long chains trailed from the rider's saddle, and at the far end of those chains, half-walking and half-dragging, was Notaras, still dressed in his ceremonial armour. Longo knew immediately what he was seeing.

'William!' Longo called down to where William was overseeing the placement of additional cannons on the rampart. 'The Turks are going to execute Notaras. Hurry to the palace and inform the emperor.'

The emperor arrived a few minutes later, with Dalmata and Sofia by his side. Longo and Sofia exchanged a look. 'She should see this,' Constantine explained to Longo. 'Notaras was her betrothed.'

By this time, the news of Notaras's impending death had spread and the walls were beginning to grow crowded. Longo heard scattered shouts of 'God bless you Notaras!' and 'God be with you!' Notaras had killed the sultan, and the people now looked upon him as a sort of saint. Soon enough, Longo reflected, he would be a martyr.

On the plain below, the Turks had stopped and stood motionless. Notaras had collapsed to the ground, and the Turks let him lay there. 'Why don't they just get on with it?' Sofia said.

'They're waiting,' Longo replied.

'Waiting for what?' Constantine asked.

'For a crowd,' Longo responded. 'They want us all to see this.'

Finally, the Turks began to move. The janissaries in front split, with half of them marching to either side. The lone horseman rode forward, dragging Notaras behind him. As the horseman drew nearer, Longo recognized him. 'I think that is the sultan.'

'My God, you're right,' Constantine whispered. 'How can this be?'

Along the walls men began to curse and women wail

as the news spread that the sultan was still alive. Below, Mehmed stopped his horse just out of cannon range and dismounted. The people on the walls fell silent as he approached Notaras.

Notaras lay face down in the dust, struggling to breathe. He had been tortured for hours the night before. His back bled from innumerable cuts, and his ribs were broken. Being dragged by his hands behind the horse had dislocated both of his shoulders. But Notaras did not mind the pain that coursed through his body. The sultan was dead. The empire was saved. That was all that mattered. And soon his pain would end.

Notaras watched as a pair of legs appeared next to the horse in front of him. The legs approached and stopped before him. Hands grabbed Notaras's arms from behind and lifted him to his knees. The pain in his shoulders was so great that he almost fainted. He began to fall, but the men behind him held him upright. As the pain receded, he found himself looking at the belt of the man before him. The man bent down so that he was face to face with Notaras. It was the sultan.

Notaras could not understand what was happening. He had seen Mehmed die. 'How?' he managed to gasp.

'I told you that you would kneel before me, Megadux,' Mehmed said. 'All of Constantinople will kneel before me.'

Mehmed stepped to the side so that Notaras now had a view of the walls of Constantinople. They were crowded with people, and squinting, Notaras could just make out individual faces; he scanned the crowd, looking for somebody he knew. The men behind him released him, and he sagged but stayed upright on his knees, his eyes still on the walls. Behind him, he heard the whisper of a sword as it slid from its scabbard. He did not turn. He thought he saw Sofia standing on the wall. His eyes fixed on her, and then . . . nothing.

'My God!' As Notaras fell, Sofia turned and buried her head in Longo's chest. Longo put his arms around her and then glanced over at Constantine. The emperor was studying them carefully.

'Perhaps the princess should return to her room,' Constantine said. 'The shock of Notaras's death has clearly overwhelmed her. Guards!' he called. 'Escort the Princess Sofia back to the palace.' Sofia left, and Longo and Constantine turned back to watch the Turks.

Mehmed had taken Notaras's head but left the body of the megadux where it had fallen. As Mehmed rode back to the Turkish lines, followed by his escort, two janissaries stepped forward and began to drag Notaras's body towards the walls. They headed for the gate of Saint Romanus, just below Longo and Constantine.

'Shall I have the archers deal with them?' Dalmata asked.

'No, let them come,' Constantine ordered. 'At least we will be able to give Notaras a proper burial. He deserves as much.' The janissaries reached the gate and dumped Notaras's body there before turning and running back towards the Turkish lines. 'Come,' Constantine said. 'Let us go and retrieve the megadux, or what is left of him.'

They reached the gate, and Longo ordered it opened just enough for one man to pass through. Longo went himself to retrieve the body. There was a piece of paper tucked into Notaras's armour, but Longo did not have time to read it. No sooner had he reached the body than thousands of Turks began to pour over the Turkish ramparts, marching towards Constantinople. Most carried shovels and picks. Others led horses pulling wagons filled with dirt and rocks.

Longo hurriedly dragged Notaras inside the gate and ordered it shut. Constantine was waiting for him. 'Do you think this is an attack?' he asked. 'Should I ring the bells?'

'No, they are not attacking,' Longo answered. 'They carry shovels, not weapons. They are coming to create a path across the moat, to make their attack easier.'

'Then something must be done. We will use the cannons.'

'No. It will be better to save our powder and shot for when they are truly needed. If the Turks are filling in the fosse, then the attack will come soon. We must be prepared to defend Constantinople tonight.'

'Then there is much to be done and little enough time,' Constantine said. 'Dalmata, have the megadux's body taken to the Haghia Sofia and prepared for burial. When you are done, you will find me on the wall.'

'My Lord, I found a message on Notaras,' Dalmata said and handed Constantine a sheet of paper. 'I believe that it is in Notaras's own hand. He asks that he be buried by the monk Gennadius.'

Constantine looked at the sheet of paper. 'This is Notaras's last wish. It should be honoured. Have his body delivered to the Church of Saint Saviour Pantocrator.'

Gennadius sat at his desk and watched as the papers before him burned in a brazier, their edges curling, then blackening and finally collapsing in a pile of ash. Just like his grand plans, Gennadius frowned. He still did not understand what had gone wrong. Notaras had done his part, and yet the sultan lived. Gennadius was sure that Halil would not have betrayed him. What could the vizier hope to achieve by aborting their plot? And if Halil had not failed him, then that left only one possibility: somehow the sultan had learned of their plot. If that were true, then Gennadius's life would be worth less than nothing if the city fell.

Gennadius was taking no chances. He would leave this very night while the Christian forces and the Turkish army were locked in battle at the walls. He could bribe his way past the sea walls, and he had already paid a Venetian merchant to ferry him from the harbour to Pera on the far side of the Golden Horn. From there, Gennadius would hire a ship to take him to the court of Demetrius in Clarenza. And if Constantinople stood, then all was lost anyway. The Union would be vindicated, and Gennadius would never be made patriarch.

Gennadius added a last sheet of paper to the brazier. There were certain secrets – lists of bribe payments, inventories of his private fortune – that were simply too important to be carried with him or to be left here untended. Better that they burn. As the page crumbled to ash, there was a soft knock on the door. 'Enter,' Gennadius called, and Eugenius opened the door and stepped into the room. Eugenius wore chainmail under his monk's robes and a sword hung from his side. 'Is everything ready?' Gennadius asked. 'I wish to leave as soon as the battle begins.'

'All is ready, Father Gennadius. But there is something

427

else: the body of the megadux, Lucas Notaras, has been brought here to be prepared for burial. The emperor has asked that you perform the service.'

'And when is this burial to take place?'

'Today. The body is to join the city's holy relics in procession through the streets to the Haghia Sofia. The megadux is to be buried in the crypt there.'

'And do you know why Constantine has chosen me, of all people, to perform this task?'

'I was told that Notaras's final request was that you preside over his funeral.'

'Were you indeed? That is odd.' Gennadius thought back to his final meeting with Notaras. The megadux had told him that he despised the monk's hypocrisy, and that what Notaras did, he did for Constantinople alone. 'Where is the megadux's body now?'

'He has been placed in the crypt.'

'Take me to him.' Gennadius followed Eugenius down into the dank catacombs beneath the monastery, where he found Notaras's headless body in a small room, laid out on a stone table. He was still in full armour. 'Was anything unusual found on his body?' Gennadius asked. 'A message of some sort?'

'Nothing other than the note asking that you bury him.'

Gennadius nodded, lost in thought. Perhaps he had been wrong: there was no mystery behind the megadux's odd request. Unless there was another message, one that had not been written on paper. 'Help me to take his armour off,' Gennadius ordered.

He and Eugenius undressed the megadux, pulling off first his plate armour and then the chainmail beneath it. Finally, Gennadius peeled off the blood-stained cotton tunic undergarment. The skin of Notaras's chest was grey and bruised where several of his ribs had been broken. Gennadius heaved the body over to reveal Notaras's back. There, carved into the megadux's flesh, was a message: *Gennadius, open the city and you will have all you seek. Mehmed.*

Mehmed stood on the Turkish ramparts with his back to Constantinople and gazed out at the army assembled before him. The day was clear and fair, and the afternoon sun glinted off the men's armour, creating the impression of a giant sea spread out at Mehmed's feet. Nearest to him, the sea of men appeared dark and deep where the neat ranks of the black-armoured janissaries stood. Behind them were the Anatolian cavalry, their chainmail glittering. Further back, stretching all the way to the hills that ringed the Turkish camp, the disordered crowd of bazibozouks in their brown leather armour seemed to form a distant shore. There were nearly seventy thousand warriors in all – the greatest army in the world.

In his right hand, Mehmed held the head of the megadux. He raised it high, and the soldiers before him burst into frenzied cheers. The noise was deafening. Mehmed let it wash over him, filling him with a sense of power. These were *his* men. He would tell them that they fought for Allah, because that is what they wished to hear. But they did not; they fought for him. He would tell them that Allah would watch over them during the battle, but it was he, Mehmed, who would observe their every move. And when the city fell, the glory would be his, not Allah's. Finally, Mehmed raised his other hand, gesturing for silence. The cheering faded, and the camp fell silent. When Mehmed spoke, the only sounds were his voice and the faint echo of innumerable voices relaying his message to the furthest troops.

'Yesterday, one of the Christian infidels tried to assassinate your sultan,' he shouted. 'You have seen what comes of such treachery and deceit.' He cast the head of Notaras aside, letting it roll down the slope of the rampart. There was another roar from the army. 'The infidels wished for my death, but Allah would not allow it,' Mehmed continued. 'He protected me, as He will protect you. Allah is with us, and we are the sword in His hand. In the face of their armour, He gives us strength. In the face of their cannons, He gives us strength. Even in the face of the great walls of Constantinople, He gives us strength! Each fighter who falls before those walls will have a place in paradise. Each fighter who lives will have the riches and women of Constantinople at his feet. And the fighter who first breaches the walls will have wealth beyond his wildest dreams!' His men roared their approval.

'The walls of Constantinople will crumble before our cannons. The defenders of Constantinople will tremble before your might. Tomorrow, the Empire of the Romans shall fall, and you shall be its conquerors. Allah is with us! We cannot fail!' The men cheered wildly. Mehmed waited until the cheering had passed and the men had fallen silent. 'Prepare yourselves today. Sharpen your weapons, eat and sleep. Tonight we will attack and Constantinople will be ours!'

The sound of Turkish cheering reached Emperor Constantine as a distant, barely perceptible roar, like waves crashing on a distant shore. He stood atop the Golden Gate and

430

looked down at the men who had gathered to hear his final words before the coming battle. Greeks, Venetians and Genoese stood crowded together, their battered and tarnished armour gleaming dully in the light of the setting sun. There were less than eight thousand of them to fight almost ten times that number of Turks. But Constantine had witnessed the bravery of these men. Their armour might be dented, but their heads were not bowed. They would sell their lives dearly, and, God willing, they would hold the city one last time.

'Gentlemen!' Constantine called out, and his voice carried over the rows of men. 'We now see the hour of battle approaching. You have always fought with glory against the enemies of Christ. Now I ask you to fight one last time in defence of your homes and of a city known the world over!'

'Hear! Hear!' a few men yelled. The rest showed their approval by thumping the butts of their spears against the ground, creating a loud rumbling. When the rumbling faded, Constantine continued.

'Be not afraid that our walls have been worn down by the enemy's battering. For your strength lies in the protection of God. In this battle you must stand firm and have no fear, no thought of flight, but be inspired to resist with ever-greater strength. Animals may run from animals. But you are men, men of stout heart, and you will hold at bay these savage brutes.' Again there was the heavy thumping of spears.

'You are aware that the infidel enemy has attacked us unjustly,' Constantine continued. 'He has violated the treaty that he made with us; he has slaughtered our farmers at harvest time; he has cut off our commerce and sunk our ships in the sea. Now he wishes to profane our city's holy churches by turning them into stables. Oh my brothers, my sons! The everlasting honour of Christians is in your hands. The fate of the oldest empire the world has ever known lies with you. Fight in the knowledge that this is the day of your glory – a day on which if you shed but a drop of blood, you will win for yourselves crowns of martyrdom and eternal glory. Fight for each other! Fight for Constantinople!'

'For Constantinople!' the men roared, and the low rumble of spears resumed. The pounding grew so fierce that Constantine could feel the wall vibrating under his feet. Finally, he held up his arms, and the rumbling ceased. His tone was sombre.

'If you have anyone you care for in this city, I suggest you go now to bid them farewell. When it is time, the city bells will call you to the walls. I will see you there.'

The servants of the imperial household had been called to the great octagonal hall of the Blachernae Palace. Everyone was present, from the cooks to the wash maids to the palace blacksmith. There were some forty people in all, standing in four rows. In another row before them stood the most honoured members of the household, including Sphrantzes and Dalmata. The sides of the hall were lined with members of the emperor's Varangian guard. All present knelt as Constantine entered, dressed in full armour and wearing his crown.

'Rise, my friends,' Constantine told them. 'I have asked you here to thank you for your service over the years. Many of us will not survive tonight's attack. Because we may not see one another again, I wish to say goodbye to you all now.' He went to the end of the furthest row, where a young stable boy shifted nervously, his eyes fixed on the floor. 'What is your name, boy?'

The boy looked up. 'Petrus.'

'Goodbye, Petrus,' Constantine said. 'I thank you for your service, and I ask that you forgive me any unkindness that I may have shown you.' The boy nodded, unable to speak. Constantine moved on to the next person in the row, the blacksmith. He was a tall man, with strong, muscled arms.

'Goodbye, John. You have served me well, and I ask your forgiveness for any unkindness that I have shown you.'

'There is nothing to forgive, My Lord,' the blacksmith replied. 'I'll see that your sword is sharp for tonight.'

'Thank you.' Constantine continued moving person by person until he had bid farewell to his entire household, save Sphrantzes and Dalmata. He came to Sphrantzes first and placed his hand on the older man's shoulder. 'Goodbye, old friend. You have been my most trusted advisor. Forgive me if I have not always followed your advice.'

'You have done what you thought was right,' Sphrantzes replied.

'If I do not see you again, then let the world know what we have done here. Let them know how we fought, and how we died.'

'I will, My Lord,' Sphrantzes replied. Constantine nodded and moved on to Dalmata. The two men clasped hands.

'Do not say goodbye,' Dalmata said before Constantine could speak. 'There is no need. I shall not leave your side during the battle so long as I live. And do not ask my forgiveness either. It has been my honour to serve you, and it would be my greatest honour to die beside you.'

Constantine gripped Dalmata's shoulder and nodded. 'Thank you,' he said at last. Then he stepped back and addressed the entire room. 'Thank you all. You have each served me well, and I know you will do the same in the hours ahead. Now I suggest that you rest while you may. We shall have need of all our strength for the coming battle.'

The city was dark when Tristo and William reached their destination: a nondescript inn near the central market-place of Constantinople. The three-storey building was centuries old and leaned perilously to the right, looking as if it might collapse if not for the building next to it propping it up. William raised his torch to illuminate a weathered old sign that hung over the door, displaying a barely recognizable bed beside a loaf of bread. 'Are you sure this is it?' William asked.

'I paid good money for this information,' Tristo replied. 'The Spanish assassin is staying here. His room is on the second floor.'

William drew his sword. 'All right then. Let's take care of this now. I don't want to worry about taking a knife in the back while I'm fighting the Turks.' He opened the front door and stepped into a large, rectangular room cluttered with tables and benches. A single old man sat at one of the tables, his head back as he drank straight from a pitcher, red wine spilling out of the sides and staining his white tunic. He slammed the pitcher down with a thud and gave William and Tristo a bleary-eyed stare. William put his finger to his lips, but the man ignored him.

'Well, come on and help yourselves,' he bellowed, then belched. 'No sense in saving any wine for the Turks.'

'Maybe later,' William told him. He and Tristo headed to the staircase that ran up the wall to the right. They mounted the stairs and found themselves in a narrow hallway with two doors on each side. 'Which one?' William whispered.

Tristo shook his head. 'The second floor was all I was told.'

'You take the two on the left then. I'll take the right. On three: *one*, *two*, *three*!'

William and Tristo each kicked open the door in front of them. The small room in front of William was empty. Behind him, Tristo had walked in on a couple, and the woman was now screaming hysterically while the man struggled to put on his clothes. 'I didn't know she was married!' the man exclaimed. Tristo pulled the door shut and moved on.

A grey-bearded Greek man had emerged from the next room on the left. 'What's going on?' he asked. Tristo showed his sword and the man disappeared, slamming the door behind him. Tristo and William turned to the last door.

'This must be it,' William said. He kicked the door open and they rushed in. There was a crust of stale bread and a bottle of wine on the table, but no sign of the Spanish assassin. 'He's gone.'

'Looks like he left in a hurry,' Tristo said, pointing to a chest that had been left open in the corner. Inside, they found a few shirts, a pair of boots and a jar. William unscrewed the jar's lid. It was empty save for a few traces of a viscous, black substance that clung to the sides. William sniffed at it.

'Poison,' he said. 'Carlos was here all right.'

'What're you two doing up here?' a voice called from behind. William turned to see the man from downstairs swaying unsteadily in the doorway. 'If you want a room, you'll have to pay.'

'We're looking for someone,' William said. 'A Spanish man, just shorter than me, with dark hair.'

'Carlos,' the drunk innkeeper slurred. 'He was an ill-tempered bastard, but he paid in gold. Anyway, he's gone now, cleared out earlier today.'

'Gone? Where to?' William asked.

The man shrugged. 'Said he was going home. Said his work was done here.'

'Did he say anything else?' Tristo asked.

The innkeeper leaned on the door jamb and scratched his nose. 'Aye,' he said at last. 'He said that there was no sense in risking his life to kill someone who was going to die anyway. He said that the city is doomed, and we're all of us going to die.'

Midnight had long since passed, but Sofia could not sleep. She stood at the window of her quarters and looked out on the city, the only home she had ever known. She was dressed in leather breeches, a chainmail shirt and boots. Her sword hung at her side. She was prepared to fight, prepared to flee if need be. But she still could not imagine leaving Constantinople behind. She tried to picture the city before her filled with Turkish soldiers, the markets filled with the sound of Turkish voices.

Behind her, she heard the door to the secret passage open and turned to see Longo. He was dressed in full chainmail, with a solid steel breastplate. Sofia smiled as she moved towards him, then frowned. 'You should be at the walls.'

'I had to see you,' Longo replied. 'Besides, the bells will ring long before the final assault begins.'

'I am glad you came.' Sofia kissed Longo, and he held her tightly to him. For a second, she lost herself in that kiss, safe in Longo's arms. Then she pulled away. 'Tell me truly,' she said. 'Is there hope? Can the city be saved?'

'The walls are strong. Our armour is superior.'

'But can we defeat them? Do not lie to me.'

'I do not know,' Longo said, shaking his head. 'The Turks are many, and our men are tired of fighting. But I believe we can win. We must win.'

'I fear the worst.' Sofia turned away and shuddered, holding her arms as if struck by a sudden chill. Longo put his arms around her. 'You know the fate of our women if the city falls,' she said. Longo nodded. 'I will kill myself before I let the Turks defile me, or I will die fighting.'

'No,' Longo said, turning Sofia so that she faced him. 'You must keep yourself safe, Sofia. Fight if you must, but fight to live. I must know that whatever happens, you will be waiting for me. I came to Constantinople to fight the Turks, but that is not why I am fighting now. I am fighting for you, for us.'

'And if the city should fall? . . . If you should fall? . . .'

'Then you must reach safety. You are a princess. After this battle, you may well be the last of your line. The fate of the Roman Empire rests with you, and your life will be worth nothing if you are found. I will send William to help you. If you hear the bells ring, then the city has fallen. Get to my ship as fast as you can. If you can make it across the Horn to the port of Pera, then you will be safe.'

'I will not leave without you.'

'I pray to God that you will not have to. But if I die . . .' Longo fell silent as outside, the city bells began to ring. 'I must go. Remember, if the city falls, you must reach Pera. Do not wait for me.'

Longo began to leave, but Sofia stopped him at the entrance to the secret passage. She took his head in her hands and kissed him. He put his arms around her waist and pulled her close. Tears welled in Sofia's eyes, and she clung tightly to Longo, desperate to memorize the feel of his body, the taste of his lips. Finally, she pulled away and looked him in the eyes. 'I love you,' she whispered. 'Remember that when you are on the walls.'

'I will,' Longo said, then turned and left. Sofia waited until the light of his torch had disappeared and the sound of his footsteps had faded from the dark passage. Only then did she allow the tears to fall from her eyes. She wiped them away, angrily; she would not cry for Longo, not while he was still alive.

Sofia closed the door to the secret passage and went to the window. The bells were still tolling, and the streets were filled with men rushing to the walls. As she watched, Sofia felt a twinge below her belly, then another. She had not bled for just over a month, but only now was she certain. She put her hand on her stomach, and this time she did not try to stop her tears.

Chapter 23

Sunrise was still more than three hours off when Longo mounted the outer wall of the Mesoteichion. There was no moon and the night was dark. Torches illuminated the wall at regular intervals, revealing hundreds of armoured men. Some knelt in prayer, while others sharpened their swords or spoke quietly to friends, exchanging messages to give to their loved ones in case they were killed in the coming battle. Dozens of unarmoured men were busy carrying rocks up to the wall to be used as shot by the cannons. Longo recognized Nicolo, his steward, amongst them.

'Nicolo!' he called. Nicolo turned and dropped the heavy stone that he had been carrying. Longo had hardly seen Nicolo since the siege began, but the rotund steward had not changed. In fact, despite the shortage of provisions in the city, Nicolo seemed to have put on weight. 'Where have you been?'

'Serving you, of course, signor. After all, somebody has to look out for your business interests while you're off fighting.'

'My business interests?'

'There's always money to be made in a war, signor,' Nicolo replied. 'There are several grain merchants . . .'

Longo held up a hand, stopping him. 'I don't want to know. I'm just glad to see that you've finally made yourself useful.'

'Hmph. They forced me into it.' Nicolo pointed to where William and Tristo stood further along the wall.

'Well, keep at it,' Longo told him. 'And once the fighting starts, get back to *la Fortuna* and make her ready to sail. This battle is no place for you, Nicolo.'

'I could not agree more, signor,' Nicolo replied, but Longo was already past him, heading for Tristo and William. Tristo, as huge and lively as ever, was talking to one of the gun crews. His giant sword was sheathed in a scabbard across his back and he carried an enormous battle-axe in his hands. William stood beside Tristo, shouting orders down to the men between the walls, telling them where to place the mantelets – portable wooden barriers. William had grown from the awkward, scrawny runaway that Longo had first met five years ago into a lean, muscular man and a confident leader.

'What news, William?' Longo asked. 'How are the men?'

'They are in good spirits. I've put most of them on the wall with spears to hold off attackers. As you ordered, I'm keeping a hundred men in reserve to act as archers and to plug any gaps that open.'

'And the cannons, Tristo?' Longo asked.

'The cannons are ready and charged, but we'll have to use them wisely,' Tristo replied. 'We have collected plenty of stone for shot, but our supply of powder is low. We have enough for maybe thirty rounds, more if we half-charge the cannons once the Turks get in close.'

'Make it so,' Longo said. 'And don't let the men fire until the Turks are at the walls.' Longo turned to look out in the direction from which the Turks would come. The plain was dark and empty. Where the thousands of lights of the Turkish camp should have been, there was nothing – only a few flickering torches here and there. 'Where are they?'

'The lookouts saw them forming ranks, and then the lights in the Turkish camp went out. That is when we rang the bells,' William said. 'They're coming. Just wait.'

'You have done well, William,' Longo told him. 'But now I have something else to ask of you. I fear you will not like it.'

'Whatever it is, I will do it.'

'I ask you to leave the walls. Go to Princess Sofia and protect her.'

'But my place is here!' William protested. 'I owe it to my uncle and my friends to avenge their deaths.'

'There is more to life than revenge, William. How many Turks have you already killed? Twenty? Thirty? Believe me, no matter how many you kill, your anger will not fade. Your revenge will never be complete.' Longo grasped William by the shoulders. 'You have a wife. Think of her. We must all protect that which we hold most dear. I am asking you as a friend to protect Sofia for me.'

William looked away, his jaw tight. Finally, he nodded. 'Very well.'

'Thank you,' Longo said. 'If the bells ring to signal the retreat, take her aboard *la Fortuna* and sail for Pera.' William nodded again. 'Good luck, William. May God be with you.' The two men embraced.

'And with you,' William replied.

'Keep yourself alive,' Tristo told him, engulfing William in a hug. 'I still have money to win back from you at dice.'

'Not if I can help it,' William replied with a grin. Tristo and Longo watched him descend from the ramparts and pass through the gate of the inner wall. A moment later, the emperor emerged through the same gate. He was followed by Dalmata and the Varangian guard. Men in the courtyard between the two walls knelt, and Constantine strode past them to cries of 'Hail Constantine!' and 'Long live the Emperor!' Longo went to meet him on the causeway leading to the top of the outer wall.

'Greetings, Emperor. Have you come to inspect the troops?'

'No, signor, I have come to fight.'

'You would be safer elsewhere. The Turks will focus their attack on this point.'

'That is why I am here,' Constantine said firmly. 'If we can hold the Mesoteichion, then we can save Constantinople.'

'But if you die, then all will be lost. It is too great a risk.'

'We must risk everything, even my life, if we wish to win this battle,' Constantine replied. 'Are the men all here?'

'Yes. Save for one or two stragglers.'

'Good. Then close the gates of the inner wall.'

'But My Lord, with the gates closed, how will we retreat?' Dalmata asked.

'There will be no retreat. Close the gates.'

*

442

Mehmed stood on the Turkish ramparts and looked out across the plain to where the torchlit walls of Constantinople loomed out of the darkness. Tonight, for the first time in a thousand years, those walls would fall. Tonight he, Mehmed, would fulfil his destiny. Mehmed thought back to nine years ago, when he had been driven from the throne and sent to rot in Manisa. The generals had laughed at him then, calling him 'Mehmed the Scholar'. After tonight, nobody would ever laugh again.

He turned to face the generals who were gathered around him under the light of a single torch. 'Are the men in position?' he asked Ulu.

'Yes, My Lord.'

'Then give the signal for the cannons to fire. After they have done their work, then you may send in your bazibozouks, Mahmud Pasha.'

Mahmud Pasha bowed. 'Thank you, My Lord, for the honour of the first attack.'

'And what of the Anatolian cavalry?' Ishak Pasha asked. 'My men have not waited these two months only to watch the bazibozouks steal their glory.'

'Patience, Ishak,' Mehmed replied. 'There will be glory enough for all today. I have something special in mind for you and your men.'

The soldiers around Longo had fallen silent as they waited nervously for the Turkish attack to begin, so silent that Longo could hear the hiss of the slow match burning next to the nearby cannons. The quiet was shattered by the roar of Turkish cannons. They fired all together, dozens of tongues of flame piercing the darkness along the Turkish ramparts. 'Take shelter!' Longo yelled as he ducked behind

443

the low stone barrier that fronted the outer wall. A second later, he felt the wall tremble beneath him as several cannonballs slammed into it. Twenty feet to his right, a section of wall some ten feet wide shook and then collapsed outward in a pile of dirt and rubble, taking a cannon with it.

'Bring forth the mantelets!' Longo yelled to the men who stood in reserve behind the wall. 'Fill that gap!' Men took up two of the mobile wooden walls and moved them into place. The mantelets were hardly in place, however, before another cannonball hit one of them dead on. It exploded in a shower of splinters, leaving several men down and screaming in pain. More men rushed forward to drag them to safety, while another mantelet was brought forward.

'We can't take much more of this!' Tristo shouted over the boom of the cannons.

'You're right,' Longo agreed. 'Take all of the men off the wall save for the cannon crews. Have them take shelter at the base of the wall.' Tristo nodded and hurried away. Within a few minutes the top of the wall around Longo was empty. He sat alone, huddled behind the low stone barrier while the wall shook beneath him. Finally, the Turkish cannons fell silent.

Longo stood immediately and peered out into the darkness. He saw nothing, but as his ears recovered from the sound of the bombardment, he heard the rumble of thousands of marching feet. 'Back to the wall!' he shouted to the men below him. 'Here they come!' He had no sooner spoken than a wave of noise burst forth from the darkness: the ululating scream of '*Allah*! *Allah*! *Allah*!' mixed with the sound of drums and wailing bagpipes. The noise grew louder and louder, yet still Longo saw nothing. A nervous cannoneer down the line touched off his cannon, sending shot flying into the darkness. 'Hold your fire, damn it!' Tristo roared. 'Wait until they're in range!'

The sound of the onrushing Turks grew deafening. Finally, a solid wave of Turks emerged from the darkness, only some forty yards from the walls. They ran in no formation and wore a hotchpotch of old armour. Some carried swords and spears, while others were armed with scythes or pitchforks. Longo recognized them as the bazibozouks, untrained peasants who formed the bulk of the Turkish army. What they lacked in training, they made up for in fanatical bravery. There were thousands of them.

'Archers!' Longo turned and shouted. 'Now!' From behind him, he heard the twang of hundreds of bows and the hiss of the arrows as they flew overhead. Bazibozouks began to fall by the dozens. Longo saw an arrow fly clean through the chest of one Turk and lodge in the groin of the man behind. He saw a huge mountain of a man whose bellowing war cry was cut short by an arrow through his throat. The screaming howl of the bazibozouks was now peppered with the anguished cry of men in pain, but the Turkish charge did not falter. They were close enough now that Longo could see individual faces: a white-haired, wild-eyed man, his face disfigured by countless battle scars; a bare-chested farmer waving his pitchfork, an arrow protruding from his shoulder; a child no older than twelve, lugging a sword he could hardly carry. The first bazibozouks had reached the wall and were pressing against the mantelets that filled the gaps. Christians from atop the wall on either side of the gaps stabbed down with spears, and a pile of dead began to mount before the mantelets.

The main wave of attackers reached the wall where Longo stood and began to raise ladders. Longo shoved one of the ladders back, and the Turks climbing it fell backwards and were crushed under the press of their comrades. Longo glanced down the wall to either side. Everywhere the walls were crawling with Turks. 'The cannons!' he yelled. 'Fire!'

All along the top of the wall the Christian cannons fired, spraying chunks of stone directly into the mass of Turks before them. The carnage was both exhilarating and appalling. Stones blasted through shields and ripped through armour as if it were cloth. Longo saw a Turk's sword broken in half by a fist-sized rock, just before another stone took his head clean off. The space before the walls was transformed into a hellish scene of mangled bodies thrashing on the blood-soaked ground. The Turkish charge slowed as the bazibozouks closest to the walls turned and tried to retreat, but the press of their comrades behind them pushed them forward into the teeth of the cannons. Wave after wave of bazibozouks continued to surge towards the walls, struggling over the bodies of their fallen comrades, only to be cut down in turn. Finally, after an hour of slaughter, the Turkish attack began to falter. Longo struck down a Turk who had managed to mount the wall, pushed over a last ladder and paused. There were no more ladders to topple, no more Turks to fight. The last of the bazibozouks were in full retreat, leaving the field behind them littered with the bloody bodies of thousands of their comrades. The Christian troops cheered.

Longo saw Constantine approaching along the top of the wall.

'We did it!' Constantine shouted. 'They're retreating!'

'That was only the first wave, to test the walls,' Longo replied. 'They'll be back.' He turned to Tristo, who stood a few feet away, wiping blood from his axe. 'How many men have we lost?'

'Less than fifty,' Tristo replied.

'So few!' Constantine rejoiced. 'And look, they've lost thousands.'

'Aye,' Tristo grunted. 'But that's only the half of it. We're out of powder. There'll be no more cannons to hold them off.' As if to emphasize his point, there was a tremendous boom as one of the Turkish cannons fired. The wall shook as the cannonball slammed into it. The Turkish bombardment had started again.

Gennadius had ordered Eugenius to the walls when the bells rang to signal the impending Turkish attack. Now, dressed in chainmail, Eugenius marched through the city, followed by a dozen hired thieves, similarly dressed. He stopped before a tall, round tower that sat where the double wall met the single Blachernae wall. Inside the tower, Eugenius knew, was the Kerkoporta – a small sally port that led outside the wall.

Eugenius entered to find the ground floor of the tower empty and dark. There were no other doors, nor any windows. On one side of the tower a staircase curved up to the floor above. On the other side, another staircase ran down into the floor. 'Follow me,' he said, leading the way down.

The lower level was crowded with a dozen soldiers.

They were grouped around a thick, wooden door that was studded with iron supports – the Kerkoporta. Three huge beams of wood lay across it, barring it against attack, and a tall, well-muscled man stood leaning against it. All the soldiers were Greeks, which was a good thing. They would be easier to handle than the Latins.

'Who is in command here?' Eugenius asked.

'I am,' the man leaning against the door answered.

'Your men are needed at the Mesoteichion,' Eugenius told him.

'We were told by the emperor himself to stay here and guard the Kerkoporta.'

'My men and I have been sent to hold the door,' Eugenius responded. 'We were manning the cannons but ran out of powder. We are not well armoured and are of no use at the Mesoteichion. They need brave men in strong armour.'

The Greek leader looked sceptically at the unsavoury lot with Eugenius, but finally he nodded. 'Very well,' he said. 'We will go where we are needed. Guard the door well, and if there is trouble, send for help. Whatever you do, do not let the Turks inside the walls.'

'We will fight to the death,' Eugenius told him. The Greek captain led his men up the stairs and when the last of them had left, Eugenius turned to the thieves. 'Help me unbar the door.'

'But the captain said to let no one through,' a thin thief with a pock-marked face replied.

'You are not being paid to think,' Eugenius snapped. 'If you want the money I promised you, then you will do as you are told.' The thieves nodded and set to work, helping Eugenius slide the heavy wooden beams that barred the door from their supports. Then Eugenius unbolted the door and pulled it open. In the dim twilight he saw the wall stretching before him down towards the sea. Turkish dead and wounded littered the ground. The fighting appeared to have momentarily stopped, but Eugenius could hear the loud roar of Turkish cannons. He closed the door but did not bolt it.

'It is time to go,' he told the thieves. 'To the cistern, where you will be paid.'

'But we can't leave the door unbarred,' the pock-marked thief said. The others nodded their agreement.

'You will do as you are told,' Eugenius ordered.

'I will not betray my emperor or my city,' the pock-marked thief said defiantly.

'Very well,' Eugenius replied. In a blur of motion, he drew his sword and slashed through the pock-marked thief's throat before the unfortunate man's weapon was halfway out of its scabbard. The thief dropped to the ground, gasping and twitching as his blood pooled on the stone floor. The other thieves drew their weapons. 'If you fight me, then he will not be the last of you to die,' Eugenius told them. 'And what will the emperor give you for your heroism? Nothing. But if you do as I say, then you will be both alive and well paid. Which will it be?'

The thieves looked one to another, then one by one sheathed their daggers and swords. 'You have chosen wisely,' Eugenius told them. 'Now come. Let us go and see that you receive your reward.'

The sun had yet to rise, but the sky had lightened enough so that Longo could just see the Turkish cannons on the distant ramparts. The cannons had been firing without pause for half an hour, and the wall trembled beneath him with every cannonball that struck it. Longo turned and watched the men below. They were placing mantelets in a long line, using the mobile wooden barriers to create a third wall in the space between the inner and outer walls. 'Move those mantelets closer together!' Longo ordered.

Tristo approached along the wall. 'The lancers are ready. If the cavalry breaks through, then they know what to do.'

Longo nodded. 'And the emperor? He is safe?'

'As safe as can be. He's behind the wall of mantelets, along with Dalmata and the Varangian guard.'

'Good.' Longo turned to shout more orders to his men when he felt the ground beneath his feet shift violently. He and Tristo just had time to leap off the wall before it collapsed, spilling earth, stones and wooden supports outwards towards the Turkish cannons.

Longo landed on his stomach and rolled over. As the dust settled around him, he could see that a section of the wall some twenty yards wide had collapsed. Through the gap he caught sight of the Anatolian cavalry, who had poured out from behind the Turkish lines and were charging hard for the break in the Christian defences. They would be on him in seconds. He felt himself grabbed by the shoulders and hauled to his feet. He turned to find Tristo standing beside him. 'Come on! Run!'

They turned and sprinted for the line of mantelets. Behind him, Longo could hear the rumble of hooves coming closer. As Longo and Tristo ran, a line of Christian lancers stepped out in front of the mantelets and braced the butts of their long spears against the ground, creating a wall of spears. Longo ran hard for the line of lancers. The thunder of hooves was deafening, and he could almost feel the point of a Turkish spear in his back. And then he was through the Christian line to safety.

A second later, the charging Turkish cavalry reached the wall of spears. The better riders managed to turn their horses aside. Others were thrown as their horses stopped short before the spears and reared up in protest. Still others fell victim to the lancers. Within seconds the Turkish charge had been reduced to a chaos of frightened, riderless horses and trampled men. A cheer went up from the Christian lines.

'Steady men!' Longo yelled. 'They'll be back!' Sure enough, the Anatolian cavalry quickly regrouped as more and more horsemen flooded into the space between the walls. They advanced more slowly this time, firing arrows as they approached. More and more lancers fell under the rain of arrows, and the Anatolians surged into the gaps. 'Behind the mantelets!' Longo yelled. 'Retreat! Retreat!'

The lancers fell back through the spaces between the mantelets and the Turkish cavalry surged forward. 'Now!' Longo yelled. 'Light them!' He himself took a torch and touched it to the nearest mantelet, which burst instantly into flames. All of the mantelets had been covered with Greek fire, and now as they were lit one after another, they formed a semicircular wall of towering flames. Faced with the wall of fire, the Turkish horses panicked. Riders were thrown as their horses backed and reared, refusing to approach the inferno. The Anatolian ranks were thrown into chaos.

'Now, men!' Longo yelled. 'Charge!' Longo led the

Christians out from behind the flaming mantelets and into the mass of struggling horsemen. He pulled the first Turk he came to from his saddle, finished him, and then mounted the horse. He rode into the confused crowd of Turks, striking out to either side. Behind him, the lancers were progressing through the Turkish ranks, spearing Turk after Turk off their frightened horses. The Turks gave ground, slowly at first and then faster until they were in full retreat. The Christians surged after them, pushing the Anatolians out past the gap in the walls.

Longo reigned in his horse in the gap. Before him, the Anatolian cavalry were retreating across the plain, lit by the rays of the rising sun. 'Halt, men!' Longo yelled to the Christian forces around him. 'Let them run! Prepare to hold the gap against the next attack!'

'Well done, signor!' Constantine said as he rode up beside Longo. 'The sun rises and the city still stands. They have failed again. This day will be a glorious one in our history.'

Longo shook his head. 'Something is not right. They attacked with small numbers and retreated too easily. It is almost as if they expected the cavalry to fail, as if they were only trying to distract us.'

While the bulk of his men were busy attacking the Mesoteichion, Ishak Pasha led a select group of three hundred Anatolian cavalry further north. As he galloped towards the Kerkoporta, grapefruit-sized stones joined the arrows that were raining down from the wall ahead. One struck the rider to his right, crushing his skull and killing him instantly. Ishak spurred his horse on, pushing it towards the narrow crevice where the sea wall ran behind the last great tower of the double wall. The Kerkoporta was still not visible, and Ishak was beginning to think that he had been sent on a fool's errand. Then he saw the door, set into the wall of the tower, far back in the narrow space.

Ishak dismounted and hurried forward, rocks falling all around him. He put his shoulder into the door and pushed hard. The door swung open, and Ishak found himself in an empty room, lit by a single torch. A staircase ran up the far wall. 'Come on!' he called to his men, who were filing in behind him. 'Follow me!'

Ishak hurried up the stairs to another empty room and then out into the city. To his left stood the palace of the Christian emperor. Before him, a maze of empty streets wound their way further into the city. Ishak took a moment to get his bearings. 'This way, towards the Mesoteichion!' he ordered and began jogging along the wall to the right. Most of his men followed, but two dozen broke off, heading for the palace.

'Stop! What are you doing?' Ishak yelled after them.

'You fight. We're going to get rich!' one of the men called back. The rest simply ignored Ishak.

'Should we go after them?' one of Ishak's lieutenants asked.

'No, let them go. We are needed elsewhere.'

Sofia stood at the window of her apartments while William sat nearby, fidgeting with a dagger. The window looked out on to the city, away from the walls, but standing there, Sofia could hear the sound of the distant battle. The cannons had stopped some time ago, and now she heard only a dull roar, marked by the occasional shout that carried to her room. Eventually, these noises gave way to a rhythmic pounding – the sound of thousands of men marching. The sounds told her little of what was happening, but as long as the bells near the walls did not ring, she knew that the walls held and the Christian soldiers fought on. But the bells could not tell her if Longo was alive.

Suddenly there was silence outside the window. Sofia strained to hear, but there was nothing. Then, from behind her, in the hallway outside her quarters, she heard shouting in Turkish, followed by a woman's terrified scream. 'What was that?' William asked.

'Turks!' Sofia gasped. 'They are in the palace.'

'Then the walls must have fallen,' William responded. 'We must get to the ship.'

'Wait. The bells have not rung to sound the retreat. This is something else. If the Turks are inside the city, then Longo must be warned. We must . . .' She was interrupted by a pounding on the door to her apartments. William and Sofia backed away into Sofia's bedroom as the door to her sitting room shook under heavy blows. Then the wood around the lock splintered, and the door swung open. Six Turkish soldiers stood in the doorway.

'What have we here?' their leader leered when he saw Sofia. 'It's been too long since I've had a woman, especially one so tasty.' The other Turks grinned in agreement as they stepped into the sitting room.

William drew his sword and stood in the doorway to the bedroom. 'Come and get her, you bastards,' he growled.

'No, there is another way,' Sofia said, pulling William away. 'Follow me.' As the Turks surged towards the bedroom, Sofia rushed William across the room to the secret passage and pushed the door open. They entered the tunnel, and Sofia slammed the door shut. Almost immediately there was a pounding on the hidden door. 'We must hurry,' Sofia said.

They had no light, so she took William's hand and led him down the dark passage. Behind them, the secret door was smashed open. Light flooded the tunnel, followed by the Turks. 'Run!' William yelled. They sprinted down the tunnel. Sofia took them into a side passage and down a spiral staircase. By the time they reached the bottom, the tunnel was again pitch black. Above them, Sofia could hear the Turks coming after them. She led William to the left and then turned right down a long corridor. They came to a door, and Sofia fumbled for the handle in the darkness. Finally she pushed the door open and they stepped out into the morning light. Looking back, Sofia saw that the Turks had just entered the tunnel behind them. She slammed the door closed.

'Quick. Over here,' William called and headed across the street to the nearest house. He kicked the door open and they entered, slamming the door shut behind them. Sofia went to the window and peered out through the closed shutters. Across the street, the Turks poured out of the secret passage. After a brief discussion, they moved off at a run, heading for the front of the palace.

'We're safe,' Sofia said. 'They've gone.'

'Come, we must get to the ship,' William urged.

'No, we must warn Longo that the Turks are in the city. Our men cannot hold the wall if they are forced to fight on two fronts.'

William shook his head. 'There is nothing that we can

do, Princess. If the Turks are in the city, then it is too late to warn Longo.'

'But we must try.'

'The Turks could return at any moment,' William insisted. 'And I told Longo that I would protect you.'

'I am not some weak girl that you need protect!' Sofia said, her eyes flashing. 'I am a princess, and you had best do as I say. Go, William. Warn Longo. I will be safe enough until you return.'

'Very well.' William opened the door but paused before leaving. 'I will return soon. Wait here.' Sofia nodded, and William left. She closed the door after him, shoved a heavy oak table in front of it, and sat down to wait.

Longo stood in the gap where the outer wall had collapsed. In the golden morning light, he could see thousands of black-armoured janissaries marching towards the walls in tightly grouped battalions. He turned and looked along the line of Christian soldiers who stood filling the twenty-yard-wide gap in the wall. In the centre stood Constantine and Dalmata, surrounded by the Varangian guard. The men to either side of them were a mixture of Greeks, Italians and Turks who lived in Constantinople and who fought to defend their city. They had all proven themselves in battle today, but still, their numbers were few. The other commanders of Constantinople were hard pressed and had only been able to spare a few men to reinforce the Mesoteichion. The ranks of men filling the gap could not have been more than ten deep, and they would have to hold the gap against a force of thousands.

Longo stepped out from the line and addressed the men. 'Stand strong, men!' he shouted. 'This attack will be the Turks' last. We no longer have a wall to fight from. But if we fight as one, then we can defeat them. We have but to hold this gap, and the day will be ours. Are you ready to fight?' The men roared. 'Fight, then, for Constantinople!'

'For Constantinople!' the men roared back. 'For Constantinople!' Then, in the midst of the Turkish ranks, a horn sounded, and the janissaries rushed forward with a deafening roar that drowned out the Christians' cheers.

'Stand firm, men!' Longo yelled, readying his sword and shield. 'Good luck,' he said more quietly to Tristo, who stood to his right. 'I am sorry that I got you into this.'

Tristo hefted his giant battle-axe. 'There's no place I'd rather be,' he grinned. Then, his smile faded. 'I've chosen a name for my child: Benito. If I fall, look after him for me.'

'I will,' Longo said.

A second later, the charging janissaries stopped short twenty yards from the Christian line and raised their bows. 'Shields up, men!' Longo yelled as the janissaries released a volley of arrows and crossbow bolts. An arrow embedded itself in Longo's shield and another skittered off the back of his armour. The man to his left fell screaming as a crossbow bolt struck him in the thigh. Then the hail of arrows ended, and with a roar, the janissaries resumed their charge. They slammed into the Christian line, driving it backwards. Longo got in a few good blows before the press of Turks became so great that his sword was useless. He was sandwiched between Tristo to his right and another Christian to his left, and crushed between two janissaries in front and two Christians behind him. The battle had become a shoving match, and for now, the Turks were winning, their numbers and momentum pushing the Christians backwards.

'Push men!' Longo yelled. 'Don't give ground! If they breach the gap then we are lost!' The two Christians behind Longo put their shields into his back and pushed hard, shoving him forward. All along the line the Christians dug in. Their armour, made of solid steel plates, protected them against the press of men, while the Turks in their lighter leather and chain armour were being slowly crushed to death in the crowd. As the leading janissaries ceased pushing, the Turkish advance ground to a halt. All along the gap the tightly packed Christians shoved against the crowd of janissaries, with neither side giving an inch. More and more janissaries poured into the attack, but the Christians held firm. 'Keep pushing, men!' Longo yelled. 'We're holding them!'

Then, there was a sudden commotion in the ranks behind Longo. 'The gates are opening!' someone shouted. 'Reinforcements! Reinforcements have come!' another cried. Soon, the entire Christian line had erupted into cheering. Then, just as suddenly, the cheering stopped.

The men behind Longo gave way, and he glanced behind him to see what had happened. 'Mother of God!' he cursed, for the gates had not opened to reinforcements. Turks were pouring through them and attacking the Christians from behind. The Christian line dissolved under the two-way attack. Longo found himself isolated in a small group with Tristo, Constantine, Dalmata and six members of the Varangian guard. They formed a circle with Constantine in the middle. Turks swarmed around them, eager to win the glory of striking down the emperor.

Longo fought with Tristo and Dalmata on either side of him. Tristo had dropped his axe and was now wielding his huge, four-foot-long sword. The heavy sword smashed through leather and steel alike, shattering swords and removing heads with every swing. Dalmata fought with a short, curved sword in either hand, parrying and slashing in a deadly blur of activity. Longo fought with his thin, slightly curved Asian sword and a small shield, dealing out death with lethal efficiency.

Next to Dalmata, one of the Varangian guards was impaled by a spear and slumped to the ground. The group closed the gap, forming a tighter circle. 'We won't last much longer like this!' Tristo shouted. 'We must do something!'

'We must get to the gate!' Constantine shouted back. 'If we can hold it then we still have a chance to defend the city from the inner walls.'

'To the gate! To the gate!' Longo shouted, echoed by Constantine and the others. All around them, the other remaining Christians were also fighting towards the gate. The Turks however, soon realized what was happening. As the Christian forces neared the gate, the janissaries rallied. They surged forward, led by a huge janissary wielding a giant, curved scimitar. Just before the wave of janissaries hit, Longo recognized the man as Ulu.

The janissaries drove a wedge through the middle of Longo's group. He found himself alone, fighting for his life. He ducked a sword, then blocked a spear thrust and spun away from two more Turks, slashing each across the gut as he did so. Another janissary charged him, screaming '*Allah*! *Allah*!' Longo ducked under the man's sword, then slammed his shoulder into the Turk's gut and stood, flipping the janissary head over heels. Longo stabbed down, finishing the man. Then, as he turned to find his next foe, something slammed into his chest, causing him to stagger backwards. He looked down to see the feathered tail of a crossbow bolt protruding from his armour, just beneath his right collar-bone. Blood was already oozing from the wound, staining his armour red.

The janissary who had fired the bolt had drawn his sword, and now he moved in for the kill, slashing at Longo's gut. Longo managed to parry the blow, but as their swords clanged together, agonizing pain shot through Longo's chest. He stumbled backwards and sank to his knees. The janissary raised his sword to finish Longo. Then the man's weapon fell aside as he was struck from behind, cleaved almost in half by Tristo's huge sword. Tristo stepped past the dead man and knelt beside Longo.

'Come on, let's get you out of here.'

'Tristo, behind you,' Longo whispered, pointing past his friend to where Ulu was striding across the field towards them. Tristo rose and turned to face him.

'Don't worry. I'll take care of this bugger.'

As Ulu approached, he grabbed one of the other janissaries running to confront Tristo and pushed him aside. 'This one is mine,' Ulu barked. The two huge men faced off, each pausing to size the other up. Tristo was a good three inches taller than Ulu and heavier, but whereas Tristo was bulky, the janissary general was tightly muscled, without an ounce of fat. Ulu held his long *yatağan* sword with one hand and swung it lightly from side to side. Tristo gripped his own mighty longsword with both hands.

Ulu attacked first, springing forward with surprising speed and slashing for Tristo's gut. Tristo knocked the blow aside with his sword, then spun and chopped down at Ulu's head. Ulu jumped back out of the way, and Tristo pressed the attack, slicing upwards towards Ulu's chest. Ulu blocked the blow, and their swords locked together, bringing them close. Each man strained against the other, their teeth gritting and biceps bulging. 'You're a strong son of a bitch, aren't you?' Tristo growled. 'But the bigger they are, the easier it is for me to do this.' And with that, he head-butted Ulu in the face, and at the same time, brought his knee up hard into the janissary's groin.

Ulu stumbled backwards, his guard open, and Tristo stabbed for his chest. For a second, Longo thought that the blow would succeed, but then Ulu's sword swept back, deflecting the blow at the last second. Still, Tristo's sword sliced through the side of Ulu's armour, which was soon wet with blood. The injury, however, seemed to only enrage Ulu. With a roar, he went on the offensive, forcing Tristo to retreat under a series of heavy blows. Despite all his fury, however, Ulu could not penetrate Tristo's guard. Then, Ulu made a mistake. As Tristo retreated, Ulu lunged too far forward, tripping over a dead body. Tristo stepped in for the kill, slicing down for Ulu's neck. But the janissary had only pretended to stumble. Ulu sidestepped the blow, knocked Tristo's sword aside, and then reversed the direction of his own sword. He caught Tristo in the side of the head, cleaving his skull open and killing him instantly.

A wordless, primal scream burst from Longo. His heart pounded and rage coursed through him, washing away the pain in his chest. He stood and cast his shield aside, gripping his sword with both hands. Then he charged. Ulu waited for him to come and at the last second swung hard for Longo's head. Longo ducked the blow and thrust at Ulu's gut. Ulu parried, and as their swords met, pain knifed through Longo's chest, almost making him drop his sword. Longo staggered back, and Ulu took advantage, attacking with a vicious overhead blow. Longo spun away from the sword, and as he completed his spin, kicked out, catching Ulu square in the stomach. Ulu hardly moved. It was as if Longo had kicked a wall. Longo bounced back, barely managing to avoid another slicing blow from Ulu's *yatağan*. The two men paused, and their eyes met. 'I spared you before,' Ulu said. 'I will have no mercy this time, Longo.'

'Nor will I,' Longo growled, and gritting his teeth against the pain in his chest, he went on the offensive, pressing Ulu with a series of quick lunges and slashes. Ulu gave ground, but Longo could not penetrate his defence. Again and again Longo thought that his sword would surely strike home, only for Ulu's huge *yatağan* to sweep back at the last second, deflecting Longo's blow. Longo felt himself weakening, but then caught sight of Tristo's body out of the corner of his eye. At the sight of his fallen friend, he attacked with a renewed fury. He slashed down to lower Ulu's guard, and then, mustering all of his strength, swung for Ulu's head. Somehow, Ulu again blocked the blow. Their swords locked, bringing them close together, and with his free hand, Ulu grabbed the crossbow bolt protruding from Longo's chest and twisted it. Longo gasped in pain, his knees weak and the world momentarily dim. He recovered just in time to duck a blow that would have decapitated him.

Now Ulu was on the attack, and each time Longo was forced to parry, he grunted as blinding pain tore through him. He gave ground steadily, dodging and ducking so as to avoid having to parry. Ulu slashed at Longo's belly, and this time when Longo retreated back out of the way he came up against the wall of Constantinople. There was no more room. Ulu swung hard, and when Longo parried the blow, their two swords locked together. Longo cried out in pain as he strained against Ulu, but he was no match for the janissary's strength. Ulu pushed Longo into the jagged stonework of the battered wall, and gradually the two locked blades began to inch closer to Longo's face. 'Goodbye, old friend,' Ulu said.

'Not yet,' Longo replied. 'This is for Tristo.' He let go of his sword and dropped to one knee. As Ulu fell forward above him, Longo grabbed the crossbow bolt in his chest and with a scream, tore it free. Then, before Ulu could recover his balance, Longo rose and drove the bolt into the janissary's throat. Ulu dropped his sword and staggered backwards, clutching at his neck. He pulled the bolt out, and a fountain of blood gushed after it. Ulu stared at the bolt for a moment, and then tumbled forward, dead.

Longo picked up his sword, took a few steps, and then collapsed beside Ulu. He looked down to where each beat of his heart was pumping more and more blood out of the wound in his chest. He let his sword fall from his hand and waited for one of the janissaries to finish him. But to his surprise, none attacked. Instead, they kept a wide berth, looking at him with expressions of open-mouthed awe. One of the janissaries cried out in alarm that Ulu had fallen, and as word of Ulu's death spread, the Turkish attack began to falter. Longo watched as many of the janissaries near him began to retreat. Those that fought on seemed confused and unsure of what to do. Not far from Longo, Constantine had rallied the men and was beginning to push back the janissaries.

'Longo!' someone called, and Longo looked to see William running towards him.

'William,' Longo gasped, wincing in pain as he spoke. 'Where is Sofia?'

'In the city,' William said as he knelt beside Longo. 'You're hurt! We have to get you out of here. Can you stand?'

Longo nodded. 'You should not have left her,' he said, gritting his teeth as he grabbed his sword and struggled to his feet with William's help. He stood unsteadily, covering the wound in his chest with his left hand. 'She may be in danger.'

'She made me come, and I'm glad she did. You wouldn't have lasted much longer out here. Now come on. Let's get back to the line.'

With William's help, Longo staggered to where Constantine and Dalmata had formed a new line of troops and were pushing the Turks back towards the gap in the outer wall. As Longo and William passed through the line, Constantine stepped away from the battle to join them.

'Longo, you're alive!' he exclaimed, then frowned as he noticed Longo's wound. 'You are injured.'

'I live,' Longo grunted. He shrugged off William's help. 'I will fight so long as I can stand.'

Constantine looked at Longo sceptically. 'That is no minor wound, Longo. There is nothing more that you can do here.'

'It is my duty to fight,' Longo insisted. 'I will not fail you.'

'You have not failed me, Longo. You have done all that you can. Now, there is only one last thing that I ask of you: go to Sofia, make sure that she is safe.' Longo began to protest, but Constantine held up his hand, cutting Longo off. 'Say nothing. I have eyes, and I am not a fool, Longo. I know love when I see it. Go to her. I will hold the wall.'

'Thank you, Emperor,' Longo said. The two men clasped hands, and then the emperor returned to the battle. Longo turned to William. 'I will look after Sofia,' he told him. 'You may stay and fight if you wish.'

'And leave you on your own? Not a chance.'

'Very well,' Longo said. 'We must hurry. Sofia may have need of us.'

Chapter 24

Sofia crouched on the floor, wedged in a tight space behind a chest and beneath a broad windowsill. She concentrated on breathing steadily and quietly, despite the violent beating of her heart. Two Turks in full armour had just burst into the single room of the house where she was hiding and were ransacking it for loot. She heard the larger of the two men walk towards her. He stopped before the chest and pulled it open.

'There's nothing here,' he said in Turkish. He slammed the lid closed and moved away. 'Let's move on.'

Sofia peeped out and watched as he strode to the door. The other Turk was sawing at a candlestick with his knife, trying to determine if it was solid gold. He was short and thin, with a large wart on his cheek. He looked up, and his eyes met Sofia's.

'What have we here?' he said, dropping the candlestick. 'Finally, a real treasure.'

Sofia wriggled out from behind the chest and drew her sword. 'Stay back,' she warned in accented Turkish. 'Or you will regret it.'

'We don't have time for her,' the larger Turk said from the door. 'Let's gather what treasure we can before the rest of the army arrives to pick the city clean.'

'Nonsense,' the thin Turk insisted. 'This one will fetch a pretty price at the market once we're done with her. Besides, there's still plenty of time to have a bit of fun before the city falls.' He loosened his belt and stepped towards Sofia.

'I am a princess,' Sofia told them, raising her sword. 'Do not dare touch me!'

'A princess?' the larger Turk repeated. He drew his sword and joined his comrade. 'Then you should be worth a pretty penny indeed.'

Gennadius knelt before the altar in the chapel of the church of Saint Saviour in Chora, his head bowed as if in prayer. The church stood only fifty yards inside the high walls of the Mesoteichion, and Gennadius could clearly hear the clash of arms, the screams of the wounded and the battlecries of '*Allah*! *Allah*! *Allah*!' Behind him, women, children and men too old to fight huddled together in fear and prayed for their city. But Gennadius's mind was not on prayer. He was waiting impatiently for Eugenius's return. If all had gone as planned, then the prayers of the people here would do them little good. Constantinople would fall, and Gennadius would be made patriarch. Finally, the Union would be dead, and he would drive the Latins from the city once and for all.

Gennadius heard the door of the chapel swing open, and a moment later Eugenius knelt beside him. 'It is done,' Eugenius whispered. 'The Turks are in the city.'

'And the thieves you hired?' Gennadius asked. 'There must be no witnesses to what we have done.'

'They have been trapped and drowned in one of the cistern's flood rooms.'

'Well done, Eugenius. What you have done will win you favour in the eyes of God. Now there is only one thing left to do. Come with me.' Gennadius rose and led the way out of the back of the chapel to a staircase that spiralled up to the bell tower. He gestured for Eugenius to go first and then followed him up the stairs. 'I wish to thank you for your many services over the years,' Gennadius said as they climbed. 'You have been a faithful friend.'

'I have only sought to serve our Lord.'

'And you have. Our Father will welcome you in heaven.' Gennadius grabbed Eugenius from behind, covering his mouth with one hand while he slit his throat. He released him, and Eugenius slid to the floor, his eyes wide and his mouth working silently as blood poured from his neck. Gennadius made the sign of the cross over him. 'I am sorry, my friend, but no one can know what I have done. God have mercy on your soul.' He wiped his dagger on Eugenius's robes and then continued up the spiralling staircase.

The stairs ended in a small, dark room. A single ladder led to a hatch in the ceiling. Gennadius climbed up into daylight, emerging into a belfry, open on all sides. High above him hung the heavy bronze church bell. Gennadius went to the railing nearest the walls. From this height he had a good view of the Mesoteichion, and he could see that the fighting beyond the gate was fierce. However, the Christians seemed to be holding their ground. In fact, they appeared to be pushing the Turks back. Despite all he had done, the walls of Constantinople were holding.

Gennadius pulled a broad piece of white cloth from his robes and tied it to the side of the belfry. It unfurled in the breeze, revealing a Turkish battle flag – a white background with golden lettering in Turkish script. Then Gennadius turned back to the bell and seized hold of the thick bell rope. 'What I do, I do in your name, O Lord,' he said. 'Have mercy on my soul.'

'We have them now. For Constantinople! God is with us!' Constantine roared as he led another Christian charge. Dalmata ran at his side, and the two of them fought like men possessed, hacking their way through the Turkish ranks. Inspired by their example, the other Christians surged after them, and the janissaries fell back faster and faster. Constantine and his men reached the gap in the outer wall of the Mesoteichion, driving the last Turks out on to the plain.

'Hold the line!' Constantine yelled, and the men stopped, spreading out across the gap. Where once they had been ten deep, now their line was spread thin, but if they could hold the gap only a little longer, then the day would be theirs. 'Stand firm, men!' Constantine shouted. 'Let no Turk pass!'

The loud tolling of a nearby bell swallowed up his last words. 'My God!' Dalmata said. 'The bells.'

'But the wall still stands.' Constantine was confused. 'What could this mean?'

'Look!' Dalmata pointed behind them. 'A Turkish standard flies above the walls.'

Around them, the Christian warriors began to panic.

'The Turks have taken the city!' one of the men shouted. 'We must retreat to the inner wall!' another cried. One by one, men began to leave the Christian line, running for the city gates.

'Stand and fight!' Constantine yelled. 'We must stand and fight!' But no one listened. The Turks surged forward, and the Christian line broke apart as the soldiers turned to run. Constantine found himself swept away with the rest, running hard for the gate. When he reached it, he stopped and tried to rally his men one last time.

'To me, men! To me!' he yelled. 'We must hold the gate! For God's sake, stand and fight!' But the soldiers did not stop. They streamed past Constantine, heading for the harbour and the safety of the ships. All along the walls now, the Christians were in retreat, and bells were ringing throughout the city.

Constantine was joined by Dalmata and only a dozen other men. They stood in the gate as hundreds of janissaries rushed towards them. 'The battle is lost,' Constantine told them. 'There is no need to stay and die for me.'

'I will stand with you until the end,' Dalmata told him. The others nodded their agreement.

'Then if we are to die, let us die fighting. For Constantinople!' Constantine screamed as he turned and charged towards the onrushing Turks.

'For Constantinople!' Dalmata echoed. They met the charging janissaries side by side. For a moment they held their own against the onslaught. Then the Turks surged forward once again, and Constantine and Dalmata disappeared in the crowd of men.

*

Longo staggered through the empty streets of Constantinople, forcing himself onward even though each step brought a sharp stab of pain that stole his breath away. William walked beside him, supporting him when the pain grew too much. The palace had just come in sight when they heard the bells.

'The bells,' William said. 'The city has fallen.'

'We must hurry,' Longo said. Despite the stabbing pain in his chest, he broke into a jog. The streets, empty only a few seconds before, filled quickly as panicked men and women fled their homes. Some ran for the docks, others towards the nearest church. William led Longo through the crowd to the small house where he had left Sofia. The door to the house had been forced. It hung crookedly on its hinges.

'Sofia!' Longo called and rushed inside. He found her standing at the back of house, her sword drawn and bloodied. At her feet lay two dead Turkish soldiers.

'Longo!' she cried when she saw him. Sofia sheathed her sword and raced across the room. Longo embraced her and held her tight. 'Thank God you are safe,' she said, then she stepped back and noticed Longo's blood-stained armour. 'You are hurt!'

'It is nothing,' Longo replied, although his pale face and ragged breathing said otherwise. 'Come, we must get to the ship.'

Sofia and William supported Longo as they hurried towards the Horaia gate, which led through the sea wall and out to the harbour. The crowd in the street had thinned to almost nothing. Behind them, the sounds of wailing women signalled the approach of the Turks.

'This way,' Sofia said, leading them into a side street

471

that led down towards the harbour. They had not gone far when eight janissaries spilled out of an alleyway and into the street thirty yards ahead. Two carried a heavy chest between them, and several others dragged women. When they saw Longo, William and Sofia, the Turks dropped their loot and drew their swords.

'I cannot outrun them,' Longo said. 'I will stay and hold them off as long as I can. You two circle around and head for the docks.'

'I told you that I would not leave you,' Sofia replied. 'And I will not.' She drew her sword and stepped forward. William joined her.

The janissaries attacked all together, driving the three friends apart. Longo found himself surrounded by four men. Slowed by the racking pain that accompanied his every breath, it was all that he could do to fend them off. He felt a sword blow nick off his armour and gave ground until his back was against the wall of one of the buildings lining the street. He was light-headed and weak from the loss of blood, and he could feel his arm slowing. He was late to parry a blow, and a sword glanced off his chest-plate. Another Turkish attack slipped past his guard and slashed him across the thigh. He dropped to one knee.

Then, out of the corner of his eye, Longo saw Sofia go down. A sudden rage coursed through him, and the pain in his chest vanished. With a roar, he sprang to his feet and went on the offensive. He ducked the attack of one Turk and slashed him across the chest; parried another blow and kicked out, knocking a janissary off his feet and then finishing him with a downward thrust of his sword. Longo left his sword in the dead man's chest as he spun away from another blow. He grabbed the attacking Turk's arm and hurled him face first into the wall of the alley, knocking him unconscious. The last janissary facing him fled for his life.

Across the street, Sofia sat propped up against the wall, fighting desperately to fend off two of the janissaries. Longo sprinted forward and slammed into the first Turk from behind, knocking him sprawling face first into the wall. As the other Turk turned to face him, Sofia lunged forward, burying her sword in the janissary's back. She collapsed back against the wall.

'Where are you hurt?' Longo asked, kneeling beside her.

'My leg.' Sofia showed Longo a shallow gash on her left thigh.

Longo ripped off one of the sleeves of her shirt and tied it around her thigh to slow the bleeding. 'Can you stand?' She nodded and Longo helped her to her feet. They stood leaning on one another for support. William had just finished off the last of the Turks. He retrieved Longo's sword and then placed himself between Sofia and Longo, propping both of them up. The three of them had just set off when far away down the street behind them, the janissary who had fled reappeared leading another troop of Turks.

'There are too many to fight,' Longo said.

'And we cannot outrun them,' William added. 'Not with two of us hurt.'

'Follow me.' Sofia, supported by William, led them into a narrow alley, barely wide enough for two people to walk abreast. They had only gone a few dozen feet when she took them on an even narrower side path. Behind them, they could hear the sound of footsteps filling the alley-ways.

'Where are we?' William whispered. 'Are we near the docks?'

'I am not sure,' Sofia whispered back. 'But this is an old part of the city. The alleyways here are all connected. As long as we head north, we should reach the harbour . . . so long as we don't hit a dead end.'

The alley ended at another passage, and Sofia took them to the right. The footsteps of the Turks now sounded as if they were right on top of them. They took another left turn. After a dozen feet the passage swung sharply to the right, finishing in a dead end. Behind them, they could hear Turkish voices approaching. 'We can't go back that way,' Longo said.

'In here,' Sofia urged, pointing to a door on the left-hand side of the passage. She tried the latch, but it was locked. William stepped forward and kicked the door hard. It swung open and they all hurried inside. They found themselves in a small kitchen, barely large enough for the three of them. William shut the door behind them and they shoved a heavy table in front of it. Limping, Sofia led the way through the next room to a door. She cracked it open. Before them was an empty square, and at the far end of the square, the Horaia gate. 'We've made it,' she breathed. 'Come on.'

They hurried through the gate and into the harbour. Most of the boats had already left, and the docks were crowded with men and women desperately seeking a way across the Horn. Some were jumping into the water to swim. The few small rowing boats that remained were filled until their sides barely cleared the water and were then rowed frantically towards the far shore. Longo paused to look for his ship.

'There she is!' William shouted, pointing to *la Fortuna*, which floated at a pier some two hundred yards down the harbour. There were sailors in the rigging, preparing the sails. 'Thank God she's still here.'

They hurried towards the ship, but had not got far when behind them the first Turks began to pour out of the gate and into the harbour. They spread out, killing the men and dragging the terrified women away. 'Hurry!' Longo yelled. He tried to run, but his legs refused. The world went dim and began to spin. William grabbed him and hauled him over his shoulder, staggering towards the ship. Sofia limped after them.

As they approached, they saw that most of the ship's crew was at the railing, fending off a crowd of Greek men and women who were desperate to get on board. William shouldered his way through the crowd, carrying Longo with him and with Sofia close behind. They rushed across the gangway, and Nicolo stepped aside to let them on board.

'Thank God you're here!'

'You have done well, Nicolo,' Longo breathed as he slumped against the railing and then slid to the deck. Sofia rushed to his side. 'Set sail.' Longo pointed to the dock. 'And let as many of those people on board as the ship will carry.'

The sailors stood aside and the people poured on to the ship. The Turks were close behind, and before the last of the Greeks were on board, the sailors found themselves fending off Turkish soldiers. 'Shove off!' William yelled from the quarterdeck, where he had taken the wheel.

As the ship floated away from the dock, he called out, 'Set the sails!' The sails fell and were tied home. Within seconds the ship was making way towards Pera.

Longo sat near the railing, his head cradled in Sofia's arms. Together, they looked back upon the city. A hundred yards to their right, soldiers were marching across the floating bridge, joining the other Turks already swarming around the harbour. The Christians left trapped at the harbour were being slaughtered. Further off, past the sea walls, fires were rising up near the palace, casting plumes of black smoke into the clear spring sky. Other than the fires, the city looked almost peaceful. The bells had fallen silent. After watching for a long time, Sofia turned her head. There were tears in her eyes.

'I cannot believe that Constantinople has fallen,' she said. 'I fear I will never set foot in my home again.'

'But you are safe,' Longo said. 'That is all that matters. You will live a long life, a happy life.'

'We all will,' Sofia replied and placed Longo's hand on her stomach.

Despite the pain coursing through his body, Longo smiled. 'I have seen this day only in my worst nightmares,' he said. 'I never dreamed that it would give me reason for joy.'

Sofia leaned forward and kissed him lightly on the lips. 'Nor did I,' she whispered. She turned and gazed once more at the city through eyes full of tears. 'Nor did I.'

Chapter 25

Mehmed rode his horse towards Constantinople through fields crowded with the bodies of the dead, already food for crows and scavenging dogs. When he reached the fosse, the scene was even worse. The deep, dry moat was filled with the bodies of thousands of dead Turks, and the stench was already overpowering. Mehmed spurred across the fosse and through the broad stretch of the outer wall that had been brought down by cannons. The courtyard between the inner and outer walls was littered with dead janissaries and Christians. The charred remains of portable barricades lay smouldering around the gate to the city. Mehmed rode though the carnage to the gate, where he was met by Ishak Pasha. Ishak's armour was stained with blood and an ugly gash ran across his forehead; but he sat tall in the saddle, his head held high.

'Congratulations, My Lord,' Ishak Pasha said. 'The city is yours.'

'What of the emperor?'

'His body has disappeared. There are many who say they saw him fall, but amongst all this' – Ishak pointed to the dead littering the ground around them – 'he will be difficult to find.'

'And what of his family? Are there any survivors?'

'Few, My Lord,' Ishak Pasha replied. 'The emperor had no son. We have gathered those members of the imperial household that we found living.'

'Execute them,' Mehmed ordered. 'I want no pretenders to the throne coming back to haunt me.' Ishak Pasha nodded. 'And Ulu?'

Ishak Pasha pointed to where the giant man lay, not far from the gate into the city. 'He was the first of the janissaries to breach the outer walls and reach the gate.'

Mehmed dismounted and walked to where Ulu lay. He stood gazing down at him for a long time, lost in thought. Constantinople was conquered, but it had taken from him all those he held closest. Mehmed himself had sacrificed his father to his ambitions. Gülbehar had betrayed him, then Sitt Hatun, and finally Halil. And now, Ulu too was dead.

'Farewell, friend,' he whispered. Then he spoke more loudly. 'Bury him where he lies. From this day forth this gate shall bear his name, to honour him.' Mehmed returned to his horse and remounted.

As he passed through the gates into Constantinople, a cheer went up amongst the Turkish soldiers nearby. Other soldiers stopped their pillaging and came to line the road as Mehmed rode down it. 'Mehmed *fatih*!' they chanted. 'Mehmed the Conqueror!' Indeed, Mehmed thought, I am a conqueror now. He had lost much, but it was a price he was willing to pay. It was the price that one had to pay for glory. And this was glory. Mehmed straightened in his saddle and held his head high as he spurred his horse forward at a trot. As more and more men lined the road, chanting his name, Mehmed continued into the city, alone, triumphant.

Gennadius knelt inside the chapel of Saint Saviour in Chora, praying alongside the frightened men and women who had crammed themselves inside before barring the door. Outside, he could hear cries of agony and loud shouting in Turkish. Then, there was a great boom, and the doors to the chapel shook violently. A woman screamed, and the people nearest the doors scrambled back towards the altar. Another boom, and this time one of the bars on the door began to splinter. The praying had now dissolved into hysterical screaming and wailing. Gennadius stood and backed away into a shadowy alcove behind the altar. A final boom, and the doors burst open.

Turkish soldiers spilled into the chapel, their swords drawn. The people tried to scramble away, but in the limited confines, they had no chance to escape. The Turks cut down the defenceless old men and dragged the women and children outside, where they were shackled together in long lines to be sold as slaves. Gennadius stood in the alcove, trembling despite himself. One of the Turks was only a few feet away now, using his dagger to strip gold foil from the sides of the altar. He looked up and saw Gennadius. The Turk grinned and drew his sword.

'Wait!' Gennadius called out. 'The sultan promised me his protection! He promised! Stop. Stop!' But the Turk did not stop. He stepped towards Gennadius and raised his sword. 'But I am to be patriarch!' Gennadius squealed in terror. 'I am Gennadius! Gennadius!' He crouched down and closed his eyes.

But the blow did not come. Instead, he heard a series of sharp orders in Turkish and looked up to see an older Turk, with steely grey hair, striding towards him. 'You say you are Gennadius?' the Turk asked in Greek.

'Yes, yes!' Gennadius nodded vigorously. 'I am the monk, Gennadius. The sultan promised to spare my life.'

The Turk looked Gennadius over and then shouted an order in Turkish before turning and walking away. Two men stepped forward and took hold of Gennadius's arms, shackling them together at the wrists. 'Wait! What are you doing?' Gennadius cried. One of the Turks punched him hard in the stomach. As Gennadius doubled over, the other Turk attached a long chain to the monk's shackles. The Turks jerked on the chain, pulling Gennadius after them.

They left the church and marched to the forum of Constantine – the heart of ancient Constantinople. A thick crowd of Turkish soldiers surrounded the square. The man leading Gennadius pushed through to the front of the crowd. Gennadius was surprised to see Halil in the centre of the forum. The former vizier sat slumped on his knees between two guards. He still wore his robes of rich golden *serâser*, but everywhere his skin was bleeding and red, as if he had been badly burned. Halil's eyes were glassy and vacant.

Around Gennadius the crowd began to chant rhythmically: 'Mehmed *fatih*! Mehmed *fatih*!' The crowd parted, and Mehmed himself emerged, riding a tall horse and surrounded by janissaries in black armour. The sultan rode to the centre of the square and dismounted. He drew his long, curved sword and held it high. The crowd cheered loudly.

'Behold!' Mehmed shouted. 'This shall be the end of all

who dare to betray their sultan!' He walked to where Halil sat. The two guards holding Halil took hold of his arms, stretching them out to either side and lifting Halil up. He slumped between them, his head hanging. Mehmed bent down and whispered briefly in Halil's ear. Then he stepped back, raised his sword, and with one vicious downward blow, severed Halil's head. The crowd roared its approval. Halil's head rolled away and came to a stop only a few feet from Gennadius. Halil's eyes seemed to be looking right at him.

'Come,' the guard leading Gennadius barked. He yanked Gennadius forward into the centre of the square. Ahead, Mehmed stood waiting, his sword dripping blood. Gennadius felt a flood of warmth around his loins as he wet himself, a stain spreading across the front of his cassock. The crowd of Turks hooted and jeered. Gennadius's legs went weak, and he collapsed. Two janissaries rushed forward and picked him up. They deposited him at Mehmed's feet.

'You are the monk, Gennadius?' Mehmed asked in Greek.

'Yes,' Gennadius croaked. His mouth had gone dry, and it was all that he could do to speak.

'Rise, then, Gennadius. It is not fitting for the patriarch to grovel.'

'The patriarch?' Gennadius asked as he climbed unsteadily to his feet.

'I am a man of my word, Gennadius,' Mehmed said. He barked an order in Turkish, and a servant came forward carrying the white, conical hat of the patriarch. Mehmed took it and placed it on Gennadius's head. 'I declare you Patriarch of the Orthodox Church.'

'You are most kind, Sultan,' Gennadius said. He could hardly believe his good fortune. The patriarchy was his. Now, he could destroy the Union and return the Church to its rightful state. He held up his hands, still shackled together. 'Please, these chains – they are very heavy.'

'The chains stay, Patriarch,' Mehmed replied. 'I do not trust any man who would sell his own city for the price of a hat. Take him to his church and see that he stays there.'

'But Sultan . . .' Gennadius began.

'You are lucky to be alive,' Mehmed cut him short. 'That is more than you deserve. Take him away.' The guard jerked the chain, pulling Gennadius away. 'Farewell, Patriarch,' Mehmed called after him.

Longo lay in his cabin aboard *la Fortuna*, struggling against the pain that radiated out from his chest with every breath he took. When they had reached Pera, two days before, William had found a doctor to treat Longo, but it quickly became clear that no medicine could help him. Longo's fate was in God's hands.

Longo heard footsteps on deck, and a moment later William entered. 'Good news,' he said. 'The sack has ended. The sultan has declared that any further pillage will be punished with death. Some of the merchants of Pera have already been to Constantinople to trade and have returned. One of them told me that Grand Vizier Halil has been executed by Mehmed himself. The merchant saw Halil's head on a spike in the forum of Constantine.'

'Then my revenge is complete,' Longo whispered. 'I never dreamed that it would be the sultan who avenged me.' He closed his eyes. He had dreamt about this moment

482

for so long, but now that it was here, he felt nothing. Halil's face had already ceased to haunt him; his death made little difference. And besides, Longo had more pressing matters to attend to. 'If the sack of the city is ended, then we must lose no time,' he said. 'William, prepare the ship to sail. We will leave as soon as possible.' William left, and soon Longo could hear the hurried steps of men on the deck above, preparing *la Fortuna* to sail. More quickly than he expected, however, his cabin once again fell silent. Sofia appeared in the doorway, her eyes flashing.

'What is the meaning of this? I leave you for but a second, and you order the ship to sea?'

'We have no choice. It is too dangerous for you to stay here. You know what happened to the rest of the imperial household. And now that the sack has ended, the Turks will turn their attention to Pera.'

'But if we sail, you will die,' Sofia responded. 'You can hardly breathe as it is. A voyage on the open sea would be the end of you.'

'I will die regardless, Sofia. I have seen my share of battlefields. I know a fatal wound when I see it.'

'You may or may not die, but I will not be the death of you. We will not sail. That is final.' There was a knocking on the cabin door. 'What is it?' Sofia called.

William entered. 'It is the sultan,' he said. 'He is at the docks of Pera, and he is coming here.'

Mehmed stepped off the dock and on to the gently swaying deck of *la Fortuna*. His guard had already gone before him to search the ship. The crew had been disarmed, and they stood huddled together on the deck, surrounded by janissaries. A particularly beautiful woman stood amongst them. Mehmed studied her for a moment, admiring her lithe figure and perfect olive skin, then looked away. After all, he was not here to examine the Italian's crew. 'Where is Giustiniani, the defender of Constantinople?' he asked.

One of the crew – a lean young man – stepped forward. 'What do you want?' he asked. 'Have you come to kill him in his bed?'

'If I wished him dead, then he would be dead already,' Mehmed replied. 'I wish to speak with him.'

'Very well. I will take you to him,' the young crewman said. 'Follow me.' He stepped down a hatchway that led below decks.

Mehmed approached the hatchway, and his guard hurried to follow him. 'Stay where you are,' Mehmed ordered. 'I will be safe enough here.' He followed the young man into the dim light below decks.

The hold in which Mehmed found himself was crowded with rows of cots, one atop the other, swinging with the motion of the ship. A hatchway in the floor led deeper still into the ship, to where Mehmed presumed supplies were stored. Before him, at the far end of the hold, a door stood open.

Mehmed's guide stopped at the doorway. 'The sultan is here,' he called into the room. Then he stepped aside and motioned Mehmed inside. Mehmed entered to find himself in a small stern cabin. An oil lamp hung from the ceiling, illuminating the scene. There was a desk against the far wall, with charts and a pitcher of water upon it. A chest sat against the wall to the left. To the right hung a cot in which lay Signor Giustiniani, his face pale. His chest had been heavily bandaged, and his breath came in

484

ragged gasps. He looked nothing like the man that Mehmed had met before the walls of Constantinople only a few days before. A stool stood by the cot, and Mehmed sat down on it.

'Greetings, great Sultan,' Longo wheezed. 'You honour me with your presence. What brings you to my ship?'

'I wished to see you,' Mehmed said. 'To honour you for your brave defence of the city. You are a great warrior, signor. You were a worthy adversary.'

'Not worthy enough, it seems. The city has fallen. It is you who have been proven the great warrior.'

'Perhaps you are right, but you fought bravely with few men. Your deeds will long be remembered, by my people as well as yours. Your sword will always be welcome in my service, if you so choose.'

Longo shook his head. 'I fear I shall not wield my sword again. Not in your service or in any other.'

'I see,' Mehmed said gravely. The two men fell silent. Finally, Mehmed spoke again. 'Perhaps you are the lucky one, signor. It is a strange thing: to fight for one thing for so long and then to suddenly achieve it. Constantinople is conquered, yes, but what now do I fight for?' He shook his head sadly, his creased forehead making him look far older than his twenty-one years. 'I do not know.'

'You are young yet,' Longo replied. 'And there are other things to fight for besides cities and glory. You will learn that in time.'

Mehmed smiled. 'You are right, I am sure. You are as wise as you are brave, a rare combination indeed. I wish to honour you, to pay tribute to the defender of Constantinople. I had planned to offer you a place in my army, but since you cannot serve, is there anything that you wish of me, land or titles? If it is within my power, I will grant it.'

'My crew,' Longo said. 'They have served me well. All I ask is that you swear to spare the lives of all on this ship and to allow them safe passage to Chios.'

'It shall be as you say.' Mehmed rose to his feet. 'And, I shall tell my men to bring you whatever provisions you need for your journey.'

'You have my thanks, Sultan.'

'It is nothing less than you deserve,' Mehmed said. 'Farewell, Signor.' He turned and left. The young man was waiting to lead him back up to the deck. Once there, Mehmed called the captain of his guard to him. 'Give this ship safe passage, and see that it receives whatever provisions it needs,' Mehmed ordered as he stepped on to the dock.

'Yes, Sultan.'

'And have my baggage prepared and my horses readied,' Mehmed added. 'I wish to leave the city tonight.'

'For where, Sultan?'

'For Edirne.'

Moonlight fell through the open windows of Sitt Hatun's apartments, illuminating her as she lay in bed, unable to sleep. Mehmed was to arrive tomorrow, and she feared his return. She had heard that Halil had been executed, and Sitt Hatun worried that Isa had betrayed him. Had Isa betrayed her as well? Sitt Hatun shuddered at the thought.

A loud cry from somewhere in her apartments startled Sitt Hatun, and she sat up. A few seconds later, Anna burst into the room, a sword in her hand.

486

'What is it?' Sitt Hatun asked.

Anna tried to speak but no words came. Blood trailed from her mouth, and she slumped to the floor, revealing a deep wound in her back. Sitt Hatun knelt beside her. 'Who has done this?' she asked. 'What happened?'

Anna managed to mouth one word – *Selim* – before she choked on her own blood and went still, dead. Sitt Hatun took Anna's sword and hurried into Selim's room. Two members of the sultan's private guard stood over a third who lay on the floor unmoving, but Sitt Hatun ignored them. Her eyes were fixed on Selim. He was floating face down in his bath. Sitt Hatun dropped the sword and pushed past the guards. She lifted Selim from the water and held him to her, cradling the boy in her arms and gently rocking him. 'Selim, my angel,' she whispered to him. 'Wake up, my son. I am here now. Wake up.' But it was no use. Selim was dead. Sitt Hatun sank to the floor.

'The sultan is waiting for you,' one of the guards told her. 'You must come with us.'

The sultan: he had done this. Mehmed had killed her child. Sitt Hatun's grief transformed into rage, and she rose from the floor, still clutching Selim to her. 'Take me to him,' she told the guards.

Mehmed stood in the hallway outside Sitt Hatun's quarters. Behind him stood several of his private guard, and out of the corner of his eye Mehmed noticed Gülbehar arrive with the boy Bayezid. No doubt Gülbehar had come to witness Sitt Hatun's fate.

The doors to Sitt Hatun's quarters swung open, and Sitt Hatun stormed out, holding Selim's lifeless body in her arms. 'How could you!' she screamed at Mehmed. She tried to slap him, but he caught her arm. 'He is only a child!'

'He was a bastard and the son of a traitor,' Mehmed replied.

'Look at him,' Sitt Hatun urged, thrusting Selim towards him. 'Look at him! He is your son!'

Mehmed looked at the boy. Selim's large, brown eyes were open and seemed to stare accusingly at Mehmed. They were Mehmed's eyes. There was no mistaking the resemblance.

Mehmed felt sick and looked away. 'Dispose of the boy,' he ordered his guards. He was suddenly desperate to have Selim gone, somewhere where the child's sad eyes would not be able to haunt him. 'Cast him into the river.'

The guards stepped forward to take Selim. 'No! No!' Sitt Hatun screamed as the guards wrested Selim from her. 'Selim! My child! Bring back my child!' As the guards disappeared with her son, Sitt Hatun collapsed to the ground, her energy gone. 'Kill me,' she said quietly, 'and be done with it.'

'You shall not die,' Mehmed replied. 'You saved my one true son, Bayezid, and so I shall spare your life. But you are dead to me, Sitt Hatun. You shall live out the rest of your life in exile, and you will never see my face again.' Two guards grabbed her arms, lifted her to her feet and dragged her away. Mehmed saw Gülbehar smirk as Sitt Hatun was dragged past her.

When Sitt Hatun was gone, Gülbehar stepped closer to Mehmed and slid her arm around his back. 'It is nothing less than she and her bastard child deserved,' she whispered.

Mehmed turned and slapped her hard. 'Do not think

that I have forgotten your treachery, whore,' he said, his voice cold. He pulled Bayezid away from his mother. 'You may return to your quarters.' Mehmed walked away, pulling Bayezid after him.

'But my son!' Gülbehar cried.

'He is my son, and mine alone,' Mehmed told her. 'I will not let you poison him against me. Take her away.' The remaining guards stepped forward and pulled Gülbehar towards her quarters.

'Bayezid! My son!' Gülbehar cried as she was dragged away.

Bayezid began to cry. 'Selim,' he sobbed. 'Sitt Hatun.'

Mehmed lifted the boy and held him. 'Quiet, child,' he said. 'You must always remember: a sultan has no family, no friends, no lovers. He is married to the empire, and all are jealous of his bride.'

Longo weakened rapidly after his interview with the sultan. He slept more and more, and even when he was awake he drifted in and out of consciousness. In his delirium, he sometimes spoke out loud, yelling for help to fend off the Turks. Mostly, however, he called out for Sofia, and she was always beside him to take his hand.

On the evening of the 12th of June, fourteen days after the fall of Constantinople, Longo's delirium broke, and he woke suddenly lucid from a troubled sleep. He felt tired, almost relaxed despite the burning pain in his chest, and he knew that his time was near. Sofia was seated in a chair beside him, asleep. She had drifted off keeping watch over him. Her eyes were dark from too many tears and too many sleepless nights. 'Sofia,' Longo whispered hoarsely, barely able to speak. '*Sofia.*'

489

She awoke with a start and took his hand. 'You are awake,' she said. 'Are you thirsty? Shall I bring you water?'

Longo shook his head. 'Send in Nicolo. And tell him to bring a quill and parchment.' Sofia nodded and left. A minute later Nicolo entered the room.

'How are you, My Lord?'

'Never better,' Longo said and smiled weakly. Nicolo chuckled, but there were tears in his eyes. 'Write what I say,' Longo told him. Nicolo nodded and took a seat at the small table in the cabin. Between laboured breaths, Longo dictated his last will, leaving his title and all his property on Chios to William. Once William was dead, the lands would revert to Longo's children.

'William is young,' Longo said when it was done. 'Look after him for me, Nicolo. Make certain that his lands prosper.'

'I will,' Nicolo replied.

'Good. Now leave the paper and send in William, alone.' Nicolo left, and William entered and sat beside Longo. 'The paper,' Longo said, nodding towards his will. 'Take it. It is yours.'

William took the paper and read. 'But Sofia should have your lands.'

'No. You have more than earned them,' Longo said. 'I see myself in you, William. You have made me proud.'

'Thank you,' William said, looking away to hide his tears.

'Watch over Sofia for me. Watch over her and my child. You will be all the father that he ever knows. Promise me that you will protect him and treat him as your own.'

'I swear it.'

Longo nodded. 'Thank you, and goodbye, William. Send

490

in Sofia when you go.' William took Longo's hand and pressed it; then he rose and left. Sofia entered and sat beside the bed. She carried a cup of water, which she held to his lips.

'Try to drink something,' she said. 'It will help.'

Longo shook his head. 'It is no use. It is too late for that.'

'Do not say that. You must fight.'

'This is one fight that I cannot win, Sofia,' Longo said. She took his hand, and they both fell silent. A wave of pain hit Longo, spreading out from his chest and contorting his body. The wave passed as suddenly as it had come, leaving him exhausted. He lay with his eyes closed, and Sofia leaned close to speak to him.

'Are you still there?'

'I am,' Longo whispered. 'I was thinking of that night on Corsica, our first kiss.'

'I remember. It was the first time that I ever kissed a man.'

'I thought that I would never see you again,' Longo said. 'But here we are, all three of us.'

'Yes, all three of us,' Sofia agreed, placing his hand on her stomach. 'If it is a boy, he shall have your name.'

'If it is a girl, name her Sofia.'

'I will.' Sofia turned away as tears filled her eyes.

'Do not weep for me,' Longo told her. 'My entire life has been one of battle and bloodshed, revenge and honour. You have given me something more. I am prepared to die.'

'I do not weep for you,' Sofia replied. 'I cry for myself and for our child. He shall never know you.'

'You will tell him about his father,' Longo said. 'About

how he lived, and why he died. Our child shall know me through you.' Sofia nodded. Longo winced suddenly, his body again racked with pain. When the agony faded, it left him feeling tired and distant. He closed his eyes and sighed.

'Do not leave me,' Sofia said, squeezing his hand. 'I need you.'

'No, you are strong,' Longo whispered. 'And you have William.'

'But I love you.'

'I know,' Longo said. 'I . . .' But the words died on his lips as another spasm wracked his body. This time when the pain passed Longo felt himself letting go, embraced in a warm darkness. The world seemed far away, and it was all that he could do to open his eyes. He saw Sofia's face leaning over him, wavering but beautiful.

'Thank you,' he whispered. 'Thank you for saving me.' He paused, struggling to take a last breath. 'I love you,' he said and closed his eyes. Longo felt himself falling away into darkness.

As he slipped away, he heard Sofia's voice calling to him: 'I love you, too. I love you, Longo.' The last thing he felt was the touch of her lips on his.

The next day Longo was cremated, and *la Fortuna* sailed for Chios, bearing his ashes. The seas were smooth and the journey a swift one. Shortly after they arrived, William was installed as lord of Longo's lands, and he and his wife Portia took up residence in Longo's villa on the island. Tristo's wife Maria joined them, keeping house and raising her young son, Benito.

Sofia moved into the villa with them, and as the months

passed her stomach grew large with the life inside her. Finally, on a cool evening in late January, her time came. Maria acted as the midwife, and Portia stayed to comfort Sofia. William stood outside the closed door of Sofia's room, pacing nervously as he listened to Sofia's cries.

Sofia had never known such pain. Her labour lasted all night. She was exhausted, but still she kept straining and pushing. 'That's good,' Maria said gently, as Sofia pushed hard again. 'I can see the head. You're almost there.' Sofia bit down hard on the strip of leather between her teeth and pushed again. Finally, the child emerged, screaming. 'It's a girl!' Maria announced. She cut and knotted the umbilical cord, and then held the baby up for Sofia to see. But Sofia was not looking. Her eyes were closed tightly, and she was still straining. 'William!' Maria yelled. The door opened almost instantly. 'Take her and be gentle,' Maria said. William took the crying baby and stood holding her awkwardly. 'Well what are you waiting for? Go!' Maria snapped at him. 'There's more work to be done here. Twins, from the looks of it.'

Maria returned to her stool at Sofia's feet. 'That's it,' Portia encouraged softly in Sofia's ear. 'Keep pushing. You're almost there.' Sofia moaned with the pain and exertion, but she kept pushing.

'That's good. One more push,' Maria told her. Sofia strained one last time, and the second baby was out, wailing unhappily. 'A boy!' Maria declared happily. 'It's a boy!'

Sofia smiled weakly. She was exhausted and numb with pain, but also happy, happier than she had ever been. 'I want to hold them,' she said. Maria gently placed the crying child in her arms. Sofia rocked him, and the boy quieted. 'Hello, my little Longo,' she whispered. William entered the room, and the baby girl was placed in Sofia's other arm. 'My beautiful Sofia,' she whispered and kissed the child on the forehead.

'They are perfect, Sofia,' Portia said.

'Two children,' William said. 'Longo would be proud.' Tears formed in Sofia's eyes. She nodded happily, unable to find the words to speak.

'I suppose they are the heirs to the empire now,' William continued. 'The last of the Romans.'

'No,' Sofia said. 'They are my children. Nothing more, nothing less.'

'Well, that's enough gabbing,' Maria said tartly. 'Now everybody out and leave her be. She needs her rest.' She shooed William out of the door, then she carefully lifted up the infant Longo, and Portia took the baby Sofia. 'We'll look after them,' Maria told Sofia. 'You try to get some sleep. You'll need your strength to keep up with two little ones.'

They left, and Sofia lay alone, exhausted but too happy to sleep. She stared up at the ceiling and smiled. 'Thank you, Longo,' she whispered. 'Thank you.'

Mehmed ruled to an old age. He is known to history as Mehmed Fatih, or Mehmed the Conqueror. His son Bayezid followed him as the Ottoman Sultan, but Gülbehar never reigned as valide sultana. She died having not seen her son for many years. As for Sitt Hatun, she lived out her life alone, far from the Turkish court.

The Emperor Constantine's body was never found. Constantine's brother, Demetrius, became Emperor of the Romans after Constantine's death. He had a brief reign.

He ruled from Mistra for two years before Mistra fell to the Turks, and Demetrius was executed.

Gennadius's reign as patriarch lasted eight years. In those eight years, he only left his cell for mass. He never left Saint Saviour Pantocrator.

William prospered as the lord of Longo's lands. In time, he would leave to fight again, this time in Spain, with Longo's and Tristo's sons by his side. Longo's daughter, Sofia, would become an empress in time. But that is another story . . .

As for Sofia, she lived to an old age. In 1497 she took Longo's ashes and returned to Constantinople. She died a month later. Sofia and Longo were buried together just outside the city walls, at the Shrine of the Virgin at Zoodochos Pege. The engraving on their tomb read simply: Here lie two Romans.

Historical Note

The major events and characters in *Siege* are real. The historic Longo was a Genoese lord and mercenary who Constantine elected to lead the defence of the city. His adversary, the Sultan Mehmed, was a young man who had been driven from the throne at an early age and wanted to prove himself by taking the queen of cities, Constantinople – *kizil elma* or the 'red apple', as the Turks called it. The characters of Constantine, Notaras, Sofia, Gennadius, Dalmata, Ulu, Sitt Hatun and Gülbehar are also based on real people. William, Tristo and Isa are the only purely fictional characters in the book, but each could have existed – English prisoners were occasionally sold at the slave markets in Constantinople; as a lord and soldier, Longo would have needed a lieutenant like Tristo; and poison dealers like Isa also existed, particularly in the Muslim world and the East, where techniques to distil and separate chemicals were more advanced. The white powder and the liquid that Isa uses in the book are both forms of cyanide, which was obtained at the time from cherry laurel leaves. The antidote given to Mehmed would have been a solution of hot water, sugar and saltpetre, the chief component of gunpowder.

The events leading to Constantinople's fall in 1453

happened much as I describe them: the last crusade was crushed at the battle of Kossova; Constantine's brothers did plot for the throne. While I simplified the theological disputes, the conflict over Union was a very real factor leading to the fall of Constantinople. The siege of Constantinople was spectacular: it needed little embellishment on my part. The chain across the harbour, the giant Turkish cannons, the transport of the Turkish ships over land, the Turkish tunnels into the city and the bridge over the Golden Horn are all authentic. Constantine's farewell to his household is also based on history, and I drew on his actual words in recounting his final speech to his troops. The siege was so action-packed that I had to omit a few battles. I combined two of the Turks' early attacks into one, and left out a night assault when they brought huge towers up against the walls. The only other major change was to make Longo arrive with the ships that fought their way through the Turkish fleet. In reality he arrived at the start of the siege.

I followed the historical record closely in reconstructing the final battle. The Turks did attack in three waves: bazibozouks, Anatolian cavalry, then janissaries. Longo was forced to leave the walls after being injured by a crossbow bolt. Still the city's defenders seemed to have won the day until the Turks gained access to the city through the Kerkoporta. The Christian lines broke when they saw a Turkish flag flying from the ramparts behind them. To this day no one knows why the Kerkoporta was left open, whether it was a simple mistake, a chance of fate or treachery. After the city's fall, Mehmed had his grand vizier Halil executed. Again no one knows precisely why.

The history of the siege remains very much alive in the

modern city of Istanbul. You can still walk the full length of the land walls and, at certain points, you can climb atop them and look out upon the plain where Mehmed's army once sat. Near the middle of the walls, keep your eyes open for the gate which is named after Ulu, who really was the first Turk to breach the city walls. You can explore the ruins of the Blachernae palace. Gennadius's monastery – the Church of Saint Saviour Pantocrator – still stands, although it is now the mosque Zeyrek Camii. The cisterns underneath the mosque have been filled in, but you can visit another Roman cistern near the modern bazaar which encompasses the 'Street of the Colonnade', where William was held prisoner upon his arrival in the city. And, of course, the Haghia Sofia still stands as the glory of Istanbul.

The Topkapi palace did not exist at the time of the siege, but is well worth a visit. When you enter through the Imperial Gate, look directly above you for the seal of Mehmed, who began construction of the palace shortly after conquering Constantinople. The inscription above the seal reads: 'By the Grace of God, and by His approval, the foundations of this auspicious castle were laid, and its parts were solidly joined together to strengthen peace and tranquility . . . May God make eternal his empire, and exalt his residence above the most lucid stars of the firmament.' The palace was greatly expanded by later sultans, but its basic layout remains the same as in Mehmed's time. In the palace's portrait gallery, there is a painting of Mehmed by the Venetian Gentile Bellini. You can also visit the palace harem, a more ornate version of the structures found in Edirne and Manisa during Mehmed's time.

While the framework for the story is fact, *Siege* is a

work of fiction and should be read as such. The personalities, motivations, plots and loves of the characters are fictional. Longo's quest for revenge is my addition. While a princess Sofia did exist, the particulars of her character and certainly her affair with Longo are fictional. (What is true is that in 1469 a young Byzantine princess named Sofia – her daughter, in my story – married Ivan the Great, the first Tsar of Russia.) History tells us that Halil really was at odds with Mehmed and Gennadius was a firm opponent of the Union of the Catholic and Orthodox churches. However, the plots and conspiracies they hatch in *Siege* are of my own invention. The Turkish harem certainly was a place of intrigue, a strange mix of people where everyone strove to rise from *jariye* slave girl, to *odalisque* at the court of a favourite, to lover of the Sultan and perhaps even mother of one of his sons. Mehmed really did have his young rivals drowned when he came to power, and there are stories of unfortunate harem women being placed in sacks and thrown into the sea. Again, however, the particular plots of Sitt Hatun and Gülbehar are of my own imagining. In this spirit, all of these characters should be treated as fictional, as should their story.